STEALING FIRE FROM THE GODS

STEALING FIRE FROM THE GODS

SIX SPECULATIVE FICTIONS

RAYMUND EICH

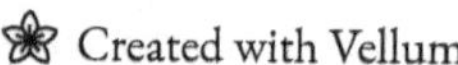 Created with Vellum

For Holly,
For helping me learn who I am when I'm being someone else.

CONTENTS

INTRODUCTION

Even after medical school, doctors must continue to take classes on new treatments and refinements of old ones. Lawyers also are required by state bar associations to take part in continuing education.

Writers should be no different. No matter how skillful we are at telling stories—or how skillful our egos tell us we are—something always gets lost in translation between our thoughts and the page or screen. There's always room for improvement.

In that spirit, in the summer of 2019, I took a self-paced writing workshop taught by Holly Lisle: *24-Hour Intensive: Find Your Writing Voice*. Unlike many writers-cum-instructors, Holly has a wealth of experience, having published over thirty novels across the fantasy, science fiction, and paranormal genres in the past three decades. Her career started with a bang—her first novel won the Compton Crook Award for best first novel. Her career has grown through the ups and downs of freelancing, the slow strangulation of traditional publishing's midlist, and the pivot to creative and business freedom of the indie era.

Because of that, I went into the workshop with high expectations.

I soon discovered my expectations for the workshop weren't high enough.

The third exercise assigned me a "simple" male character and an opening line about him being on a beach without looking back. I set a ten minute timer and started writing. Ten minutes later, I had the first two hundred words of what turned into my space adventure/first contact novel *Azureseas: Cantrell's War*.

And not just the opening words. By the end of those ten minutes, I knew the broad strokes of the entire novel: its plot, its conflict, and above all the choices that "simple" Ross Cantrell would make to do right by the planet's native intelligent species.

Excited by my early results, I continued through the exercises. Some were forgettable. Some sunk into the creative ooze of my subconscious, forgotten for the moment, though they may emerge into stories some day. (I don't think Viliana will end up naked amid ravenous tigers, but my muse is mulling over her world and what she will do instead to oppose it). But as I did the exercises, I knew some were spawning fun-to-write stories. That's a good thing.

Here's a hint, my friends: if you don't enjoy reading a story or novel, the author probably didn't have fun writing it.

Another plus of the workshop is that the exercises forced me to write about characters I would never have gotten to. The workshop short-circuited my critical voice, my *that's-not-my-kind-of-character* or *that's-not-my-kind-of-story* bit of ego blather that I paid attention to far too long.

It's just an exercise. It's just a ten minutes. Thoughts like those were enough to bypass my inner critic and just have fun with the characters and situations Holly gave me.

A woman gets a call from a ghost? My muse told me she was a middle-aged lawyer in metro St. Louis, and the ghost was a literal one, and her long-dead teenage boyfriend to boot.

A woman wishes she was someone else? My muse told me the woman was black and barely out of her teens, and desperate to flee the asteroid colony where she was born and raised.

A man regrets getting into a gamble for his friend? Within ten minutes, that man became Gordon, and I knew he and his friends would end up in Vegas. The same things happened when my muse took the seeds Holly had sown and harvested the tales of Faraday and Barnet in an alien derelict, and Jeffrey and the alien who wants him to *return blessing*.

As Holly says, your writing voice is you, when you are being someone else, existing somewhere else, and doing things you have never done. And while the works collected here have brought me some good fortune, such as inclusion in a StoryBundle and two bylines in *Analog*, the act of writing these works brought me even more emotional rewards. Joy in the moment of creation. Humble pride when I read over what flowed from my mind, or rather, *through* my mind, onto the page or screen.

Enough of my talk. You're here for science fiction and fantasy tales of adventure and wonder. Turn the page, and happy reading!

- Raymund Eich
Houston, June 2024

AZURESEAS: CANTRELL'S WAR

1

Ross Cantrell stood with the ocean before him and the cluster of huts on the beach behind him. He didn't look back.

The boxy deployment boat squatted in waist-high water twenty meters out. He could see a slice of the men at the front corner turrets through the machine gun slits. The ocean was so clear and the orange-yellow sun so bright he could see beach sand heaped up where the front end had pushed in.

Prow. The word sneaked into the top of his mind like an infiltrator passing barbed wire and sensor drones. The front end of a seagoing boat was called the prow.

He shook his head, like a cow back home twitching its tail to shake off a fly. No need for fancy words.

The line of human soldiers splashed into water warm as a bathtub and the shade of blue that gave the planet the name Azureseas. For a reason he couldn't fathom, Cantrell sounded it out in his mind. A-zhoor-sees. To avoid any discharge of the boat's reactive armor, they followed a looping path to the boat's open ramp at the back. Cantrell sucked protein goo from the straw inside his helmet and trudged along. He got deeper and the water seemed to make his legs heavier inside the boots and the shin plates of his battle armor. Little blue crawly things burrowed away from his feet.

He tried not to step on them. They didn't threaten people so why not leave them alone?

He didn't look back at the cluster of huts. He didn't need to. From behind came the smells of fire and smoke. Just like being around the burn pile in a field just cleared of brush back home. There was another smell, like roasted meat, but different. Something fruity in its smell too, like a banana or that yellow thing like a banana his buddy Armando talked about from his homeworld. Plant- something?

This time, the defenses in Cantrell's brain kept the word from reaching him.

Whatever the word was, funny how a creature looking like a cross between a dinosaur and a six-legged chicken could smell like both meat and a piece of fruit.

Cantrell shrugged shoulders bearing his slung rifle and thirty-kilo pack. His platoon had been given its orders. The creatures in the village—

He blacked out for a second or two. His legs carried on without him, brought him another sloshy step toward the extraction boat. Fear followed for a moment, but just a moment. The civilian contractors at the island base told them blackouts were normal, a side effect of hypno training and the trauma care nanobots deployed in their bloodstreams. Nothing permanent. They'd go away after their tour of duty on Azureseas.

The creatures were a threat to human visitors to this planet. He'd been told that but couldn't remember where. They'd built the cluster of huts from palm-like fronds and bark by instinct. Like beavers and dams. Burning the huts and killing the creatures was pest control. Just like plinking tree cats threatening the chicken coop, back home.

And he'd get the same hug and kiss from Nanette when he got back.

And maybe this time, as a man and a soldier, she might give him a little more.

But he wasn't home yet. He trudged on through the water. The boat's engines idled. The gunner at the front right corner kept his medium machine gun trained on the beach but turned most of his attention to the line of soldiers. A thumbs-up. Over the radio, he said, "Good hunting?"

A murmur of agreement and good cheer. "Tree cats," Cantrell said.

In front of Cantrell, Armando laughed. Ravi said all boastful, "No, more like neo—!"

An explosion on the shore. The gunner jerked his head up. All the soldiers in the water twisted around. Cantrell's rifle ended up in his hands without him noticing how.

No creature stirred on the low dunes fifty meters behind the beach. Flames still devoured what was left of the rounded huts. Now, where the biggest hut had stood in the middle of the cluster lay a hole clouded by a lot of white smoke. Little pieces of leaves and bark floated in the hot air of the fires. The smoke spread quickly, like a fog. It hid the sensor drones watching the perimeter. It reached over the beach and the shallow water.

Cantrell sniffed with his mouth open. His helmet allowed some of the smoky air in so the air must be free of toxins.

He remembered his dad grilling hamburgers over charred wood. And for a moment he thought his suit's waste management system leaked, because he picked up the smells of rotten eggs and pee.

He relaxed. Amazing the six-legged dinosaur chickens could combine saltpeter, charcoal, and sulfur in the right proportions, by inst—

Another blackout. He couldn't tell how long, but short enough that nobody in line moved.

A voice as young as any soldier's spoke over the platoon's radio net. Lieutenant Liebrandt. "Sensors pick up evidence of an accidental explosion... of.... Proceed with remount."

The soldiers swung back to face the boat. Not in unison, because they weren't robots, they were free men. Cantrell turned only when the man in front of him took his next step toward the boat.

As he turned, a little piece of something drifted down, no longer held up by the cooler air near the boat. An air current made it hover for a moment about half a meter in front of his face.

Cantrell reached up and grabbed it and took a step toward the boat, all in one motion.

He glanced at the thing in his palm.

A piece of bark. Dried and crinkly. Blackened edges where it had burned a little. Markings on it a darker shade of the yellow of the berries growing on their island base that gave men diarrhea if they broke standing orders and ate them.

He looked closer. The stroke of the markings reminded him of fingerpaintings made by his baby brother in kindergarten. But what was—

Cantrell saw it. The head and upper body of a dinosaur chicken. One front paw raised. Crude lines but he could see it. Wise eyes, like an old dog wanting to herd with its master once more. Face upturned. Long and pointy ears perked. It reached up for something. Not toward a thing. Toward....

God?

But he only held a picture of an animal. A picture made by instinct by another animal.

Animals couldn't know God—

Even after the next blackout ended, his thoughts stayed fuzzy. Getting too hot in his suit? He sipped water through the straw and told his battlesuit to run a self-check on its climate control system.

Despite the blackout, his grip held tight on the piece of dried bark.

The line of soldiers passed the reactive armor's keep-out zone and turned to the boat's open ramp. Lieutenant Liebrandt and Sergeant Ronaldson stood on the three-meter slab of alloy, near the remount ladder flipped down and over the side. Incoming ripples of water pushed thin puddles onto the ramp and against the officer and NCO's boots. Sarge held in one thick gloved hand a can about the size of a thirty-round magazine with a funnel on top pointing sideways.

"Dammit." A muffled voice, not over the radio. From the second man in line ahead of Cantrell. The heads-up display in Cantrell's helmet labeled the squat figure with wide shoulders as Vasquez. Cruel and crude. Cantrell avoided him when he could.

Why did Vasquez swear?

Cantrell peered around Armando. Vasquez moved his left hand behind his back. He held something tapered. Fifteen centimeters long, streaked yellow and green, jagged on the wide edge. The jagged edge oozed red.

The animal life here used iron in its blood, just like Earth life.

Vasquez had taken a trophy. An ear of a dinosaur chicken. Against regs.

And wrong, too. A man may kill an animal when he has to, but he shouldn't gloat about it.

The line stopped at the foot of the ladder. The first soldier, Ravi, went up. Sarge moved the can with the funnel up and down. Liebrandt pulled back his shoulders in trying to strike an authoritative pose.

Sarge nodded and moved the funnel-can away. "Clear to remount," Liebrandt announced over the platoon network. Ravi went into the boat's shadowed hold.

The line moved slowly. Men up and down grumbled. Cantrell said nothing. Yes, his feet ached after hours of soldiering while humping a pack, but after discharge and return to New Ozark, there wouldn't be any white sand beaches, warm oceans, and salty air. Without thinking, he swayed side-to-side in rhythm with the gentle waves.

He glanced back at the shore. If you ignored the dwindling fires and stench from the huts, you could imagine a resort hotel or a leisure condo on the sand under the deep blue sky. Maybe he could take Nanette on vacation to a world like this, someday.

The line advanced. Only five men ahead of Cantrell now. In front of Armando, Vasquez groped with his right hand for a zipper on his pack. One of the small pockets near the bottom. Vasquez yanked the zipper and shoved the dinosaur chicken's ear into the pocket.

Cantrell's stomach soured. The piece of bark in his hand. Was it a trophy too? No, but....

He stayed aware, but his mind seized up, like gears of an unoiled machine.

Throw it away—

—I got a pocket too—

Though he wobbled, light-headed, Cantrell's free hand mirrored Vasquez' actions. Zip open. Shove in the piece of bark. Zip closed.

He hunched forward and sucked tepid water and protein goo around hard breaths.

"C'mon up, Vasquez," Sarge said.

The ladder clanged under the soldier's boots. Vasquez waited on the open ramp with a *who-me-officer?* pose.

Sarge pressed a button on the funnel-can. A fan whirred, barely audible to Cantrell. Sarge moved the funnel-can around Vasquez. He stopped when the funnel faced the zipped-up pocket hiding the dinosaur chicken's ear. The sniffer beeped, loud enough for Cantrell to hear over the slosh of water and the crackle of the dwindling fires on the shore.

"What's that?" Vasquez asked like he didn't know.

Lt. Liebrandt puffed up his voice. "The sniffer detects circulatory fluid of an indigenous life form in your pack."

"I don't know what all those big words mean," Vasquez said in accented Standard. He had to be grinning inside his helmet.

Sarge loomed closer to Vasquez. "Play dumb with me and you will regret it. Toss out the trophy," Sarge said. "And God help you it better be only an ear."

Vasquez stood taller for a moment, until his shoulders hunched and his hands groped for the zipper pocket. He showed the dinosaur chicken ear to Sarge. "You mean this? I didn't know there was a reg against it."

Sarge's voice grew deeper. "Toss. It."

Vasquez shrugged. He flicked his wrist and the ear went spinning into deeper water behind the boat. Maybe some little blue crawly things would lay eggs on it.

Vasquez made his way to a seat inside the boat. Armando went up next. The sniffer found Armando was clean. Of course it would. *He's a good soldier.*

One gloved hand on the ladder's railing, Cantrell hesitated. The piece of bark seemed to weigh down his pack.

Are **you** *a good soldier?*

His sweat suddenly sour in his nostrils, Cantrell trudged up the ladder. Sarge worked the sniffer around. The funnel paused near the pocket... and moved on.

"Clean," Sarge said.

Lt. Liebrandt transmitted an interior view of his helmet to the augmented reality rig in Cantrell's suit. Cantrell could see the officer's face, smooth but for a mole on his jawline near his chin. "Good job today, soldier," the lieutenant said.

"Thank you, sir," said Cantrell, certain his guilt came through in his tone.

But apparently it didn't. The augmented reality view of Lt. Liebrandt's face vanished. The lieutenant turned his head to the man at the base of the ladder and said, "Next."

Cantrell trudged into the boat. Two aisles of seats, like the departure lounge at the space elevator station on New Ozark. But less comfortable.

He mounted his rifle in the storage locker, then found a seat next to Armando and slipped off his pack. The piece of bark in its pocket seemed to double the pack's weight. The pack raced down his shoulders and thudded on the deck.

He slumped into his seat and pulled the pack under. Clearing the aisle. Really, hiding the piece of bark.

Armando lolled his head back. Cantrell knew his squadmate well enough to know Armando didn't want to talk.

Gratitude trickled through Cantrell. He didn't want to talk either.

Cantrell frowned. A thought lumbered through a mental fog. *What's the big deal about a piece of bark? Is there something on it?*

Another lumbering thought. *Of course not... but hide it anyway.*

He pushed up the visor on his helmet and stared at the far bulkhead. Two hours, forty klicks, across the deep blue sea back to the island base. Most men dozed. A few talked in low and tired tones. Vasquez grumbled to one of his buddies, words inaudible, anger at the lieutenant and Sarge plain in his tone.

Cantrell dozed, or blacked out, or just let his thoughts wander. He and most of the others jolted upright in their seats when the boat's motors whined higher and the boat slewed about. Backing up to dock. The whine of the motors dropped to normal but got an echo. The walls and high ceiling of the pen.

The boat stopped. The ramp eased down with a whish of pneumatics and clomped on the concrete dock. The pen's interior was shadowy except for the orangey brightness of an open man-sized door in the corner.

The sunlight tugged on Cantrell like a magnet. But first...

Sarge and Lt. Liebrandt stepped onto the dock and waited under spotlights mounted high up, where the pen's ceiling met the walls. They waited with four civilians, three men and a woman, clad in cargo pants under white lab coats. The lab coats had blue logos on them. A line ran side-to-side from a brain. Some words, maybe made up or maybe from some dead language.

One of the men, though the shortest of the three, was obviously the leader from the body language of the other civilians and the lieutenant. Stitching on his lab coat named him Dr. Fitzhugh. He cracked his knuckles and turned green eyes cool as a menthol vape on the solders.

Cantrell swallowed thickly and lined up with the other men of the platoon. They filed to the storage locker for their rifles, then out of the boat, past Liebrandt, Sarge, and the civilians. The civilian contractors sometimes did inspections after missions and this must be one. Sarge waved men through. "Come on, back to your racks. Hustle! I want off this boat too."

Lt. Liebrandt and green-eyed Dr. Fitzhugh said nothing. Maybe it wasn't an inspection after all?

"Vasquez," the lieutenant said. "Step aside and wait."

Vasquez glowered for a moment, but when he turned to Fitzhugh he dropped his eyes and slumped his broad shoulders. He shuffled out of the way as the line filed past.

"Armando."

Arched eyebrows arched even higher. Armando bobbed his pointy chin. "Me? Why?"

"Random check," said Dr. Fitzhugh in a brisk voice. "You know it won't hurt."

They all knew the inspections didn't hurt, but nobody liked them. Armando's face fell. He took a step aside.

Cantrell clamped his jaws together. *They're going to pull me out next.* But he manned up and slapped Armando on the shoulder. "See you back at the rack."

Armando nodded. Cantrell went forward. He just knew the lieutenant would call his name... but this time the lieutenant didn't even make eye contact as he went by.

Outside. Orangey rays of afternoon sun were no match for the cold sweat on his cheeks and nape.

Get rid of that pic—spots swam in his vision—*piece of bark.* But where? Leave it on the ground, even toss it in a waste hopper, and someone would notice. Brass and more civilians would come down. The investigation would make an inspection look easy.

Cantrell trudged toward the armorer's warehouse. He shuffled through the line, handing over his rifle, setting down his pack so that a civilian tech could extract him from his battlesuit. In his undershorts and T-shirt in the air conditioning, he shivered even after he pulled on his fatigues and pushed his arms through the straps on his pack.

On his way to the soldier's dormitory, he felt like an enemy lurked amid the maintenance garages and the training sheds, preparing an ambush.

He made it to the wide three-story building and trudged up to the room he shared with Armando. Two twin beds on plastic frames. Afternoon light made an angled geometry-class shape halfway down his bed. Shelves with a few mementos from home, a paper-thin display showing a video loop of Armando's family, a handwritten card from Nanette.

Even the card seemed oppressive. He clomped forward on the plastic-tile floor—

—Ouch—

At least his boots kept his toe from stubbing badly on his trunk.

For the first time in hours, Cantrell felt like he could wriggle out of his anxiety. He shrugged off his pack and kneeled at the foot of his bed. He pulled his trunk all the way out from under, then shifted it and his position as if getting more comfortable. But really, to happen to block the view from the hidden camera in the corner.

He pressed his thumb to the biometric lock. The trunk lid popped up an inch. Cantrell yanked it up the rest of the way. A jumbled mess greeted him. Civilian clothes, toiletries kit, a trucker hat with the family farm's logo. Further down, a printed Bible pressed on him by Nanette's mother the last time he'd seen her.

With trembling hands, Cantrell pulled the piece of bark out of his pack. He glanced at it and spots again swam in his eyes. Color leached out of his peripheral vision.

What was it about the piece of bark that brought a risk of blackout? He tried to look at it full on, but a blind spot formed in the middle of his sight and turned the piece of bark into a blur.

Was the piece of bark marked in some way?

Why couldn't he remember?

Hurriedly, he shoved the piece of bark toward the bottom of his locker, under the Bible, and snapped shut the lid. A thud as the magnetic lock resealed. The scrape of the trunk against plastic tile. The creak of his bed under his rump, his back. The warmth of sunlight across his bare forearm, abdomen, and hand....

...Warmth on his cheeks. A bright orange glow through his eyelids. Cantrell opened his eyes and squinted against sunlight on his face.

His mouth tasted cottony. How long had he napped? And one hell of a weird dream, about, about, what was it about? And the mission earlier today...?

Cantrell sat up. Alone in the narrow room. Despite the late afternoon warmth, he shivered. Get out of here and join the rest of the platoon in the rec hall. He'd earned it. Today he'd been a good soldier. Today they all had been.

2

Ross Cantrell strode up the jetway toward the concourse. His feet sprung on the spongy surface. Yes, his backpack massed only ten kilos, much less than the pack he'd humped on Azureseas. But the main reason he strode with easy steps and a grin cracked open the sides of his mouth lay in an inner pocket of his baggy blue cargo pants, zipped up and secure.

For a moment, his mood dipped. Something else, something secured in a zip pocket. But what? He hadn't worn these pants since before he'd left home, almost two years ago.

Another step. A quick shake of his head. Whatever that something else might have been couldn't be as important as what was in that pocket now. He touched the thin, rigid case through the fabric of his pants. His grin returned.

He rounded the last corner, went from spongy jetway to the carpeted concourse. His grin widened into a toothy smile even before he heard them shout, "Ross!"

He jogged forward to the group of five. He swept up his parents in a both arms. His dad, Big Jim, squeezed Ross back harder. The older man's beard scratched his cheek. Mom sobbed tears of joy against his chest. He held them a long time. After Dad slapped him on the backpack, Ross broke away. He extended his hand to the Bauers, Nanette's father and mother.

"Welcome back," her father said. His crows'-feet deepened around his eyes and his goatee turned into a scrutinizing pointer. His voice boomed amid the chatter of conversations and the whistle of a cappuccino frother up the concourse. "Looks like Ground & Suborbital turned you into a man."

"I enlisted with Planetside Security," Ross said, and Mr. Bauer's narrowing eyes told him it didn't matter at all which of the Consortia's ground combat companies he'd served in. "...and I'm definitely a better man for it."

Mrs. Bauer smiled up at him with her baggy eyes. She wore a dress over her trim form and Ross wondered if she'd just been or was just about to go to church. "You look quite handsome," she said. "The Lord kept a guardian angel watching you."

His soldiering days blurred in his memory, like looking out a window in a heavy rain. Ross certainly couldn't remember any touch of the divine while he'd been on Azureseas, but the best answer when Mrs. Bauer said something like that was, "I'm sure He did, ma'am."

"You read that Bible I gave you?"

Ross' mood dipped for a moment and he didn't know why. Maybe because he was about to lie to Mrs. Bauer. He jammed his smile in place. "Every day."

The Bauers each took a half-step back. That was all the opening Ross needed. His grin widened as he pivoted to Nanette. Blond hair in a ponytail to her shoulder. A smile of straight and gleaming teeth. Blue eyes, wide and bright and dripping tears.

He gripped her upper arms and pulled her close. They kissed. Her tears trickled down his cheeks and into the corners of his mouth.

"I missed you so much," Ross murmured into her lips.

She wrapped her arms around his shoulders. "Me too."

"I love you so much."

"Me too."

His heart swelled. He almost did it right there, but it wasn't time yet. Instead he said, "I'm never going away again."

She stepped out of his embrace. "Good." The word broke up into half a chuckle and half a sob. Her smile widened and her tears flowed faster.

Dad cleared his throat. "We're going to take you out for dinner, son. Here in Taney Creek, before we head home."

"I'd like that," Ross said. Maybe he'd get a chance to talk privately with Mr. Bauer before dessert.

The chance came much sooner than that. Twenty meters up the concourse, with the scent of ground espresso buoyant in their noses, Bauer said, "Get you a cup, Ross?"

"Thank you, sir.... Let me help you carry."

After Bauer ordered himself a cappuccino and Ross, an americano black as space near a jump point, and the two of them waited near the counter for the articulated robot arm to deposit their drinks, Ross blurted out the words. "Sir, I'd like your permission to marry Nanette."

Crow's feet wrinkled. "You would."

"Sir, you said it yourself, my service made me more of a man. I saved almost every penny they paid me, it's enough to buy some ranchland when Bioseeding opens up the next territory—"

"*Almost* every penny?"

"I bought a ring." Ross moved his hip closer to the counter, further out of sight of Nanette and the others waiting in the concourse. He patted the pocket and said, "Red diamond. From Ophir. It's got a nanochip with proof it's natural." Ross gave Bauer a hopeful look.

"Do you have a guilty conscience about something?"

Ross blinked, but then stood taller. "I would know if I did, and I don't."

The older man said nothing. The robot arm whirred and set down their drinks. Bauer reached for his and paused with the cup near his mouth. "I approve."

A block of ice melted inside Ross. "Thank you, sir."

Bauer jutted out his goateed chin. "Don't make me regret it."

"I won't, sir."

For the first time Ross could ever remember, the corners of Bauer's mouth turned up and he patted Ross on the shoulder. "Now let's treat our returning soldier to the dinner he deserves."

. . .

THE BEST RESTAURANT in town jutted out from a bluff overlooking the small river that gave Taney Creek its name. They sat at a table upstairs, where the windows gave views of thousands of houses. On the roofs, ink-black solar panel arrays soaked up the yellow rays of Beta Can. Ten miles away, a tiny dot of a plane leaving the airport climbed over green fields and pastures, then banked in front of the End-O'-The-Biosphere Mountains. Deep green forest blanketed the reddish-brown foothills. Thick clouds masked the upper slopes below the glittering diamond peaks.

Azureseas might be prettier, but New Ozark was home.

After the robotic cart wheeled up with beers, glasses of wine, and Mrs. Bauer's iced tea, Big Jim asked from across the table, "What was it like out there, son?"

Ross lacked interest in talking about his security stint, not when the woman he loved sat next to him and smiled at him like she wanted him to be happy more than anything else. Nanette angled her head and laid her hand on his forearm. "You don't have to talk about it if you don't want to."

"It wasn't like that," Ross said. "There's some old line, soldiering is 99% boredom."

Bauer's voice carried from the far end. His tone hinted at stories he'd never told. "And 1% terror."

Ross looked down, with an aw-shucks look on his face. "It was a little scary at times. The—" He enunciated the word the officers used. "—in-di-ge-nes could fling rocks, really fast—"

"Like David with his sling," Mrs. Bauer said.

Ross' head suddenly ached. He rubbed his forehead. "Like that, yes ma'am."

Mom's voice was tight with retroactive hope. "You were never in much danger?"

"No. It was like plinking tree cats."

"Tree cats." Big Jim's voice rumbled. When Dad used that tone, he grabbed the steering yoke of the conversation. "The eco department people still won't admit they fouled up when they made those critters.

They're making *us* gather data on habitat invasion and attacks on livestock...."

Tension eased from Ross. His soldiering experiences blurred together when he tried to think about them, and he talked as much about them as he cared to. It felt good to hear older men from his community talking about the challenges facing them. And facing him, now. Tree cats might menace farms and ranches in the new, more arid lands opened up towards the briny sea. He lifted a hoppy beer toward his mouth and savored the aroma for a moment.

Ross glanced at Nanette. His heart thumped and he smiled around his sip.

After they finished their steaks and potatoes, and ordered two slices of pie, one tiramisu, and six forks, Ross cleared his throat and glanced at Bauer. The older man's eyes narrowed. He nodded once.

Ross quietly unzipped the pants pocket with the ring, then cleared his throat more loudly. Conversation faded. Five faces turned to him. "Everyone, there's something I want to say." He turned to Nanette. "Before I enlisted, I thought I loved you. Two years later, I *know* I love you."

He pushed back his chair and lowered himself to one knee. He pulled out the ring case from his pocket. Her mouth opened wide and her blue eyes glinted and the thousands of show-me-dollars he'd spent on the ring seemed the greatest bargain ever. "Will you marry me?"

Nanette gasped, then said, "Yes, oh yes," before tears ran down her smiling cheeks. She put on the red diamond ring from Ophir, then they kissed, longer and more deeply even than they had in the airport.

The older people spoke, to Ross, to one another. He barely heard. His mother and hers wanted to admire the ring and Nanette held out her hand to show them. He barely saw. The slice of apple pie for Nanette and him came, a la Canadian, and he barely tasted the slice of cheddar cheese on top. He only had eyes for his girlfriend. His fiancée. The only woman he'd ever love for the rest of his life.

Some time later, after their fathers split the check, Big Jim held out a hand to keep Ross and Nanette from standing to go. A wise look came to his face. "Your mother and I, and the Bauers, are going to get hotel rooms here in town tonight. You and Nanette can take our truck and head home."

Bauer and his wife held hands. "Nanette, Ross," he said, "it's important that the two of you prayerfully reflect on the commitment you're making, to make sure it's in line with God's will." Mrs. Bauer nodded, like a fine lady in a costume drama might nod over tea. From where she couldn't see, Bauer winked at Ross.

Nanette squeezed Ross' hand. With a proper voice, she said, "Thank you, Dad, Mom."

They stood then and filed for the door. Ross took one last glance out the window, toward the distant iron hills and the surmounting diamond mountains covered over by water and life. Nanette excused herself and took her purse to the ladies' room. Waiting for her in the front lobby, Big Jim shook Ross' hand, said, "I'm proud of you," then leaned closer and whispered, "I messaged Tommy and Ellie to sleepover at the Evans' house tonight."

Ross' face grew warm. Big Jim grinned. "Thanks, Dad."

"Got to give you peace and quiet to be prayerful." Big Jim slapped Ross on the back. Nanette returned from the ladies' room with a smile for Ross. The party filed out and parted ways in the parking lot.

A minute later, after the air conditioning took the edge off the long afternoon heat inside Dad's pickup, Nanette said from next to him on the bench seat at the rear of the cabin, "I *cannot* believe my dad got my mother to agree to this."

"She's a good woman and she believed him."

"She can't be that naive. Can she?" Nanette squirmed a little on her seat.

"You okay?" Ross asked. "If you're having second thoughts, we don't have to do it tonight. I know I want to do it with you the rest of my life—"

She touched his lips with a manicured finger. "No second thoughts."

"I brought home some prophylactics," he blurted. The pickup made a right turn, toward the two-lane highway leading out of Taney Creek toward home. "The service handed them out." Cheeks suddenly hot, he said, "I never used—"

"I got a prescription. I thought you might propose, so I called a teledoc in New Springfield—" The planet's capital and largest city, at the foot of the space elevator and a thousand miles from small-town gossip. "—and lied that I was already engaged. It came in the mail. I put it in before we left the restaurant—"

His turn to stop her from talking with a touch to her lips. With his mouth, in the deepest kiss yet. His body yearned for much more. From the way she leaned into him, it seemed like she yearned for more, too. But not here, in a pickup truck on a public road. It would be too cheap.

Desire glowed inside Ross for the next hour. The two-lane road, purple-black and whisper-quiet under the truck's tires, followed the creek south out of the town. Farms, ranches, fenced-off sections of wilderness with Department of Ecoengineering signs on eight-foot high chain link. Bald knobs of gray basalt showed through on high spots of the terrain, and made the work of human hands seem thinly rooted on this world. To take his mind off his urges, he talked about the ranch they would buy, the house they would build. The roots they would grow deeper into New Ozark.

Forty miles out, the truck turned left, away from the creek. Nanette talked about the children they would have, and how soon she wanted them. She squeezed his hand then, and said, with her head angled away from him and a coy smile on her lips, "But not tonight."

Their home town, Saddlepoint, nestled on a small plateau between two high hills fifteen miles from the creek. Nothing much had changed since he'd left. Not that he had eyes for anything but Nanette. So close. Just six miles on asphalt, then the truck slowed for the driveway to his parent's ranch. The truck rumbled over the cattle guard, a pit crossed by three-inch pipes about three inches apart. Through the seat, tonight he felt the bumpy pipes more than ever before.

The pickup let them out at the front door, into the golden light of late afternoon. A glance told him his parents hadn't yet built the second floor or the new master bedroom suite they'd always talked about. Other than that, he didn't care what might have changed.

The front door recognized him and opened. He glimpsed in the sunroom his trunk, deep green plastic with *Cantrell, J.R.* and the Planet-side Security logo printed on it. But other than that, he had tunnel vision. He led Nanette by the hand, down the hall, past the quiet and empty rooms of his younger siblings and toward his.

Closed blinds cast diffuse light across his narrow bed. Their lips met in wet kisses tasting of seared beef. Their hands tugged at clothing, their own or each other's. Ross lost track.

After their clothes lay in a heap, he gazed into her blue eyes. "Ready for this?"

She met his gaze. "More than anything." She tugged on his hand and took a step toward his bed.

Afterward, as they lay together, still breathing heavily, she gave him a wry smile.

"It wasn't good?"

"I heard a girl's first time usually isn't."

"Funny. It was great for me."

She quirked her mouth, then punched his upper arm with the side of her knuckles.

Ross grinned back. "Hey, maybe your next time will be better."

An hour later, it was.

Full dark had settled by now. They daydreamed aloud in giddy afterglow about their future life together as they drifted off to sleep.

Ross woke when the first rays of dawn lightened the sky. The first time since he'd debarked at the top of the space elevator that he'd slept through all the longer New Ozark night. He lay there, Nanette's body snug against him, and felt more at home than he ever had in years.

She woke then. Despite the dim light her smile glowed. "I love you, Ross Cantrell."

Like a valve opened, a warm feeling poured out of his chest and down to his toes and fingers. His ardor rose, undimmed by their couplings the night before.

"I love you." He kissed her, and quickly discovered her ardor flowed in complement with his.

Afterward, with more light in the sky and more color in his room, the bull bellowed in its pen. Ross sighed. "It's been good to taste the perks of married life, but we've got to do the duties of it too."

She gave him a kiss. "Take care of the chores. I'll cook up breakfast."

He found old clothes from his closet. Baggy and a little short, but they fit well enough. He went to his dad's office. A bank of dark monitors lined one wall. He gave voice commands and the controller tucked away in the cabinet set the monitors aglow. Camera feeds of the cattle grazing in the south field. The high-def images brought up the smells of bovine hide and manure. Biotelemetry from the herd. Charts of spot and futures prices from the stockyard in Taney Creek. Ross checked the water tanks and pumps, the automatic feeder dispensing grain for the penned bull, and the other systems checking the systems that checked those things.

Which wasn't enough. He went into the kitchen. Bacon sizzled on cast iron and the oven's cooling fan whirred. He stole up behind Nanette and wrapped his arms around her waist. "I'm going to check the livestock in person."

She turned at that, a quizzical look on her face. But then her blue-eyed gaze darted over his expression and she nodded. "Food'll be ready in fifteen."

He kissed her, then went to the mud room for rubberized boots.

The morning had a cool edge, but from the clear sky and the first rays of sunlight on his face, Ross knew it would warm up quickly. At the chicken coop, the spring closure of the door twanged like an untuned guitar. The smell of feathers and chicken dung permeated the rough wooden walls but the chickens were gone. Did Dad talk about that at dinner last night?

Ross grinned. He'd had other things on his mind.

At the barn and checked on the bull, which eyed him insolently while its jaws mashed grain pellets. Out the back of the barn and along the outside of the barbed wire fencing in the bull's pen, he came to the south field. The gate opened for him. He walked onto grass hummocked by hooves after the last rain. Cows and calves perked up their heads and watched him.

Ross watched them back. He couldn't remember all the things his dad said you should look for, but he looked for the things he did remember. And one of the calves limped, with the tatters of a biodegradable bandage on its back left foot. A tree cat attack.

Ross' head jerked up. He checked the clump of maples and oaks growing downslope, near the gully. The only movement came from birds and squirrels.

Home didn't mean his challenges were over. It just meant he faced different ones, now.

Back in the house, Nanette ladled cream gravy over steaming plates of bacon and biscuits. "Your folks sold off their last chickens a couple of months ago."

Ross crossed the kitchen and gave her a kiss. A glance out the window and his eyes crinkled. He couldn't see the chicken coop from this side of the house. "How did you know I checked out the coop?"

"Heard the spring scritching when you opened the door," she said with a smile.

"I knew you had sharp hearing—"

"Especially when I'm listening for you." An apologetic look filled Nanette's face. "You didn't tell me what you wanted to drink with breakfast."

"Coffee."

"Since when? Creamer, sugar?"

"Black."

Her eyebrows jumped. She bustled into the kitchen and returned in a moment with two hot mugs. The red diamond on her finger sparkled in the warm glow of the ceiling panels.

They sat, and ate. Everything tasted good. Everything felt good. Maybe not every day with Nanette would feel this good, but remembering moments like this would help them get through the days when their marriage would get some rust on it.

After breakfast, she cleared the dishes and refilled their coffee. "I'd like us to go to the sunroom."

"Sure." Ross put on a lazy grin. "We don't have to do it in the bedroom every time."

She grinned for a moment, but quickly grew serious. "I gave you my body, even though it was a little scary, because I love you and I trust you and I knew it would bring us closer. I'd like you to do something that might be a little scary for you but would bring us closer too."

Ross set down his mug with a clunk on the table's tile top. He took her hand in both his, rested his thumbs on the ring. "I've already done things for you more scary than anything in the house."

"I want to go through your trunk with you."

He felt light-headed for a moment. He pulled a hand away from her to steady himself on the tabletop. "No reason to do that."

Nanette reached for his hand. "Don't worry, I'm not going to judge. Whatever might be in there, whatever you did or didn't do on Azureseas, I'm going to love you, Ross Cantrell, come hell or high water."

Her touch seemed foreign, as if he wore an invisible glove. "Judge? There's nothing in there I feel bad about." His legs swayed like saplings in a breeze. "There's nothing in there worth looking at."

Her eyes crinkled. "Let me look at nothing worth looking at. With you."

Dark spots drifted at the edges of his vision. He took shallow breaths. The crinkle left her blue eyes. Her gaze became a lifeline, reminded him of man-overboard recovery practice during training on Azureseas.

A deep inhalation, scented by conditioned air and her presence. The spots faded out and full color returned to his peripheral vision. He took her hand and squeezed gently. "With you."

"Are you okay?"

"Travel, gravity changes, it all just caught up with me for a second. I'm okay now."

They took their coffee mugs to the sunroom. On their second steps in, the hardwood floor squeaked in the same spot it always did. Light slanted through the south-facing windows and glinted off the trophies and prizes earned by Ross and his siblings and crowded into the display case by his mother. The couch and chairs still matched. The tan plaid pattern might come back in style someday.

His trunk, rigid lines, deep green, plastic, squatted next to the couch like an interloper. Nothing worth looking at? He couldn't even remember what was in it. Empty it out, keep what was worth keeping, then throw the rest of the contents and the trunk too in the recycling hopper.

They sat on the couch together. The cushion sagged under their weight and rippled like a gentle sea when he dragged the trunk around to the front of the couch. At the touch of his thumb, the biometric lock popped open.

He and Nanette looked inside.

Ross let out a breath.

T-shirts, a lightweight jacket, blue jeans. "We got to wear civilian clothes sometimes."

She playfully arched an eyebrow. "Was there a house of ill repute on base?"

Warmth flushed Ross' neck, cheeks, and earlobes. "I went in there once, with my buddies, but I never left the lobby. I swear to God."

"I believe you."

"They knew their trade, but I could see through their sweet voices. I wanted to save my money. And myself. For you."

Nanette eyed him for a moment, then nodded as if he'd passed a lie-detector test. She gave him a kiss, loving, not lustful, then turned her attention back to the trunk. "Hey!" She grabbed a trucker hat with the Cantrell Ranch logo and pulled down over her blond locks. "I'm going to be a Cantrell, I should advertise."

Ross grabbed the brim of the trucker hat and twisted it side-to-side. "No."

"A girl can look country if she wants."

"Hell yes. The problem is, the hat's for Big Jim Cantrell's ranch. You're going to advertise Ross and Nanette Cantrell's."

She dropped the hat to the couch next to her. She teased out her hair with her fingertips, then kissed him again. Lust sparked, but after the exertions of last night and earlier this morning, he was out of kindling.

Ross pulled out a bag of toiletries and tossed it into the recycling hopper. He reached into the trunk and pulled out the Bible given to him by Mrs. Bauer. "We're going to tell your mom I read a couple of chapters every day."

"I tell her the same thing." She winked. "Though there is a lot of wisdom. Better to marry than to be consumed by lust."

"Even better would be both," Ross said.

She laughed like bubbly music. He shared a chuckle, then sat back and sipped coffee around a smile. He was with the woman he loved in a place he wanted to be.

Nanette reached deep into the trunk for something. "I didn't know you drew."

"Draw? I don't."

"One of your buddies, then. He's pretty good. Is this a creature from Azureseas?"

She held out to him a crinkly tan piece of some tree's scaly bark. Black marks scorched the edges, as if from fire. More black marks showed. Not from fire. From charcoal, maybe. Lines by an inhuman hand, showing a creature—

—*Creature? Like hell.*

An intelligent alien life form, pricking its long slender ears and raising one front paw toward the same God he and Nanette prayed to....

"Ross. Ross!" Nanette's voice, laden with more fear than he ever wanted to hear in it.

He opened his eyes. His body felt like a suit of old clothes, ill-fitting and wrinkled. He squinted around the room, confused. The blackouts were supposed to stop after leaving Azureseas—

He jolted upright.

"Are you okay? You had me so worried."

He nodded absently. His gaze locked onto the picture of the dinosaur chicken. The intelligent, worshipping, dinosaur chicken. He took it from her loose grip and cradled it in his palms.

"They messed with our minds."

"Ross, I don't understand."

Dr. Fitzhugh, the short one who cracked his knuckles and pierced you with his green eyes. "They messed with our minds to make us think the dinosaur chickens were just dumb animals. As if animals could build huts or make gunpowder by instinct."

"You mean...." Nanette squinted at the drawing on the piece of palm-like bark. "The dinosaur chickens are intelligent? But who would want to make you think they weren't? And why?"

"Why? So we could hunt them and kill them. Like good soldiers. Just following orders."

The picture felt heavy in his hands. He couldn't unsee it. The dinosaur chicken was the third intelligent life form in the room.

His heart felt heavy in his chest.

The dinosaur chicken would follow him and Nanette everywhere for the rest of his life.

He shivered, suddenly cold all over. Except for a warmth spread across his crotch. A residue of making love with Nanette? Guilt lashed him, that he'd taken a dry run at bringing new life into the universe while the dinosaur chicken in the picture lay dead on a beach, smelling of burned plantains—

No. Not from sex. The warmth in his crotch? He'd wet himself.

"I need to clean up," he said.

"Oh? Oh. Don't feel bad. It happens sometimes when people faint."

Ross gripped the arm of the couch and pulled himself up. He teetered for a moment before letting go.

"I can help you—"

"I'll make it, honeypie."

He did. Through the house, to his room for new clothes, to the bathroom to wash up. He took the picture of the dinosaur chicken with him. When he needed to use both hands, he laid the picture down. On his rumpled bed, on the back corner of the bathroom counter where water wouldn't splash on it.

Even when he turned away from the picture, he felt the dinosaur chicken's presence.

By the time he pulled a yellow T-shirt with the logo of his high school's ultimate flying disc team over his head, he knew what he had to do. A last splash of water on his cheeks. A last dab of an embroidered hand towel on his face.

Nanette sat on the couch, her hands fidgeting in her lap and worry in her blue eyes. She looked up at him and the worry didn't go away.

Ross sat next to her. His heart pounded as he took her left hand in his right. The red diamond glinted in the morning light. "You can keep the ring."

She looked puzzled, then her mouth fell open. "What?"

H held up the piece of palm-like bark and turned the picture of the dinosaur chicken to her. "I did wrong. I've got to set it right."

Her mouth worked. Her eyes glistened. "How?"

"I'll go to Azureseas. I'll go to the dinosaur chickens and help them fight back."

Tears flooded from her eyes. She groped for a tighter grip on his hand. "Ross, how can that work? Don't the dinosaur chickens hate people now? And how can you fight back when people have more armor and better guns? You'd be a traitor to the human race and you'll get killed for nothing."

He held the picture closer to her eyes. "Not nothing."

Nanette's gaze darted around, avoiding the picture. Until she couldn't. She stared at it then. Sniffling, crying, her shoulders hunched, her mouth tight. "It's sad, I know. The rich and powerful used you, like they've always used us. But you can't solve all the problems in the universe. You can't solve all the problems of the dinosaur chickens." She tugged down on his forearm. He lowered the picture.

"Stay with me. I love you, and I don't care what you might have done, especially when the rich and powerful made it so you didn't know what you were doing. Let's just build our lives together."

Her words tugged at him. He could see a new ranch, a new house, new life with her hair and his eyes, for decades and decades to come.... and with the ghost of the dinosaur chicken haunting him every step. Even though the ghost would ignore him as it permanently reached out for God to help it and its people.

"If I don't try to make it right," Ross said, "I won't be worth a damn. I won't be a man you'd want to live with." And as true as the words were, as much as he loved her, it mattered even more that he wouldn't want to live with himself. "I've got to do this."

She pulled away from him. Her tears still dripped, but a cold fire burned in her eyes. "Then go," she said. "And hell yes I'll keep your goddamn ring."

$$3$$

THE WORKERS on Azureseas lived in a town of lumpy plastic buildings grown near the maintenance sheds and the nanoassembleries, ten miles inland. No cool breezes there. No views of the vast blue ocean that gave the planet its name. Just flat terrain and clouds of native insects the workers called sandflies. They didn't bite or sting. Most of the native life's proteins and carbs and DNA were mirror images of Earth life's. But they still landed and crawled on exposed skin for ticklish and itchy seconds before buzzing away.

Ross Cantrell quickly learned the routine when off shift. He wore a bandana around his neck and pulled it over his mouth when a thousand buzzes sounded nearby and got louder. The sap of a bush with coiled, dark green leaves made a sandfly repellent. It worked, but made his arms sticky. By the end of the day dust covered his arms like cornmeal breading on catfish.

One of the more enterprising workers chopped and parboiled the leaves and sold a more effective, and less sticky, repellent extract for a tidy profit. Management turned a blind eye. If it made the workers more productive, and didn't use any nanoassembler time, they didn't care.

The nanoassembleries made a much better sandfly repellent. They even made portable dispensing drums that synthesized the repellent from sunlight and processed garbage. But Ross and the other workers only deployed the repellent drums along the shore, at the construction sites. Outside the glass lobbies of two-story condo complexes and high-rise beachfront hotels. Near the tables and chairs of sidewalk cafés. At the driving range tee boxes and around the practice green of the golf course. Every place with a transponder beacon pinging out the name Mammoth Construction LLC.

No tourists strolled the beaches, yet. Only a few advance-team employees from the hotel and entertainment companies scurried around the sites, scowling into midair at checklists displayed by their augmented reality contact lenses. For Ross, it was like working in full-scale architectural models.

You leave for eight months and everything changes.

His first weeks back on Azureseas, he'd looked for the site of the village where the proof the dinosaur chickens were intelligent had fallen into his hands. No luck. Planetside Security, his former employer, must have scraped the ground of charred huts and dinosaur chicken remains. High-powered nano could break up the mirror image proteins and rebuild them into molecules Earth life could use. A disposal of remains more thorough than any crematory could manage. And any other traces that might have survived would have been plowed under by the construction equipment that built the empty hotels and restaurants and shops.

There were days, early on, when Ross wanted to shout at the advance teams. Grab the young women hotel clerks by the upper arms of their navy blue skirt suits, slap the effeminate male restaurateurs and shopkeepers across their exfoliated faces. *Intelligent beings lived here. We killed a lot and drove off the rest so your corporate masters could get richer. You should be ashamed.*

He held back. The ethnic cleansing wasn't their fault. And more important, he couldn't do anything if he blew his cover.

Planetside Security had traded its base on the nearby island for one five miles inland, on the road to worker town. A fake ID identifying him as *Stuart Havlicek* from New Prague, the capital and only major city on Masaryk; a retro-nano-viral-vector treatment to disguise the bits of his DNA used for forensics; more nano to change his retina, his fingerprints, and his facial bone structure; all fooled Planetside's automated sensors. Well worth the large chunk of his enlistment bonus he'd spent on them, even though he sometimes woke up with phantom pain shooting through his cheeks and eye sockets. But all that work wouldn't fool a suspicious person accessing Planetside's records and finding there a photo of Ross Cantrell.

Instead, he worked by day and he planned by night. He hadn't seen a dinosaur chicken anywhere near worker town. From time to time, armored personnel carriers—wheeled, boxy like his old deployment boat, but lacking mounted guns—rolled up the road and set off cross-country to the north, raising clouds of dust visible for miles. Ross angled an ear that direction but never heard gunfire. Making the rounds like a cop or a night watchman? Or combat operations out of earshot? Ten or twelve miles.

A chance meeting at a bar in worker town confirmed what he suspected. A solitary Planetside soldier, out of uniform and into his third bomber of beer, perked up when Ross offered to buy him his fourth. Five steps to the ordering kiosk. Thirty seconds for the robot arms to deliver a beer for the soldier and a radler—beer cut with a lemon-lime soda—for Ross. He carried the tall glasses back to the table and sat.

The soldier adjusted his off-duty baseball cap over his sandy blond buzz cut, then extended a tattooed arm for the beer. Inside Ross lodged a nugget of hate. Unlike the employees of the hotels and shops, the soldier had taken part in the ethnic cleansing...

...and judging by his chewed nails and the haunted look lurking around the corners of his eyes as he gulped beer, the soldier did his foul duty as unknowingly as Ross had.

Ross drank his sweet, diluted beer. "They didn't tell me there'd be a war on when I signed the work contract, or I would've asked for higher pay."

The soldier scrunched up his face. "It's not a war. Pest control. We're keeping big native animal life away from the new hotels on the beach."

"I didn't know they were a problem."

"You're welcome." The soldier gave an inebriated grin. "Really not much to it. We drive up and down the dirt track along the fence, mostly. We'll go out one of the gates if we see dinosaur chickens nearby to scare them off. We don't even have to shoot any anymore. They're learn...."

The soldier's eyes turned glassy. His mouth went slack.

Ross thumped his glass gently on the table. "Hey, man. You okay?"

The soldier blinked groggy eyes. "My bad. Happens sometimes. Trace molecules in the air mixing with the med nano they pumped into us. The civilians say the blackouts go away after you leave." The soldier paused with the glass near his mouth. "You don't get them, do you?"

The cold green eyes of Dr. Fitzhugh came to his mind's eye. Ross suppressed a shudder. "Nah. They wouldn't make this a tourist planet if everyone got them, would they?"

"On vacation and you blackout? Hell, that would be fun, wouldn't it?" The soldier emptied his drink. His smile faded as he set down the glass.

Ross kept him talking. A fifth beer loosened his tongue even further. Twice daily patrols. Double fences, both with razor wire pointing out, twelve miles north. Cameras and microphones every ten meters. Gates big enough to drive an armored personnel carrier through, every four miles.

Hundreds of miles of terrain beyond, where sandy plain gave way to rolling hills.

Where thousands, maybe even tens of thousands, of dinosaur chickens needed help to form an army and reclaim their rights.

Ross gathered more intel and swiped survival items to add to the pack locked in his personal luggage during the next weeks. He always kept an eye out for the men he'd known from his stint with Planetside. Lt. Liebrandt. Or Vasquez. Vasquez seemed like the guy who'd renew his contract for the chance to shoot more guns and kill more things.

Old faces turned out to be no problem. Instead, a new arrival to worker town disrupted his planning.

He met the guy in the chow hall. Young, Ross' age, give or take a couple of years. A nose as squashed as a bad boxer's dominated the guy's broad face as he swiveled his head, up at the glass dome and from side to side at the ordering kiosks and serving stations. The guy's pallor showed a lot of recent time spent in ships and space elevators.

Had rumors about the dinosaur chickens spread off Azureseas? Only one way to find out. Ross went over with a tray of vat-grown chicken breast and fried hydroponic okra, and a hi-new-guy smile.

A pop-up into Ross's augmented reality contact lenses, showing data pinged out by the new guy's nametag, made Ross stutter-step. *Jan Cech, New Prague, Masaryk.*

The stutter-step swung Cech's gaze to Ross. Half a second later, Cech's blue eyes widened. In a smooth voice, he said over the echoing clatter of conversations and utensils on plates, "Ahoy! Yak say maa tay?"

The air suddenly tasted dry. Software in the wearable dangling on a chain round Ross' neck needed two seconds to feed the translation to his earbuds. *Hello! How are you?* At least it caught up with Cech's next words almost in real time. "What, are you German?"

Ross blinked and put on an awkward smile. "Sorry. Gets noisy in here, and I haven't heard the language in a long time." His mind raced over the info packet he'd memorized from the identity engineer. "I grew up in the Americanek neighborhood."

Cech nodded as if that explained his fumbling with the language, then squinted one eye at him. "You look familiar. You play on the Americanek junior football club? I was on the New Karlin club and we played you guys a bunch."

"I didn't play sports in high school," Ross said. Which might have been a bad answer, from the way Cech's squint turned into a confused look.

Ross went on despite his thudding heart. "We can swap stories later. You look hungry now." He pointed out the food stations around the chow hall, told Cech to avoid the meat loaf, and pointed to a table with half a dozen guys Ross kind of knew. When Cech joined the group, Ross introduced him, then said as little as possible as the conversation turned to liquor and sports. Ross gobbled down his food and left as soon as his plate was bare.

For the next two weeks, he avoided Cech when he could. And got one-eyed squints when he couldn't. If Cech got suspicious, the construction company—or, worse, Planetside—might notice and investigate.

Earlier than he'd planned, on a night lit by the Milky Way and

Azureseas' small gray potato-shaped moon, he set out. Before leaving his single room, he took off his augmented reality contact lenses and earbuds. He slipped his wearable from around his neck and dropped it in the trashcan. His backpack weighed down his shoulders and reminded him of his soldiering days as he slipped down the hall and out of the building.

It would look really odd if someone noticed him walking around worker town with a backpack, but most people slept through the white noise of air conditioning. He avoided the gambling hall and bars on the east side. He avoided the security cameras, too, when he could. When he couldn't, he pulled a wide-brimmed gray hat he'd never worn before on-planet lower over his eyes, lifted a sandfly bandana higher over his nose and his earlobes, and twisted his gait.

Soon he left worker town behind him. Parallel to but about fifty meters from the dirt track Planetside's AFVs, armored fighting vehicles, used, he crossed a terrain of native grasses thinly rooted in sandy soil. Thick air blanketed him. Sweat trickled down his neck and flooded his armpits. His work boots found good purchase but the pack slowed him. When he paused for swigs of water, he checked the sky for the lumpy moon. Always lower in the sky than he'd hoped.

Walk faster, Cantrell.

A thin line of predawn edged the eastern horizon by the time Ross reached the first of two fences. A brief pang struck him. It had been this time of day when he'd made love with Nanette for the last time.

He paused and set his shoulders. A man's got to do what he's got to do.

Right now, that meant crossing the double line of fences. Ten feet tall with strands of normal barbed wire—still sharp enough to draw blood—spaced about a foot apart. The razor wire was on top, coiled like a picture of DNA and angled out, ready to slash the veins of any dinosaur chicken trying to climb over. Atop every third pole, and under a square meter of solar panels, a turret housing a camera and a microphone panned across the view to the north.

Ross turned his head in the opposite direction. Small native animals rustled amid tufted grass. A sandfly swarm buzzed. A faint smudge of light on the southern horizon came from worker town. No rumble of an AFV's motor came to his ears, no dust from wheels obscured his view.

He sluffed out a breath. He had an hour or more, not ten minutes or less.

He dropped his backpack to the ground and opened it up. He dug out the radio frequency jammer and the wire cutters, then put the pack on again.

He turned on the jammer and shoved it into a pocket of his shorts. He tried opening the pocket flap's hook-and-loop fabric quietly, but the ripping sound still seemed to carry for hundreds of yards.

If he'd planned right, it wouldn't matter. The cameras and microphones might pick him up, but the jammer would block them from reporting his next actions to the Planetside base.

Planetside hadn't bothered with a wired backup line. Which meant its brass on Azureseas was either lazy, or also believed with its enlistees that the dinosaur chickens were just dumb animals in need of pest control.

Ross filed that thought, then turned to the fence with his wire cutters.

Snick. One strand of tense wire recoiled with a *sprang*. Another snick. Another *sprang*. From atop the poles came whirring sounds. The cameras had noticed him now.

His gut clenched, but he kept working. No turning back, now. Four more quick cuts gave him a hole he walked through.

The two fences were farther apart than an armored fighting vehicle's turning radius. The stars and faint moonlight cast the gray shadows of vehicle tracks across his path.

Ross went straight ahead. Sandy ruts slumped under his boots. A camera and microphone turret stopped whirring. It was locked on the back of his head like a handgun's laser sight.

He let out a tight breath. Whether it saw him now or not, Planetside Security would figure out soon enough that Stuart Havlicek had deserted from the human occupation of Azureseas. It wouldn't matter, if he could reach the dinosaur chickens in time.

His wire cutters opened the second fence as easily as the first.

He stepped through, took one deep breath, and started jogging.

Ross didn't pick a destination, at first. Just trying to put distance between him and Planetside. He jogged up and down low swells in the ground, sand dunes held in place by thick cover of native grasses. His pack weighed him down and his boots weren't meant for jogging. Soon he breathed heavily and sweat stuck his clothes to his skin. After five minutes he glanced backward from the top of a swell. The sandy path between the fences showed as a thin line in the grayscale light.

He slowed to a walk and untied his bandana. While he caught his breath, he studied the terrain ahead. The swells in the ground became low hills, which two or three miles ahead rose into three higher hills, two to the west, his left, and one to the east. From maps he'd glanced at, the three hills were the tips of ridge lines extending southward like a giant's fingers. Enough light spilled over the eastern horizon to show the fuzz of tree-sized foliage covering the hills' slopes.

High ground for defense, a forest for concealment and food supplies. The dinosaur chickens must live up in the hills.

Drying sweat on his arms made him shiver. Which hills? The drunken soldier had been vague about Planetside's operations north of the double fence.

Planetside would track him starting with the line he'd followed jogging away from the cameras, right? But then they would expect him to veer off that line when he was out of camera view. Which meant he should go fairly straight. That meant the hill farthest to the west was out.

He made his decision and nodded to himself. The middle hill, slightly west of north from where he walked. He jogged that way, staying in dips in the ground wherever he could to lower the chance a camera at the double fence might see him. He jogged past thicker clumps of grasses. Little animals scurried away from his boots.

The orange-yellow sun rose quickly, filling the terrain with dark greens. During one walking break, while he munched an energy bar, he took a closer look at the native plant life. The leaves were a darker green than he expected from the terrestrial plantings along the shore. The slender, coiling blades of one native grass turned almost black at the tips. Insect-like creatures buzzed and hopped, but the plants had no flowers for the native insects to pollinate.

This was a *place*, just like his family's farm on New Ozark. Embedded in the minds of the dinosaur chickens same as the farm was embedded in his. It belonged to them.

He cinched the straps of his backpack tighter, and jogged again.

The landscape changed as he neared the middle hill. The canopies of trees fanned out a foot or two above his head. The trees had pale yellow trunks, scabbed and mottled like some kind of skin disease. Some scientist could tell him why the trunks weren't made of wood, but simpler to think of them that way. A sandpaper texture when he ran his fingertips over a trunk confirmed it.

Steeper slopes in the rolling plain showed eroded limestone layered like a birthday cake had slumped over while cooling. Water seeped from the limestone and made a patch of ground soggy.

Ross went around the damp patch. Don't leave footprints if you can help it. He glanced up for his bearings, then set out for the middle hill.

The trees grew thicker, plunging most of the rolling, rising terrain into welcome shadow. He pushed his gray hat off the back of his head. Sweat matted his hair and trickled into the hat's strap crossing his neck. His legs ached. He walked more than he jogged, now.

He didn't need to hurry. The tree cover would help conceal him if Planetside's ground forces tracked him, or if the company launched a recon drone or rented time from an orbiting satellite. And if the dinosaur chickens lived close enough to approach the fence, it wouldn't be much longer till he met them.

Walking gave him a chance to study the alien forest. He'd hunted back home and knew what to look for. Snapped branches, bent stalks of grass, footprints, scat. After his mind got over the forest's strangeness, the presence of small animals somewhere in the undergrowth or in the tree's branches became clear. But nothing the size of a dinosaur chicken had come this way.

At least, not without covering its tracks.

In the distance, undergrowth rustled. Ross snapped his head up but couldn't see the source of the noise. He stopped walking, opened his mouth and relaxed his throat to breath as quietly as he could, then cupped his hand around his ear.

No other sound.

He kept going.

Glimpsed between trees, the bulk of the hill darkened the sky like a low storm cloud. Soon the last roll of the terrain gave way to a steady upward slope. His quads burned. He looked to each side and cupped his ear again, seeking a sign. Not finding any. A glance to the sky showed the yellow-orange sun past the zenith.

He'd push on for a while. Even though night came quickly at this latitude, before dark he only had to unroll his sleeping bag and eat an energy bar. He had enough food for three more days. Tomorrow he'd walk farther. Day after tomorrow, he'd take a rest day and set up the solar-powered food synther.

Deep in thought, he rounded a heap of fallen limestone. A dinosaur chicken hopped out.

4

Ross froze. For a moment that seemed to last half his life, he studied the dinosaur chicken.

Centaur shaped, about six feet from its tail flap to its long snout and five from its four toes to the pointed ears atop its V-shaped head. Covered with thick hairs or thin feathers, he couldn't tell which. The hairs were deep green in color fading to yellow at the tips.

Yellow-green also its eyes without whites. Eyes set in the front of the head, to give binocular vision like a human being or another predator. Not to the sides like a cow always on the lookout for threats.

Long ears twitched toward him. The paws on its triple-jointed front legs—the hands on its arms—had four digits each, two opposable thumbs and two long fingers with three knuckles each.

Easy to focus on its knuckles when its left hand held a donut-shaped grip around the barrel of a long firearm.

The thing it held could only be a weapon. A tube four feet long and too dull-looking to be metal. Fired clay? Some hardened wood? The tube open at the end nearest Ross, like an unblinking dark eye. The other end, closed, had a hole on the right side maybe an eighth of an inch wide. Dark scorch marks radiated from the hole along the tube.

Near the hole, the dinosaur chicken held between a thumb and finger of its right hand a slender stick, straight and just narrower than the hole. A slender column of smoke rose from an orange glow at the tip of the stick.

A *punk*, Ross and his buddies called it growing up on New Ozark, when they sneaked off to the hollow of a creek with bottle rockets.

Forget that for now. Assume in the tube, just inside the hole, a wad of gunpowder and a projectile.

A primitive firearm.

Primitive? Advanced enough to kill.

How did Dr. Fitzhugh and his psych-hackers make us think the dinosaur chickens carried blowguns or spearchuckers?

Ross raised his hands. "I come in peace. Take me to your leader."

The dinosaur chicken—no. That's what he and the other soldiers had called them when they believed they were animals. The *alien* opened its snout to reveal a mouth of yellowed teeth, the rear ones flat for mashing vegetables, the front ones pointed for tearing meat. It barked out a mix of gargling and throat-clearing.

Ross wanted to shake his head, but for all he knew, that gesture could be a challenge for a fight to the death. "No hah-blah. No parley-me."

The alien pricked one its ears. Not at Ross. At something behind Ross's right shoulder.

He heard them then. Three or four aliens behind him. Their smell overpowered the stink of his own sweat and flooded his nose. Not burnt plantain, thank Christ. Alive, they smelled peppery and musty.

The one behind his right shoulder replied to the first alien in the same language. Its voice sounded deeper and more resonant.

Others behind Ross spoke. One repeated a sound, *Khaw, khaw,* in the back of its throat.

The one with the deep voice roared something. The others turned silent, as did creatures flitting in the nearby trees.

One of the others grabbed the straps of Ross' backpack and yanked backward.

Ross staggered and dropped his arms toward his sides to balance himself. He kept his hands open and behind his back, in view of the one with the deep voice. The leader, he presumed. "I'll take off the backpack for you," he said. Slowly, he dropped to his left knee and moved his right hand up to his shoulder.

A pit gaped in his stomach. They might say the hell with it and put a bullet in him. To give up a life with Nanette for nothing....

His pulse pounded. He looked at the alien in front of him through a tunnel walled by swirling gray dots. Intelligent creatures would be curious, right? At least eager for intel. Heck, intel, intelligent, they meant the same—

Ross took a breath to calm himself. He'd been at their mercy since he'd crossed the fence. And his thoughts proved accurate, at least for the ten seconds it took him to take off his pack and set it down. They were curious enough for him to stay alive.

He raised his hands, rose to his full height, and turned.

Six feet away, the leader stood three inches taller than the others. Broader across the chest, too. Yellow ran farther down the tips of its feathers. The way it carried itself reminded Ross of his father, still nearly as strong as in youth but with a commanding presence earned by middle age.

The leader raised its right hand. A sheen rippled through the green and yellow of its hair or feathers, like oil on water or special editions of the ultimate flying disc trading cards Ross collected as a kid. Irri- something? Iridescence....

It wrapped its fingers over its thumbs, making a fist, and punched the air in Ross's direction about a foot in front of it.

Ross' mouth felt dry even though the alien leader hadn't tried to hit him. But what did the gesture mean?

The alien jabbed the air again. One spot on its arm didn't ripple with the movement. A closer look showed Ross something had gouged out a straight, thin line through its hairs or feathers, leaving behind what he guessed was a scar, puffy and bluish over pallid yellow skin.

A grazing shot by a Planetside bullet?

Another jab at the air, this one with more force behind it. The alien growled something in its language. It stared at a spot on the ground behind Ross, about five feet away from the backpack.

"I get it. I'll back away." Hands still raised, Ross shuffled backward, moving carefully to not trip over rocks or roots. The first alien, now behind him, moved backward too, keeping its distance from him. Most of the others raised their firearms.

One ducked forward with its weapon slung across its back. It kneeled at his backpack like a camel in a living nativity scene. It jabbed the unlit end of its punk into the soil, then tugged the backpack's zipper pulls and yanked the hook-and-loop flaps like it knew what it was doing.

Ross squinted for a moment. Then he realized how. The aliens had seen Planetside soldiers do the same things.

The kneeling alien reached into the backpack, pulled something out, raised it high in its right hand. A plastic water bottle, glistening with condensation.

"Water," Ross said. He remembered the fad for sign language for infants, from when his youngest brother was a year old. He held down his ring finger with his thumb so that the other fingers made a *W*, then tapped the side of his hand to his mouth. "Water."

The kneeling alien worked its left thumbs on the bottle's twist-cap. The cap turned, popped off, and dangled on its strap. The alien rocked back, then leaned forward and opened its mouth. It dabbed its sinewy tongue in the air over the bottle's mouth.

It turned its yellow-green eyes up to the leader and said something.

The leader fixed its gaze on Ross.

"Water," he said, and again tapped his mouth with a *W* of fingers.

The gaze drilled into him.

Try a different gesture. Ross opened his hand as if holding an invisible bottle, then raised it to his mouth as if taking a drink. "Water."

The leader grunted some monosyllable. It turned back to its subordinate and made a stern reply.

The kneeling alien's head slumped. It angled its neck, opened its mouth a couple of inches, and held the bottle high. It tipped the bottle toward its mouth. A trickle of water landed on its teeth and tongue.

It swallowed and looked up to the leader. It said something that sounded like "*Harek.*"

The leader grunted again, then aimed its gaze and its ears at the pack.

The kneeling alien reached back into the pack. This time it pulled out an energy bar, a sticky mass of protein and slow-digesting carbs in a foil wrapper.

The leader returned its imperious gaze on Ross.

He pressed the tips of his thumb and fingers together and aimed them at his mouth. "Food."

The kneeling alien gingerly nibbled at a corner of the wrapped bar.

"No, no!" Ross waved his hands like the mediator at an ultimate flying disc game signalling a pass hit the ground. Unlike water which he could get anywhere on Azureseas and have the bottle purify for him, he carried only a few kilos of food. He couldn't eat anything from the native biosphere.

Which meant the aliens couldn't eat anything terrestrial.

"Food for me." He made the sign for food, then tapped his chest with his index finger. "My food will make you sick." Ross made the sign for food and extended a flat hand to the kneeling alien. He mimed vomiting, making hand signs of barf exploding out of his mouth. Then he repeated the hand signs behind his butt.

The kneeling alien's ears pivoted to him. Its gaze followed his hands while he moved them, then studied his face.

A moment later, the kneeling alien lowered its hand holding the energy bar.

Another alien spoke to the kneeling alien in a gruff voice. As it growled out its words, its snout and nostril wrinkled.

The kneeling alien spread the fingers of its open hand and replied with a softer tone. *Softer* being relative, like fine grit sandpaper instead of coarse.

The other one growled again. It stuck the unlit end of its punk between its teeth, then flicked its thumbs at the kneeling alien.

A deep and firm stream of words erupted from the leader. It brought the thumbs of its right hand together, carefully as a drunk, and made a slow-motion flick of them at the growler.

All ears pivoted to the growler.

The growler lifted its shoulders as if it sought to regain some lost status. It stalked toward the kneeling alien, and yanked the wrapped energy bar from the other's grip.

Foil rustled. They'd seen Planetside soldiers tear open packets before.

"No!" Ross said again, but with less vigor. "You'll regret it." He mimed vomiting and explosive diarrhea again. Part of him wouldn't mind if the growler puked his guts out.

The growler's sharp front teeth ripped off a corner of the bar. It chewed for a moment before its eyes squinted. Muscles bulged in its neck. It glanced at the leader—

—who raised its hand high and held its thumbs together for all to see—

—and mashed the bite of energy bar between its teeth like it wanted to grind it into oblivion. Though not aimed at the growler, the last alien tapped its thumbs together, spreading them wide between each tap.

The growler swallowed, then flung the rest of the energy bar to the ground.

"Hey!" Ross said. "My food!" He turned to the leader and repeatedly pointed at the energy bar and made the food sign.

The leader grumbled something. It pointed at the food, then at Ross' mouth.

Ross took that as a yes. He scampered forward and picked up the energy bar. He brushed off a clot of soil and an eight-legged little crawler. Two puffed-out breaths didn't actually make the fallen bar any cleaner, but at least he could imagine it was clean enough. Ross stepped back and chewed a bite. Not very hungry, but he had too little food to waste any until he got the food synther on line.

He chewed another bite. The bar clogged up between his jaws. He extended his hand toward the backpack. "Water, please."

The kneeling alien looked up at him. Its yellow-green eyes looked skeptical.

"Water." Ross made the sign-language *W*. He took a chance. "*Harek?*"

The kneeling alien turned its head and pivoted its ears to the leader. "*Khaw.*"

The leader made a bunch of noises. *Harek* might have been in them.

The kneeling alien made no sound. If its body language said something, Ross couldn't read it. But when it lifted his water bottle from the ground next to his pack, warmth buoyed his torso. The kneeling alien tossed the bottle. Despite the condensation, Ross caught it between his left hand and his chest. He popped the cap and drank, not minding the plastic taste left behind by the purifier.

He'd communicated with them. Not much, but it was a first step. He munched another bite of the energy bar, more relaxed than he'd been—

The kneeling alien shouted in its language. It lurched to its feet without using its arm. It carried two things, one in each hand. It brandished them at Ross and shouted again.

Ross swallowed the bite of energy bar, then raised his water bottle. "Rifle." The alien held the barrel in its right hand and the stock in its left. Unloaded, but even if it slid the magazine into the slot, the safety mechanisms would disable the trigger unless the barrel was threaded onto the stock.

The alien holding his rifle shouted again. Its companions drew back their lips, showed meat-ripping teeth. They hissed. The growler raised its weapon to its chest. It brought the glowing tip of the punk closer to the firing hole.

"Hey!" Ross said. He held his hands face-high, palms facing out and as open as he could around the energy bar and water bottle. "I come in peace!"

The alien holding the rifle shouted again. *"Tark rehonnet! Tark rehonnet!"*

Swallowed bites of energy bar felt like rocks in Ross' gut. "I come in peace! Dammit, if I meant to use the rifle, I'd assemble the damn thing before entering indian country!"

"Tark rehonnet!" the alien shouted. Its ears twitched toward the leader. It shouted something else, followed by *"Khaw."*

The leader peered at Ross.

More aliens raised their weapons to firing position.

Oh Jesus, what do I—

The answer came to him. He dropped the bottle and the energy bar. He heard a glug of spilling water as if from dozens of yards away.

Ross threw all his effort into raising his hand and his gaze to the tree-screened sky. The piece of bark with the drawing of the praying alien burned in his memory. He twisted the muscles in his fingers, tightened the muscles of his face, trying to look as much like the praying alien as he could.

Oh Jesus, I wish I could perk my ears the way they can.

When he got as close to the praying alien's body position as he could, he froze. Small muscles in his shoulders and sides ached but he held the position. The only thing he moved was his eyes. He looked down at the leader's stern face. *Come on, you see what I'm doing, don't you?*

The yellow-green gaze drilled into him. All of a sudden, the leader's eyes widened. It jutted its hands up and out and called something in their language.

The muzzles of the aliens' firearms wavered upward. The smoking tips of the punks pulled a few inches back. All except the growler's.

Despite the hot day, Ross' face turned clammy with gooseflesh. "Yes, I was a soldier with a rifle. The bosses of my people told us you were animals. Then God showed me the truth." He extended his raised hand toward the tree canopy, aiming for the sky beyond. "God."

"*Khott,*" the leader said.

Ross grinned. "Yes. I don't know what you call Him but we call Him God. He showed me the truth. And He sent me here to fight at your side against my people's bosses."

The growler kept its weapon raised. It said something gruff and cold, and pricked one ear toward the leader.

The leader's voice rumbled. It aimed an ear at the growler yet kept its gaze on Ross.

The growler spread the fingers of its right hand toward the leader as wide as it could while holding the smoldering punk near the firing hole of its weapon. It hissed at Ross, then spewed out a stream of harsh sounds.

Another rumble in reply. The leader raised its right hand toward the sky and repeated its words.

The growler lowered its firearm. It gave Ross one last glare from its yellow-green eyes, then turned its head toward the leader.

The leader gave a command, emphasized by pointing into the forest up the slope of the hill. The alien who'd first stopped Ross took point.

After a barked order, the growler followed. Ross couldn't tell if they walked more like horses or camels on their rear-hinged knees and four-toed feet.

Behind him, the one still holding the halves of his rifle shoved them into the backpack. It zipped it up.

Ross extended a hand, but the alien slung his backpack over its right shoulder and unslung its firearm. His gut squirmed—those were his only possessions inside the backpack, including his only source of food after the energy bars ran out—but his shoulders did feel lighter for the first time all day.

The leader grumbled something at Ross, then pointed in the direction followed by the first two aliens. Ross set out. The one with his backpack came three yards behind him. His backpack thudded against its shoulder with every step. A glance back showed the leader followed, and the last alien brought up the rear.

Ross set out, through the warm and still air under the forest canopy. He studied the surrounding aliens, the dark green leaves and pale yellow not-wood, and the places where soil had eroded to show the limestone layers forming the bones of this world. New Ozark, brought to life after a billion years or more of waterless runaway greenhouse, had nothing like limestone.

How many ages did this world roll, to make layers of rock like that?

Did it matter? This world unfolded the way God meant it to. The lives of the aliens did too.i

At least, they had, until the big human money behind Planetside and the resort hotels saw illicit profit here.

As he loped up the hill, veering around trees and sweating in the warm air, a wave of calm swept over Ross. He'd make enough food to eat. He'd communicated with the aliens. Not much, but enough for them to know his heart.

In time, they'd learn what was in his brain, about weapons and how to use them.

A faint clatter sounded from downslope, behind and to his right. Ross slowed his pace and turned his head. Another alien trotted between the trees and straight toward the leader.

The alien carrying his backpack came closer. It said something to

Ross. About as intelligible as a rock polisher. Its tone sounded guarded, but with a hint of openness. It pointed at the path taken by the two lead aliens.

Absent-mindedly, he nodded and moved forward as the alien asked.

Farther behind Ross, trotting footsteps slowed to a walk. The new alien growled to the leader. A couple of hisses. Ross couldn't pick out any words.

The leader spoke. Quieter than usual. Its voice still carried command up and down the line. All the aliens froze and turned to the leader. Even the chattering animals in the forest grew quieter for a moment.

Ross couldn't understand a word, but he could tell something was wrong. The growler ahead of him in line hissed something. At him.

His mouth felt dry. *The hell?*

A moment later, from far in the distance, he heard the rumble of a Planetside armored fighting vehicle.

5

Ross swore. Four words, a nice combo. Enough to get the emotions out of his system.

"They're looking for me," he said to the leader. "Because I ran away."

The growler spoke. Ross whipped around his head. Wrinkles creased the growler's snout. It brandished its firearm at him with a hiss. It aimed a deeper hiss toward the far-off AFV.

"I didn't bring them," Ross said.

The growler took a step toward him. Its snout wrinkled further, showing the cutting points of its teeth.

"I said, I didn't bring them! God told me to run away from them and fight them! God!" Ross raised his hand and his gaze to the sky.

Feathers rippled in the alien's arms. Ross tensed up, one eye on the butt of the alien's weapon, readying himself in case the growler tried to club him.

Instead, it hissed and gestured at his pockets.

A frown twisted Ross' face. He turned his palms to the alien. *His pockets?*

The alien suspected Ross used a gadget to summon Planetside. They might have only developed primitive tech surpassed on Earth a thousand years ago, but they'd figured out that the human soldiers used gadgets to communicate among themselves.

Ross allowed himself a small smile. "They're empty." He lowered his hands and pulled his pockets inside-out.

The growler feinted a clubbing blow with the butt of its firearm. Its skin and feathers smelled more peppery than musty, now.

"Are you blind? My pockets are empty!"

The growler made a low noise, deep in its throat.

An alien voice barked out, strong and firm. The leader. Ross yanked his head around. The leader's snout wrinkled at the growler. Its breaths sounded like the breeze rustling the leaves above them.

The growler stood firm. It rattled off a stream of grunts and growls, punctuated with hisses aimed at Ross and the distant sound of the Planetside AFV.

The leader responded in kind.

Ross watched their faces for clues to what they said. No luck.

He glanced around. None of the other aliens looked ready to dispute the leader, but did they show sympathy for the growler? And fear or hate of Ross?

Sweat trickled down his nape. How could he prove he was on their side?

The growler made a noise that caught Ross' attention. It jabbed its fingers at him, then at his backpack. After that, it aimed its firearm up into the foliage. Then it lowered its weapon and pointed toward the rumbling engine of the AFV. It held its gaze on Ross for a moment, then spoke in its harsh language to the leader.

The leader regarded Ross for a moment with its intense yellow-green eyes. "*Khaw*," it said.

Fire on his former brothers-in-arms? Not as easy to imagine now than it had been back home. But the choice he'd made, that morning with Nanette, remained in him like steel. But tempered with good sense.

He could fire on human beings. He would fire on them. But knowing Planetside's capabilities, not today.

"Bad idea," Ross said. He spoke and gestured. "If I—" He tapped his chest. "—shoot at—" He mimed firing a rifle. "—the human soldiers —" His left hand waved in the direction of the Planetside personnel.

"Many more will come." He made a fist and bobbed it through the air. "With bigger weapons." Another mime of a rifle. Then he spread his hands apart to indicate the wider barrel of an AFV's main gun. He flung his hands wide, like Vasquez tossing the alien ear into the sea, then toward the ground. Like the children's rhyme. *Ashes, ashes. All fall down.*

The alien holding his backpack hunched its shoulders. The leader squinted at him. The growler's snout gnarled around ragged breaths.

Ross swallowed around a dry mouth. "Instead," he said, "I'll show you how to build more of my rifles. And how to use them." He pretended to screw the barrel of his rifle onto the stock and to fire again. Half a dozen repeats of the gesture, moving his invisible rifle a couple of inches each time. "Then we all can fight them." A big circle with his hands, indicating all the aliens around him. He shoved his hands toward the AFV's faint sound.

The growler grunted. The leader peered at him.

"Later. Not now. Now we hide until they give me up for dead." A hunch of his shoulders, then he mimed pulling a cloak over his head. After a few quiet seconds, when the only sounds came from the shifting bodies of the aliens and the growler's ragged breaths, Ross remembered to exhale.

The growler reacted first. It turned to the leader and spoke in its language, interspersed with hisses aimed in the direction of the AFV and a flick of its thumbs at Ross.

The leader growled back low in its throat until the other fell silent. Its yellow-green eyes regarded Ross for a time, then said a few words.

The growler protested. A sharp look from the leader cut it off.

The leader lifted its head. It spoke at medium volume, but its meaning thundered. "*Baget rakh.*"

At the front of the line, the alien walking point turned away from the leader and set off.

The growler tensed its arms. It gave Ross a cold look, then trotted away to keep its place in line.

And, judging by the spumed breaths coming from back in line, to avoid the leader's wrath.

Ross resumed the march. The trees blanketed almost the entire ground with shadow, save for ragged patches of sunlight that found the forest floor. He cupped his hand around one ear, trying to listen for the Planetside AFV. Tough to hear over the rustle of feathers and the thump of feet from the moving aliens, but the military vehicle didn't seem to be coming closer.

The patrol wound its way through the trees. After ten minutes, the ground leveled off under Ross's boots. Top of the hill. The forest remained dense, the ground shadowed save for jagged patches of sunlight.

The alien at the back of the line jogged off with a crackle of feet on dried flakes of pale yellow bark. Probably trying to see the AFV with the help of the long line of sight.

Which meant the AFV had a better chance of seeing the alien.

Would Planetside suspect the aliens of kidnapping Stuart Havlicek? No, of course not. The dinosaur chickens were animals.

Would Planetside shoot at a visible alien just for the hell of it? The soldier from the bar had said nothing about that. But some things you might feel so guilty over, not even five stiff drinks can loosen your tongue enough to confess.

He listened for the AFV again. It sounded quieter than before, though tough to tell given the forest cover and the distance. But certainly not closer.

Ross let out a breath and kept walking.

Behind him, the alien lugging his backpack made a sharp whisper, sounding more like some small creature in the undergrowth than a creature nearly as tall as a man.

The patrol froze. Ears perked toward the sky. The alien walking point shuffled to its left, away from a small clearing where a dead tree had toppled.

The alien carrying his backpack stepped toward Ross. It whispered something. A question, it seemed.

He whispered back, "I don't understand."

The alien's whisper turned harsh, slicing into his hearing. Ross made out *"Renoot bareketukh"* in the stream of growls and grunts. Its left ear twitched, tracking something above.

"Drones?" he whispered back. He pressed the fingers of his right hand together, then splayed the thumb and pinkie. Not at all what a Planetside drone looked like, but the best he could do. He banked his hand, hovered it, rolled and moved, hovered again. "Drones?"

"*Derones.*" The final *s* hissed out.

Ross swore again. The soldiers in the AFV would write him off if they didn't see him. But a patrolling drone gave them eyes in the sky that could range for miles. And see not just in visible light, but infrared too. If the aliens' body temperature wasn't around 98.6°, he'd stick out. Plus, the drone carried microphones. The only thing in his favor was that it couldn't smell him.

He caught the leader's gaze. He touched his chest, walked his fingers in the leader's direction, and held out open hands.

The leader made one low growl. It pointed at the ground in front of it.

Ross took the gesture as permission to approach. He stepped through the deepest shadows he could. Not that it would help if a drone found a viewing angle from a different direction of the sky than the orange sun. The alien carrying his backpack followed.

Ross stopped where the leader had pointed and bowed his head before he spoke in a low voice. "If the drones—" He made the hand sign again. What had the alien called them? "—the renewed barry catlikes see me, the soldiers will come after us."

He gestured at the leader's slung firearm. Another game of charades. The hand sign for drone held high. Touching an imaginary punk to the firing hole of an imaginary weapon. The sign for drone. His hand wobbled down like a dead bird. "Can you shoot them down?" And if they couldn't tell from his inflection that he asked a question, he took a guess and said, "*Khaw.*"

The leader copied his drone hand signal, spreading wide its thumbs. With its other hand, it acted out firing its weapon and went "*Grr*" in time with the gesture. Twice, three times. His other hand kept making the drone sign. Finally, it dropped its hands to its sides.

They rarely, if ever, shot down a drone. Not a surprise. Their firearms couldn't be very accurate. The drones were small and tough to see.

Tough to see....

And if they still doubted his intentions, he could give them a gift....

"Try this." Ross turned to the alien holding his backpack. He unzipped the main pocket and dug in, past the halves of his rifle, for an item the alien hadn't found earlier. His fingers felt its curves and hard plastic body.

He grinned and lifted out a pair of binoculars with anti-reflective lenses. He gauged the separation of the leader's eyes and moved the scopes apart to match. He raised the eyepieces to his own face. The rubbery cups bumped the outsides of his eyesockets. "Like this," he said, and held the binoculars out.

The leader plucked the binoculars from him with its left hand. It moved them to its eyes. The stabilizing motors whirred. It yanked the binoculars away and peered at Ross.

He showed open palms. "It's doing its job," he said.

The leader studied the binoculars from multiple angles, then grunted and looked through them.

It panned through the forest. The anti-reflective lenses looked like pits of night. The leader settled on Ross' face and jerked the binoculars away again. "*Neere!*" came from the back of its throat. It tapped its right thumbs together. "*Neere!*"

Around Ross, the other aliens pricked their ears to the leader and each other. The growler peered at the binoculars, then at Ross.

The leader called out something in a low voice. The alien on point lifted its gaze and trotted toward the leader. The leader held the binoculars to the other alien's eyes and spoke at length.

The alien grunted and grumbled. Its feathers rippled over its chest. The aliens' peppery smell flooded Ross' nose.

The growler raised its voice. It brandished its firearm at the leaves above them.

With a wrinkle in its snout, the leader replied in the aliens' language.

The growler shuffled backward. Its fingers spread wide for an instant.

The alien looking through the binoculars spoke quickly.

The leader made a pleased sound. It took the binoculars back from the other, then jutted out its scarred arm at Ross. It pointed at deeper shadows under a tall, gnarled tree five yards off their path.

Ross nodded. He went to the tree, watched all the way by the chill gaze of the growler.

He stiffened his shoulders and met the growler's gaze. *I don't much like you, either.*

He would put aside the feeling, of course, for the more important goal of helping the aliens get a fair deal.

Could the growler?

The leader and the other alien moved now, into the clearing around the dead tree. When they stopped, the other widened its stance and bent its torso backward. Its snout pointed almost straight up. The leader stood next to it, holding the binoculars with the eyepieces facing out.

A hush settled over the others, and Ross.

From somewhere above came a faint buzz.

The alien staring at the sky raised its firearm and moved the punk close to the firing hole. The leader held the binoculars to the other's eyes. Fine movements of barrel and binoculars.

A bang. A cloud of white smoke plumed out of the muzzle of the alien's firearm. The faint buzz in the sky took on a ragged note, then turned silent.

Every alien ear pivoted.

Plastic and metal clattered somewhere in the forest.

"*Neere!*" called out the alien carrying Ross' backpack. Others echoed the word.

Goosebumps raised Ross' beard stubble. A whiff of sulfur reached his nose and tongue. They'd done it.

The leader and the marksman hurried out of the clearing. The leader barked out commands and made emphatic gestures in the direction of march.

No time to celebrate. Planetside might investigate the fallen drone.

Would the soldiers realize the aliens shot it down? Or would Dr. Fitzhugh's mental block make them think it broke down and crashed?

Under the leader's firm gaze, the marksman trotted to the front of line and kept on at that pace.

The growler gave Ross a last cold look, then trotted after. It took the expression off its face before the leader peered at it going by.

Ross jogged between the trees. Near the leader, he tried sign language. Drone, shot down. With his other hand he picked it up. "*Khaw*?"

The leader called out an order to the alien at the end of the line. It and the backpack carrier trotted into the forest toward the crashed drone. The leader then followed Ross in line.

They jogged through the forest. Roots tried to make Ross stumble, but he had enough energy in his aching legs to jump clear.

Energy and high spirits. He'd made contact with the aliens. The growler had started off hating him, but it would come around. Together, they'd struck their first blow against Planetside and Dr. Fitzhugh. More. Against the big money who hired Planetside and Fitzhugh to exploit Azureseas.

His feet slowed for a moment.

The big money wouldn't give up easily.

How would it fight back?

6

AFTER A NIGHT OF FITFUL SLEEP, when insects tickled his skin with their crawling feet and Ross relived the day's events a dozen times, the patrol broke camp in the slanted orange rays of morning. A few barks from the leader, and they handed Ross his pack back. He took it as a sign of trust and bowed before they set off.

Their weapons at the ready, the aliens watched the forest, just like the day before. They moved slower now. Ross hoped he wasn't the only one whose legs ached.

He wasn't the only one who suffered, at least. Whenever the leader called a halt, the growler took a dozen uneven steps off the trail. It held its hands on its belly and a low whimper came from its throat. Through the trees, Ross made out a flash of iridescence from a rapidly-raised tail flap. When it returned, it shot Ross angry looks undercut by lingering whimpers and a bitter tang to its musty smell.

Ross shrugged with open palms. He bit back on laughter. *I don't eat your food. Now you know not to eat mine.*

Late the second day, they climbed a hill where trees sank their roots between outcrops of limestone. From the aliens' tone of voice and jittering heads, he knew the patrol drew close to something. What? Good or bad?

At the top of the hill, something Ross had first thought was a bush turned out to be a hunter's blind, when an alien came out with a firearm on its shoulder and excited noises coming from back in its throat. A sentry, Ross guessed. He listened for hisses, heard a few. But after a few words from the marksman walking point and the leader's voice carrying from the middle of the line, the hisses went away. When the line resumed its march, the sentry gave him a close look. Its yellow-green eyes focused on him despite a rapid shaking of its head.

Ross passed between trees, crested the hill, and saw what the sentry guarded. And why the aliens had approached with excitement.

A hollow, maybe half a mile wide and cleared of trees. On the near slope, a juvenile alien and a knee-high six-legged creature with russet brown feathers sat on the grass near a herd of fat grazing animals. An uneven checkerboard pattern straddled a small creek on the valley floor. He forgot the names of the shapes, trapalaterals, quadrizoids? He'd apologize to his high school geometry teacher after he got home.

On shapes of bare dirt, plants grew in straight lines. Some areas held rows tall and bearing maroon fruit. Others, short plants bowed with greenish-black pods. Deep green ground cover blanketed about a third of the rows.

Ross' gaze went up the far slope of the hollow. At the ridgeline, a wooden palisade surrounded a cluster of huts. Smoke streamed up from a dozen cooking fires.

He remembered coming home from Taney Creek, Nanette beside him, when his parents' farm came into view. His eyes grew moist.

Of course the aliens were excited. They were *home*.

They headed down into the hollow, to the tilled fields open to the angled rays of the afternoon sun. Scattered clouds tumbled overhead. Hundreds of yards away, the juvenile shepherd ignored its flock and stared at him.

Ross' head snapped up.

The alien behind him spoke. From the stream of growls and grumbles, Ross made out *derones* and *renoot bareketukh*.

He turned his head. The alien held its right hand far from its body, in the direction of the human settlement, and made the sign for drones.

It guessed at his thoughts, but still Ross winced. "Not drones." He pointed high overhead and hopped. "Satellites."

The alien angled its head. Its yellow-green eyes showed no sign of understanding. It said something. "—*burknen regnentorke khaw.*"

Ross made a forget-it gesture. The aliens could comprehend drones —mechanical birds—but satellites were outside their ken. He'd have to be careful and stay out of sight as much as possible. He didn't know the satellite cameras' resolution, but didn't want to chance being seen more than he had to.

His steps slowed as they reached the edge of the fields. The satellites must have seen the aliens' farm. And all the other farms of all the other alien villages within a thousand miles of the barbed wire fence. Animals didn't farm. Anyone reviewing sat footage would realize they were intelligent.

How many people knew the truth?

Ross and the aliens filed up the slope toward the palisade. Chatter went back and forth from the aliens around him to the village. Taller and thicker versions of their firearm barrels made up the walls. Ropes and dried mud bound them together. The walls might stop a round from his rifle, but the main gun of a Planetside APC would rip them to shreds.

His pack pulled down his shoulders. The walls protected the village against other villages. Every creature's fiercest rivals were other members of its same species. High school xenology.

Unifying the natives of Azureseas into a fighting force would be his first challenge.

They approached an open gate crowded with aliens. Tall, short, skinny, plump, different shades of feathers. The voices of the crowd ran together, like machines on the construction sites on the beach. The crowd pressed back, making room for the returning patrol. Most of the crowd shied farther back from Ross. Hisses and wrinkled snouts, yes, *I wouldn't trust me either*, but plenty of heads jittered and thumbs tapped. Some were pleased. And all of them, combined, smelled like an explosion at a pepper factory.

Too much to take in. His chest felt tight. Could he, all by himself, really help them get what they deserved?

The drawing of the praying alien came to his mind's eye.
He stood taller. He wasn't by himself. With him was God.

THE PATROL LED Ross through the crowd to a thatched hut. Two feathery hides, lumpy with stuffing, lay each in a back corner. He stowed his backpack where the aliens pointed. The one who'd gone through his backpack on their first meeting opened it up again and pulled out his rifle. It handed his weapon to the leader, who then left with most of the others.

Ross opened his mouth to protest, but stayed silent.

Other than confiscating his weapon, the alien acted more like a host than a prison guard. Ross spent ten minutes miming and making hand signs before the alien gestured for him to set his food synther in sunlight. And the alien seemed apologetic when it had conversations with passerby before guiding him out of the hut to the latrine pit at the west end of the village.

He spent three days learning to communicate with them.

More accurately, teaching them to communicate with him. Through hand signs and repetition, the aliens borrowed some of his words. Drones, rifle, soldiers, workers, tourists, God. He tried their language, but though he heard the difference between *gh* and *kh* and *k*, his mouth couldn't make the sounds. He managed a few words, badly pronounced, like *harek*, water, and *tark rehonnet* for a human rifle. Though why they didn't call rifles, plural, *tark rehonnets* he had no clue.

He spent the next days learning about his hosts. They came in two sexes, male and female. The patrol that found him were all male. He wasn't surprised. More high school xenology. His teacher, Mr. Cantrell, no relation, would be proud Ross actually remembered something. Convergent evolution.

Like people, most aliens had two sexes, enough to mix up genes for the next generation without getting even more complicated than relationships already were. Almost always, one of those sexes invested more of its body, its time, and its mind in offspring than the other. Regardless how its genitals combined with the other's, the xenologists called that sex *female*. That fundamental division of labor usually led to the different sexes doing different things to keep their communities running. And males usually hunted animals and fought rival tribes.

He'd gloated about that to Nanette and her friendgirls in the school hallway after class. Nature, God, whatever you wanted to call it, made it universal, that males get the glory.

Now he knew males didn't get glory. They earned it. By taking a hell of a lot of risks along the way.

Like people and most other intelligent life, the natives of Azureseas —they called themselves *Banakhenner*—lived in groups with roughly equal numbers of males and females. Watching from the door of the hut, and talking with ones passing by, Ross soon developed an eye to tell the sexes apart. Not from obvious body parts. The tail flaps of both sexes stayed close to their rumps except when they went to the latrine pit. He also saw no sign, from sight or smell or male behavior, that any of the females were in heat.

Intelligence didn't come cheap. Large brains required long pregnancies and childhoods to form and a lot of food to keep running. In most cases, large brains only helped creatures if males could cooperate most of the time and no one could tell when females were fertile.

Mr. Cantrell said that, but if he explained why, Ross didn't remember. Probably he'd been sitting in class, staring out the window, wondering whether Nanette was fertile....

He shook his head and refocused on Azureseas and the Banakhenner. The females were a bit smaller and duller in color than the males. Some looked a little wider across the hips. He assumed the wider-hipped females were carrying offspring. The Banakhenner looked too poor for any to be fat. He couldn't figure out if they were pregnant with live young or laid eggs. At least their young didn't gnaw their way out of their mothers' bodies. He didn't think. And between the language gap and good manners, he couldn't ask.

At least the language gap closed a little each day. Ross realized the Banakhenner grasped what satellites were. *Burknen reghnentorke*. Small, fast moons. "Humans put them sky," his host said.

Mouth open, Ross blinked. "Yes. They're like drones. They fly thousands of miles up but they can still see me—"

"We watch they. We let you out hut when they go."

Ross winced. "Some may be tiny. Very small." He held his hands a couple of feet apart.

The alien paused a while. "You stay here when day."

While he waited for the orange sun to set, Ross learned the names of the males who'd found him. Ross' host was named Merghunek. The leader of the patrol was named Lerbot. Lerbot had earned leadership by fighting well against other villages. He'd led teams to recon Planetside's fence and take potshots at soldiers, and brought most of his subordinates home alive. All the males, from young adults to the elderly, respected Lerbot. Juvenile males bickered in their equivalent of cowboys-and-indians over who would play as him. Females fluttered the bottom edges of their tail flaps at the mention of Lerbot's name.

Merghunek told him about others. "Kibkhal, he talk lot, much females."

Ross munched a sandwich of a cold protein patty between starch cakes. After days of energy bars, it tasted better than anything he'd eaten since the dinner when he'd proposed to Nanette.

He shook his head. "Who's Kibkhal?" Wait, they didn't ask questions by inflection, they added a word. "Khaw?"

"Lerbot hold binocular. Kibkhal shoot drone."

"He's a good shot? He shoots well, khaw?"

"Yes. More good in village. More good than Harkhmal."

"Harkhmal is...?"

"He no like you. He want lead, not Lerbot."

"The one who ate my food and crapped much?"

"Yes." Merghunek puffed out the feathers on its shoulders and wrinkled its snout. It flicked its thumbs to show mockery. "Most we no like him."

"Why does he think he could replace Lerbot?"

Merghunek took a few breaths. Maybe he misunderstood *replace*? But before Ross opened his mouth the alien said, "He father lead we fighters before Lerbot."

"I see."

Merghunek craned its neck, squinting at the corner of the hut Ross faced.

Ross waved his hand. "Back to Kibkhal. Much females, khaw?"

"He want make love much females. Much females say no."

Ross laughed. He remembered to tap his thumb and little finger together. "Do *you* have much females?"

Merghunek splayed his fingers and looked away. "One. I want make love. She want make love. When Old One say she just me, me just she, we will."

Marriage, or something like it. More convergent evolution. You could only get large numbers of males to work together if the social rules gave most of them a chance to court and keep mates. And if both sexes mostly followed the rules.

Rules he'd broken back on New Ozark.

As the days wore on, and Ross ventured out of the hut, he heard more about the Old One. He lived alone, in a hut next to the eastern wall of the village. He rarely ventured out—the Banakhenner considered it an honor to bring him food and water and carry his chamberpot to the latrine. Ross, one night, unable to sleep and feeling cabin fever, sneaked away from sleeping Merghunek and wandered around the quiet village. Until Merghunek ran after him and tugged him by the forearm. "Old One no say yes."

Ross wondered about him on his way back to the hut, and for an hour lying on his lumpy pallet staring at the thatched ceiling. The Old One was a king? A priest? Both?

Whatever he was, the Old One held the key to Ross' release.

Two days after that, Ross dozed through the warmest part of the day when alien footsteps at the entrance to the hut woke him. Merghunek, but not alone.

Lerbot peered into the hut and growled something. Merghunek translated. "Talk we khaw."

Ross pushed himself to a sitting position. What brought the patrol leader to him? "Yes, we can talk." He beckoned Lerbot in with a wave of his hand.

Lerbot entered. His presence filled the hut and pulled Merghunek in behind him.

Heart thumping, Ross climbed to his feet. Fully awake now. The first time he'd seen the patrol leader since they'd entered the village.

"Seet," Lerbot said. Merghunek echoed him with better pronunciation.

Ross sat. Lerbot went to the other pallet and folded up his four legs to sit. Merghunek sat on the dirt near the entrance and threw a long, scanning look out the doorway before turning his attention to his leader and Ross.

Lerbot spoke, mostly in the Banakhenner language. Merghunek translated, with difficulty. They talked about concepts, not things.

"We meet you, know good come to we. Maybe."

"I only want to do good by you and all Banakhenner."

Feathers flattened on Lerbot's chest and head. "You say. We believe. But want good not make good."

Ross gave them an opportunity, not a guarantee. "I understand."

"Harkhmal meet you, know bad come to we."

Though Ross knew Harkhmal's opinion of him, he still rankled at it. "Why?"

Merghunek spoke before Lerbot could. "I tell you, Ross."

"He's that ambitious?" He turned to Lerbot. "He wants your job so much that if you say something is black, he'll say it's white, khaw?"

It took a minute of awkward conversation for them to get his point, but when they did there was no doubt. Lerbot peered at him and said, "Yess."

A nugget of spite at Harkhmal lodged in Ross' gut.

Through Merghunek, Lerbot said, "Banakhenner leaders say yes, we fight *kutel bakhelrebten* with you." Ross had picked up enough of their language to know their term for humans literally meant *ones without legs*. The alien went on. "One Banakhenner leader say no, we no fight with you."

"Which leaders must agree for us to fight together, khaw?" Ross swallowed down the question of what the Banakhenner would do with him if the leaders failed to agree.

"I. Retkhmal. Old One."

"Who's Retkhmal, khaw?"

"Father Harkhmal. He no fight. He talk."

Ross scrunched up his face. "Seems like Retkhmal would side with his son against you, Lerbot."

For the first time ever, Lerbot hesitated before speaking. But his voice sounded confident when he said words translated as, "Retkhmal know good for village and Banakhenner. We say you make good, he know." Lerbot gently tapped his thumbs together. Ross thought he looked pleased, though Merghunek struggled to translate. "He know and, we make good, Harkhmal make much good, khaw."

"If we fight together, Harkhmal may benefit? Good may come to him."

Merghunek spoke on his own. "He shoot *tark rehonnet*, he hit target." He quickly translated his words to Lerbot.

The leader tapped and flicked his thumbs and said "*Neere!*" The hut interior smelled more peppery.

Ross laughed too, though better weapons were not the benefit he had in mind. If Harkhmal fought well against Planetside, he might earn as much respect as Lerbot.

The aliens' good spirits turned more solemn. They too knew fighting would give Harkhmal a chance to rise in status. And if Lerbot fell in combat, Harkhmal would probably take charge.

Despite the warmth of the day, Ross' skin suddenly turned clammy. Instead of Lerbot falling in combat, could Harkhmal push him? No. However ambitious Harkhmal might be, he wouldn't dare frag his commander. Right?

"Sounds like Retkhmal will agree," Ross said. "It comes down to if I can persuade the Old One."

"Old One know yesterday, today, tomorrow. He know good and bad all we."

"Getting my people to treat you as our equals is very good for the Banakhenner. Today my people think you are animals. They can kill you, drive you away, and take from you anything they want. Tomorrow, if they know you are intelligent—" He tapped his temple. "—they must give you things to make up for what they did before, and must trade with you for anything they want in the future. Rifles, tools, vehicles, medicines, knowledge. Much good for all Banakhenner."

Merghunek's head rapidly shook. Excited by the list of good things. But his delight faded as he translated Lerbot's next words. "We win fight much good come. Rain summer. We lose or win fight, bad come. Sunrise morning. You know."

The sulfur and plantain smells of the burning village came back to Ross. "We might not win. Bad will come if we lose."

"Bad come we win. I lead, I speak, males die." Merghunek let the leader's words hang.

"I risk death, too," said Ross.

"Much we die khaw? AFVs come village, burn huts, burn fields, females and childs die."

"We'll have to build up our defenses—"

Lerbot's voice filled the hut. "Old One say fight not worth khaw? AFVs no come, drones no fly here today. We eat, we drink water, we make childs, oldest die in peace today. We fight, much die, Banakhenner suffer."

Ross shook his head. "Yes, you live in peace today. The children born today might even live in peace and die old and in peace. Might. Like rains falling in summer. Just as summer may bring drought, my people might want more land, and think they take it from animals. You might not have the chance to live in peace tomorrow."

Lerbot spoke in Ross' language. "I know." He switched to his native tongue, but Ross guessed what he said even before Merghunek translated. "How we make Old One know."

7

WHEN THE TIME CAME, Lerbot strode to the hut. He spoke in Banakhenner, low yet forceful, and capped it off with one human word. "Come."

Merghunek unfolded his legs and Ross suddenly flashed to why few intelligent species had more than four limbs. It took a lot of brain to coordinate six arms and legs. Merghunek extended a hand and helped Ross up. The way his feathers flattened made the alien's palm feel like burlap.

"Good to talk?" he asked Ross.

Ross pulled on his backpack and brushed dirt off his shorts. The mint flavor of toothpaste lingered in his mouth. "Yes I am."

They stepped outside, where Lerbot stood and about ten Banakhenner waited behind him. Males, mostly. Wide yellow-green eyes, deep green feathers, jittering heads. Some looked fighting age, others, even younger. Their words jumbled out. "*Neere*! Good!"

Ross hunched his shoulders and squinted at the sky.

"Is good," said one of the males. Ross recognized him from near the back of the line on the patrol. "No drone."

A juvenile with a smoother voice said, "No sat light!"

"That you can see."

"I see much," the juvenile said. He raised his hand and showed Ross the binoculars. "Lerbot say I sat light watcher!"

Lerbot grumbled out words. "We go." He strode forward. Ross loped to keep up on Lerbot's left. Merghunek walked next to and half a step behind Ross. The crowd followed. The aliens' uncoordinated footfalls thumped the packed dirt like a master's drum solo. Their scent pushed Ross forward on a wave of peppery air.

The alien leader took a winding path through the village. Banakhenner watched from the entrances of huts or while standing near cooling firepits. More Banakhenner joined the procession. Ross saw Kibkhal holding hands with a female. Near the village's north wall, in an area Ross had never seen before, an older male wearing a satchel and a belt laden with hammers and other tools left a cluster of huts clanging with work hidden from sight. Smells of burning wood and sulfur filled the air.

Lerbot paused the procession. He and the older male spoke respectfully with each other. The older male's gaze landed on Ross and never left.

The older male joined them, a step behind and on the other side of Lerbot. The satchel and the tools in his belt rattled with each step of his front feet. His breath wheezed and Lerbot slowed the procession's pace.

"Who is he?" Ross whispered to Merghunek.

"Arkhtes. He lead workers. They make tools. They make guns."

Although Lerbot's path meandered through the village, the procession drew eastward. Ross squinted at the morning sun.

Eventually, Lerbot led them into an open area of packed dirt. Memories of parades around the courthouse square in his hometown came to Ross.

Huts ringed the open area on three sides. He barely noticed. What he saw in front grabbed all his attention.

A wooden platform, about forty feet wide and twenty deep, butted against the village palisade. Two huts stood on the back corners of the platform. In the middle, a larger pavilion, framed with timbers and open to view, roofed over a higher platform. On either side of the higher platform, two candles burned in braziers suspended from the pavilion's ceiling.

In the shade of the pavilion's roof, the light of the candles guttered over the Old One.

Of *old*, Ross lacked any doubt. Yellow ran far toward the bases of his feathers, and the muscles under his skin looked shrunken. The Banakhenner equivalent of cataracts clouded both eyes, especially his left, like silt spilled into clear water. How much could he see of the material world?

Ross also instantly knew the Old One was attuned to God. Around his neck dangled a pendant of four intertwined metal rings glinting in the candlelight. He struck the same pose as the unknown Banakhenner in the drawing. And as much as one could tell the breadth and depth of faith of the drawing figure, it was ten times more powerful to see it in person. Ross' breath caught. Hairs stood up on his nape.

Lerbot flattened his upper body feathers. The Banakhenner with him did the same. Ross bowed his head as Lerbot spoke in a raised voice. Merghunek's voice murmured to Ross's ear, "Old One, you see yesterday and today and tomorrow. You see we and God. We ask you help we decide."

Age rasped the Old One's voice, but it still carried over the crowd. "I help."

Silence took over, save for the wheezing breaths of Arkhtes the gunsmith. Lerbot shifted his weight. A few murmurs around Kibkhal and the others.

Ross muttered sidelong, "What are we waiting for, khaw?"

"Retkhmal and Harkhmal." Merghunek perked his ears to the south. "They come."

Feet tramped not far away and grew louder. Through gaps between huts around the open area, Ross glimpsed a crowd of Banakhenner approaching.

Into the open area strode Harkhmal at the head of the crowd. Next to him, an older male with a family resemblance matched the younger one's face despite a limp in his right front leg. They came to a stop. Retkhmal took an extra step forward and flattened the feathers on his chest and head. He gave the Old One the same ritual greeting as Lerbot had, but with a touch less respect in his tone.

The Old One took an extra second before speaking. "I help. Come you."

Lerbot beckoned for Ross and Merghunek to follow him to a set of three steps leading up to the platform. Arkhtes the gunsmith came along with a rattle of his tools.

They reached the foot of the steps at the same time as Retkhmal and Harkhmal. The two leaders growled and grumbled at each other, until Lerbot said something that sent Retkhmal half a step backward and led Merghunek to tap his thumbs.

The way clear, Lerbot went first up the steps. Ross followed. He passed three feet from Retkhmal and Harkhmal. The son eyed him with as much dislike as he'd shown on the patrol. The father peered at him. Not with dislike. With the gaze Ross' father turned on bull calves when deciding which ones to castrate and fatten for the slaughterhouse.

Up on the platform, Ross whispered to Merghunek, "What did Lerbot say?"

"You second here, you second up."

He crossed the platform next to Lerbot. Boards creaked under Ross' boots. The Old One held his head steady as he flexed his ears toward Ross and studied him with rheumy eyes.

Despite the morning warmth, a shiver went over Ross' arms. The Old One saw both very little, and everything.

From the back corners of the pavilion, two males of middle age came around the Old One. Junior priests, obviously. They wore pendants with the same pattern of intertwined metal rings. Not the infinity symbol, not a simple circle. Their lives had cycles but you didn't end up at the same place you started from. So God had ordained for the Banakhenner, just as He had for humankind.

The junior priests stopped at the far side of a line of translucent, smoky white quartz laid in the platform just outside the corner timbers of the pavilion. On the near side of the line, Lerbot halted in front of one junior priest. A pungent smell, like frying onions, came from the candles hanging in air.

The junior priest raised his pendant high. Lerbot flattened his feathers and lowered his head. The priest spoke. Lerbot replied. The priest said a final phrase, then brought the pendant down and side-stepped to Ross.

Instead of raising the pendant, he puffed out the feathers of his chest and turned to the Old One. The two aliens spoke.

Ross shared a glance with Lerbot. Everyone in the village, even those who'd never come by Merghunek's hut, knew a human had lived there for a week. The Old One and the junior priests were not suddenly surprised by him. They'd planned out their response.

A smile turned up the corners of Ross's mouth.

With Lerbot's approval, he'd planned out his response, too.

The junior priest turned away from the Old One. The pendant remained in his hand but under his snout. His muscles bunched, preparatory to move to Merghunek—

Ross raised his gaze and his right hand toward the sky. "Only one God set all the stars in the sky." Merghunek translated.

The junior priest spoke again to the Old One. The high priest's aged yellow head jittered as he replied. The junior priest flattened the feathers of his head and chest to Ross.

Ross lowered his arm and bowed. The priest raised the pendant of interlinked circles and said the same words he had to Lerbot.

With practice the night before, he'd eventually pronounced the ritual reply well enough for Lerbot to leave the tent. He repeated it now.

The junior priest said the final phrase of the greeting ritual. Yellow-green iridescence rippled as he lowered the pendant.

Warmth spread in Ross' belly. First obstacle cleared—

A growl from Retkhmal froze the junior priest. Merghunek translated, "Is proper, khaw?"

—Here came the second.

The Old One pivoted his aged head to Retkhmal. The high priest looked unamused now. "He know same God we."

"Yesterday he know we God, he no fight Banakhenner by sea, khaw?"

The Old One's voice held steady. "He no come yesterday. He come today. *Baget rakh.*"

The junior priest turned to bless Merghunek and Arkhtes. After that, the other junior priest performed the ritual for Retkhmal and his subordinates, Harkhmal and an older female.

"Who is she?" Ross murmured.

"Subanagh. She help female lay egg."

A midwife. "Why is a female allowed in a war council?"

"Female face risk foe take her. Female nurse hurt we. Female mourn dead son."

Females pine for their boyfriends gone off to fight, too. Ross' shoulders slumped. They rose back up with a thought.

That's why you only fight a war worth fighting.

Greeting rituals complete, the junior priests stepped backwards to flank the Old One. In his raspy voice, the high priest said, "We much talk about. War and peace. You must agree." He spread his withered arms to take in Lerbot, Retkhmal, and the other Banakhenner on the platform. "I help you agree."

The night before, Lerbot and Merghunek had explained the protocol as well as the language barrier allowed. The Old One presided over the debate but had no vote. Yet almost always, the other leaders of the village would agree on the plan of action the high priest wanted.

The Old One extended his arm to Ross. "We not talk yet. Visitor come we. Welcome. Please tell you we."

Ross took a step forward. He felt like he had as a young child meeting the church's new pastor. He spoke up to make sure he was heard.

"Thank you for your welcome. I'm really grateful given the bad history between your people and mine. I hope we can change that."

Merghunek finished translating. Ross said, "My name is James Ross Cantrell. I am a human being. My ancestors come from a planet called Earth, which goes around a star called Sol. Now, my people live on thousands of planets going around hundreds of stars."

In the hut, learning to communicate, Merghunek had taken to the idea of interstellar travel surprisingly quickly. He translated into Banakhenner without hesitation. A silence settled as Ross waited for the Old One to question. Or Retkhmal to call b.s.

The Old One spoke. "We know stars are distant brothers of we sun.

We think they shine on planets, sisters of Kurnekht, Azureseas, spinning and going around them. We think humans come from there."

Retkhmal muttered something. Merghunek whispered, "He say we not stupid."

Ross ignored the jibe from Retkhmal... and his surprise. *How did they guess?* He bowed to the Old One. "You know and you are wise."

He went on. "My people are the only ones who build ships to travel between the stars—"

The Old One rasped out a question. "You know or you think, khaw?"

"We know only us. My people have found much other intelligent life. They speak, they think." He made gestures. Words flowing from his mouth, finger tapping temple. "We treat them fairly. They let us use part of their planets, we give them tools and knowledge."

Retkhmal growled out something. The Old One raised his hand to him, then turned back to Ross. "Today your people no treat Banakhenner fairly, khaw?"

Why?

Sweat ran down Ross' neck. Why, indeed? He knew his one sparsely settled planet—actually, only a tiny part of it. He knew other human worlds by name. A complex web of planetary governments, treaty organizations, non-profits, corporations, churches, and secular groups hashed out policies relevant to all human worlds. But half the time, the left hand didn't know what the right hand was doing.

Kind of like....

"Each human world is like a Banakhenner village. Just like each village of your people has leaders who don't always agree—" Ross extended his hand toward Lerbot and Retkhmal. "—our worlds are the same. A few human leaders decided not to play fair with your people. All other human leaders don't know."

Retkhmal cleared his throat and shifted his weight, favoring the leg with the limp. Harkhmal flattened his upper body feathers and met the Old One's gaze.

To Ross, the high priest said, "Few leaders only, khaw? Much your people hunt and kill Banakhenner."

"The few leaders fooled us. They scrambled our thoughts so that we believed you are animals." Ross put his head in his hands and waggled it.

Harkhmal muttered something to his father. Retkhmal raised his hand to speak.

The Old One gestured at him. In the air near the high priest, a drop of wax overran the brazier and plopped on the wood. The onion stench from the candles struck Ross' nose with more force.

Rheumy eyes swung back to Ross. The Old One's words scraped like sandpaper. "He think thought he no want think, khaw?"

The high priest didn't believe him. Ross blurted, "It's technology! Like the binoculars, my food synther...." He clawed the air for more words.

A wheezing breath, then Arkhtes said, "*Torke barehonner.*"

"Yes, my rifle! Technology!"

A stir went through the crowd. Retkhmal and Harkhmal brought their heads together in low talk.

Silence returned when the Old One raised his pendant like a judge raising a gavel. He let it drop back to his shallow chest, then said to Arkhtes, "Maker, you make gun?"

"Yes."

"You make thought scrambler?"

In the corner of Ross' eye, Lerbot next to him spread the fingers of his hands.

The war leader was nervous? Ross' stomach flopped. Only Arkhtes' wheeze sounded for a moment.

"No," the gunsmith said. "And I no make satellite. And I no make ship travel stars."

Merghunek rested his hand on Ross' shoulder. Lerbot's head shimmied. Ross could breathe again. The onion scent from the candles now made him hungry for a hamburger and a beer.

The Old One's voice rasped. "Tell we, Ross, why few human leaders make soldiers think thought they no want think."

"If the soldiers could think straight, they'd know you're people like us. They would fight against you if you attacked them, but they would refuse to attack you first." Most would, at least. Some kids on the playground growing up had used insulting slang to describe aliens they'd seen in videos from distant worlds. And was Vasquez the only soldier in the platoon to try taking ears as trophies?

Ross added, "They only burn villages and kill Banakhenner because they think you're animals who hurt our livelihood. Like my ancestors way back when killed wolves that threatened their sheep." He had to converse with Merghunek for a moment before the alien understood the metaphor enough to translate.

The Old One considered. "How you straighten thoughts, khaw?"

"The wind blew the truth to me. A drawing of an Old One praying to the one God who set all the stars in the sky. Only a thinking creature could make that drawing. Only a thinking creature could know God. Because of that, you deserve a fair deal from my people."

"You tell human leaders on Azureseas, khaw?"

"No."

The Old One's clouded eyes narrowed. "Khaw." *Why?*

"They know they're doing wrong and they want to keep it secret." He pictured the green eyes of Dr. Fitzhugh peeling back the layers of his mind. "They'd arrest me. Scramble my thoughts even worse than they do to the soldiers. Or kill me."

"You tell human leaders at stars, khaw?"

"No. Because it would take too long for me on my out-of-the-way planet to get the attention of enough important people on Earth and major worlds to investigate. The bad human leaders on Azureseas would block them at every step. Ten years? How much land could the bad leaders take by then? How many fields could they burn? How many villages could they bulldoze? How many Banakhenner could they kill?"

The Old One took a breath. "Can we fight human bad leaders and soldiers no think straight, khaw?"

Ross opened his mouth to speak. But the question wasn't for him. The debate had started.

Iridescence rippled on Arkhtes' aged yet still stout arms. He opened the flap of his satchel and drew out two pieces of formed alloy.

That's where Ross' rifle had ended up.

Arkhtes showed the parts to the high priest, then threaded the barrel onto the stock. "We learn much from Ross rifle. We make better weapons."

The Old One fixed his gaze on Arkhtes. "Soldier weapons or we weapons better, khaw?"

The gunsmith splayed his fingers. The feathers on his head flattened. "Soldier weapons better."

The Old One angled his head to Ross. "Soldiers think we animals we shoot firearms, khaw?"

Ross nodded, remembering. "Yes. The thought scramblers make us think you are animals who can throw rocks very fast."

To Lerbot, the Old One asked, "We better weapons, we kill all soldiers, khaw?"

"No."

"We fight, soldiers live, what soldiers do, khaw?" The high priest addressed Retkhmal.

"They come. They fight. We—"

"Who win fight, khaw? I no ask you. I ask you son."

Harkhmal puffed up his feathers, but his father growled something. Harkhmal replied to the Old One. Ross knew Banakhenner mannerisms well enough to tell Harkhmal didn't want to answer the way he did. "Soldier weapons better. Soldier armor better. We fight well but no win."

The Old One's voice rasped once more, to the midwife, Subanagh. "Today how many females carry egg, khaw?"

"Eleven," she replied. "Much flee, soldiers come tomorrow."

"All hear all," the Old One said. He raised the pendant of interlocking circles away from his withered chest. "I ask no more questions now. Talk, you, you." He brandished the pendant in turn at Lerbot and Retkhmal. "Know I listen. Know God listen."

The leaders flattened their feathers and spread their fingers to the Old One, then pivoted to face each other.

The orange sun climbed into the sky while the leaders argued, sometimes calling on their allies for support, other times demanding the other's allies answer questions, like lawyers cross-examining hostile witnesses. Merghunek struggled to keep up, and Ross knew he missed a lot of fine points.

In overview, Harkhmal counseled caution. The soldiers stayed mostly on the human side of the fence. No workers built anything on the human side within sight of any Banakhenner patrol.

"*Kaht kulrabt!*" he called at one point, and Ross knew the words meant *human*. "How much tomorrow when you people build over all land beyond fence, khaw?"

Ross spread his palms wide. "I don't know."

"Answer you. Lerbot, he answer."

Lerbot turned to Ross and deepened his voice. "He answer what he know."

Ross bowed his head to the war leader. He inhaled to calm himself, then faced Harkhmal.

"Know you," the Banakhenner asked, "how much yesterday you people build, khaw?"

"About one year." Terran standard. He and Merghunek had worked out the math. He trusted him to translate accurately.

"Know you how much land have building today, khaw?"

"A small amount along the shore. I don't know how much of the fenced-off land that is."

"We agree one finger on two hands, on four hands, on six hands, khaw?"

Ross needed a moment to think through the Banakhenner number system based on eight fingers. "Maybe one-sixteenth."

"We agree, khaw, four hands of years? Until bad human leaders want more land. If they want more land."

Ross' mouth hung open a moment. Damn, what had Retkhmal gotten him to admit?

His self-criticism faded when Lerbot's voice rumbled. "When they do, Retkhmal, you grandson fight them, khaw?"

The debate flowed back and forth for a time. Lerbot called on Ross to describe the goods and knowledge humans would give to the Banakhenner as payment for buying land on a planet from its intelligent natives.

Ross played it up. Tools to grow more food. Gadgets to carry speech, even pictures, instantly through the air from one Banakhenner village to another. He caught the eye of Subanagh, the midwife, then talked about medicines to help a female lay an egg and keep a hatchling healthy.

She flattened her feathers at him. Retkhmal, though, puffed up and snarled, "How you make all humans give all things, khaw?"

"We trade instead of take because God likes when we treat aliens the way we want them to treat us." Maybe he put words into the mouths of billions of people on Earth and the oldest colony worlds who never set foot inside a temple or church, but at least the Banakhenner understood.

Over the next minutes, Retkhmal's faction came to agree with Lerbot. Action now could give them great benefits, while doing nothing meant the threat of more land grabs and obliterated villages would always hang over their heads. Yet even if it were better to act now, what could the Banakhenner do? The soldiers thought them animals.

Lerbot clapped Ross on the shoulder to speak. They'd gone over this point the night before. Ross met his yellow-green eyes and nodded before turning to Harkhmal.

"There are two things we can do," Ross said. He held up his index finger and pinkie like the horns of a bull. "Go to others whose thoughts are not scrambled. Show the soldiers so well how you think, it gets through their scrambled thoughts."

Harkhmal glared. "Which is it, khaw?"

"Both."

"How." Harkhmal's snout wrinkled. He emphasized his next words with flicking thumbs. "We cut through fence and walk over eight miles south, khaw?"

Into the sights of a Planetside armored fighting vehicle scrambling to intercept them. The civilians on the beach wouldn't even hear the AFV's main gun. Or smell the burned plantain stench of Banakhenner dead.

Ross shared a knowing glance with Lerbot.

"We no go through fence. We go around it."

8

IN A GLASS WALL three stories high, one of a dozen pairs of double doors swung open, and Nanette entered the grand hall of the convention center in New Springfield, the largest room she'd ever been in.

The polarized glass shaded the afternoon rays of Beta Can, but still let in enough to light up the vast space. Cool air spilled from vents high above. She pulled her bare arms closer to her body, but not out of cold. Hundreds of voices bounced off the triple-height ceiling and echoed off the booths of companies and agencies in a cacophony of accents.

Her ears strained. She couldn't hear her name spoken anywhere across the two acres of ceramic tile floor.

Which meant someone whispered it, somewhere.

Nanette got in line for the check-in table and shuffled forward. The man ahead of her, maybe a couple of years older than her, gave her figure the once-over with hooded eyes. She turned her head with a little sniff. A scrawny little guy. Not half the man Ross was.

You've got to forget Ross— and then it came her turn to check in under an augmented reality banner floating in midair. *Interstellar Employment Opportunities Fair.*

The attendant at the front table looked to be from off-world, judging by her long, narrow, curved nose and her skin tone, a shade of warm light brown that Nanette would sunburn if she tried to tan to it. The tag pinned to the lapel of the skirtsuit jacket pinned over her generous bosom read *Illyria*. "Your name, please?" Her accent trilled the *r*.

"Nanette Bauer," she muttered. Her gaze darted to the scrawny guy, who stood with open mouth as a robot swabbed inside his cheek for a DNA sample. *Thank God* he didn't react to her name. Even here in New Springfield, the planet's capital a thousand miles from her home town, people sometimes asked if she was related to the Bauers from Saddlepoint.

Illyria said, "Allow me to share the floor plan and guidebook." She got the absent look of someone distracted by data flowing through her smart contact lenses and earbuds. Her hands, featuring long nails glossy with clear polish, gathered up air, like a farmer cupping water from a well, then opened them to Nanette as if she released a dove at someone's wedding—

Why do I keep thinking about him?

"I wish you the best of luck in finding lucrative and challenging employment opportunities off-world." Illyria smiled at Nanette, the corners of her wide mouth curling up and a crinkle touching her large brown eyes.

That proved Illyria came from off-world. Because everyone on New Ozark looked at Nanette with contempt.

"Thank you so much," Nanette said, her voice needy. Cheeks suddenly hot, Nanette barely noticed the second attendant and her robots take DNA samples and collect retina and fingerprint data. Her feet drifted into the grand hall. The virtual text boxes and graphics overlaid in her vision were just meaningless lines. The helpful female voice in her earbuds said something she didn't catch.

Damn you, Ross. I give you my body and you tell me a bunch of aliens are more important than me?

Everyone within twenty miles of her hometown knew Ross broke off their engagement, seemingly before she stopped crying her first batch of tears. She knew what they whispered behind her back. *He wanted what all men want and she gave it to him too soon. I wonder if Ross really was her first. I bet she was frigid.*

Wherever she went in and around Saddlepoint, she ducked her head, turned up music in her earbuds, and pretended not to notice. When the preacher one Sunday gave a sermon about the woman taken in adultery, *who was he to cast the first stone?* But without turning her head, she knew a hundred sets of eyes stared at her. She could feel a virtual target between her shoulder blades. She sat frozen on the pew for the rest of the service while sweat turned clammy on the back of her neck.

At least she had her parents.... until Dad scrunched up his mouth. He looked away, too embarrassed to meet her eyes, and asked, "Did you show him you'd be a bad wife?"

A trapdoor opened beneath her. A pit formed in her stomach. She ran off to the bathroom and vomited. Thick heaves left bile in her mouth and her forehead against the cool porcelain side of the toilet bowl.

Dad tried to take back his words. Mom crinkled up her eyes and laid the blame solely on Ross. The devil could snare anyone and come, sweetie, let us pray. But too damn late.

She couldn't stay around Saddlepoint anymore. Taney Creek was too close and too small a city for her to disappear. So off to New Spring-field. To make ends meet, she trained as a bartender just because Mom would disapprove. Yet even here, a thousand miles away and three months later, her best chance on the planet for a fresh start, everyone seemed to know she'd put out for Ross and he'd scorned her.

Her hands shook. She wanted to grab them, all of them, and yell into their faces that Ross wasn't a player, he hadn't loved her and left her. He only broke off their engagement because a large purpose called him.

And then she wanted to reach across the light-years and grab him. *Damn it, Ross Cantrell, isn't making a family with me the largest purpose of all?*

Nanette found herself at a booth where a tray of stuffed pastries smelled of beef and garlic. A lanky man, his pointed chin looking young beneath his bushy eyebrows, extended a gray sleeve to the tray. "Ropa vieja empanadas, help yourself."

Suddenly famished, Nanette picked one up and took a bite. Only then did she notice the lanky man's sleeve was part of a uniform. An old-fashioned printed nametag said *Capt. Corcoran*. On the curtain forming the back of the booth, video looped of young men of every ethnicity looking stern and resolute as they marched through jungles and crewed cannons and tanks. From a slender nanotube alloy frame hung a rifle on a retractable cord. Above everything else floated an AR banner. *Planetside Security LLC.*

She managed to swallow before lanky Captain Corcoran greeted her. "Let me guess, Ms. Bauer, you aren't a soldier, so what can Planetside do for you? We have plenty of opportunities in support services for a young woman like you."

Why did he speak with a knowing leer in his voice? She crossed her arms. "Support services? What kind of woman do you think I am?"

The skin between Corcoran's bushy eyebrows wrinkled up for a moment. Then he put on a self-effacing smile. "Not like *that*. We subcontract those services to junior priestesses from Ashtoreth." He went on, speaking quickly. "No, we'll aptitude test you and train you in any of a dozen career paths, from medtech to nanoassemblery to social coordination, or leverage your existing skills—"

"And send me to a war zone?"

He shook his head as if her question was a fly to shoo away. "Only a fraction of our personnel on a tiny number of our deployments see combat. We provide the full range of security services, from policing to pest control to—"

The words knifed into her. "Pest control? Like on Azureseas?"

Corcoran's eyebrows rose. His mouth hung open as if he tasted his next words before he spoke. "Azureseas is one of our lesser-known deployments."

She swallowed around a lump in her throat. Ross would have made it back there by now. What would Planetside do to him if they knew what he planned?

Why the hell should she care? After what he did to her reputation....

"I had to do a current events report my senior year of high school. Pick a colony world settled this century. I picked Azureseas just because I liked the name. I remember you had to clear dangerous native animals from the settlement zone."

The dangling rifle bobbed on an air current, as if it shook its head at her lie.

"Few people know about our deployment there." Corcoran angled his head and gave her a warm smile. "If you like the name of Azureseas, you could see the planet for yourself. I've never been, but I hear it's gorgeous. If there's a skill we need there, I promise we can deploy you to Azureseas. What do you say?"

Her cheeks felt hot. What could she do on Azureseas? Find Ross and beg him to return? Risk her life by helping in him in whatever battle he fought for the dinosaur chickens? Or find him to spit in his eye?

"Thank you, that's kind, but I just got here and want to look around...."

Corcoran's expression grew polite but distant, and his voice sounded flat. He'd already given up on making the sale. He turned his head to a new arrival at the booth before saying, "Thanks for your time, Ms. Bauer." His voice turned lively. "Hello, Mr. Hart, you look like a young man who knows how to handle a rifle. But have you ever fired one like this? Augmented reality only, of course, but it'll feel like the real thing."

Nanette turned away from the sound of Corcoran pulling slack the rifle's cord. She wandered the aisles, trying to forget about Ross, Azureseas, and dinosaur chickens. Trying to forget about New Ozark.

But few booths gave her an opportunity to leave. Gillett Terraforming wanted engineers for turning a newly-opened world's greenhouse atmosphere into hills of diamonds and rust. Colonia Productions wanted stage performers, mostly singers and dancers, for a troupe to tour the biggest cities of Earth.

Her shoulders slumped. Just give up. Finish bartender training and go to New Ozark's frontier. Everyone on the frontier ran away from something, just like her. And they all wanted a stiff drink. The bioseeding techs, the farmers, the ranchers....

Ranchers like Ross wanted to become. Once. When he wanted to marry her.

Her chest heaved. She stepped between booths at the back of the hall and dabbed her eyes. No. Don't cry. Not in public. Not over him.

Everything rose up in her like a wave. She jammed her fist against her clamped lips until the flood crested gently and subsided. One deep breath, one shudder of emotion. Her stomach still swam but she could face the crowd now.

Nanette wandered to a booth. Standard crew, two women barely older than her, hair in tight curls, makeup applied with robotic precision, skirtsuits cut to the latest fashion trends out of Old Los Angeles. The brunette took both of Nanette's hands with a soft grip. "Ms. Bauer, have you ever considered a career in mental health?"

Nanette stiffened. The brunette could tell she'd almost cried, was that it? "Not really." She craned her neck and noticed the AR banner floating overhead. A horizontal blue line that squiggled up in the middle to form a brain. One word on each side of the brain. Maybe Latin? "I've never heard of Anima Sana."

"We are a small but growing company in the field of behavioral optimization," the brunette said. The words came out like she practiced them in a mirror.

Nanette squinted. "Like the brain doctors where people with criminal genes go to get fixed before they commit a crime and get sued by the victim?"

"That's only one of the many markets we serve. Our relationship counseling practice helps couples enhance their emotional intimacy. We help survivors of harrowing experiences reduce their risk of post-traumatic stress disorder."

Nanette's voice sounded hollow. "Like soldiers."

"They make up most of our customer base in the PTSD market, that's right."

Nanette rocked on her feet. Her cheeks heated up. Yet the brunette seemed not to notice, and the blonde seated at the back of the booth buffed her blue nails with her fingertip as if everything was right in this world, and the augmented reality video loop projected on the back wall showed a stern man with intense green eyes talking to a hidden interviewer like relationships and soldiers were no big deal and why couldn't Nanette shake Ross off?

She choked out words. "I'm not interested." Then she hurried away from the whispers she knew the two attendants would share behind her back.

The coffee counter lacked a line. The voice-activated ordering kiosk didn't judge her. She picked an Italian word from the menu at random. The robotic arms behind the counter swung into motion. The grinder briefly sounded louder than the babbling crowd.

The robotic arms delivered her cup. Her fingertips grew hot despite the insulated cardboard. The drink scalded her lips. As oily and bitter as the vinegar the soldiers gave Jesus.

She turned away from the counter. The crowd milled about the booths. A hundred conversations full of hope and optimism. Hard work but high pay. Build that stake for your future....

Her shoulders slumped. There was no place for her. Go back to Saddlepoint or travel through twenty jump points. Become an old maid more pious than Mom. Marry an ex-con paying reparations to his victim and treatment fees with interest to a company like Anima Sana. Or become the fallen woman half this world thought she was. No matter where she went, Ross Cantrell would hang over everything she did and slide his ghost between her and anyone she might be able to love, man or child or the woman in the mirror—

She took deep breaths until her thoughts slowed down. She either had to make Ross come back to her or tell him to go to hell.

A realization came to her. She weighed it on both sides of a mental balance.

Nanette threw her bitter cup into the mouth of a wheeled trashbot, then strode to the booth for Planetside.

9

The longboat skimmed the surface of the deep blue sea. On each of port and starboard, six Banakhenner dipped and pulled long, painted oars in time to the call of Korfkhob, sea leader of the coastal village, who stood amidships on a small platform. Korfkhob's voice carried twenty yards over the water to the two longboats on the flanks of the three-ship formation. In the bright orange sun, iridescence rippled over the arms of the thirty-six oarsmen.

"*Bokha!*" Korfkhob shouted. *Stop*. Oars rose. Seawater dripped down painted pictures of Banakhenner pulling in nets of sea creatures. The oarsmen caught their wind with deep breaths of the salty air, and pounded the worked muscles of each other's shoulders. On the ship to their right, Lerbot helped a young male from his village lean over the side to catch his breath or vomit from motion sickness.

Korfkhob turned his face to Ross. Years of sunlight reflecting off water had given the Banakhenner a permanent squint and bleached the tips of his feathers nearly white. "Good is khaw," he asked Ross.

After half a standard year, most of the young males from Lerbot's village spoke as fluently as their alien mouths allowed. The sea villagers had learned much less. Ross needed a moment to answer Korfkhob's pidgin question. He shaded his eyes against the morning sun. His calves ached from trying to find his sea legs, and the three ships were alone on the surface of vast and primal depths. Despite a shudder, he said, "Yes. This is close enough."

In the distance, the blue shades of the cloud-dotted sky and the glassy ocean met at a thin line of green dotted with the unnatural colors and shapes of human construction. Tiny, from here. Ross turned to the mass of ten young males from Lerbot's village jammed toward the bow, craning their necks. "Gorekhtes, may I?"

The juvenile—despite his youth, he'd been promoted from satellite watcher to scout leader—lowered Ross' binoculars from his eyes. He worked his way back from the viewing platform at the prow. The young males parted for him. The muzzles of their slung firearms, pointing into the air, waved like a wheat field in a wind. Gorekhtes wobbled once and reached up for another male's shoulder to keep his balance.

He held the binoculars out to Ross with both his deep-green hands. His feathers flattened in respect. "There is much to see, Rossir."

"Boats? Aircraft? Soldiers?"

"No, Rossir. Just the buildings of your people."

Ross moved the eye cups closer together, then looked through them.

His people? He wished. After they terraformed New Ozark, his people busied themselves building farms and ranches and workshops. Not huge and luxurious structures like these. Rectilinear high-rise hotels turned hundreds of windows to the west, toward the three long-boats. A group of six spheres stacked three-two-one held a different environment in each, from jungle on top to snow and ice in the lower right. Ross shook his head. Rich tourists could spend so many months on Azureseas to get bored of sun and sand. A spiky mass of cubes and pyramids marked a shopping and restaurant complex. Stuart Havlicek once set out sandfly repellent stations there, a hell of a long time ago.

Judging from the bright green of manicured lawns viewed edge-on and not a single palm-like tree in sight, so much Earth life had been planted during the last six months that no sandflies lived anywhere near the beach.

He lowered the binoculars and checked a map sketched on rough-edged palm bark. Gorekhtes had sketched it on the first joint recon mission with Korfkhob's village. Dried lines of a sour root extract the

Banakhenner used as ink glistened blue-black. The scout's written notes were as blocky and clumsy as a child, and limited to shapes, sizes, and colors. Ross' notes, added three days ago, after they decided Planetside paid so little attention to the sea that they could risk him joining recon mission #2, labeled buildings and regions of the shore with their human functions. *Hotel. Mall.* He read his notes, looked through the binoculars, re-read.

Any civilians spending time in a resort on Azureseas would be rich. Which would be the richest of all?

He zoomed in on the spiky cubes and pyramids. Angled walls of glass, alloy, and mycocrete tinted in shades of white and gray. He remembered mixing water, gravel, and mushroom extract and pouring mycocrete on another building site, ten miles away and lost amid the developments now sprawling along the coast.

Back to the spiky structure. On a balcony jutting over sand and water, sunshades above café tables showed as dots of yellows and oranges. An eighth of a mile away, a tiny number of people were squiggles of movement between the fences of a private beach. Behind the beach rose twenty mansions widely spaced on lawns of Earth grass. A vast swath of green terrain beyond the mansions looked like a golf course.

Ross took a deep breath. Salt air like the bad breath of Jonah's whale bit the insides of his nose. Through the binoculars, he showed the spiky shopping complex to Korfkhob. "There."

"Yes." After Ross took the binoculars away, the sea leader's gaze locked onto the tiny spot on the horizon. He called out in his language. Oarsmen grumbled to one another while tapping their thumbs. Oars hovered over the water like seagulls looking for fish to eat.

"*Ghiagh!*" shouted Korfkhob.

The remaining miles to shore passed quickly. Bright sun, and a calm sea dappled with wavelets like the scales of a lizard's skin. Ross looked to the south and up, in the direction of the station at the top of the space elevator. Ross' stomach tightened. Gorekhtes had seen through the binoculars a ship leave the station for the jump point to 18 Bo-otis this morning. That part of the plan was in place.

He shifted his weight side-to-side more than he needed to keep his balance. But the rest of the plan? Six months of hard work to get to this point. Not just language lessons. Negotiations with other villages, to get Korfkhob's expertise at sea and enough lumber from villages higher in the hills to build the three ships. Arkhtes had designed and built new firearms, rifled-barrel breech-loaders, faster to load with new aerodynamic bullets. Trenches and tank traps now ringed the villages.

The human buildings on the shore became clearer to the naked eye. The tightness in his stomach turned sour. In an hour on the beach, could they find enough humans with enough influence off-planet? Could they persuade them to send messages to the alien affairs agencies? Could Ross and the sixty-four Banakhenner with him get off-shore before Planetside could react? Planetside probably wouldn't fire the guns of an AFV in sight or hearing of tourists.

Probably.

Unless Dr. Fitzhugh could wipe tourists' memories as easily as they hacked soldiers' brains.

Ross sipped from his canteen, but his mouth still felt dry. Rich off-worlders might choose to get memory wipes, but Planetside, Fitzhugh, and the big money behind both couldn't force them.

He wiped his mouth with the back of his hand and scraped over beard stubble. Even if the tourists sent outbound messages proving the Banakhenner weren't animals, the negotiations and back-room deals to give the Banakhenner a fair deal would take standard months. Until then, Planetside could target the villages with a punitive expedition. Could Harkhmal, his father, and Merghunek, left to lead the defenses, protect the females and juveniles before Ross, Lerbot, and Lerbot's warriors returned?

Would adding Lerbot's warriors and the rifle slung over his own shoulder make a difference?

Close to the shopping complex now. "Raise the truce flag," Ross said.

"Yes, Rossir." Gorekhtes reached down behind a rower's seating mat and pulled up a stick five feet long. Females from Korfkhob's village had stitched together pieces of bark, bleached in the sun and then softened. Gorekhtes raised it high enough for people on the shore to see.

Blots of color took shape in the glass-walled concourse and on the café's balcony. Golf shirts, pants, skirts and sundresses rippled in the breeze. Arms set down drinks. Feet pivoted and legs went to the railing. Hands rose to shade eyes from the reflection of the sun off the sea.

Ross' gut tied into a cold knot. People rich enough to spend months on an interstellar vacation wouldn't care about the plight of aliens.

He took a deep breath of salt-laced air. Even if most didn't care, just one of the people crowding the balcony or gathering on the beach in front of the longboats could be enough.

Korfkhob called, "*Bokha!*" Oars rose. The longboats coasted until their prows ground to a halt on sand.

Ross wobbled. He'd boarded the extraction boat on a day as sunny as this....

Every day in this region of Azureseas was about as sunny as this. Only he had changed, but that change was enough and more than enough.

He strode forward. His boots thumped on the deck. The squad parted for him.

He stepped on a platform just behind the prow and turned to the Banakhenner warriors. Despite his nerves, his chest swelled. "You know what to do. Be friendly. If they talk to you, tell them about your families, your customs, and the things you make. You probably won't understand what the humans say, but they'll understand you. Rifles stay slung unless Planetside shows up. We go with God!"

"With Khott!" came an uneven cheer. He climbed over the side and jumped into two-foot deep water. Warmth wrapped his legs and soaked his boots. He strode through slumping sand up the beach. The Banakhenner warriors filed off the longboat behind him. Two more lines climbed off the other ships, led by Lerbot to the right and Kibkhal to the left.

About twenty people crowded the beach amid scraggly native plants. They stood on dry sand beyond the meager high-tide line. Behind the crowd to the left rose the sheer walls of the shopping complex. A narrow garden filled with terrestrial bushes trimmed into dolphin shapes nestled between the building and the twelve-foot wall of a three-story mansion. A garden path of cultivated stone, barely glimpsed between arms and legs, probably led to the main road Ross remembered followed the coast.

As he approached, most of the crowd leaned back and eyed the Banakhenner and their slung firearms. A tall man with an athletic build stepped forward. Black sunglasses hid his eyes. Gray strands salted his wavy black hair. His white linen shirt, half-unbuttoned, showed his stainless steel wearable hung on its neck chain, cushioned by curly black hair on his chest. He had the look of a man accustomed to taking charge.

A woman half his age followed half a step behind him. Golden-brown sunglasses as huge as insect eyes. A sheer white wrap over a pastel yellow sundress over slender curves. Golden hoop earrings glittered amid her blond curls.

A squint on his face, the man asked in a deep voice, "Key diavolo say too?"

Ross showed his palms. "I can't understand you," he said in Standard. "I left my wearable behind when I joined my new friends." He gestured toward Lerbot and the other Banakhenner.

The man listened to his earbuds for a moment. He pointed to Lerbot and said in halting words, "What are these?"

Ross stiffened, then gave his head a little shake. Maybe it was just a translation error to call them *what* instead of *who*. "These are Banakhenner. Members of the intelligent species native to Azureseas."

The woman's slender eyebrows crinkled. Slowly she said, "The resort company said nothing about aliens."

The man sniffed out a breath. "Per kay no chee sono alieni, stupida ragazza."

She turned on him and punched his upper arm. He smirked back until—

Lerbot spoke. Despite his throat-clearing growl, his words came clear. "We can prove we are intelligent."

The man blinked. The woman set her hand on her hip and angled her head at him. The rest of the crowd showed confused and puzzled looks as they whispered among themselves.

Lerbot went on. "For eights of eights of eights of years we lived in our villages across this continent. We tended our herds. We growed our crops. We traded with other villages." He paused the way he'd practiced with Ross. "Then the soldiers comed."

The tone of his last words fell like a shadow on Ross. And some of the faces in the human crowd.

Ross's next breath filled his chest with warmth. They were getting their story across.

"Banakhenner villages once standed along the shore. One standed here." Lerbot jutted out his right arm toward the foundation of the shopping complex. The iridescent ripple of Lerbot's feathers caught the blonde's eyes.

Then his scar did.

Technically he lied. Korfkhob had told them a fishing village once stood on this stretch of the coast, but he couldn't remember exactly where. Didn't matter. If Planetside, the brain hackers, and the big money behind both knew where the village had really stood, they couldn't admit it.

Lerbot spoke. "The soldiers killed Banakhenner and burned the villages. The villagers who lived here tried talking with the soldiers to make peace. The soldiers did not talk and kept killing and burning. All Banakhenner know this. No Banakhenner knowed why. Until our friend comed to us." He gestured to Ross across his body with his right arm.

Troubled brows and gasping breaths revealed more people in the crowd noticed his scar.

Ross stepped forward on the soft sand. "My name is James Ross Cantrell." He had to give his real name. Planetside's records would corroborate that part of his story. No greater risk to him, and every human being he cared about lived on New Ozark, safe from the company's retribution. "I signed up with Planetside about three years ago and spent most of my enlistment here on Azureseas. I was one of those soldiers who killed Banakhenner and burned villages."

His throat tightened on the last words. The presence of his alien friends around him shamed him and relieved his shame at the same time, like the sight of the empty cross on the church wall behind the preacher. "I didn't know they were intelligent. I thought they were animals. All us soldiers thought they were animals." He raised his voice over the rustle of wavelets on sand. "Because we were brainwashed."

Ross let his words hang. He read the frowns and peering eyes of the rich tourists. Brainwashing was some barbaric thing, like cars powered by fossil fuels. Not part of the 25th century.

"Planetside worked with some brain hackers," he said. "I never knew the company name, but their man running things here was Dr. Fitzhugh. Their logo is a blue line with a brain coming out of it." His right index finger sketched it in the air.

He cast a long look over the crowd. Warmth lifted his chest. People studied him, studied the Banakhenner. Some nodded to each other or murmured in tones of belief. The blonde's fingers wrapped around her throat.

The confident man batted his hand toward Ross. "Kay storia."

"Storia?" The blonde turned on him a gaze like a fileting knife. She shot out her arm toward Lerbot. "Storia?"

He ran a hand through his wavy black hair. His voice sounded like he lectured a small child. "Uno spot-o-cola messo sue doll centro commerce-ee-ah-lay."

The blonde yanked off her sunglasses. She rattled off something in their language, tapping the edge of the sunglasses against the man's upper arm. Her final sound to him was a deep sniff.

She nested the sunglasses on her blond curls and came to Ross and Lerbot. "He thinks the aliens are a spectacle put on by the shopping complex. But why would the shops make robots or people in costumes have such a scent?"

"We are real," Lerbot said. He held out his right arm.

The blonde ran her fingers over the iridescent, hair-like feathers, both with and against the grain. She touched his arm above and below the lower elbow, then the upper, applying enough pressure each time for Lerbot to flex the joints. "No costume could allow a person to bend his arms like that."

The confident man said, "Then a robot—"

"No robot." Her high voice sliced through the air. Her hazel-brown eyes met Lerbot's. "An intelligent creature."

Doubt flickered across the confident man's face. A moment only. "A creature, fine. But intelligent?"

His disbelief seeped into faces in the crowd Ross had moments before thought were on his side. One man's voice scratched, "The developers could charge more if they told the Consortia worlds aliens lived here. They wouldn't lie and say none did."

A woman in the crowd with a shaved strip through her brown hair looked at Lerbot and the others from under skeptical eyebrows. "Parrots can talk too."

"If Dr. Fitzhugh brainwashed you, Mr. James Ross Cantrell," said the confident man, and damn him and the smug tone in his voice, "how did you break it?"

"Thanks to God, I found proof they were intelligent." Ross glanced at the woman with the shaved strip in her hair. "Yeah, parrots can talk and beavers can build dams, so maybe animals can build firearms and ships as big as those." He pointed over his shoulder at the three long-boats beached in shallow water, and the dozens of sea village oarsmen ogling them and the giant angular shopping complex.

Ross reached into a pocket of his cargo shorts and pulled out a clear plastic bag holding the drawing of the praying Banakhenner. He raised it high. "But only an intelligent alien could pray, and only another intelligent alien could have drawn him praying."

The blonde extended her hand to the drawing. "See prega," she said. A little shake of her head and she switched languages. "I record with my contact lenses and share with all?"

"Please do." He held the drawing in front of her. She studied it, absently reached for it. Her soft fingertips brushed his hand. Her perfume trickled a flowery note into his nose. He hadn't been this close to a woman since he'd left Nanette on New Ozark.

Over the rustle of plastic, her voice flowed like wine. "Bella art-ay."

The confident man cocked his head. Plainly looking at video shared by the blonde to his augmented reality overlay. He scoffed. "A human artist draws this."

Ross chuckled. He'd prepared for that reaction. He nodded at Lerbot and the two of them turned to a Banakhenner with wide-set eyes and long snout, named Neerokh. "Your turn," Ross said.

Neerokh unslung his firearm. He nudged the warrior next to him, to pull his comrade's attention away from the glass wall of the complex, and handed over the weapon. Neerokh came forward while he reached one-handed into a satchel. He stopped between Lerbot and Ross and held out a rigid sheet of bark and a chunk of charcoal. To the confident man, he said, "May I draw you?"

"You may attempt it, parrot."

Neerokh gave him a close look. The scrape of charcoal over the bark joined the sound of the waves, the hiss of traffic from the main road, and the murmur of conversations on the café balcony high above.

Ross glanced up, shading his eyes against the bright noontime. Tourists crowded the railing. On the other side of the glass wall, more tourists watched while robotic carts heaped with luxuries idled next to them.

Warm salt air filled him like a balloon. Hundreds of people saw the Banakhenner. No way the big money behind Planetside and the brain hackers could deny it had stolen land and slain intelligent life.

"Finished," said Neerokh. He raised the piece of bark and panned it so all the crowd, and Ross, could see.

Ross sucked in a breath. A trickle of sweat turned cold down his back. Sketched lines, and not many of them, and Neerokh missed some details of the sunglasses and the line of the man's jaw. Yet in spite of the speed and crudeness, or maybe because of it, Neerokh had captured the essence of the man. Skeptical. Assertive. For all to see, perhaps long after the man went to his grave.

Art was the nearest thing to magic, and only intelligent life could create it.

The man took slow steps toward them. He slipped off his sunglasses and hung them on the open collar of his shirt. His brown and piercing eyes studied the lines of charcoal on bark for a moment.

Suddenly, he stood tall. He turned to the blonde and spoke with as much confidence as before. "Justo, amore mio."

She smiled at him. Her eyes misted. "I knew you would see they are intelligent."

To Ross and Lerbot, he said, "What things do you want us to do?"

"Send messages out of the system," Ross said. "Tell and show who the Banakhenner are to as many people as you can. Tell your friends and family. Investigative reporters. Ombudsmen."

Lerbot's voice rumbled. "We want the same fair deal your people gived other thinking species on other worlds. And compensation and memorial for Banakhenner killed and villages burned."

"Do it now," Ross added. "When the big money realizes you know the truth about the Banakhenner, they'll try to stop you from sending messages."

An older woman stiffened her shoulders under her sea-green dress. "They wouldn't dare."

The confident man whipped his head toward her and raised an eyebrow. "Just as they wouldn't dare brainwash soldiers and lie to the worlds that intelligent aliens are animals? You are too old to be so naive. Mr. Cantrell is right. We must send our messages now."

The older woman sniffed in a breath, but nodded along with the others. Murmurs of agreement washed over the beach, louder than the rustle of wavelets.

Calm triumph flowed through Ross, as warm as the orange sunlight on his skin. He and the Banakhenner had done it. People knew the Banakhenner were aliens. Word would get out.

Just as the feeling drained away, Lerbot reached for Ross' shoulder. Ross read the question in the yellow-green eyes without whites, and nodded. The Banakhenner leader could read his reply.

Ross turned to the blonde, still near him, and the confident man a few steps away. "We must go now. Planetside will soon find out we were here. We must set sail now to make it home before they can send boats after us."

"No!" said the blonde. Her hazel eyes darted as if she searched for reasons why. "If you stay with us, you cannot be harmed. Too many of us will see."

Ross smiled gently. "It's where you can't see that worries us. We have to get back to defend the females and juveniles in case Planetside launches a punitive strike against the Banakhenner villages."

"Mr. Cantrell is correct," said the confident man. "We will do our part. Go do yours." He angled his head. "Rapid-amen-tay!"

Ross heard the sound too. A hydraulic hiss, followed by a metallic clang, coming through the narrow garden between the shopping complex and the twelve-foot wall. He knew the sound.

An AFV, deploying soldiers out its rear gate.

"Let's go," Ross said to Lerbot and Kibkhal. "On board the ships!" He cupped his hand around his mouth and called out, "Korfkhob, we need to go the instant everyone is on board!"

Korfkhob shouted orders in the Banakhenner tongue. On all three ships, some crew mounted oars in slots while others jumped out and waded to the prows. Lerbot and Kibkhal turned to their warriors and ordered them back. Ross did the same. Lines of Banakhenner splashed through the shallow water.

Heavy boots, dozens of them, tramped on the cultivated stone path through the garden. The sound grew louder every moment.

Ross remained in his spot on the beach. His head swiveled between the withdrawing Banakhenner and the approaching soldiers. Worry churned his gut. He'd wanted to time it just right, but if he'd guessed wrong how the soldiers would respond....

Lerbot rested the rough skin of his palms on Ross' shoulder. "You said it right. The soldiers will not shoot at us when your people can see."

Gray-green movement at the edge of the narrow garden. The light-swallowing black of rifle muzzles slung over shoulders. Flashes of varied skin tones of human faces. Helmets open, standard operating procedure when around civilians.

At the back of the crowd, people turned scowls to the soldiers. A woman jutted out an arm clinking with bangles. "Murderers!"

The line of soldiers paused. A male voice at the head of the line said something in a patient tone.

Ross looked over his shoulder. The last warriors waited in line at the boarding ramps. Five or six oarsmen waited at the broad prow of each longboat, ready to shove off. Korfkhob shifted his weight, a sign of nerves, as he watched the shore.

Voice raised, Ross said to the civilians, "Let the soldiers come through."

The blonde's hand covered her neck. The confident man gave Ross a nod, then laid his hand on her shoulder and whispered in her ear. Her body language eased against him.

The other civilians slowly parted. Into the gap came soldiers. Sand slumped under their boots. The first soldiers came three abreast. An e-ink rank badge, only used around civilians, showed the one in the middle was a lieutenant. Presumably the commander of the unit filing in behind him.

Ross looked at the lieutenant's open face shield. Skin as smooth as the rich folks' faces except for a mole on his jaw. Buoyed by a fresh breath, Ross grinned.

Lt. Liebrandt. Always trying to seem more forceful than his face and voice came across, but firm and fair. And as brainwashed as the enlisteds serving under him.

Liebrandt's gaze swept across the Banakhenner too quickly to notice anything. His eyes stopped at Ross and turned glossy for a moment. He blinked and pushed back his shoulders. His gaze tunneled at Ross. "What's going on here, mister...."

Ross widened his grin. "Hi, l.t. It's me, Cantrell."

"Cantrell? You discharged? You discharged. Went home." Liebrandt rubbed his temples with the thumb and middle finger of his left hand. "What are you doing back here?" He glanced at Lerbot and his head locked in place. "With—with—"

Lerbot spoke. "He finded out all soldiers here are brainwashed to think we Banakhenner are animals. He comed to help us get the same deal you give smart life around other suns."

Not just the lieutenant. Every soldier froze. Their eyes didn't see, their ears didn't hear. Even if Ross hadn't expected that response, he'd be able to tell the soldiers blacked out from some unnatural cause inside their heads.

He wasn't the only one. The civilians on the edges of the scene gave each other shocked looks and muttered in fearful tones. Words like *brainwashing* and *crime against humanity*. The blonde shook her head and her voice held pity. "Poor boys."

In the water behind Ross, the last Banakhenner clomped up the wooden ramps onto the longboats. From the middle boat, youthful Gorekhtes called out, "Korfkhob says we are ready!"

Ross nodded over his shoulder, then turned back to Liebrandt and the others. He got a little jolt when he saw Vasquez' wide face, and life returning to the man's sneering brown eyes. Why had Vasquez renewed his contract?

Because no one on his homeworld wanted him to go back.

Call him out? 'Hey Vasquez, did you ever sneak trophies past the l.t.?'

Ross shook off the thoughts. The Banakhenner had taken well to him because he'd expressed remorse and because he'd soldiered against them without malice. But bring to their attention a man who'd cut off the ears of Banakhenner dead to keep score in some sick game? It might distract one of them into trying to shoot Vasquez in the face. Miss or hit, the Banakhenner would look bad if they shot first.

He returned his attention to Liebrandt, whose eyes saw clearly again. "My friend Lerbot is still learning the language, but I know you heard what he said."

Another wave of blackouts seized the gathered soldiers. Liebrandt's eyelids fluttered and his body swayed. "Dinosaur chicken." Sweat beaded on his forehead. "Friend." His eyes glazed over. His mouth hung open.

Ross gave a sympathetic wince to the gathered soldiers. They hadn't asked to be brainwashed. They were guys just like him, wanting to earn money to do good things back home.

His gaze skimmed the corporal stripes on Vasquez' shoulder, then landed on his face. The man's dark eyes were like an angry drunk's looking for a fight.

Most of them were guys like him.

"We must go now," Ross said. "The boat captain wants us off the sea before sunset, and we need a head start before Planetside can send a powerboat after us—"

"Do not worry about that," said the confident man. He tapped the stainless steel wearable resting against his chest hair. "I tell friends who rented a pleasure boat today to ride along near you. Planetside dares do nothing in front of eyes that can see."

"Thank you," Lerbot said. "We Banakhenner want to meet all humans as friends."

"Yes, thank you." Ross held out his hand. The confident man shook it with a firm grip. Ross then held it out for the blonde. Other than her hair color and her build, she looked nothing like Nanette. But when she leaned toward him on her perfumed neck and air-kissed his cheeks, memories of his night and morning alone with Nanette washed through him like an iced drink on this hot day.

He shook off that thought too. Time to withdraw. They'd done all they could.

Ross and Lerbot sloshed through the water on their way back to their longboats. Ross remembered sloshing through similar water, on a similar beach fifteen miles away. The smell of burned plantains suddenly seemed to lodge in his nose.

He clomped up the loading ramp. Korfkhob shouted commands. The Banakhenner waiting at the prows pushed the boats off the sandy bottom, then ran to the ramps as the oars dipped into the water.

Ross raised one hand to the crowd still gathered at the beach, around the crowd of soldiers like statues. The tourists waved and gestured back.

He took a deep breath of salty air. The phantom smell of burned plantains went away. He had done all he could today to force the big money to give the Banakhenner a fair deal plus extra compensation.

What would he have to do back on dry land, to defend against the big money's backlash?

10

Nanette stood behind the bar of the empty Planetside officer's club. The clock in the lower right corner of her vision read 1355, just a few minutes before her shift officially began. The polarized windows cut the rays of the afternoon sun down to an orange glow, like a sunset or a rotting citrus fruit. A spidery cleaning robot jumped from table to table, squirting antiseptic spray. A twangy song about lost love played through speakers hidden in the ceiling. Not what she wanted to hear, alone on a planet God knew how many light-years from home.

Especially today, for some reason. When the Planetside robo-rideshare brought her onto the base, the MP at the gate had triple-checked her ID while nervously licking his lips. The soldiers she passed on the final part of the ride either hurried with hunched shoulders or milled in clumps, sharing puzzled looks as their mouths moved. A line of soldiers out the door of some gray prefab office. And had she seen a soldier sitting on the asphalt, looking up to his comrades with his eyes red from crying? What had happened?

She felt better when she lost herself in work. She ran her gaze over the bottles racked along the top, bottom, and sides of the mirrored back wall. Augmented reality overlays showed estimates of when each bottle would run out. Three weeks for the smooth bourbon from Covington?

She frowned. Only a couple of fingers remained in the bottle. But only a couple of men drank it, and then rarely. Far more expensive than the nanoassembled bourbons fabricated here on Azureseas.

A chime sounded in her earbud. Brightness in the mirror dazzled her eyes. A wave of fresh air from the open door reminded her just how much the interior of the officer's club smelled like spilled whiskey and chocolate and coffee nicotine vapor.

As she turned, Nanette put on a pleasant smile. The real job of any bartender was to brighten up the customer's day. Plus, the regs allowed officers to fraternize with civilian contractors. The next man to come in might be tall, handsome, and able to make her forget about Ross.

Her smile wavered a little. Two men. The familiar one had a turned-up nose and red cheeks from too much sun. Gray fuzz showed between his ears and his officer's cap. Each flap of his gray-green collar carried a single silver star. Usually he eyed her figure, but he never talked crude or groped at her. General Pouliot, Planetside's commander on Azureseas. She treated him like the happy drunk uncle she'd never had. "Afternoon, sheriff. Your usual?"

He turned his head to her and opened his mouth, but the other man spoke briskly. "Two of your best bourbons, neat. Make them doubles."

Her first glance, when sunlight through the open door backlit him, had been enough to tell he was a civilian, shorter than average. Maybe from a heavy-g world. As her eyes readjusted, she saw his white lab coat with blue embroidery. His green eyes gave her a cool look, then he raised one eyebrow.

"Yes sir, two double Covingtons, neat." On the ceiling-mounted track behind Nanette, a dark brown egg shape unfolded two of its arms. One wrapped articulated alloy fingers around a stubby glass while the other poured.

"I'll drink the liquor you buy off your expense account, Fitzy," said the general, "but you foobarred this and damn if I'll let you off easy."

The articulated arms carried the glasses to the bar. Nanette timed her approach to the two men for the moment after the double clunk. "Anything more, gentlemen?"

The scientist, Fitzy, cracked his knuckles while his wearable transferred payment. And a generous tip. But his green eyes looked at her the same way he might look at his lab rats. "Miss, go clean some dirty glasses at the other end of the bar."

Nanette's back stiffened. She overheard lots of talk from her customers but kept all of it secret and didn't need to be talked to like that. But despite his short stature, the scientist's green eyes burned off her resentment and left only lingering unease.

Her shoulders hunched. "Thanks for the tip," she said as if she didn't deserve it, and went to the far end of the bar. She tapped her wearable on its necklace through her peasant blouse to wake it up. Her wearable read her gestures and opened up a story bookmarked on her wearable of celebrity gossip from Earth. Superimposed on the pale, sheened wood of the bar, Salomé Wainwright wore a ribbon of shimmering silver fabric on the red carpet that barely covered the body parts it had to cover. Dressing like a priestess from Ashtoreth? No wonder Liam Kleindorfer had filed for divorce....

She made another, hesitant gesture, below the bar and to the side where the general and the scientist couldn't see. The audio playback through her earbuds muted. Overhearing the two men might explain more of what strange thing happened today.

Ross? Had he fought them? Had they caught him? Tangled emotions swirled inside her. She rested her hand on the bar to keep them from carrying her away. She didn't even know if he'd made it back to Azureseas.

Fitzy the scientist spoke in Standard. Voice low, but not low enough for her sharp hearing. "No, general, we can talk right here. Because I did my job right."

General Pouliot said in a strangled whisper, "Then how in the hell did Cantrell show up on a tourist beach with a hundred damn dinosaur chickens?"

Nanette sucked in a breath. Ross. He'd helped the aliens fight back, just like he'd sworn he would. Warmth filled her belly. Her head swam. He fought back. Good for him—

But what good was that for her?

Dozens of flashbulb reflections popped on Salomé Wainwright's tanned abs and tops and bottoms of boobs. Nanette stared at the augmented reality image without seeing it.

"I conditioned Cantrell the same way I conditioned every other soldier. What happened, general, is some competing tourism conglomerate is stirring up trouble. This is some agent of theirs posing as Cantrell—"

"Face recog software found him in the database in half a damn second. Cantrell, James Ross, from New Ozark. My former soldier parading intelligent aliens in front of a thousand tourists." The general's whisper turned haggard. "A competing conglomerate? Did they break Cantrell's conditioning?"

"I assure you, nobody broke his conditioning."

"Something made him remember—"

"General, trying to figure out why Cantrell came back to Azureseas is like checking sports scores during a hull breach. What are you doing about the real problem?"

"The cat's out of the bag," said General Pouliot. "The outbound ship left the top of the elevator. All those civilians can send messages to it now."

Fitzy spoke like he lectured a child. "The Transterrestrial Space Defense Force flotilla can order that ship to wipe its outbound message buffers before clearing it to traverse the jump point."

A jump cut to shades of white tinged with chill blue kept Nanette's eyes from wandering toward the two men. A man with tight, arrogant eyes. White-furred aliens whose arms had so many joints they moved like tentacles. The ice sculptors native to Concordia. But who was the man? The CEO of the conglomerate that hired Planetside and Fitzy to do its dirty work here on Azureseas? Or some other company hiding a vice under a camera pose of virtue?

Why did Ross think he could fight the big money?

But he'd been right to fight it. And he'd landed a hard enough punch that its minions were scrambling.

If only he could have done it from their ranch on New Ozark....

"Stop the ship? My authority ends at the top of the atmosphere." She'd never heard Pouliot whine like that before.

A cold chuckle. "Your hands are as soiled as mine from conditioning the soldiers. Both our CEOs are going to try to make us take the fall as rogue employees. You have to stop that ship from jumping to 18 Boötis until we can scrub its message buffers."

"TSDF isn't my service. I can't order them to do that."

"Then ask nicely. Call in a favor with the flotilla admiral. You're a big boy. Figure it out."

"It wouldn't do a damn thing but stall. We can't keep all the tourists on-planet forever." Childish hope filled his voice. "Unless you can...."

"Wipe their memories? If there were one or two, that would be another day at the office for me. But a hundred, who've been talking and sharing video they shot with their friends and fellow tourists? Infeasible."

A chime rang. Another customer. Nanette paused the video, looked up, and squinted at the glow of light from the doorway. One customer.

She cleared her throat. Fitzy set down his glass and turned it like a dial on the bar. Pouliot brooded. Nothing happy about him if he got drunk today. She'd find a way to cut him off, she decided as she came closer. "Doing well, gentlemen?"

"Just fine," Fitzy said with an edge.

"How can I help you?" she asked the newcomer. A lieutenant, from the silver bar on his collar. And his smooth face made him look even younger than Ross. Liebrandt, she remembered. A little distant but always polite. Usually took a pale yellow lager or pilsner.

"I'm not drinking," he said. His voice was higher than usual and crackled. He pulled back his shoulders and turned to General Pouliot and the civilian. "What did you do to us?"

Pouliot glared at him. "Rethink your tone of voice when you speak to me, son."

Liebrandt flinched, but then leaned in. "I'll use whatever tone I want with a superior who gives me an illegal order!"

"Lower your voice," said Fitzy. "You're showing signs of what may be, in my professional opinion, a psychotic episode." His green eyes darted toward Nanette. "Where were you?"

Nanette dropped her gaze. "Let me know if you need anything." She went to the end of the bar and unpaused the muted video of the man and the ice sculptors.

Liebrandt drew in a breath. His voice sounded like he stood taller.

"You can try to pull rank or threaten me with a trip to the nut house, but it won't work. I know what I saw. I know what my men saw."

Nanette trembled. *You tell them, lieutenant.*

"What do you think you saw?" Fitzy asked.

"Don't try to gaslight me, Doctor. You know what happened on the beach today. You must have known from the beginning there were intelligent aliens here on Azureseas. If the two of you want to break all the laws of man and morality, fine. But don't make us your catspaws."

"You're being insubordinate to the general. Isn't he, General?"

Pouliot said nothing for a long moment. He thunked his glass down with a finality that told Nanette he'd drained it. The general raised his voice. "Miss? I'll take another." He angled his head at Fitzy. "Put it on his tab."

She peered at the general, gauging his drunkenness, before turning on a smile. "A double Covington, neat." She pivoted to face the robotic arms, then her fingertips tapped out a pattern on the denim of her pants leg. An icon popped up in her augmented reality contact lenses, showing the system recognized the pattern. A water line inside one of the robotic arms would dilute the bourbon, but not so much that he'd be likely to notice. With luck, General Pouliot would stay sober enough to do the right thing. Admit his sins, if only to himself, and make amends for them.

Liebrandt spoke in a shrill whisper. "You broke my platoon, doctor. Your conditioning failed when we saw the Banakhenner speaking a human language and making art. It didn't fail gracefully, though. We came out of a stupor and now we have to live with what we did to them when we thought they were dinosaur chickens. I've got men in fugues, men drunk as skunks, men crying. They won't raise their weapons against the Banakhenner ever again. But if they don't get compensated for your crimes, they just might raise them against you."

"Compensation," muttered Pouliot. He took a long gulp of bourbon.

Nanette's face fell. General Pouliot would get too drunk to do anything, wrong or right.

"I've already filed a complaint with the ombudsman," Liebrandt said. "I've got men standing in line to do the same. The truth will come out. Planetside and Anima Sana will pay the price. The two of you will pay the price. Come clean, both of you. Then resign."

Another gulp of bourbon, then the thump of the empty glass. "Miss?" Pouliot over-enunciated the simple word.

"Coming up," she said. She tapped on her thigh the commands to water down his next drink even more. When the robotic arm delivered it, she followed the articulated gleam to the three men and gave each one a close look. The general, morose, hunched toward the new glass. Liebrandt, chin up, waved her off when she asked if he'd changed his mind.

The doctor gave her a green-eyed stare until she retreated to the far end of the bar.

"You've given us a lot to think about," Fitzy said to the lieutenant. "Give us some time to talk it over."

Nanette squinted at the glamorous images of an unfamiliar celebrity power couple. Fitzy couldn't give up that easily. It was only a stall.

"Don't take too long. Word is spreading wider and wider."

Nanette watched Liebrandt's pulled-back shoulders as he strode out. A better man than she'd ever known he was.

Her breath caught. Just like Ross. Only Ross had done so much more.

Ross had given up so much more.

Another chime. Another dazzle of sunlight. Nanette cleared her throat and moved closer. She hesitated and raised her hand in a stop sign. "Corporal, the enlisted men's club is—"

"Not where I belong." Set in a wide face, his brown eyes sneered at her. The nameplate on his chest read *Vasquez*.

"Corporal, I have to ask you to leave." Her right hand went out of his sight, to the small of her back. Tap out a pattern with her fingernails against her blouse and MPs would come in seconds.

Pouliot stirred out of his stupor. "Son, you heard the young lady."

Vasquez snapped a salute. His dark eyes burned with confidence. "Sir, give me a minute and I'll earn a field promotion to lieutenant."

"Son—"

"Let him speak," Fitzy said. His voice trickled like ice water down Nanette's back. Clips of an environmentalist campaign to restore some

Earth desert by tearing down solar farms and building fusion power plants on the coast failed to warm her.

Vasquez said, "Most people believe all the bulldaisies about alien rights and fair deals. Doctor, you had to do what you did for them. But I don't need it. Aliens. Carah-ho. Maybe some people call them Banakhenner but they're still just dinosaur chickens to me."

"Go on," said Fitzy.

"I know other men who don't need it either. Enough to put together a squad for a mission on the other side of the fence. Punish the dinosaur chickens for following Cantrell." His voice added a sadistic note. "Punish Cantrell."

Nanette stifled a gasp. She turned her head away from the three men. How many soldiers were in a squad? How many of those tanks that carried soldiers and fired cannons? Even with Ross' help, the Banakhenner would lose against that.

She put a hand on the bar to steady herself and gulped a mouthful of the vape-spiced air. Still hope. The general had to agree with Vasquez' plan and why would he? Even if Pouliot didn't care about the Banakhenner, ordering a massacre would just make things worse for him when the truth came out.

"I admire your initiative, Corporal," said the scientist.

A forceful thump came from the general's glass on the bar. "Christ damn it. We're already twisting in the wind and you want more blood on our hands?"

"No one's twisting anywhere. You're going to do what I said and hold the next outbound ship until we wipe its message buffer. Crack down hard on the ombudsman so he buries Liebrandt's complaint."

"I can't do that—"

"With the right combination of carrots and sticks, you can make any man do your bidding. What else would we need to do? You warn your bosses and I'll warn mine."

Pouliot sounded uncertain. "We can stop messages, but we can't stop tourists from leaving."

"Then word trickles back to the other Consortia worlds, to Earth," the scientist said. "So what? Both our bosses will inject disinformation into the rumor mill. A hoax, a publicity stunt, whatever. That gives us months before anyone comes to investigate. If they do, and there isn't an alien alive within a hundred miles of the perimeter?"

"Their villages are visible from orbit."

"Then bulldoze them and seed the sites with native forest. Do that and the investigators won't have enough proof. We can survive this. If you pin a lieutenant's bar on Vasquez' collar."

Nanette balanced on the edge of a knife. *Come on, sherriff...*

Pouliot spoke after a time. His voice didn't belong to a happy drunk, or an angry one, but to a man of too many years and too many worries. "He doesn't get a field promotion."

"Good call. That will help Planetside's CEO cover his tracks," Fitzy said. "And all of ours. Corporal Vasquez, will you still take care of our problem?"

"If you take care of me." Vasquez whistled a jaunty note with a hint of menace, like a serial killer stalking his next victim.

"How much?" Pouliot muttered.

"Hundred k in transstellar cryptocoin. Or the equivalent."

The usual general returned for a moment. "Don't joke with me, son."

"We'll find a way," said Fitzy.

Pouliot sighed, hoping for some little victory to save face. "Now clear out before the bartender calls the MPs to roust you for trespassing."

"Yes. Sir." Vasquez' salute was a languid motion in the corner of Nanette's eye.

She kept her gaze locked on the bar top, where a memorial story played about an ultimate flying disc hall-of-famer from the last century who'd just passed away. Ross would know the former player's name. She continued to watch, even after a flash of sunlight from the doorway showed that Vazquez had left.

Faint scrapes came from Fitzy rotating his glass. "We have work to do, general."

"Thanks for the drink. Damn fine bourbon," the general said without conviction.

"After we save our bosses' backsides, they'll give us so large a bonus you can drink it every day."

"Every day." The general sounded beaten.

"Miss. Miss!"

Nanette turned to Fitzy the scientist. She put on a cheerful smile. *Please God help me keep what I know off my face.* "Yes?"

"Time to settle my tab." His green eyes looked unperturbed, as if he'd just talked about the weather instead of mass murder and cover-up.

She was polite and sprinkled in friendly words. The two men soon left. After the door closed behind them, she shuddered. Her elbows sank to the hard bar and she hugged herself against a sudden chill.

Ross against that vile corporal and Planetside's full firepower. He didn't stand a chance.

—He wouldn't be in this mess if he'd done the right thing by her—

Nanette broke off those thoughts. He'd done the right thing. God had put the truth into his hands. Acting on it was the only thing he could have done. That was more important, even than their life together.

Hot pressure welled behind her eyes. She prayed no one came in because if they did she'd burst into tears.

She'd lost Ross once. Now she might lose him again.

11

THE ARMORED FIGHTING vehicle's air conditioning roared out of the vents, but still the interior baked like an oven. Especially up in the turret, where Vasquez sat cramped behind a swing-down display, between the barrel of the main gun and the glowing screens of the driver's station.

The driver and the gunner didn't call him *sir*, but their body language and tone of voice over the vehicle's radio net told him, deep in his bones, that he called the shots.

The turret might be hotter and more crowded than the troop compartment below, but he could get used to being up here.

Say the word and the driver would change course. Say another word and the gunner would fire a high-explosive shell that could shatter huts and shred dinosaur chickens into nuggets.

A grin sliced across Vasquez' face. Yes, he sure could get used to giving the orders.

The AFV tilted up. The engine deepened its growl to go up yet another hill. In Vasquez' display, trees striped the front camera view of the hillside. The driver cursed in his own language as he shoved the control sticks back and forth, aiming for gaps between trees.

"Just knock them down," Vasquez said.

"We left our bulldozer blade back at base." Vasquez couldn't tell if the driver was sarcastic or not.

Vasquez tapped the display's touchscreen. An information page came up. Time 1636. About three hours till the tropical sunset. Sure, they had night vision and the dinosaur chickens didn't, but it would already be an unfair fight. And you'd be able to see smashed huts and dead aliens better during daylight. "Clock's ticking."

The driver let out an exasperated-sounding breath. "It's faster to go around trees than to push them over."

Vasquez grunted. With another tap, he called up a map. Pouliot had sounded like a whipped dog when the old man agreed to share unfiltered satellite imagery with him. Just like a *cheto*, a rich man, back on Planeta Messi, the general needed someone to do his dirty work but wanted to pretend he had no dirty work at all.

He refocused. If he read the map correctly, from the top of the hill the AFV now climbed, they would be in sight of the dinosaur chicken village on the next hill. "How much farther?"

"Two hundred meters to this crest. The target lies eight hundred meters north-northwest from there."

Well within range of the main gun. Fire a couple of the high-ex shells, throw in an incendiary or two to set anything flammable in the dinosaur chicken village on fire. Then order the men out of the troop compartment to mop up.

He would get in on the fun, too. From the touchscreen, he could control the AFV's machine gun. Put suppressing fire on any dinosaur chickens trying to make a stand against the ground-pounders. He probably wouldn't hit any, but if he got lucky, his stream of high caliber rounds could slice a dinosaur chicken apart.

Aliens. Vasquez shook his head as if to make scorn drip off the tip of his nose. The *chetos* on every world treated them as pets. But the real reason was to keep down people like Vasquez's parents. Every square mile preserved for aliens denied some human settlers the chance to own farmland. Every law against cultural appropriation snared a human craftsman in a mass of red tape.

A fire in his belly flared hotter than the stifling air inside the turret.

The driver veered between two trees. The AFV's right-side track scraped a trunk. Brush crackled underneath the vehicle as the driver slewed the sticks to aim the AFV straight up the slope.

Clear sky and a strip of bare ground half again as wide as the armored fighting vehicle filled the front camera view. Vasquez grinned. "Almost there!"

The engine grew quieter. The speed gauge in the lower right corner of the touchscreen display dropped to zero. "What are you doing?" he said to the driver. "Gun it!"

"It's too obvious," the driver said. "We're being channeled this way."

Vasquez took a closer look. Shadows of trees spread across the strip. The low, deep green ground cover took on a gray shade. The cleared strip wasn't smooth, but rose in terraces to the crest. Rising above the ground cover, straggly plants grew, some tall, some short and leafy, a different type on each terrace.

He flicked out his left hand. His fingernails clacked on the driver's helmet. "It's a farm, you pansy."

"They'd clear more ground than this—"

"They're aliens! Who knows how they think? Who cares? Punch it! Park on top of the hill where they can see us. They need to feel fear before we open up the guns."

The driver exhaled sharply. His only protest, though. His hands worked the control sticks and the AFV lurched forward.

"Infantry," Vasquez said over the radio, "we're almost there. Prep to deploy."

The AFV rose onto the first terrace like an amusement park ride. Vasquez clamped his lips together. The maneuver exposed the AFV's thin bottom armor for a moment.

The vehicle tipped forward. He exhaled. The crude firearms of the dinosaur chickens couldn't pierce even the AFV's bottom armor. That race traitor Cantrell had been a mere ground-pounder. He didn't know enough to teach the dinosaur chickens how to make armor-piercing rockets.

Rocks lining the edge of the terrace crunched underneath. The vehicle bounced on its suspension. Alien plants thrashed weakly against the AFV's thick treads.

Another plus. Destroying the dinosaur chickens' food supply.

The AFV took the next terraces the same way. Just three more. "When we park, we'll take our time to pick a target," Vasquez said to the gunner.

The gunner's accent had a lilt from one of the African diaspora worlds. "Not too much."

"Don't you be a pansy either. Nothing the dinosaur chickens have can harm us in here."

After a pause came a scraping sound. The gunner's helmet against a storage cabinet. He nodded. Not just agreement. Submission.

Vasquez grinned to himself. Yes, he could get used to giving the orders.

One terrace remained. More bare dirt than the others, where short plants sent out a few slender, curly leaves. The AFV rose. The front end tipped forward—

A warning buzzer sounded. Lights flashed on the touchscreen display next to the words *ground-penetrating radar.*

From the muzzle of the main gun came a crack like wood splintering.

"Dammit!" shouted the driver. He jerked backward on the sticks. The AFV's engine grunted. The tracks bit into the ground, but slipped. The vehicle tilted forward, more and more.

Vasquez' fingers clamped on the thin padding of the command chair's narrow arms. What the hell? The AFV should have levelled off by now.

More cracking, splintering sounds. The front camera swept down, past bare ground to darkness, faster and faster. A clod of dirt or maybe a torn edge of thick fabric smacked into the camera.

A metallic shriek crawled along the barrel of the main gun. A jolt halted the AFV and threw Vasquez and the others in the turret against their shoulder belts.

He dangled, facing almost straight down. The vehicle no longer moved. He tried catching his breath but adrenaline played his heart like a kick drum. The front camera showed only darkness. Over the radio net, the men in the troop compartment cursed. One of them howled in pain.

Vasquez' stomach churned. What had the dinosaur chickens done?

"Tank trap," the driver said.

Tank trap. A fancy word for a ditch. Deeper and wider than an AFV. How could primitive aliens dig such a thing?

The driver worked the control sticks. The engine growled. The tracks nibbled at the back wall of the ditch. Pebbly dirt clattered down the AFV's bottom armor.

"Ambush!" yelled one of the men in the troop compartment. More shouts echoed agreement. A hydraulic hum came from the rear door. Sounds carried through the hull, handholds and footholds, men climbing up the sides of the compartment.

The next sounds were distant firecracker pops and sharp pings that rang through the AFV. Men swore to, or at, their home gods. A stumble. "You clumsy bastard." Stronger curses. Bodies slammed into each other. Another voice gave a grunt of pain and surprise that sounded oddly distant, like he had only half his mind on it. The same voice soon grunted again, accompanied by a few more pings.

Vasquez could move his arms now. He swiped the touchscreen to the troop compartment. The men were hulking shapes in green-gray battle armor. Two men lay at the front, now the bottom. One held his arm above the elbow. The other's leg looked to have a new joint between knee and ankle. Another man kneeled next to them. An open med kit at his hand showed green and red LEDs.

The rest of the men clung to the walls, gripping shoulder belts and seats tilted sideways. Three held on to the last seats near the rear gate. One of them popped up from a crouch, scanned toward the top of the hill, ducked down. More pings struck the open gate. More enemy rounds ricocheted in. A second of the men near the rear gate rose from a crouch. One hand clutched around a shoulder belt, he fired a one-handed burst somewhere into the alien trees.

The third man stood tall, as if it were a sunny day back at base. One foot on the side of a seat, the other on the alloy framing the gate. He wobbled on his feet. He could fall at any moment. What was he doing exposing himself to enemy fire? It couldn't pierce his armored helmet but it could still smack him hard in the head.

"Get him down!" Vasquez said. "Possible concussion!"

"On it," said one of the men firing out of the rear gate. More rounds ricocheted off the alloy and into the troop compartment.

Not enough to kill, but they could still hurt. "And shut the damn gate!"

"Bloody hell!" said the other man who returned fire. "We got to clear out!"

Vasquez swore, then said, "We aren't facing human rebels lugging man-portable armor-piercing–rocket launchers! These are dinosaur chickens! They can't hurt us! Cantrell couldn't tech them up high enough to hurt us!"

"They got shovels, righty? We button up and they'll bury us alive."

Vasquez' breath turned shallow. The dinosaur chickens could do it. Trap them inside here, drinking recycled pee and eating recycled poo until the power plant ran out of juice for the atmosphere scrubber. Trap Vasquez with men who knew he'd doomed them. Nowhere to run. No personal weapon in the turret, nothing except a knife on his hip, not enough to take out an armored soldier—

He caught his breath enough to find a new reason he was right. While his heart slowed its hammering, he said, "We need to shut the gate to drive out."

A fresh grumble from the engine clawed more dirt from the wall of the ditch. The AFV didn't climb an inch. Instead, metal groaned and the AFV leaned to one side.

What propped it up? The main gun?

The engine quieted down to idle. "The vehicle ain't getting out of here," said the driver.

"Main gun inoperable," the gunner added. "It got bent out of line by the AFV's weight."

Vasquez' mouth felt dry, like his older brother had shoved another sock in it. The corporal who lost an AFV.

He blinked hard. *Man up.*

"Out the rear gate!" Vasquez said. "One team sets a perimeter, another gets the wounded out. Take up a position behind the vehicle. Go!"

"Righty, then what?" called one of the men.

"We complete the damn mission. Go!"

Hydraulics whined again. More dinosaur chicken rounds pinged and panged off the gate and into the troop compartment. The ricochets might sting, leave a bruise, with bad luck wreck an elbow or knee or give a concussion, but they wouldn't kill a soldier through standard-issue armor.

Men climbed out. Bursts of covering fire chopped up the stream of grunts and curses coming to Vasquez' ears.

He swung the touchscreen out of his way and grabbed a handhold on the turret's ceiling. With his other hand he unbuckled from the command chair. He eased his feet down to the front wall, now the floor. Out the top hatch or out through the troop compartment?

The troop compartment. The circular opening lay—stood, now— in the center of the turret floor, surrounded by the high rim of the pivot joint. Vasquez contorted and slipped through.

He grabbed a handhold. Quick glance down at the front of the compartment. No one there. He looked up. The gate aimed straight into a deep blue sky. After hours in the turret, the brightness of late afternoon made him blink. He double-checked his helmet with one hand, on tight, and sucked a mouthful of protein goo through a straw.

"Clear," he said to the driver and gunner. He started climbing. Lots of chatter over the radio, but from the forest and the men's rifles, mostly silence. Saving their ammo, good. The dinosaur chickens had ceased firing, too. Without the element of surprise, they were unlikely to inflict much harm with their pop guns. Race traitor Cantrell had taught them that much.

"How smart are they?" A quiet voice. The owner never swore. Some thumper, God had made man, not aliens, in His own image, but whether he thumped Bible or Book of Mormon or Tao te Ching, Vasquez had no clue.

Vasquez neared the top of the tilted troop compartment. A line of rocks reinforced the edge of the terrace and the tank trap. While his eye measured handholds of how to reach safe ground, he growled over the radio net. "The smarter they are, the more of a threat they are. The dinosaur chickens and us are like two bulls, and the galaxy is the herd of cows we're fighting over. Remember that!"

Dinosaur chickens fired at him from the woods on that side and upslope on the other. Their fires sounded weightier now then he remembered from missions clearing the beach villages.

One round smacked his arm, midway between the elbow and shoulder joints of his armor. *Damn.* A heavier round, higher muzzle velocity than the old days. Leave a sizable bruise.

Vasquez scrambled around the rear gate and over the line of rocks. He joined the men hunkering behind the terrace edge and the alloy slab jutting into the sky. His gaze darted through the woods to left, to right. Dinosaur chickens had to be out there, but they camouflaged themselves too well. They held their fire, which meant the audio pickups on the men's helmets couldn't get enough data to triangulate the enemy's locations.

Eight riflemen and three of them wounded. Surrounded by enemy. Twenty klicks back to the perimeter, on foot. Vasquez' breath came shallower, faster. No relief mission. Lieutenant Liebrandt and all the race traitors lined up at the ombudsman's office would refuse to help.

The driver and gunner crawled over the line of rocks and joined the formation.

"Now what?" someone asked.

"Bloody hell, we bugger off, righty?"

Wincing at the bruise in his arm, Vasquez raised his hands to the side of his swimming head. Keep it together. "Don't be stupid. Twenty thousand meters through indian country?"

"We got armor and semi-auto rifles!"

"Armor can't stop a rope trap. Rifles will run out of ammo if we're playing spray-and-pray into the woods." Vasquez took another suck of protein goo. "We're going to destroy that village."

"Then ain't we gonna have even less ammo when we return to base?"

The thumper said, "The dinosaur chickens will be even madder."

A change in the radio carrier tone meant the next words were private to Vasquez from the rifleman with the med kit. "Three men need real medical attention."

"They going to die?"

"No, but they'll take a hell of a lot longer to rehab—"

Fire churned in Vasquez' gut. To everyone, he said, "Our mission is to destroy that village."

Mr. Bloody Righty reached up and tapped his rifle's muzzle against the gate of the AFV. "We lost our best tool for that job."

"I told General Pouliot and the scientist from Anima Sana they'd better make this mission worth our while. I got them up to five k transstellar for each of us."

"Tough to spend crypto when you're dead," someone muttered.

Cowards, every last one of them.

Most of the men looked away from Vasquez, watching the woods or inspecting their rifles with exaggerated body language. The driver alone stared at him, expression unreadable through his dark-visored helmet.

Vasquez leaned back and avoided the driver's gaze. Sweat trickled down his nape and smelled sour in his nose. He willed his body to not shake. Damn, he was in the oven, with french fries. Lost a troop carrier, losing authority over these men. The goddam aliens and that race traitor Cantrell would win—

He drew in a breath. His spirits rose with it. He could still get something out of this. "I'm going to see if the dinosaur chickens are willing to make a deal. Hold your fire unless they shoot."

He held his hands to the sides and stood up. His gaze swept over the woods on the right, on the left, seeking dinosaur chickens and finding none. Yet they had to be there. He activated the loudspeaker on his suit. "I'm in charge here. I want to talk to your commander."

From below the rustle of dark green foliage in the breeze came distant growls and the snap and thrash of bodies through the undergrowth. His heart pounded but Vasquez stood still. Even though the dinosaur chickens could only injure him badly if they got lucky, all his instincts made him feel naked in range of their fire.

"Go alone," called out a dinosaur chicken's harsh voice from his left. "Bottom of hill." Then the only sound was the scamper of movement away from where it had spoken.

Two hundred yards. In rifle range of his current position. "You know what to do," he said to the men.

Vasquez went down the hill. His legs ached a little when he took the steep slopes at the end of each terrace, but warmth sparked in his chest as he surveyed the mangled crop plants lying in the AFV's tread tracks.

Sparked but failed to ignite. The mangled crops were ugly things, purple and twisted, inedible by human or livestock. The forest on both sides loomed close, made him want to pull his shoulders together. The dinosaur chickens had neutralized the AFV and injured three men. No telling how many aliens hid under the trees, watching him. His hands tightened into useless fists.

He opened his hands. The dinosaur chickens would never have done it alone.

He descended the last terrace. Undergrowth rustled to his right. A dinosaur chicken emerged from between two trees. Unarmed, it came toward him on legs that looked rubbery. Vasquez craned his head to look under its belly for its junk but couldn't see any. Female, or hidden behind its broad tail, or pulled into its body when not in use.

One of the last two. Had to be. No way the AFV had gotten trapped by a girl.

The dinosaur chicken stopped in front of him. Thick hairs puffed out, making its shoulders look a darker green than usual. Greenish-yellow eyes watched him without blinking.

"My name is Vasquez." He popped open his visor. Bile rose in his throat from the dinosaur chicken's damnable stench of black pepper gone moldy.

From negotiating with an alien instead of taking what he wanted.

The dinosaur chicken's voice was even more gruff than the first one's. "I am Harkhmal."

Vasquez found enough clean air to calm his stomach. In with his breath came a sudden hunch. "Did you ask to stay here or did Cantrell and the others order you?"

Its snout wrinkled, baring the sides of yellow teeth. "My father and the other leaders of the village agreed I lead its defense."

Its father. It probably was a male, then, the way nature intended. "You mean they denied you the glory of representing your race to the rich human tourists."

Harkhmal extended his arm upslope, to the rear gate of the AFV jutting into the sky. "I get glory for *that*."

Vasquez' fists clenched at his side. He managed a calming breath. "For following Cantrell's orders?"

Harkhmal's snout wrinkled again. "Cantrell has much knowledge."

A barking laugh from Vasquez made some small creature scamper away through the undergrowth. "Cantrell doesn't know crap about soldiering."

Fingers spread on its open hands. "He came to us with what he did know."

"Maybe he knew how to channelize an AFV. And dig a big hole. But did he know what would happen next?"

"You would walk many... thousands of meters back to the fence."

A breeze made the forest canopy writhe and cooled Vasquez' face. Tendrils of cool air trickled inside his armored suit and down his neck. "No. We don't need the AFV to complete our mission. We've still got enough firepower to kill everyone in your village and burn it to the ground."

Harkhmal gave a soft hiss. Then his snout wrinkled and he puffed out the hairs on his upper body. "Do those things and we will kill you."

"You might. Your weapons pack more of a punch than I remember. You could put a lot of traps and snares across thousands of meters of forest. But how would it look for you when your co-leaders who went with Cantrell come home and find their mates and children dead and their homes and food stores destroyed?"

The dinosaur chicken hesitated. "We will defend our village. No matter the cost."

Vasquez turned his hands palms-up and shuffled them like a salesman. "I can give you a way to defend your village at no cost to you. Or any of your kind."

Harkhmal's head jittered. His scent turned a little more sour. How the hell was anyone supposed to read alien body language? The dinosaur chicken growled, "What do you ask for khaw?"

"One thing." A grin split Vasquez' face. "Give me Cantrell."

12

Yellow-orange sunset smeared across the western sky. The ocean chopped up its reflection into a thousand rippling pieces. A cool breeze from the shore brushed the hairs on Ross' forearms. His feet held him steady on the platform next to Korfkhob and the salt air left a pleasant tang on his tongue. He wished he knew some fancy words to describe all this when he returned to New Ozark.

To Nanette, if she would have him back.

He craned his head to the east. Scattered stars glittered in a sky shading from deep blue to purple. To the south, three miles behind the longboats and brighter than both the stars and the light pollution from the resorts and shopping centers farther away, an uneven line of lights dotted the sea near the dark shore. Civilian boats, curiosity roused by the sight of the longboats and, he hoped, by tourist chatter, had gathered around the Banakhenner vessels and followed them north.... until the autopilots stopped the boats in line with the Planetside fence.

"*Ghiagh!*" Korfkhob kept shouting, with a burst of energy in his voice. The rowers put a little more strength into each pull of the oars. Their fresh exertion brought more of their musty, peppery smell to Ross.

He glanced over his shoulder to the north, to the pale beach and the dark, palm-like forest beyond. Behind the beach, guarded by a double wall of sand held by woven vines, torches glowed and the roof of an old one's pavilion rose into view. Half a mile, give or take. Korfkhob and the oarsmen were almost home. One good reason to fight through their exhaustion.

The sunset backlit the other reason. A boat matched their course and speed. A forty-footer with the Planetside logo on its sleek white hull and a Planetside flag drooping on a pole rising from a cabin covering most of the deck. It rode a quarter of a mile to the west, the longboat's left.

A shrewd choice by the captain. Close enough to follow the longboats, but far enough away that the sailors' conditioning wouldn't be challenged by seeing "animals" rowing in unison, up close and personal.

The boat carried rescue equipment hooked or magnetically clipped onto the side of the cabin. Despite twilight and distance, Ross made out inflatable rafts with solar-charged propellers folded in like duck feet and the red cross of med packs. On the roof of the cabin, stretcher cradles dangled from coiled-up winches. Planetside provided the nearest thing to a coast guard on Azureseas.

The boat also carried a dozen uniformed men with rifles slung over their shoulders. They hunched over the railing, watching the longboats and talking to each other with animated arms.

Even at their distance, they could tell the Banakhenner weren't just dinosaur chickens.

Korfkhob shouted new commands, with more urgency. The rowers turned the longboat to face the beach. Careful strokes guided the longboat toward a notch in the outer sand wall. A sea gate of hardened palisade wood blocked the notch. Banakhenner on top of the wall tugged on ropes, pulling the gate out of the channel. More Banakhenner on the wall held breech-loading long arms made by Arkhtes the gunsmith.

Ross gritted his teeth. The Banakhenner warriors exposed themselves to the riflemen on the Planetside boat. The distance might be enough for the conditioning to keep the upper hand, and make a soldier think the dinosaur chickens carried sticks to poke little blue crawlers out of burrows in the sand. Might be enough for the soldiers to take a potshot.

No one needed to die, or kill. Ross cupped his hands around his mouth. "Fellow men, you know what you've seen! The Banakhenner are our equals! Go back to base! Tell everyone Dr. Fitzhugh brainwashed us and Planetside knew!"

The riflemen and sailors on the Planetside boat clumped together in agitation. They had to be speaking among themselves, but their voices didn't carry over the sea breeze and the splash of oars. The boat itself held its position. An officer climbed onto the top of the cabin and raised binoculars to watch the longboats row in through the sea gate.

His mouth dry, Ross watched back. The other two longboats entered the sea gate, first Kibkhal's, then Lerbot's.

Korfkhob's longboat followed. Over the grunts of the Banakhenner pulling the sea gate back into place, Korfkhob barked commands that echoed off the two sand walls enclosing the longboat. The oarsmen turned the vessel a quarter-circle to the right, toward the back end of Lerbot's ship. Beyond Lerbot's, the longboat carrying Kibkhal was half-hidden by an open passageway in the inner sand wall.

Triumphant shouts came from behind Ross. The Banakhenner had closed the sea gate.

Ross let out a breath. Safer, now, with thick sand and hardened wood shielding the longboats and Korfkhob's village from the Planetside boat.

Another cry, even more pleased, rose from the Banakhenner on the outer wall. "Soldier boat goes!" one called down to the longboats.

Feet thumped on the deck. Gorekhtes came closer to Ross and tapped his thumbs together. His head jittered in delight. "We broke the sailor conditioning the same as we broke the soldiers!"

"Looks like it." Ross shifted to include Korfkhob in his reply. "But keep up your guard just the same."

The sea village leader puffed up his feathers. "I keep four on wall, every night."

Ross smiled rather than try to correct him. "Even better."

Korfkhob's longboat turned to the left. Inside the gap in the inner wall, the sea villagers months ago had dug out a lagoon to beach their watercraft. Korfkhob gave a final command. The rowers lifted their oars and the longboat coasted to a stop between Lerbot's longboat and two small fishing canoes.

Flickering orange light came from torches jabbed in the sand. The torches burned a rancid oil extracted from some sea creature. The stench made Ross' nose crinkle and pulled Banakhenner curses from the mouths of Lerbot's warriors.

The rowers tapped their thumbs. Ross knew Banakhenner speech well enough now to hear the humor in their words. "Smell like home."

Home. A pang struck Ross. Sure, gravity was higher on New Ozark, and the nearest thing to an ocean was a sea of brine, but it was where his people made their home. He belonged there, same as the Banakhenner belonged here.

Sea villagers, including many females and juveniles, crowded forward, greeting the rowers with skewers of roasted meat chunks and vegetables like squashed purple golf balls. One older female, her eyes drooping, offered Ross a skewer.

For a moment, she reminded him of Nanette's mother. The burnt plantain smell of the food covered the stench of the torches, but the scent of the burned beach village made his stomach turn. He slowly shook his head. "No, thank you. *Kaht kulrabt* can't eat your food."

Her feathers, flecked in spots with white, flattened more. She spread wider the knobby fingers of her open hand, and with the other raised the skewer closer to him.

He groped for Banakhenner words but could only think of *no*. He mimed eating, then vomit and explosive diarrhea. Easy enough with the stink of burned meat in his nose. He remembered his first encounter with Harkhmal, months ago.

The female understood then. She turned toward Kibkhal but soon moved on. He'd already been offered food, by two younger females from the sea village. Kibkhal talked to them in the Banakhenner language around pieces of meat. Even though both their hands were empty, one of the females stayed.

Ross smiled to himself, but a moment later, a hollow feeling stole over him. Even though no hero's welcome awaited him on New Ozark, women impressed by his mission to Azureseas might bat their eyes at him or nuzzle against his body. But none of those women would be Nanette.

He sluffed out a breath. Coming back here had broken things off with her forever. No use crying over broken eggs. He'd done what he had to do. Right now, amid a crowd of Banakhenner jittering their heads and tapping together the two thumbs of each hand, the high price he'd paid seemed a bargain.

Through the crowd came a familiar face. Merghunek. He and other warriors had come to help defend the sea village from a Planetside amphibious assault. A less-familiar, younger male followed a half-step behind. This one's sides heaved with breaths interrupted by a swig from a water skin.

Puzzlement crinkled Ross' eyes until he placed the newcomer. From inland. He'd stayed behind as part of the force defending Lerbot's village from attack over land. He must have run hard for hours to get here.

Ross kept his voice low. "Did Planetside attack?"

Merghunek matched Ross' volume. "Yes." He raised a hand upward in the beginning of a prayerful gesture. "Denarobh will tell you."

The newcomer bowed his head. He'd caught his breath well enough to speak. "Greetings, Rossir. I comed now from village to tell you."

A movement in the corner of Ross' eye caught his attention. Lerbot came closer, a skewer now holding only purple golf balls in one hand, and a sharp look in his eyes. "The tell is good or bad, khaw?"

"Good," said Denarobh. After a swig of water, he wiped his mouth with the thumbs of his left hand and spoke.

"I guarded the approach to the village from the south. The bad soldiers sended one AFV against us—"

"Only one?" Ross asked. A lively feeling widened his eyes. "That might mean the conditioning is failing," he said to Lerbot. "They could only find a few soldiers able to go on a reprisal mission."

"One AFV is enough to make much harm," Lerbot said. To Denarobh, he growled, "Tell us more."

"It comed through the forest up the hill toward the south farms. When it finded the channel, it goed up. As close to me as we are to ships." Denarobh glanced over Ross' shoulder. "Much loud. Much fast. It falled into the tank trap."

"Yes!" Ross pumped his fist. The conversation of the Banakhenner around them fell into a lull. Dozens of yellow eyes, now gray in the dim light of the torches, turned toward them.

Lerbot asked, in a tone commanding an answer, "What happened next khaw?"

"The bad soldiers opened the gate. We fired our weapons and they fired theirs. Two us hitted. One a scratch, the other, Borekhtes right arm ripped up, no work, healer fears the rot from within."

Ross clenched his jaw. Gangrene or some other infection. Borekhtes could die in days, long before medical assistance from the Consortia could rebuild his arm. "Damn. I'll be praying for him."

Lerbot's voice deepened. "We all ask Khott for help," he said. "We all knowed risks of our mission."

"We hitted one bad soldier. We hurted his brain."

Ross' eyebrows jumped. "Your bullet got through his helmet?"

"No. It, we...." Denarobh mimed a punch to his own skull, then rolled his head. "Two more hurted when the AFV falled."

"What happened then?" asked Ross.

"The bad soldiers comed out. Their leader asked for Harkhmal. Two them talked alone."

A grin tightened Ross' cheeks. "He negotiated a surrender."

Merghunek shimmied his head. "I think you have it, Rossir."

The torchlight turned Lerbot's eyesockets into dark pits and made him look even more imposing. "What happened after they talked?"

Denarobh had fully caught his breath. "The bad soldiers walk away."

"That's it?" Ross asked.

Lerbot landed his hand on Ross' shoulder. "We need no more, khaw? The village is safe. The bad soldiers are free of false thoughts. They see us as we are and know we beated them."

"Good points. But Harkhmal better not have just let them go." Ross angled his head to Denarobh. "Three of the bad soldiers were wounded. How many could walk?"

"All."

"Say one medic goes with them back to human country. How many bad soldiers total khaw?"

"Eight plus three," said Denarobh.

"Even without the AFV," Ross said, "seven Planetside infantry could damage a village and kill many Banakhenner."

Lerbot loomed over Denarobh. "Do-ed—did Harkhmal send warriors to follow the bad soldiers, khaw?"

"I think so. He picked some to follow, then ordered me to run here before I could see if the warriors followed the bad soldiers." Denarobh's gaze cast about, until it landed on a juvenile female with a skewer of meat and vegetables. He beckoned to her and spoke in their language. As she came closer, he said, "Your pardons, Rossir, I am very hungry."

"Go ahead and eat. You just ran ten miles." Even though the stench of burned meat struck his nose, Ross put on a smile. "Then celebrate. You've earned it. We all have." Near them, Kibkhal said something that made one of the females rustle her tail and lean closer.

Denarobh nibbled at a purple bulb. "Thank you, Rossir. But I must say, Harkhmal asked you come back to our village tonight."

His legs ached after a day of standing on the longboat's bobbing deck and the slumping sand of the beach. Ross licked dry lips. "Tonight?"

"Bad soldiers can be rain in summer. Harkhmal said only you know what we can use from AFV to defend village."

True. What if the first AFV's mission was to probe the village's defenses? How many more might be readied to strike? Sore legs didn't matter compared to that. He could rest up tomorrow.

"I'll need some water," Ross said. His stomach made a hollow sound. He tapped a pocket, he still had two food bars, enough to get him to the village.

Lerbot puffed out his feathers. "I go with you."

"You don't need to. You can't help me salvage anything from the AFV. Rest up with the rest of your warriors, in case the bad soldiers come against the sea village tonight or your village tomorrow."

Denarobh gestured with an empty skewer. "I will go back with Rossir. I know the way in the dark."

Blinking, Ross said, "You just ran ten miles, khaw?"

"I can walk eight plus two more."

Gorekhtes had sidled up. "I will also go."

"You both may go," rumbled Lerbot. To Gorekhtes, he added, "Tell Harkhmal and the Old One what we did today. *Baget rakh.*"

Ten minutes later, with water bags hanging from Ross' belt and the two Banakhenner's backpacks, they set out amid cheers that sounded like a rock polisher's convention. A youthful female from the sea village, who from her height and weight alone Ross guessed was at the cusp of her fertile years, offered Denarobh and Gorekhtes more skewers of meat and the bulbous vegetable. Gorekhtes took his with a jitter of his head while his gaze darted to the curves of her rump.

The solitary guard patrolling the sand walls on the landward side offered his hand to pull them up to the top of the outer wall. The chatter of the crowd and the flicker of torches in the village suddenly seemed far away. Around a pang of sympathy, Ross said to the guard, "Lonely work, but thanks for doing it."

Gorekhtes had to translate. The guard replied, "New guard come soon. I eat and flirt then. Go with Khott."

Ross and his companions soon left behind the lights and cheerful sounds of the village. Ten thousand stars gave enough light to make their way across the coastal plain. Azureseas' single, lumpy moon, low in the west behind them, was too small and gray to cast their shadows. Like God had thrown a rotten potato into orbit. As they walked, some low plant with spiked edges on its leaves kept snagging his socks.

The wan natural light proved not enough when they climbed the first low hill and entered the forest. Gorekhtes stumbled over a root and Ross learned a couple of new Banakhenner expletives.

Ross pulled a penlight from his pocket. "This might help." He pressed the button. A glowing circle about a foot across bobbed on the ground.

"Is making a light safe?" Denarobh asked.

Gorekhtes said, "Bad soldiers can see in dark."

"Which means we need to listen up," said Ross, "if any are around. Keep moving."

They continued through the forest over hills and valleys, spending more time going up than down. The penlight beam prevented twisted ankles and denied Ross the chance to expand his Banakhenner vocabulary.

No one spoke. The only sounds were ten tramping feet and the creak of the Banakhenner's saddlebags and the strap of the human-made rifle rubbing against Ross' shoulder. He angled his head to his right, to the south, but no soldiers tramped through the undergrowth and no AFV churned up the ground. Only the sounds of nature came to him. Tiny creatures flittered through the brush. Larger ones scampered from branch to branch above his head.

Three hours after setting out, Ross, Gorekhtes, and Denarobh topped a hill. The stars and the moon, near the eastern horizon now, lit up a valley stretching in front of them, cleared and dappled with fields of crops now different shades of gray.

Ross smiled. Even in the dark, he recognized the farm. The hill they stood on curved away to the left. His gaze followed the ridgeline to the palisade ringing the village, a good four hundred yards away.

"Home," Gorekhtes said.

"You'll be the first to tell everyone the news." Ross nudged the young males' shoulder with the side of his fist. "The girls will be all over you—"

"*Bokha*," snarled a Banakhenner male in the trees behind them. The word sounded odd coming from a voice other than Korfkhob's. *Stop.*

Denarobh craned his neck around. He grunted in his native language, then said, "It's me. Back with Rossir."

Similar sounds came from Gorekhtes. "I come with news."

Footsteps thudded the soil behind Ross. Another low noise sounded like the slap of a breech-loader being slung on a shoulder. "Pardon, Rossir. You and Harkhmal say be watchful. I no know you at first."

Ross turned then. The guard's eyes seemed wide in the faint moonlight. "Well done."

"I must alert the village." The guard reached into his shoulder bag and pulled out a small object, two thumb-size pieces of animal bone held together by a cord threaded through drilled holes. He held it high and clacked them together. *Clack-clack, clack,* pause, *clack.*

Ross remembered the plastic castanets his kid brother played with in kindergarten music lessons. The clacks seemed loud enough to carry for miles.

A moment later, answering clacks came from the direction of the village. A different pattern—Ross inwardly cursed for not memorizing the Banakhenner's clack codes—but the message was clear enough even before the guard said, "Go, Rossir. Harkhmal meets you at gate."

With a spring in their steps, Ross and his companions followed the ridgeline until they reached the west end of the village. They hurried away from the smell of the latrines wafting over the wall. Gorekhtes reached up and ran his fingertips over the hardened wood.

Two guards manned the gate in the south wall. "Where's Harkhmal, khaw?" asked Ross.

"He comes. He asks you wait here."

Movement rustled amid the huts behind. Not Harkhmal, but villagers aware something had happened. Denarobh and Gorekhtes went in to cheers and chatter. Though Gorekhtes spoke in Banakhenner, Ross heard the excitement in his voice as he told the villagers about the mission to the tourists.

A warm glow filled Ross. The Banakhenner had earned their place as equals to people. The crowd moved away from the gate, flowing around Gorekhtes and Denarobh toward the Old One. To pay respects, to report on today's events, to bask in glory.

After the sound of the crowd faded toward the eastern end of the village, Harkhmal came through the gate. He carried a breech-loader in his hands. "Welcome, Ross." Despite his growling voice, he sounded like he meant it. "How goed the mission, khaw?"

"We spoke to many eights of civilians and an eight of soldiers," Ross said. "Lerbot talked in a human language and Neerokh drew a portrait of a leading civilian. In the brains of all the soldiers, what they saw and heard broke the false thoughts that you are animals. How's Borekhtes?"

"He lives if he loses arm. Healer takes him to Arkhtes, heats blade of saw. Then healer uses your bitter water on stump."

"Jesus," Ross whispered. "But if he holds on, when my people compensate yours, we'll give you treatment to regrow his arm."

"This is good. Now I ask you see the AFV."

"Your father does not need you at the place of the Old One, khaw?"

"My father, and Old One, know it is more important you see if AFV has tools or weapons to help us if bad soldiers come back."

A breeze cooled Ross' arms. His legs ached from hours of standing and miles of hiking. The lumpy cushion in the hut he shared with Merghunek would feel better than a luxury mattress in a honeymoon suite. "A male's work is never done. I'm ready."

Harkhmal turned to one of the guards. The guard sent a message with the bone castanet. Harkhmal held out his hand in front of Ross, fingers together in a *stop* gesture, until a set of clacks answered from across the valley.

Through the thick fuzz of alien forest on the opposite ridge, a single sliver of starlight touched the ground. Harkhmal went that way, steps measured. Ross kept up as they wound around the irregular shapes of the fields. Only the stars lit their way now, but Ross' eyes had long adapted to the dark.

The ache in his legs mounted as they climbed the far slope. Harkhmal said, "You were true about how better to catch the AFV. The warriors who saw say it must not have looked inside the ground to see the hole until too late."

Ross breathed hard. "Good."

After a few more steps they reached the ridgeline. The stench of firearm propellant lingering after the firefight wafted into his nose. A dark, angular shape loomed up below. If he didn't know the thing jutting out of the ground, between the tree-shaded starlight and the odd angle, he would have frozen for a second.

Instead, his grin tightened his cheeks. His aching legs and knocking heart seemed minor annoyances. He went close enough for dirt to trickle into the hole. "You did it!"

Harkhmal's next words sounded measured. "Yes. I did."

From the shadowed undergrowth came sounds. Rustling brush. A skittering pebble. And why had the forest's nocturnal animals been so quiet a moment earlier?

A human shadow resolved out of the gloomy forest. Two more followed behind it.

Ross' breath caught. It couldn't be—

It was. Planetside soldiers. He shrugged his shoulder and reached up for his slung weapon.

A hard circle jabbed him in the middle of his back, two inches left of his spine. "Drop your rifle," Harkhmal said.

The lead human emerged from the forest. Starlight landed on Vasquez' wide face and glinted on the barrel of his rifle leveled at Ross' belly. "Drop it and raise your hands. No bulldaisies. Any tricks get you gut-shot. This far from a medic, that's slow and painful death."

Ross' heart raced. His mouth tasted like ashes. Could he spin around and grab Harkhmal's weapon before the Banakhenner shot him through the heart? Maybe. But Vasquez would put a bullet in him if he tried.

He opened his hand and his rifle clattered to the dirt. "Harkhmal, what are you doing?"

"After we got out of the AFV, we were in a Mexican standoff with the dino—the Banakhenner," Vasquez said. "If they chased us for twenty klicks, they could kill us, but if we attacked the village, we could kill a lot of them. I offered Harkhmal a way out."

"A good deal," Harkhmal said. "I get rid of you. Lerbot's human ally runs off, he looks worse and my father looks better."

Ross' arms shook. "God damn you."

"Khott is words from Old One." Contempt snarled Harkhmal's voice. "Family is real. Power is real."

"Lerbot and the others will figure out what happened. Gorekhtes and Denarobh know you left the village with me."

"They goed to Old One before I comed to gate."

Words tumbled out of Ross. "The gate guards—"

"Are cousins of mine. They will say you did not wait for me. I comed after you to ask you come back but did not find you." Harkhmal shifted the muzzle of his breech-loader an inch down, closer to Ross' slamming heart.

A thought washed the ashy taste from his mouth. He could blow up Harkhmal's story. Make him fire his weapon. The sound would carry to the village and interrupt Gorekhtes' report to the Old One. How could Harkhmal explain that? Ross opened his hands and nerved his muscles to grab for the barrel.

"You would die for nothing," Harkhmal said. "I will tell the village I finded you. You raised your rifle against me and I fired in self-defense. I missed and you runned off."

Despite feeling gut-punched, Ross said, "You're such a bad shot, they'll believe you missed. But not that I ran off."

"If there is doubt, I have enough cousins to force the village to believe."

Shivers ran down Ross' legs. Nausea curdled his gut. Could he make Vasquez and the goon squad fire their rifles? Many villagers would know the difference in the sound. After Harkhmal claimed he'd let the soldiers retreat, how could he explain that?

Vasquez shifted his weight. Starlight glinted on the barrel of his rifle. "If you make us shoot you here, we'll have to attack the village. You got a lot of dinosaur chicken friends, don't you? Hell, one of them's your lover, I bet. Female or male?" He snickered. "Even if you're not an alien lover, a lot of your friends would die."

A sneer filled Vasquez' brown eyes. "I didn't ask Harkhmal to hand you over so we could kill you. Instead, I'm taking you to an appointment with Dr. Fitzhugh."

13

RINGED by rifle muzzles and helmets with closed visors, Ross trudged down the terraced, cleared strip. The metallic odor of machine oil filled his nose. He counted without making it obvious. Vasquez and six others.

He couldn't escape. Even if he managed not to get shot, they'd still fire their rifles, and then they'd march on the village. Banakhenner would die who otherwise would see a better future.

He'd done his job. Maybe he'd end up like Moses, forty years in the desert only to die within sight of the Promised Land. Not what he wanted, but he could go content to that fate.

Still, God damn Harkhmal to hell.

Going down the hill burned one set of his leg muscles. The steps up the terrace made another set ache. The ache became a burn when Vasquez led the group through the forest up the next hill. A blister chafed the inner side of Ross' right heel.

"I might have to walk twenty miles," Ross said around ragged breaths of humid night air, "but so do you guys, and I'm not wearing forty pounds of armor."

"Shut it," said Vasquez.

"What's Dr. Fitzhugh going to do? Too many civilians and Planetside soldiers saw the Banakhenner on the beach today. Even if he could make me think the Banakhenner are dinosaur chickens again, the cat's out of the bag.You're just making it worse for yourself, Vasquez. And all these men."

Body language shifted around Ross, but the rifle muzzles held mostly steady on him.

Vasquez stopped and turned. He held his weapon loosely. Soldiers parted as he came closer to Ross. "We bagged you, didn't we, *gato*? Now shut your hole and keep walking."

They went down the other side of this hill. Vasquez led them on a beeline through the trees. Tangled ground cover swallowed up their flashlight beams. Eventually their lights glinted on something colored mottled gray in a starlit clearing at the bottom of the hill.

Somethings. Two off-road vehicles on knobby tires. Parallel lines of torn-up dirt showed a third off-roader had already left. Probably a medic taking the wounded men to a hospital.

The off-roaders looked like the ones the eco department folks on New Ozark drove around to survey tree cat populations. Woodland camo paint job. Canvas roofs tied up around roll bars. Front and back bench seats. No doors, just openings with more rolled-up canvas. A steering wheel.

That was different. Hard plastic with finger-sized indentations all around it. The quarterpanels showed the logo of a dirt, water, and rock off-road driving track inside the tourist zone.

Vasquez gestured to the back seat of an off-roader. "Nothing funny from you. We're still in earshot of the village."

Ross climbed in. His gaze ran over the open doorway on the far side, to one soldier guarding him. He couldn't run for it. Here. But somewhere on the other side of the fence, he could jump out and take his chances....

The off-roader rocked as someone climbed on. "Sit," Vasquez said, right behind him.

"Glad to." Ross landed on the bench seat. His legs smoldered like a camp fire with an hour to go before it died out.

Vasquez stayed on his feet. He gestured with his rifle's muzzle. "Buckle up."

Ross pulled down shoulder straps and worked the crotch belt out from under his thighs. On the harness pieces glowed yellow LEDs. When the latches and buckles came near another, the yellow lights blinked. Servo motors whined as the closures strained for one another like blind snakes seeking mates. Low but sharp clicks sounded. All the LEDs turned green.

"Lock it," Vasquez said. Not to Ross, to a soldier who'd taken the driver's seat. His armored fingers jabbed at a touchscreen in the center of the dashboard. Suddenly, all the LEDs on Ross' safety harness turned blue.

"Like a carnival ride." Vasquez sounded proud of his cleverness. "We don't want someone unbuckling themselves and getting into trouble."

Ross' stomach fell. The blue lights suddenly reminded him of his great-grandmother's hospitalized last days.

While a final soldier, in the front passenger seat, twisted around and watched Ross, the soldier in the driver's seat worked the touchscreen. The words *Auto Drive* appeared. The pair of off-roaders soon took off.

The one with Ross took the lead. Headlights off, the vehicle took its time, following a serpentine path over the forested hills. Time to think. Wait until they arrived at their destination, and after they released him, run for it? His odds were low, but gunshots anywhere in the human zone would attract attention. Attention would help the Banakhenner. Vasquez couldn't kill human witnesses the way he could have destroyed the village.

Attention would help the Banakhenner, but might not help him. The thought of death sat like a black lump in his belly. He didn't want to die, but if God called him down a path where death could come, so be it.

But if God showed him a better way, going to his death for nothing would be a sin.

What could Dr. Fitzhugh do to him? Ross already broke the conditioning once. He could do it again.

The forest thinned out and the hills dropped away. Ross looked to the sky but the gray potato moon didn't race across it. Less than three hours since he and the two Banakhenner arrived at the village. Some time between twenty-three o'clock and midnight. Thousands of people would be awake, in the hotels and bars, in worker town, and on the base. If the off-roader drove by just one person, he could shout about his abduction.

Lights snapped on ahead. Ross lifted his head. His stomach fell with his next breath out. Only spotlights mounted on the perimeter fence.

The off-roader slowed for the gate. Metal rattled as the gate slid open. They drove through, onto gravel creased by the AFV's tracks. Vasquez gave a command and the headlights came on. The vehicle behind them turned on its lights too. The blue-white glare glinted off Vasquez' helmet and shoulder armor.

Signs of human habitation soon appeared. Light pollution from the coastal strip laid fuzzy gray along the horizon. A cluster of lights came into view to the right of the gravel road. Worker town.

Low-rise dormitories, the domed cafeteria in the center. Unfenced all around. Ross listened for sounds from bars and parties, but he heard nothing over the crackle of gravel under the tires. Not yet. When they got close enough—

"Near as we want to get," Vasquez said. Half a mile away.

The driver stopped the off-roader. The one behind also stopped. Both vehicles turned off their headlights, plunging the night into gloom.

Ross glanced out the open doorway while the driver tapped the touchscreen. As his night vision returned, his gaze traced a path across the sandy ground. If he could run into worker town, he'd be free.

The blue LEDs on his harness reminded him he couldn't.

An armored glove slapped against his mouth. Vasquez faced him. Despite the visor Ross just knew Vasquez sneered at him.

Ross squirmed. Vasquez pressed harder on his face. A metallic smell made Ross queasy. The alloy in the glove stiffened, mashing his lips.

Manual Drive, the touchscreen now read. *Virtual Tow: One Vehicle.* The driver yanked the steering wheel to the left, across bouncy terrain and native grass-like plants thwacking at the wheel wells. Away from worker town. The second off-roader followed in its tracks.

The vehicles headed east, then south, across land undeveloped by human hands and not yet colonized by terrestrial life. Vasquez took his hand from Ross' mouth. Ross could shout and no one would hear. The driver cursed under his breath while he worked the wheel over the uneven ground.

The Planetside base passed like a small island of light over a mile away. Which was another clue that a majority of Planetside's personnel had turned against Dr. Fitzhugh and Gen. Pouliot. Otherwise, Vasquez could drive down the road along the base's boundary fence with his headlights on.

Most soldiers—most people—were good enough, unless their leaders and the big money steered them wrong.

The gray haze of light pollution climbed the sky. Lit-up windows and signs showed the outlines of hotels, resorts, and shopping centers along the coastal strip. Smaller buildings, nondescript and dark in the night, popped up in clumps for a couple of miles inland.

A black strip, sharp-edged and aiming straight south, resolved out of the night in front of them. The driver turned the wheel. The knobby tires climbed onto asphalt as quiet as a whisper, as smooth as Nanette's skin.

I'll get back to you. If you'll have me.

The off-roaders stopped on the empty street. In the plots of ground on both sides, transponder stakes marked out future construction. More money to add to the bill due the Banakhenner. The driver turned off the virtual tow, turned on auto drive and the headlights.

Down the street of living asphalt, then left onto another. The only sound was the faint hiss of the tires. They passed a construction site, where nanotube alloy girders jutted out of a mycocrete foundation.

A quarter of a mile farther, the off-roader turned left onto a driveway to a sprawling building with its exterior lights off. Wings of dark windows jutted to left and right like the skulls of many-eyed non-terrestrial animals bleached pale gray in the dim light.

Not all was dark. Light glowed behind one window, on the second floor, where the main body of the building faced the driveway. Under a glowing sign. The blue-line-and-brain logo of Anima Sana.

The vehicles drove around to the back. A motion sensor light high on the building illuminated a parking lot between a loading dock and a privacy fence eight feet high.

Brakes worked without a sound. The soldiers from the second off-roader got out and spread out on Ross' side of the first one. They held their rifles in front of themselves. He couldn't see their faces through their visors, but their body language showed they were ready to bring their weapons to firing position any moment.

Vasquez and the soldier in the front passenger seat moved their rifle muzzles closer to Ross' chest. "Nothing stupid," Vasquez said.

The driver touched the screen. The blue LEDs on Ross' harness turned green. His heart pounded and his mouth felt parched.

"Unbuckle. Climb out.."

Ross released the harness with fingers suddenly clumsy. He stepped out. The microorganisms in the asphalt must have had a growth spurt, the parking lot sucked at his boots and tar clogged his nose.

He held his hands at his sides, palm out, and swept his gaze over the four soldiers in front of him. Their visors reflected the light from above, making him squint. They tightened their grips on their rifles.

He glanced at the building. Thick walls and polarized windows. They would swallow up the sound of a rifle fired inside the building... and echo it if fired outside.

A feeling rose from his gut to his heart. Fuzzy on the edges, around a core of calm. He would gladly die to help the Banakhenner earn the rewards they deserved. He tensed his legs to sprint away. He wouldn't get far before they shot him, but the gunfire would echo....

Across miles of undeveloped land before anyone might hear.

Vasquez and the soldier from the front passenger seat walked a wide circle around the four soldiers and climbed up mycocrete steps between the loading dock and a windowless wing of the building. Vasquez stopped, turned, jerked his thumb over his shoulder. "Follow me."

The soldiers backed away from Ross. Weapons aimed at his back, he trudged up the steps. When he reached the loading dock, the other soldier held open a pedestrian door next to the roll-up gate. Ross went in, to a corridor under lights redshifted for overnight and air conditioning deliciously cool after hours in the open-topped off-roader.

From behind him, the creak and clump of equipment and boots meant soldiers followed.

Vasquez held his rifle across his chest. He seemed even taller than usual. "No bulldaisies. The doctor is waiting." With that, he turned and strode down the corridor. His boots thumped eggshell-white tile veined with shades of blue.

Ross followed, aware of the soldiers behind him, ready to put a bullet into his back.

Down hallways, up stairs, along another corridor painted in soothing earth-tones and lined with canvases showing blobs of color transitioning to geometric blocks. As if Ross's baby brother had made paintings with a robot. Something no normal person would call art.

Vasquez stopped at a door slightly ajar. Sharp white light poured through the gap. A nameplate on the wall next to the jamb showed *C. A. Fitzhugh, M.D., Ph.D.*

A shiver ran down Ross' spine.

The man in charge here was not normal.

"Bring him in," said a voice that knifed him from out of memory.

Vasquez pushed the door wider and went in. Behind a broad desk of honey-yellow wood, Dr. Fitzhugh leaned back in his chair and cracked his knuckles.

Ross' feet felt glued to the floor. A rifle muzzle jabbed him in the ribs near his spine. He shuffled into Fitzhugh's office.

Fitzhugh regarded him through eyes as green as a pond smothered with algae. A cup of coffee, a roast so dark it smelled burnt, steamed on a coaster on the desk. He reached an arm shrouded in a white medical coat for the cup. "James Ross Cantrell. The source of all this trouble." The doctor took a sip.

"Is you."

One handed, Fitzhugh swiped at the air, then angled his head that direction. "I don't see mouthiness in your psych profile. Or altruistic heroism."

"Your techniques can't see everything."

Vasquez, tall and in his body armor, hulked between Fitzhugh's desk and the windows. Like the doctor's pet giant. The external speakers on his helmet amplified his snort. "God made him do it."

"God showed me the Banakhenner deserved respect and fair treatment. That's the only miracle He worked in this, far as I can tell."

As the words came out, the meaning sank in. Ross stood taller.

Vasquez could break his body. Dr. Fitzhugh could hack his brain. But neither could touch his soul.

Fitzhugh shook his head sadly, as if God were a bad habit he could wipe away. "Cantrell, Vasquez and I are going to take you downstairs to a treatment room. There will be a technician there whom. I've told her you are a mercenary hired by a competing tourist conglomerate to fake native intelligent life on Azureseas by using robots and aerosolized suggestibility drugs."

Ross' eyes widened. A tech. Another person to tell the truth to.

"If you try to tell her otherwise, you will be killed. And, sadly, she would also be killed. That would be a shame. A young woman's life cut short because your mission from God matters more to you than an innocent's life."

"You're a sick bastard."

"The impotent insult tells me you'll do the right thing, Cantrell." Fitzhugh raised his hand to Vasquez. "You and two others, bring him after me. Dismiss the rest of your men."

The doctor picked up his coffee, then led the way out of the office and down the nearest stairs. A door buzzed open. Beyond, triggered by motion, Ross guessed, soft warm light lit up a wide, pastel blue corridor. Music played by a fiddle and a piano, slow and quiet enough to put someone to sleep, came from speakers hidden in the ceiling.

Fitzhugh strode over fake wood flooring with clacks and jangles from his monkstrap shoes, black leather with buckles instead of shape-memory closures. Vasquez shoved Ross by the shoulder to keep pace.

In the rooms they passed, small shelves holding cacti and glass trays of sand and rocks, and black and white photographs of wooded and watered landscapes, together looked down on chairs like thick white pods slit open and their seeds pulled out. Behind the pods stood cabinets locked and shrouded by darkness.

Ross shivered. What Fitzhugh did was so wrong, he worked hard to make it look right.

"These are the main public exam and treatment rooms," Fitzhugh said. "We don't treat criminals here."

He led Ross and the soldiers on a winding path toward the back of the building. At an unlabeled door, he sipped his coffee, then pressed his thumb to a bulky security panel, looked into a tiny but bright light, and spoke his name.

A mechanical lock whirred and made a snapping sound. A magnetic hum stopped. The door swung open.

No music played. The motion-sensor lights in the ceiling gave a white glare. The soles of boots and the doctor's fancy shoes scraped over the unfinished mycocrete floor.

More harsh light came from one open doorway near the back. The walls were bare gray and looked gritty. No soothing decor. The body cushion inside the white pod looked thinner and harder than what he'd glimpsed in the spa rooms. The pod's plastic shell swallowed up the glare from the ceiling.

Some cultures said white was the color of death. Ross suddenly understood why, deep in his gut.

Behind the white chair, a metal cage, its door open, held racks of transcranial stim probes, syringes, and vials of pale liquids. A keyboard and an old-fashioned video monitor mounted on an articulating arm meant a computer was hidden somewhere in the room.

Standing at the cage, one hand on the door, stood the tech. A squat, stout young woman in light blue scrubs. Azureseas' yellow-orange sun had pinked her skin and sandy brown hair hung in a braid to her shoulders.

Brown eyes turned to Ross. She pulled in her lower lip. Her free hand went to her nape and stroked her braid.

"Tonight's client, Marli," Dr. Fitzhugh said. "Don't worry, the men from Planetside will keep him from harming you."

Marli glanced over her shoulder, as if she hadn't noticed what her hand did. She let go of her braid. Her voice sounded more high-pitched than Ross expected from her build. "Of course, doctor."

"Standard prep for the criminal interrogation protocol," Fitzhugh said. He turned his head to Ross. "Shirt off. In the chair."

Near the door sounded a creak of armor. Vasquez must have shifted his weight to echo the doctor's words.

Ross pulled his shirt over his head. Marli's presence made him conscious of his uneven tan. He shuffled his feet until he was next to a notch in the side of the pod. He sat, grabbed the sides, and squirmed back into the pod.

The cushion felt as uncomfortable as it looked. He squinted at the harsh light directly above him in the ceiling. The sides of the pod blocked his peripheral vision and nearly enveloped his body, like floating in the brine sea back home.

"Hands below the rim," Dr. Fitzhugh said. Behind him, Vasquez stood taller.

Ross did as he was told. The padding under his hands and wrist felt rough, as if patched with some cheap fabric.

Dr. Fitzhugh went to the keyboard. With his index fingers he slowly pressed keys. Each stroke gave a high-pitched click echoing off the mycocrete.

Five snaps sounded inside the pod. Something slapped each wrist and ankle and all the way across his forehead. Ross jerked his hands, but couldn't move them.

His heart slammed. Security straps. Exactly what you'd use for a dangerous criminal.

He took a deep breath and shut his eyes. Despite the orange glare of the overhead lights through his eyelids, he felt calmer. Persecuted by the enemies of God, like Daniel in the lion's den, or Jesus carrying the cross.

Dr. Fitzhugh spoke briskly. "Marli, begin."

The rim of the pod kept Ross from seeing her for long seconds, until she stood next to him. A rattling sound came from the outside of the pod, maybe she pulled out a tray. She lay down a small item with a clunk, then reached into the pod with a spray bottle in one hand and a rigid strap in the other. Close enough to smell fake-flower deodorant. Her lower teeth tugged at her upper lip. She didn't speak and didn't look at Ross' face.

Damn Dr. Fitzhugh and his lies.

She slapped the strap two inches above his elbow. It tightened around his arm enough to make him wince. She sprayed something from the bottle into the hollow of his elbow. He heard a bubbly hiss, felt a cool tingle. A phantom taste of raspberries crossed his tongue.

A second later, she injected him with the syringe.

The first syringe. Ross lost track of time as she worked in his peripheral vision and occasionally reached into the pod. Not just more injections. She pressed flat electrodes on adhesive discs onto his cheeks, the sides of his neck, and his chest hair. Rhythmic sounds droned in his ears. Their tempos didn't match up. A third, ghost sound with a different beat started droning in his head.

His heart knocked in his neck. He really had to pee. And the raspberry taste still clung to his mouth.

Damn Vasquez too. And Harkhmal while you're at it.

"He's ready, doctor."

Fitzhugh spoke with authority. "You're certain."

"I checked off the entire protocol through augmented reality and his brain wave traces—"

"A statement, not a question. You did good work and should be proud of it. I'll give you a bonus in addition to your overtime wage."

"Thank you."

Dr. Fitzhugh's shoes clacked on the hard floor. He appeared over the edge of the pod, facing away from Ross, and laid his hand on the rim.

If I wasn't locked in, I could grab his... I could... could....

"Head home, Marli," Fitzhugh said. I'll take care of him from here."

14

THE LIVING ROOM of Nanette's apartment wasn't home. It would never feel like home.

Nanette sat on the couch, bare knees tucked under her chin. Her eyes felt gritty but even in her pajama dress she couldn't sleep. Everything looked ghostly in shades of gray, dimly visible in the wan light coming through the polarized windows in the dining room and the kitchen behind her. The off-white walls, the sofas and the coffee table, all looked the same as every other apartment in worker town.

The framed slideshow of her roommate's family, marked by a wide black frame, look tiny on the wall, like an Ecoengineering well in the desert on New Ozark. From the droop of its leaves, Nanette knew her potted plant needed water.

Not now. Not at three in the morning. Not with Ross out there and Vasquez after him.

Her wearable projected in AR the first frame of the video on the wall next to her roommate's closed bedroom door. Next to a Banakhenner stood Ross. More tanned, leaner and more muscular than she'd ever seen him. She'd watched the whole video a dozen times and knew it by heart. Straightforward words, spoken in earnest, overcoming the resistance of rich and powerful people through the force of truth.

Ross had done the right thing. He was the kind of man who always did. That's why she'd said *yes* to his ring and *yes* to his bed. At the end of the video, when he sailed off with the Banakhenner, her heart went with him.

She wanted him back. Maybe she didn't deserve him. Maybe God had called him to a level she could never reach. But she would wait here until he came back through the fence in triumph and peace. If he turned her away a second time, so be it.

But please, God, move his heart to take me back.

Footsteps in the hallway outside the front door. They slowed. The locks hummed open.

Nanette kicked her heels backward, lodging the small of her back against the sofa's arm. The gray light seemed harsher. She squinted at a widening strip of light coming from the door.

Her records showed she came from New Ozark, just like Ross, and Dr. Fitzhugh and Planetside had put two and two together and come for her—

Silhouetted by the hallway lights, only one figure stood in the doorway. Shorter than Nanette, wider too. A shake of the head set a braid in motion. Marli came in.

"You startled me," Nanette said. She waved a hand toward the closed door to the other woman's room. "I thought you were asleep. What were you doing out?"

The door shut behind Marli. The ceiling lights came on, dimmed and reddish. Her features were nothing to write home about, and the light made her complexion even more plain. "Called into work."

"Work?" Why did her voice sound surprised in her own ears? Marli didn't get asked on many dates and half the time she turned men down for not being good enough.

"The soldiers from the security company caught the guy. The one who faked aliens this afternoon."

A strangled gasp came from Nanette's mouth. "What did they do to him?"

"He looked unhurt. Must have given up without a fight. Guess he knew he didn't stand a chance. One of the soldiers stood guard the whole time."

A cold feeling trickled down Nanette's gut. Her hand cradled her belly. "I mean, what did Anima Sana do to him?"

"Just a criminal interrogation protocol. To make sure he tells the truth."

Nanette frowned. Why would Fitzhugh want to do that? "What did he say?"

"I don't know. I only prepped him. Dr. Fitzhugh told me to go home when I was done."

A shiver went over Nanette's bare arms. She knew where Ross was. A few miles away. But God knew what they were doing to him. Not making him tell the truth, that was clear.

Making him tell a lie, then. To cover up their crimes.

Nanette pulled her knees closer to her chest. Her head sagged sideways against the back of the sofa.

"You okay?" Marli asked.

"Tired. So much happened today and I don't know what it all means."

"At least they caught the guy."

A hope came to mind. Nanette felt silly as she asked, "Are they sure it's him?"

"He looks like the guy in the video going around from the beach." Marli yawned. "When he tells the truth, they'll figure out what company or planetary government or NGO or whatever is behind it. I'm really tired. You going to be okay?"

Nanette managed a little nod. "If I can't fall asleep soon, I'll go to the cafeteria. Grab a snack and see who's around."

"Lots of guy bartenders are coming off shift now." Marli's voice sounded wistful. "Night."

Nanette might have replied good night. A moment later she couldn't remember. Marli had done what she thought had been the right thing. She couldn't get angry at her. If Marli had really prepped Ross to tell the truth, she'd done what really was the right thing.

Unless Fitzhugh would make Ross confess everything he knew, then kill him.

But what could she do? Storm into Anima Sana to rescue Ross? Life wasn't a fantasy movie where she could karate chop half a dozen men taller and heavier than her and in body armor. She needed help. Preferably armed.

There were a lot of armed men on the Planetside base.

And at least one of them knew Ross was right.

She jumped off the couch and was halfway to the door before she realized she only wore her pajama dress. Two minutes to change into the blouse and flare-bottom jeans from her bartending shift that afternoon. Two more to go to the taxi pickup lane outside her building. A two-door jitney, a boxy little car with seating for two over the electric motor and four wheels, pulled up to the curb as she came out.

Perfect timing, thank God.

She climbed in. The jitney took off but seemed to crawl through the streets of worker town to the main road. The electric motor whined like a child's toy. She wrung her hands together in her lap. At one point, her index finger and thumb pinched the base of the ring finger of her other hand. With a jolt she remembered wearing Ross' engagement ring for one night.

Her eyes misted. Yes she would take him back. Of course she would take him back.

If there was enough of him left to take back, after Dr. Fitzhugh finished with him.

She could cry later, if, if.... Not now. She sniffled back the urge to cry and steeled herself for what she had to do.

Six minutes after leaving her apartment building, the jitney drove up to the Planetside base. Inside the perimeter fence, the gray, unadorned buildings huddled under the security lights mounted high on poles. No one stirred. But something struck her as off.

The fluorescent red gate arm blocked the entry lane. The jitney stopped. A touchscreen telescoped out of the guard kiosk. Nanette told the jitney to roll down a window.

A synthesized female voice, as cool as a man's daydream, said, "The base is closed to visitors and civilian contractors until further notice."

It could tell who she was, then, and it knew the officer's club would be closed by now. "I'm here to see Lt. Liebrandt."

"The base is closed to visitors until further notice."

Her eyelids blinked rapidly while she searched for words. "It's extremely important."

Unflappable as ever, the voice said, "The base is closed—"

"Who ordered you to close the base?"

"General Pouliot, commander of Planetside forces on Azureseas."

Hiding behind the kindly uncle act while all the time he was a monster. And now blocking her only chance of saving Ross.

The red glow in front of her caught her eye. No, the general wasn't blocking her path. A gate and a computer's voice did.

She gave the guard kiosk another look. No one inside, when there was always a pair of soldiers on duty.

"Where are the guards?" she asked in a bossy tone, even though she knew it wouldn't change the computer's mind.

The voice sounded more robotic now. "Information access denied."

A change in the corner of her eye brought her attention to the jitney's dashboard. The meter rolled over to a new minute.

"I'm getting out here," she told the jitney.

The vehicle opened its door for her. She climbed out on legs tense with coiled energy. She stared at the camera mounted on the touch-screen's bezel while drawing in a long breath.

Nanette ducked under the gate arm and ran.

"Miss! Stop! Miss! Stop!" called the computerized voice. "Alert! Central security station! Intruder on base...."

Except she was an intruder who knew her way around. Her footsteps and the flap of her jeans against her ankles echoed off a garage for AFVs. If only she'd known to change into sweatpants. At least her shoes had cushioning for long shifts on her feet.

She passed the garage. On both sides stood more garages, plus drone hangars and supply warehouses. Air conditioning units kicked off and on, but the only other sounds she heard came from her.

Something seemed odd in her peripheral vision. She pulled her arms against her flanks and cast nervous glances side to side until she figured it out. The garages and hangars should be locked at this hour of the night. Normally, the security LEDs on the locks blinked slowly. Now, they double-blinked, and the pauses between one pair of flashes and the next seemed shorter.

She'd never seen that before. What did it mean?

Part of the general's lockdown of the base?

The same pattern of rapid double blinks came from the locked doors of office and service buildings, the officer's club among them.

Where was Liebrandt? Probably in his cottage in the officer housing zone.

Nanette slowed down and gulped a breath of the warm night air. An insect-sized creature flicked through the dark and spiraled native ground cover.

Which cottage?

On her wearable, she opened the base directory. Or tried to. An hourglass icon projected into the lower left corner of her eye slowly spun. No sign of progress.

Had Pouliot locked down the base's internal network?

She gasped. Closing the base meant he was worried about outsiders. Closing the intranet meant he was worried about his own men.

A good thing? Probably. Except it didn't get her any closer to rescuing Ross.

Nanette broke into a jog until she sucked in breaths, then walked for a few seconds. She continued the cycle, grumbling at herself for doing too much pilates and not enough cardio, as she headed for the officer's housing zone. Start at the smallest cottages, because that's probably where the most junior officers, the lieutenants, lived. Knock on doors and ask men grumpy from getting woken up which cottage belonged to Lt. Liebrandt.

Not much of a plan, but what was Dr. Fitzhugh going to do to Ross?

As she approached officer's housing, noises other than the usual nighttime mix came to her. Male voices, from deeper in the housing zone, where the cottages were bigger.

Gen. Pouliot would live in the biggest of all, right?

With more energy, she ran past the cottages of junior officers and most of the way toward the sound of the voices. The streets curved over the flat terrain. Only when she was almost there did she see the crowd.

The wan glow of streetlights showed some men wore body armor, others, plain khaki fatigues. Most carried slung rifles. They stood on the street facing a house of slanted metal roofs and mycocrete walls that zigged and zagged. The house's many windows gave no light.

She came closer, pace slowing and breaths coming hard. Two men in khakis at the back of the crowd heard her, she guessed when they turned at the same time.

"Who might you be?" asked the shorter one. He spoke Standard with a lilting accent. His eyes showed tiny pits in his pale, bullet-shaped head. His jaws mashed a piece of gum while he waited for her answer.

"I'm here to see Lt. Liebrandt. Can you show me where he is?"

The other one, either deeply tanned or naturally swarthy, looked more friendly, with hazel eyes and a mouth curled up at the corners. A question flowed smoothly from his mouth. "How did you get on base, miss?"

"I ducked under the gate and ran."

"And you happened to run right here? A map of the base is restricted information."

"I'm a contractor." Her voice rose in pitch. "I tend bar in the officer's club."

The shorter one's jaws stopped. His eyes seemed even narrower. "Do you now?"

Sweat felt cold at the small of her back. "Why would I lie? Who do you think I am?"

"The general holed up in his place," said the taller, darker man, "demanding that the lieutenant and the other officers guarantee him fair treatment in protective custody in exchange for showing us evidence against Planetside corporate and Anima Sana. He's looking for a way out. Anyone can see it." He waved his hand at the men milling in the street. "He might see a strike on enemy command and control as his best play."

"I don't know what that means," Nanette said.

The shorter man said, "Did the general hire you to kill the ell tee?"

"Did he...." Why couldn't they see how misplaced was their concern? "Do you know what's going on? Dr. Fitzhugh captured Ro— the man fighting for the aliens."

"Cantrell," said the shorter man.

The taller one shook his head. "I heard it was Havlicek."

Nanette raised her voice. "His name doesn't matter. If we don't do something, Fitzhugh will screw with his head to make him say the aliens are a hoax." Intuition formed a icy pool in the pit of her stomach. "And then he'll kill him."

"That'd be a damn shame," said the shorter man. His tone sounded sincere.

The taller man spoke. The turned-up corners of his mouth now mocked her. "Look here. The aliens are no matter to me. It's the general using a brainhacker to mess with my thoughts that matters to me."

Nanette drew herself to her full height and stared the taller man in the face. "You look here. You want to spend the rest of your life thinking how you let a good man die because you were selfish for five minutes? No? Than show me to Lt. Liebrandt."

"I'll do it," said the shorter man.

The taller man's hazel eyes took on an expression like a house cat toying with a mouse. How had she ever thought he was friendly? "We ought to frisk her."

"Jesus Mary and Joseph!" the shorter man said. His fingers closed on Nanette's elbow. "Follow me."

The shorter man pushed through the crowd. She pressed close behind. Soldiers gave her puzzled looks. By the time she neared the front of the house, most of the men watched her and not the dark windows tucked under slanted roofs and peering out of jagged mycocrete walls across the terrestrial grass lawn.

The men in camouflage fatigues waiting on the sidewalk watched her too. Nanette knew almost all their faces: officers of various rank who mostly battled databases and spreadsheets. In the middle of the group, Liebrandt stood between two men who were three or four ranks above him. But Liebrandt held his position like he belonged there, and didn't do his usual of pulling back his shoulders to seem more in command.

Despite being outranked, Liebrandt was in command now.

Her guide stopped chewing his gum and saluted. "Ell tee," he said, "this lady has news about Cantrell and Dr. Fitzhugh."

A squint creased Liebrandt's smooth face, but soon vanished. "You're a bartender at the officer's club," he said in his youthful voice. "I never caught your name."

"Nanette Bauer."

"What's your news?"

"My roommate is a tech for Anima Sana. She came home less than an hour ago and told me she'd prepped Ross for a criminal interrogation. Soldiers had caught him, one stood guard."

A colonel, a full one with eagle pins on his collar, regarded her through one normal and one lazy eye. "Why did you call him Ross?"

"I knew him. On New Ozark. I loved him. We were going to get married until he realized he had to help the Banakhenner first."

"Really?" asked an owlish major. "Caught him?" He said to Liebrandt, "Vasquez and his lot haven't returned."

"No one's seen or heard the AFV come back." Liebrandt went on, thoughtfully. "They could have come back in civilian vehicles."

Hope bubbled through Nanette's voice. "That must be it."

"Unless she's making up this story to distract us from the general."

Her eyes went wide. "All I've ever done is pour him drinks. He seemed nice until I overheard him talking with Fitzhugh in the officer's club today. I wouldn't help him now for anything."

Liebrandt turned to the major. "She was there today. At the end of the bar, not listening. Or trying to make them think she wasn't listening." He pivoted to the colonel. "Sir, I can take my platoon over to Anima Sana to investigate. That leaves most of the men here or guarding the far end of his bolthole if he tries to escape off base." He glanced over his shoulder at the house. "The general isn't going anywhere."

The major blinked and said, "Neither is Ross Cantrell, if what she says is true."

Liebrandt stared the major in the eye. "That's why he have to rescue him. We know what happened when Fitzhugh made us believe his first set of lies. What would happen if Cantrell believed his second?"

15

A FLORAL SCENT WOKE HIM. Soft music, next. Fiddles and other instruments, like fiddles, but bigger. A soft sheet over him, a plush surface under him, luxuries hadn't felt for a—a—a long time.

How long?

The question didn't matter. He let it drift away.

Cool air flowed over his bare face. Another luxury. He let this one go unquestioned.

No questions mattered. He didn't know why, but it was true.

Pale orange glowed through his eyelids. Slowly, he opened them.

Light the color of sunlight on Earth came from the ceiling panels. He turned his head, leaned it backward. Windowless walls of pastel blue behind him and to the sides. He tried lifting his head to see more of the room, but that was too much work. His head eased back against the pillow and he shut his eyes for a moment.

From somewhere in the room came calm breaths. Then a creaking, maybe someone on a chair shifted his weight. Or hers? There'd been a woman with a braid....

He jolted upright, eyes wide.

He was a criminal.

Two men were in the room with him. One, seated, watched him

with intense green eyes. He wore a white lab coat with some blue stitching over his heart. Near the door stood the other man, a soldier in body armor, visor down and rifle in his hands. Though the soldier had more height, weight, and muscle mass than the green-eyed one in the lab coat, this place belonged to the green-eyed man, the way a web belonged to a spider.

The green-eyed man in the lab coat spoke as if in a hurry to get this over with. "Do you know who you are?"

"My name's Ross Cantrell."

"Where are you from?"

"New Ozark."

"Never heard of it. Why did you come to Azureseas, Cantrell?"

The answer flowed out of Ross' mouth before he could think. "To stage a hoax to make the Azureseas Development consortium look bad."

Plastic and alloy creaked. The soldier shifted his weight. Something about his body language made Ross think he sneered.

The green-eyed man did not blink. "Enough for now. Cantrell, come with us."

Ross read the man's name in the blue stitching. *Dr. Fitzhugh.* The man's words sank in. Ross' brow crinkled. "Where?"

"To a more comfortable room. There, you'll tell us the whole story."

"Then...."

"Then we're done with you."

"But...." Ross' face drooped. He couldn't look Fitzhugh in the eye. "I committed a crime. I owe—" He made sure he said the word right. "—rest-i-tu-tion."

"The wheels of justice will turn, Cantrell, in time. Don't worry about that now." Fitzhugh rose. "Follow me."

Ross pushed the sheet off his legs and got off the bed. His clothes felt unfamiliar—the shirt's sleeves were too long and balloony, and never in his life could he remember wearing orange pants that didn't reach his ankle. He stepped into a pair of sandals.

Fitzhugh led the way out the door and down the hall. Ross followed. The soldier brought up the rear, filling the hallway with his clomping step and shadows jumping on the floor and walls.

Ross didn't need a guard. He couldn't hide from what he'd done.

He'd pay the price when the wheels of justice turned. Attacking Fitzhugh would only make things worse for him.

They came to a spacious room mostly filled by a long conference table. Windows lined one long side. A rock fountain burbled on a countertop along one wall. At the far end of the room, two chairs in a swoopy organic style faced each other.

Fitzhugh went to the rock fountain. "Water, Cantrell?"

Ross noticed his dry mouth. "Yes. Please."

"One water," Fitzhugh said. A machine whirred under the countertop. Fitzhugh reached down for a clear plastic bottle. His hand made a claw around the cap. He gestured with the bottle at the chair facing the windows. "Sit there."

Ross crossed the room and took his seat. The chair's motors conformed to his back. Fitzhugh sat opposite him, then tossed him the water bottle.

Ross took a sip. Ergonomic chair, cold and filtered water, more luxuries after months of—

Of?

He shook his head and took another sip. Just one, he didn't want to pee. He caught a glimpse of the soldier, who stood near the wall behind him now, between Ross and the door.

Fitzhugh sat back, right ankle on left thigh, right knee jutting out. He locked his green eyes on Ross. His fingers nudged the air in the direction of the soldier.

Equipment creaked. The soldier shifted a few inches, Ross guessed. Why?

To get out of Fitzhugh's view. The doctor would record the interview and wanted the soldier off-camera.

The interview where Ross Cantrell confessed his crimes.

"Now we begin," Fitzhugh said. His voice took on a tone like God talking to Moses on the mountain. "First, for the record, state your name."

"My name is Ross Cantrell...."

Ross lost track of time under the power of Fitzhugh's voice. His answers flowed out of his mouth without thinking. He'd served in Planetside on Azureseas, working pest control. He returned to New Ozark but needed money.

Then, a woman representing "a major player in interstellar tourism" came to visit. She offered him a large sum to return to Azureseas under a false identity, Stuart Havlicek, and smuggle a nanoassemblery package into the native wilderness.

Which giant conglomerate backed her? He asked. She pulled her sunglasses out of her handbag as if to leave.

He never asked again and accepted her offer. He didn't have a wife or girlfriend to keep him home, after all.

Six months of prep, transit, and work on Azureseas under his false identity passed before he made his move. Outside the fence, he avoided Planetside's patrols until they assumed him dead. The nanoassemblery made robots that looked like dinosaur chickens but passed the Turing test. The nanoassemblery also made tools, and pieces of buildings and ships. The robots' programming let them build villages, plant native plants to look like crops, and row longboats.

Ross remembered putting solar panels out for his fabricator. And how *real* the robots and their village had looked, sounded, even smelled.

To cap off the mission, he led a team of robots on the mission to the beach, to sell the hoax to gullible tourists and workers. Even a few soldiers believed it.

"Final question, Mr. Cantrell. Is there intelligent life on Azureseas?"

The enormity of his hoax made Ross' mouth taste like sand. "No."

Fitzhugh nodded. The corners of his mouth curled up. "You have served the cause of justice by telling the truth." The words sounded like something cops said to criminals in police stories.

Shame flooded Ross. That's all he was. A criminal. Before, he'd only had his family on New Ozark, but now, even Dad and Mom would reject him and he'd be alone in all the Consortia worlds.

Fitzhugh kept his green-eyed stare on Ross while he extended his fingers to the soldier. "This man will take you to a secure location. You will remain there until the next stage of the proceedings against you."

"Yes."

Fitzhugh stood and stalked out. A cold smile formed on his lips. *He's glad he served the cause of justice.* Ross' face fell. *He should be.*

The soldier hulked over him. A gauntleted hand reached for his upper arm to pull him up but stopped short. Through the speaker grills below the closed visor, the soldier said, "You heard the man."

Something about that voice made Ross' mouth even drier. He shook the water bottle back and forth. "I'm really thirsty."

"Drink up."

Ross guzzled the last half of his water. He stood and started toward the door and his mouth still felt parched.

The soldier followed a step behind, like an avenging angel over his shoulder. With words, the soldier guided Ross down a hallway and a stairwell. They emerged into the warm night next to a loading dock. An off-roader hunkered in the mycocrete hollow.

"Get in," the soldier said.

The off-roader was the color of dust and had a business' logo on the side. Not a real police car? Must be a busy night busting drunk tourists and loud parties.

The bigger question, where had he heard that cruel voice before?

Ross took the front right seat. The soldier climbed in behind the steering wheel next to him. He held his rifle straight up with his left hand, its butt on the floor and the stock outside his left leg. His right hand jabbed at the touchscreen with clumsy armored fingers but eventually set a nav location.

Ross glimpsed green and blue on the nav map. Maybe his prison would have a seaside view.

He puzzled briefly. Wasn't there a jail on the Planetside base? Yes, but they couldn't keep him there. That's the first place the people who'd hired him to hoax would look for him, when they came to Azureseas to silence him forever. The soldier took him to protective custody at an undisclosed location.

Made sense. Fitzhugh and the soldier served the cause of justice, after all.

The off-roader beeped at Ross to buckle up. He snapped his harness connectors together. The soldier didn't. Instead he mashed softkeys on the touchscreen until the safety alarm cut off.

They rolled out of the parking lot. The off-roader drove alone between the empty lots where buildings would stand someday. Lights from the hotel strip along the shore washed out the glow of the Milky Way above.

Moisture welled in Ross' eyes. God made immensities lasting billions of years, and he'd done wrong for the sake of a moment's bite of the apple or thirty pieces of silver.

His cheeks burned. He hung his head while shame and guilt washed through him.

He'd done so much wrong with his life, maybe it would be for the best if it ended now.

The soldier let the off-roader drive itself. His head swiveled to face Ross. In the dim light, Ross couldn't see where the helmet ended and the visor began. He kept the rifle pointing straight up.

The off-roader turned a corner. Lights from ahead of them glinted on the soldier's visor. The helmet's matte alloy swallowed the glow. Ross squinted his right eye. Both of them turned their heads to the source of the lights.

Headlights an eighth of a mile ahead. Two trucks in column. Hulking thirty-footers riding on street tires. From his previous deployment, Ross recognized them as utility vehicles from the Planetside base.

In front of the trucks rode an off-roader twin to his. The headlights of the lead truck silhouetted two figures inside. Just like them, a soldier and a civilian. But the soldier wore his visor up, and the civilian was a woman. Blond hair pulled back in a ponytail, but strands had escaped and the wind through the open top batted them around her forehead.

"Next turn!" the soldier next to Ross yelled at the nav. Why did he sound so panicked?

The off-roader drove straight another couple of seconds, toward a side street angled off to the right. Ross kept his gaze on the woman. She turned her head from the soldier next to her and looked at Ross' oncoming vehicle. Despite the distance, her gaze met his.

A fog descended on his mind. A name fought through the murk. *Nina...?*

Nanette.

The fog swallowed him.

The jerk of his harness against his body woke him up. The off-roader bounced over open ground, going faster than any normal programmer should allow it.

How long had he been out? Long enough to leave the streets behind. The hotel strip glowed far to his right. Was the soldier taking him to protective custody at some rustic eco-lodge?

Sweat bloomed on his forehead. The fog came back, but not fully. A beacon burned in his mind to dispel it.

Nanette. Nanette had come for him. Come after he'd loved her and left her.

The off-roader went hard over a bump. His head slammed against the headrest.

Left her to help the Banakhenner fight for their rights as intelligent beings.

More sweat. His heart knocked in his neck. The soldier, Dr. Fitzhugh, the story he told about a hoax... *that* was the hoax. Fitzhugh forced lies into his brain and he'd repeated them as truth.

For a few smooth seconds, the only sound came from native plants whisking and thwacking against the tires and side panels.

After recording his false story, Fitzhugh's best play would be to make sure Ross could never tell the truth.

The soldier didn't drive him to protective custody. He drove him to a shallow grave or a burial at sea.

The terrain kept rattling and bouncing the off-roader. The soldier wrestled the hard plastic steering wheel with both hands. His right leg stiffened on the accelerator pedal. The soldier muttered curses in a half-familiar language.

Ross swallowed. Vasquez.

If anyone wouldn't need Fitzhugh's conditioning to kill Banakhenner, it would be him.

Kill Banakhenner, or a fellow human being in cold blood.

Why did Vasquez drive? He'd let the autopilot and the AFV driver handle the off-roader from the village to Anima Sana.

Another bounce showed the answer. Pinpoints of light glinted on the frame of the off-roader's windshield. The headlights of a vehicle behind them. Nanette and the soldier helping her followed?

Ross wanted to look back, to see her again. He locked his neck. One glance back might alert Vasquez that he'd broken tonight's conditioning. Instead, he studied the glint of Nanette's headlights. How far behind?

Far enough that Vasquez could kill him before the soldier with Nanette could come to his aid.

He froze. Where was Vasquez' rifle? From the corner of his eye, he saw Vasquez kept both hands on the steering wheel. Still in the off-roader, but where?

Resolve pooled in Ross' gut. The rifle was out of Vasquez' hands and that was good enough. Ross gauged the distance to the steering wheel. Could he reach it with both hands? Better to yank it toward him or turn it away?

Bad idea. The off-roader had a low center of gravity. The jolts and jounces of the terrain that lifted Vasquez from his seat made the off-roader's speed seem higher than it really was. He couldn't make it roll and throw Vasquez out.

But he could use the steering wheel a different way.

He slowly turned his head. Vasquez hunched over the wheel. From the angle of his head he focused on the ground in his headlight beams. His hands stayed locked on the wheel, working it a few inches from side to side. Wait until he had to turn hard, reaching one hand over the other—

The instant Vasquez lifted one hand off the wheel, Ross twisted and reached for the back of Vasquez' head and shoulder. He used all the strength he had. He slammed Vasquez' head into the steering wheel, then pushed him toward the open door.

Vasquez' upper body leaned out over the uneven ground. His arms flailed, groping the air for handholds.

Ross lifted his legs and gave an extra shove with the soles of his sandaled feet on Vasquez' armored thigh.

Vasquez twisted to face Ross. Oh hell, had the shove low to his body straightened his center of balance? For one instant, Ross stared directly at the dark visor... and then Vasquez overrotated and he reached out to break his fall. His legs whipped out of the off-roader. He was down.

But not out. The off-roader's brakes squealed and the touchscreen read, *Driver absent. Emergency stop. Autopilot mode on.*

"Keep going," Ross said. He unbuckled his safety harness. Where was Vasquez' rifle?

The off-roader didn't move. Ross slid into the driver's seat, still warm from Vasquez' body heat.

He peered out. Vasquez lay five yards away. He rotated onto his front and moved his hands toward a push-up position.

Ross scanned the ground between them for the dark metallic shape of a rifle against the native grass and sand. "Keep driving!" he said.

The off-roader's knobby tires bit the sand. The vehicle rolled forward at a speed its programmers intended.

Ross put his knees on the seat and looked over the backrest. A long dark object lay across the shadowed back seat. Vasquez' rifle. He must have tossed it there when he needed both hands to drive. Ross reached between the front seats and picked up the rifle.

Same model he'd fired during his Planetside days. He sat and ran standard checks. The e-ink screen on the stock showed results. One round in the chamber and eight in the fifteen-round magazine. All hollow-points, for soft targets. Like loyal Banakhenner. The screen also read *Maintenance needed*, but this model always said that after you fired even once.

Nine rounds. But not armor piercing. If he needed to shoot Vasquez, he'd have to aim for the visor.

The autopilot worked the steering wheel from side to side. Still bound for that shallow grave by the sea.

"New destination. Where you emergency stopped."

The off-roader turned in a tight circle. In front of him now, the headlights of Nanette's stopped vehicle silhouetted the armored hulk of Vasquez. He'd made it up to one knee, yet his hands wavered and his legs wobbled.

Ross' off-roader rolled to a stop five yards away, slightly off-line from Nanette's. Vasquez reached his feet, hands at his sides, helmeted head turning from one vehicle to another.

"Ross!"

A thrill of gooseflesh ran over his arms. Nanette. The glare of his headlights washed out her blond hair but etched in his memory the expression on her face, overjoyed and frightened at the same time.

"Nanette!" His mouth worked, hunting for words.

Vasquez looked her way for a long moment, then turned back to Ross. He would know Ross had the wrong sort of ammo in the rifle. If he charged now...

Ross had another weapon, one a hell of a lot more powerful than hollow-point bullets. But one he'd barely trained on.

Fight with what you have.

He jammed the brake pedal to the floor, then touched the *manual drive* softkey on the off-roader's screen.

A male voice, young but surprisingly authoritative. "It's over, Vasquez."

Vasquez' voice remained as cruel-sounding as ever. "Liebrandt. Go to hell, you *trolo*."

"I can add insubordination to the list of charges against you. No skin off my nose. Lie face down with your hands behind your back. I'll spray you down with police gel. The MPs will take you into custody soon enough."

Vasquez faced him. Ross sized up the situation. If Vasquez chose to fight, Liebrandt was his biggest threat. He might have loaded his pistol with armor-piercing rounds. Instead, Vasquez slumped his shoulders, as if giving up.

"Face down," Lt. Liebrandt said.

Vasquez turned away from Liebrandt's side of the other vehicle. He bent at the waist and reached for the ground.

And broke into a sprint.

Not toward Liebrandt in a bid to disarm him.

Toward Nanette.

Ross put both hands on the steering wheel and moved his foot to the accelerator pedal. The off-roader lurched forward. Ground cover lashed at the tires and the quarterpanels. The steering wheel bucked in Ross' hands. If he couldn't keep it straight and collided with Nanette's vehicle instead of—

Vasquez loomed in his headlights. An alarm beeped, faster and faster. Brakes squealed while Ross kept his foot down. The soldier looked back, once.

A loud crunch. Arms and legs flailing at the air. A muffled bang.

White airbag rushed at Ross' face. His head bounced backward, slamming against the headrest hard enough for him to see stars.

Ross blinked and caught his breath. Alarms blatted in the off-roader's dashboard. His foot still jammed the accelerator pedal but the off-roader didn't go anywhere.

Not that it needed to. He stood up as far as he could against the pressure of the airbag. Vasquez lay just beyond the back fender of Nanette's vehicle. An arm and both legs twitched at unnatural angles.

Liebrandt stalked toward him, pistol in one hand and a spray canister in the other. Pink gel shot out. Glop covered Vasquez' hands, then his feet.

Someone called his name. Through a daze he realized it was Nanette.

He lifted his head. She sat in the dimness of the other vehicle. Her teeth gleamed but her eyes were closed and her voice cracked as if she cried. "Hey, no tears," he said.

"They're happy tears. You're alive. You're safe. You did the right thing and I'm so proud of you and I know I don't deserve you but please take me back...."

She begged *him* to take her back. He couldn't believe it. "You came all this way for me?"

Nanette nodded, then broke into a sob.

He pushed out from behind the airbag and slid toward her. He reached for her shoulders and tugged her against his chest.

"You've always been the woman I wanted to spend my life with. I've done what I had to do for the Banakhenner. Soon we can get back to the life we dreamed about. But it will be even better than our dreams."

Motion caught his eye. Liebrandt appeared at the front door on the far side of Nanette's vehicle. "Vasquez is restrained. I called Planetside's MP and medical teams with his coordinates."

"Let's go home," Nanette said.

Ross pulled her closer. "Not yet, love. Looks like we still have business to take care of."

Liebrandt gave a crisp nod. "Fitzhugh."

Nanette shuddered against Ross' chest. "Yes. You have to."

With thumb and middle finger, Liebrandt rubbed his temples as his gaze landed on Ross' airbag. "Climb in, Cantrell. Time to finish this."

Ross went in the back of the vehicle, behind Nanette's seat. Liebrandt rode next to him and filled him in on events. Ross listened and asked questions. All the while he laid his hand on the console between the front seats, over Nanette's, squeezing.

He wished he had nothing more to do right now than squeeze her hand, but he forced himself to pay attention to Liebrandt.

While crossing open ground, her free hand suddenly clamped on his. Two pairs of headlights bobbed toward them, along with the distant wail of a siren.

"They're coming for Vasquez," Ross said.

"Do they have to?" she replied.

"He's going to have a long and healthy life ahead of him to pay restitution for everything he did to the Banakhenner."

"And you."

"Not me. Us."

She softened her grip on his hand, and nestled her weight deeper into her seat.

When they reached the first paved road, the lumpy potato moon hung nearly overhead. Gray predawn crept along the eastern horizon. Despite what Liebrandt told him, he half-expected the vehicle to turn toward Anima Sana's offices. Instead, it went straight south, toward an extended-stay hotel rising fifty stories above the beach.

The vehicle crossed the empty coastal road into the hotel's parking garage. The two military trucks Ross glimpsed before his blackout waited near the exit. Soldiers with their visors up milled about, but snapped to attention when the lieutenant climbed out. They exuded smells of machine oil and male sweat along with an air of grim readiness.

Liebrandt assigned teams to watch the stairs, the elevators, and the outer sides of the building. He, Ross, and Nanette rode up an elevator with a team of three men, along with a tourist in dripping swim trunks and towel, with pool-damp hair and goggling eyes.

Forty-fifth floor. They were on their way to Fitzhugh's suite when Liebrandt raised his hand. Everyone stopped with him.

"Vasquez suffered a major brain injury. He'll live but won't remember anything."

Nanette squeezed Ross' hand. "That won't change our plan," he said.

"No." Liebrandt's expression turned shrewd. "Unless it's for the better."

Suite 4505. Soldiers took positions on both sides of the door. Liebrandt waved Ross and Nanette down the hall, then rang the buzzer.

A 2d display in the door came to life. Dr. Fitzhugh looked odd without his lab coat. From his polo shirt and clear green eyes, he looked like he'd stayed up since recording Ross' false confession. His voice sounded alert. "Who are you?"

"Lt. Liebrandt, with Planetside. We're here to talk to you about the accusations going around. May we come in?"

"There are a lot of rumors and outright falsehoods going around. I'd be glad to set the record straight. I will be exercising my rights to livestream our conversation, you understand."

"We wouldn't have it any other way."

The door opened. Liebrandt and one soldier went in. Ross ached to follow.

Liebrandt's voice came through the open doorway. "Doctor, would you object if some civilians observed our conversation?"

"No. Not at all. With enough eyes, all bugs are shallow. Bring them." Feet shuffled on synthetic hardwood floors, presumably making room for the newcomers.

Ross patted Nanette's shoulder. She went first. In the hallway, the carpet swallowed her footfalls, letting the sound of waves and sea breeze come to Ross from inside the suite. Her shoes squeaked softly on the floor inside Fitzhugh's suite.

Silence reigned for a long moment. "Miss, I don't believe we've met," Fitzhugh finally said with care. "And you said 'civilians,' plural?"

"Yes," said Liebrandt. How much had he grown as an officer this day? Out the doorway, he called, "Come in."

Nerves and anger jostled in Ross' gut. A grim certainty overlaid them both. If a man had to make sure the wheels of justice turned the way they should, that's what he had to do.

He strode into the room. Furniture made of straight metallic lines and round organic shapes, all in shades of gray. Minor blemishes showed the furniture came from the work of human hands. A fountain burbled over rocks. A framed picture on the wall of two tiny figures on a craggy oceanside golf course. Paint thick enough to show texture in gray rocks. Open balcony doors revealed a balcony with two lounge chairs facing the night sky over the ocean. A cool breeze rippled the doors' silk curtains.

The doctor has all this and it's not enough? Ross wondered as he met Fitzhugh's green eyes.

Dr. Fitzhugh's eyelids fluttered. He forced one final blink, then managed to speak with his usual vigor. "Cantrell. Yes, if you want to separate truth from lies, he is the right man."

"Ms. Bauer tipped us off that you had Mr. Cantrell in custody. On our way to Anima Sana, we crossed paths with Mr. Cantrell and Vasquez."

"Who?" Fitzhugh said. He almost sounded authentic.

"They were on their way, we presume to the location where Vasquez would kill Mr. Cantrell and dispose of his body, when Mr. Cantrell overcame the conditioning you imposed on him and overpowered Vasquez."

"I still don't know who Vasquez is." Fitzhugh's voice wavered a little.

"In the struggle, Vasquez suffered a severe brain injury. His brain can be reconstructed but his memories of today will be lost."

A grin split Fitzhugh's face. "Whoever he might be, I'm glad he'll make a full recovery from whatever injury Cantrell inflicted on him."

"As far as we can tell, the two ringleaders were you and General Pouliot."

"What ring did we lead? I'm at a loss."

Liebrandt paused for a moment. "General Pouliot surrendered to military police about fifteen minutes ago. He's making a full report to the MPs and the base ombudsman about his role in brainwashing soldiers into not believing the Banakhenner are intelligent. His role, of course, was to bring those soldiers to you."

Fitzhugh's face crumbled. He didn't blink. Instead, his green eyes turned as cold as the jade eyes of a statue unearthed from ancient ruins of Earth. As cold as the last breeze of night coming behind him.

"It's over," Ross said. "Come clean, make your amends, let a brain-hacker with a moral compass rewire your brain, and then it's up to God to forgive you or not."

Fitzhugh gave them a haggard look. "Allow someone to rewire *my* brain? As if I were a simple soldier from a nowhere planet?"

"Cantrell's right," said Liebrandt. "It's over."

Fitzhugh shuffled back a step. His calves bumped into the edge of a sofa. He straightened then.

Ross' stomach flopped like a caught fish in the instant before Fitzhugh spoke.

"You're right. It's over. And I don't need your housewife's God to forgive me."

Fitzhugh turned and ran for the balcony.

"No!" Ross shouted. Nanette gasped. Liebrandt and the soldier ran after the doctor.

The curtains on the open doors stirred in the air currents the doctor caused as he ran onto the balcony. Fitzhugh grabbed the railing and flung himself over.

He didn't scream, not a peep, until a distant *splat* sounded over the waves rustling the beach far below.

The breeze sighed through the open balcony doors. Liebrandt looked ashen. "My God. He... our bluff...."

Nanette asked in a ragged whisper, "Bluff?"

Ross held her in his arms. "General Pouliot didn't surrender. He stuck his pistol in his mouth and pulled the trigger."

"Oh. They all escaped justice."

"No, baby. They inflicted on themselves a worse punishment than they would get from the law." The wind sighed again. Gray dawn seeped along the eastern sky. "And there's a higher justice they hurried off to meet."

16

A SINGLE ROAD, two lanes wide and monitored by sensors every twenty yards, snaked over the hills. The purple-black living asphalt contrasted with the bright green of native vegetation.

The two-seater coupe carried Ross and Nanette around a curve. Native forest shaded and crowded a clear strip rising up the hill. The coupe downshifted and climbed. The cuts through the terraces flashed past. Near the top of the hill, the angular shape of the AFV jutted out of the tank trap now filled with rubble. The two-lane swung wide to the left around the AFV.

"Can we stop?" Nanette asked.

Ross checked the time projected by his new wearable into the corner of his eye. It matched what he'd guessed from the nearly vertical angle of Azureseas' yellow-orange sun. "Stop next to the AFV," he told the coupe.

The car eased to a halt. A clear plastic fence laden with sensors ringed the rubble-filled hole. Two signs were mounted on the side of the fence, both hard-printed, one in Standard and the other in the intricate, swirling script the Development Assistance team had co-created with the Banakhenner priests.

Ross couldn't read it, and he didn't need to read the one for humans. He knew what it said. Pride filled him, tempered with humility.

Nanette's gaze traced the hulking lines of the AFV, then skimmed the words in Standard. She turned to him with her face aglow. "You get the credit you deserve for defeating Vasquez' attack."

He slowly shook his head. "I told the Banakhenner how to do it. They did the work."

"I want to see it up close." To the coupe, she said, "Open the door."

The door didn't budge. She tugged on the manual override handle. The handle moved but the door stayed shut.

"DA and the Banakhenner leaders don't want people on foot north of the fence."

"Even you?"

"Even me."

A thoughtful look crept into her blue eyes. "Let's go."

The coupe rolled forward, topped the hill. The dark purple ribbon ran down and up the valley between fields ripe for harvest. It stopped at the village gate, where five DA vehicles, off-roaders and light trucks, stood on a gravel parking lot.

More than human vehicles waited outside the gate. Seven, no, eight Banakhenner stood in the afternoon sun. And one other thing hung nearby, dangling from a bar mounted on the village wall and a pole placed for this one purpose.

Ross recognized the hanging thing first. He reached for Nanette's hand.

As the coupe slowed to turn onto the parking lot, her fingers clenched around his hand. "That's a dead Banakhenner."

"Harkhmal. The one who betrayed me to Vasquez." Not that Ross could recognize Harkhmal's corpse. Tied up by his feet, after months of exposure to sun and rain, his feathers had fallen out and sandfly larvae had eaten his eyes. The side of his neck bore multiple slashes. He'd struggled in vain away from the executioner's blade. Had he growled or whimpered, at the last?

Gravel crunched under the tires, then grew still. The doors unlocked. Nanette stayed in her seat. "He did wrong but did they have to...?" Her hand fluttered in the direction of Harkhmal's corpse, now mostly obscured by the DA vehicles. Then it went to her mouth.

"The Banakhenner don't have our criminal rehabilitation tech. They won't for centuries. That's the only way they could work justice on him now."

She swallowed hard, the nodded and pushed on the door. Ross hurried out and around the coupe. Heat baked him and sunlight on the gravel made him reach for the sunglasses tucked into the unbuttoned collar of his linen shirt. At her door, he reached for Nanette and helped her out of the low-slung car's leather bucket seat. Her smooth skin felt cool from the coupe's air conditioning.

They walked side-by-side, holding hands, to the gathered Banakhenner. Though she walked on Ross's side farthest from Harkhmal's corpse, she still stole glances at it, then looked away, like a child probing a loose baby tooth.

The group of Banakhenner came toward them. Ross recognized them from his time in the village. Among them was Borekhtes, whose regenerated right arm bore a fuzz of light green feathers. Merghunek and Gorekhtes led the way. The pair of binoculars Ross had given Gorekhtes hung around the Banakhenner's neck, bobbing with each of his steps.

Their musty, peppery scent filled his nose. They stopped a few feet from him and Nanette. They flattened their feathers tight against their heads and chests.

Humility washed over Ross. "I'm not an Old One. It's just me."

Merghunek relaxed. "It is better to see you again, Ross."

"I wish you could have made it to the ceremonies yesterday."

"Lerbot told us about them," said Gorekhtes. "Your Old Ones blessed the place where we landed on the beach, and the rebuilt village where Khott revealed our intelligence to you? Elders talking for long times, and no Banakhenner females my age? It was better I was too young to be invited."

Ross laughed and idly swept a sandfly off his forearm.

Merghunek's snout veered toward Nanette. "Speaking of females, khaw...?"

"This is Nanette."

"Your mate?" Gorekhtes asked. The other Banakhenner tapped their thumbs together.

"My wife. Nanette, may I introduce—" Ross identified each of the Banakhenner in turn. She said a few words to Merghunek and Gorekhtes, citing anecdotes Ross had told her about them, and gave a warm smile to the others.

A breeze picked up. A creak came from the rope holding Harkhmal's ankles to the crossbar.

Nanette's gaze flicked that direction. Her smile shrank.

"It is a sadder thing, what he did," said Merghunek.

Nanette stared for a long moment. "I'm glad you punished him for what he did to Ross."

"Yes, that too."

A dormant unease stirred in Ross' gut. "What happened around here? Lerbot wouldn't tell me the entire story."

Merghunek and Gorekhtes shared a look. Merghunek spoke. "When you went missing, Lerbot and many of us suspected Harkhmal harmed you. But we did not know, until word came you lived. Even then, we could have let him kill himself with the Old One watching. But instead of accepting Khott's judgement, he fought it still. He recruited warriors loyal to him and his father to attack Lerbot and the rest of us."

"A civil war in the village?" Ross said. Unease mutated into anger, and pity for females and juveniles caught in the crossfire. "Jesus."

"The fight was short. Harkhmal's warriors turned their loyalty away from him when they learned he'd betrayed you to the soldier who hated us all. Harkhmal fled to his father's hut, but Retkhmal could not hold out. He handed over Harkhmal to us. We made him watch as we ended Harkhmal's life."

"Retkhmal lives?"

"He did not help Harkhmal's fight against Lerbot. He lives, but no warrior follows him. He never again feels pride. All he feels is weakness and shame."

Gorekhtes spoke, voice rapid. "Harkhmal had so much yet did all his crimes to get more. Why khaw?"

Ross sucked in a breath. He'd mulled the same questions, late at night in the recent months. Despite the suicides of Pouliot and

Fitzhugh, webs of evidence extended to the big money behind them. The CEOs of Planetside, Anima Sana, and the Azureseas development conglomerate faced charges of conspiracy and cover-up. Bribery and corruption charges could bring down high-ranking personnel in the Exploration Service and the Transterrestrial Space Defense Force. Men and women who had far more wealth and power than the richest rancher on New Ozark.

"Some people can't be happy, even if they have every reason they should be. Some Banakhenner too. I guess God or nature made it possible for them to be that way. I wish I knew why, but I don't."

Merghunek held out his hands. "It is better to not trouble ourselves with things known only to Khott. Come, please. The Old One wishes to bless you before you return home."

Still hand in hand, Ross and Nanette took a step toward the village's open gate. Merghunek turned with them, and Borekhtes and the other Banakhenner at the back of the group parted to give them way.

Only Gorekhtes didn't move. "You are leaving Azureseas, Rossir, Nanettema'am, khaw?"

Ross paused and gave the young Banakhenner, on the cusp between juvenile and mature male, a warm smile. "We love Azureseas," he said. He strengthened his grip on Nanette's hand. "But it isn't our home."

"You say a wise thing," said Merghunek.

A faint whimper came from Gorekhtes, but then he stood taller and said, "I understand."

"New Ozark is where we belong," Ross said. He moved his hand and Nanette did not resist. The tips of his fingers, curled around her hand, rested on her silk blouse. Over her belly, where no bump yet showed. "All three of us."

A FISTFUL OF MONOPOLES

A SPACE ADVENTURE SHORT STORY

A FISTFUL OF MONOPOLES

With a last surge of *Winona from Pomona*'s main drive, Barnet matched our bearing and speed with the alien derelict.

He shut down the engine and the dregs of thrust-gravity ebbed away. My feet drifted off the floor of our cramped command station. I grabbed a strap. Two meters away, Barnet did the same, showing off the sweat stain in his armpits.

I sniffed, though I didn't smell much better. For a two-man crew in deep space, it's easier to noseblind yourself through your neuronal interface than to bathe regularly. Then I forgot about our lack of hygiene as my neuronal interface projected a 3d image of the derelict onto my optic nerves.

Constructed by our ship's computers from reflections in the EM spectrum and active detection using the neutrino radar, the alien vessel seemed to float in the air between Barnet and me. 1:200 scale. Despite the dim light here, 4000 AU from Margolin's Star, there could be no doubt of what we saw. No human ship had lines that looked once alive.

Twisted lines of tubing and conduit curled around the hull like a nest of flash-frozen snakes. Most of the outer skin had flaked off, leaving great scabrous patches dangling in vacuum. After a billion years of ultraviolet light, the remaining skin bore a yellow-brown tinge. Micrometeor collisions had sandblasted the exposed inner hull to a dull, matte finish.

But behind that battered surface might lurk exotic materials beyond the manufacturing capability of any human world. Magnetic monopoles, dyons, condensed matter. Even a tiny amount delivered to Earth or a major world could set up a crew for life.

A smudge on the hull caught my eye, near twisting conduit just forward of the drive dish. The outer skin looked peeled away from the smudge.

My heart quickened. I confirmed my hunch with a glance at the radar signal. A hole in the hull, left by some chunk of space debris.

I checked the size against the scale. About three meters high by two wide.

Our way in.

Barnet's right hand worked the buttons and switches of a fidget cube. He spoke slowly, as if he'd fallen out of practice. We hadn't talked much during the six-month journey here from the station near the jump point. "Mac, how about I turn on the external spots to give us a better look."

"No!" From similar disuse, my voice came out somewhere between a growl and a croak. I cleared my throat. "The neutrino radar is the only safe active sensor. The most innocuous things, like visible light, can trigger their defenses."

He squinted his gray eyes at the bulkhead behind me. Probably pinging his neury for what *innocuous* meant. Then he swept a callused hand across his shaved scalp and gave a wry grin. "You know more about them than me, old man."

By a decade, sure, but I'd been able to afford a rejuve treatment. The age difference didn't matter. My five prior prospecting missions to his two mattered a lot more.

Maybe I had an old soul. But if it kept me alive, I'd take it.

"And don't you forget it, whippersnapper," I said, grinning back. We'd met on my previous mission and hit it off in the low-key that's-cool manner of men since the first mammoth-hunting party left camp.

Through my neury, I checked the incoming data feed. Numbers and text scrolled down a translucent pane overlaid in my vision between me and the derelict's image. Too much to process right then, which was a good sign in itself. "Data collection looks good."

"Then let's get going."

"Hold your horses," I said. "We'll follow the standard checklist. The expert systems will pore over the data from the derelict, then I'll double-check what they tell us. By then, the drive will be cool enough for me to go outside for maintenance. Always be ready to run before you explore a derelict."

Barnet nodded without seeming to hear me. He smoothed his ragged brown beard with one hand and clicked and clacked the fidget cube with the other. His gaze lingered over the derelict's image.

I gave a chin-nod. "What?"

"I got a good feeling about this mission."

I peered at him. Overconfident men got sloppy, and sloppy men got dead. But I knew him well enough to tell he wasn't overconfident. He had hunches, and more often than not, they panned out.

"Yeah. Whatever we find, we only have to split the profit two ways, not twenty."

He grinned at that. My neury simulated reflections of the derelict dancing in his eyes.

I knew him well enough, or so I thought.

———

A DAY PORING over the inside of the drive parabola checking for defects in the gamma ray reflector surface. Another day lugging a tank of reflector gunk from defect to defect, dispensing squirts, and curing the gunk with a handheld UV flashlight. The monopole had been retracted into its immaterial storage cage of electromagnetic force, but still I moved cautiously. Three tethers spaced evenly around the rim of the drive dish were all that kept me from drifting away to a lonely death.

Back inside *Winona*, I found Barnet had loaded the sled. Everyone called it that, though it looked nothing like the flat slabs of plastic I'd ridden down snowy hills on Planter's Punch. The intership sled looked like a canister of compressed gas because that's what it was. A valve at one end, a control panel sensitive to the touch of vacuum-gloved fingers at the other. It would respond to our neuries, too, but I'd trained in virtual to use the control panel or even to manually override the valve, and ridden Barnet enough on the way out here from the jump point for him to do the same.

He shoved his fidget cube into his pocket. "How'd I do, Mac?"

Tools and equipment dangled from rubbery black webbing hooked onto the sides of the canister. Detectors for electric and magnetic fields. Cutters and welders. Aid kits for suit punctures and routine medical emergencies.

Two handguns, each with a fifteen-round magazine, in case we found something not routine.

Or it found us.

I checked the packing list and the readiness of each item through my neury, then spot-checked it with my own eyes and hands. "Looks good."

"Ready to go?"

"Patience. The derelict's floated for a billion years, it can wait till the morning." I flexed aching shoulders and winced. "No one's going to get there ahead of us." We were the only ship within a thousand AU. We were the first to piece together the data from deep space neutrino scans that suggested this derelict was here.

A grin showed in Barnet's beard. "Looks like you need to take a break, old man."

I rubbed my upper arms. "The reflector tank is weightless but still has inertia." I turned serious. "We want to be as fresh as we can when we board the derelict."

The grin died away. I had a good guess why. I slipped past him to the galley, for a dinner of naan and tandoori chicken recycled from our feces.

A night of fitful sleep. A dream of a field of yellow flowers and the oldest oak on Planter's Punch led me into a mechanical tunnel of jagged edges. I knew before I rounded the last corner that I'd see Erdmont, the poor bastard. I woke with the straps of my free-fall sleep net soaked by sweat. When I blinked, I saw the panic in Erdmont's face as the nano consumed his skin.

Why did I do this? I could have settled down to an honest living. Hell, even a normal spacer's living would be a damn sight more honest than this.

That morning, 0500, a squeezebulb of lukewarm coffee covered up my fatigue. Next to the airlock, my neury reminded me of the full checklist for suit prep. Air tank full, air valve properly responsive, CO_2 scrubber above minimum flow rate. We could stay in the derelict for a week if we had to.

Not that we wanted to. Get in, find something valuable, and get out.

I suited up, then put on my helmet. *Winona*'s background sounds, a chorus of reactor, pumps, and cooling fans, turned muffled as I dogged the helmet seals. I checked Barnet's suit, then gave him a thumbs-up and a "Looks good" over the suit-to-suit radio.

He gave me the same checks, then slapped me on the shoulder, near the external controls for my suit's life support system, and nodded.

We wrestled the sled into the airlock. Through my neury, I told the airlock to cycle. We hunched together around the sled as *Winona* sucked back the air around us. We turned on the electromagnets in our boots and they thumped onto *stand here* tiles.

A minute later, the outer airlock opened, and we saw the alien derelict with our own eyes.

A hundred thousand stars wheeled behind it. My stomach flopped, until my neury triggered something in my brain. I felt then in my gut what my mind knew, that *Winona* spun in synchrony with the alien derelict.

We moved. The stars remained fixed.

I nodded at the attitude-matched derelict. "Good job parallel parking," I said.

He gave a puzzled grunt at the idiom, then nodded.

My attention returned to the derelict. Impossible to eyeball its size and distance against the backdrop of stars, but knowing it was about two hundred meters from front micrometeor shield to rear drive nozzle, it lay about three hundred meters away. In the wan starlight, its flaked skin and pitted curves made it seem even older than it had in virtual projection.

A shiver ran down my back. The derelict seemed to have congealed out of some broken symmetry in the moments after the Big Bang.

I shut my eyes. My breaths sounded ragged inside my helmet. The truth was awesome enough without getting poetical. Built when my ancestors were microorganisms in the seas of Earth, when nothing lived on land and the atmosphere had just become oxygenated. Built by life-forms who'd harnessed energies beyond the reach of twenty-sixth century man. Life-forms now reduced to desiccated mummies, from a planet long sought but never found.

A ditty of beeps played in my ear. A green LED flashed on the sled's control panel.

"Sled checks out," Barnet said.

I slipped my hand into a strap dangling off the sled's gas canister. "Out we go."

More *stand here* panels dappled *Winona*'s hull. I followed a path of the panels and kept my eyes down until we were both on the hull with the sled between us. I looked *up* at the derelict and the wheeling background of stars.

"Ready?" Barnet asked. His helmet's heat-trap visor hid his face behind a bronze-tinted mirror. He looked like a one-eyed giant mantis. I knew I looked the same.

"Yes." I pointed with my free hand at the meteor puncture near the derelict's drive nozzle. "See our target?"

"Yeah...."

"What?" I asked.

"You sure that's a way in? We won't get stuck cutting through a fuel tank wall?"

My gaze ran over the derelict's lines. I didn't know for certain, but it felt right. "The airlocks have more defenses."

Barnet grunted in surprised agreement. "Got our target. Boots off."

I repeated the words, then with a thought through my neury I turned off the magnets in my boots. I drifted, untethered from *Winona*, untethered from everything except the gravity of Margolin's Star and the galactic disk. My stomach flopped for a moment.

With nudges by his dexterous hand, Barnet pointed the front of the sled toward the meteor puncture and let out a long jet of gas from the back valve.

My gut relaxed as we moved. Slowly, two meters per second, but we moved. Public data lacked any incident of a derelict's defense systems activating against any inbound object traveling so slowly. Barnet adjusted our course with millimeter nudges and tiny puffs of gas.

Over two minutes of coasting. The derelict grew, blotted out stars behind it. My eyes made out small details. Intricate curlicues of piping and plating. The brittle edges of skin flakes shot through with tiny micrometeor holes like some exotic cheese. A snapped flange of some long-gone instrument, showing spiky edges of nanotube alloys around a straw-like hollow core. I'd heard of caves, on worlds with natural oceans and landscape transformations over geologic time, and this sight seemed a spatial inversion of stalagmites and stalactites, though even more foreign and even more old.

"Turn and burn," Barnet said. He swung the sled around and let of a long puff to slow us down. We crept the last half-meter. A final whiff of gas stopped us next to the jagged meteor puncture. Sharp-edged star-shadows smothered the interior with darkness. The jet of gas kicked up ancient dust that drifted into the puncture and out of sight.

"Anchor the sled, then we load up." I worked with him, keeping one hand on the sled because derelict hulls were non-magnetic. Our boots wouldn't hold. He moved more easily than me in untethered free fall as he spray-mounted hook fabric on the alien hull, then moved the sled to mate a patch of loop fabric to it.

He gave a gentle tug. The fabric held.

"Good." I unhooked mesh bags from the sled and mounted them on carabiners on my suit. Magnetometer, reflective paint, laser cutter, medkit, suit patch, adhesive, UV cure lamp. With hook-and-loop fabric I stuck one of the handguns to my right hip. "In we go."

I pushed off the anchored sled and slipped through the meteor puncture, careful to avoid jagged edges. Barnet followed as I flexed elbow and knee to softly contact a splotch of starlight illuminating an inner bulkhead. I pressed a glove and a boot against the alien alloy to hold myself in place, then looked around.

Left, right. Dust skittered into darkness in both directions, down an off-white corridor curving out of alignment with the coils on the outer hull.

"Helmet lamps on low," I said.

Barnet snapped his on first. Though low, our beams still outshone the stars outside. Sharp edges of jutting flanges and low conduit flung double shadows along the corridor and out of sight.

Nothing came zipping out of darkness to attack our lights.

"Which way?" he asked.

"Scans first," I said. "They might tell us something."

He jerked up his head. His visor reflected the glare of my helmet lamp. "The drive monopole would be that way." He raised an arm toward the corridor twisting away behind me.

"We'll go there if the scans come up empty." I gestured at one of the machines hanging off his suit. "Run the portable neutrino radar. I'll use the magnetometer."

We worked in silence for a while. I was a quarter of the way through a magnetometer sweep when he spoke flatly. "Compressed matter near the drive."

"How much?" From his tone I guessed the answer.

"Five, ten kilos?"

"Better than nothing." I moved the magnetometer through its sweep. Flat, flat... then abruptly the numbers spiked and an alert tone squelched in my ear. "Damn!"

"What?"

The solid-state display on the magnetometer showed all 9s. My neury dialed down the volume of the alert tone, but still it droned. My mouth scrunched up and I frowned at the magnetometer's plastic box in my gloved hands. "Son of a whore. Did we come all this way to find one of our two magnetometers failed?"

His voice came a little quicker. "You sure it failed?"

A quick diagnostic showed the magnetometer passed a self-check. I moved the device back and forth along the sweep path. The numbers fell back near zero and the alert tone stopped blaring. Until I brought the device back to the position where it first spiked.

The numbers jumped again. This time I cut off the alert tone the instant it started.

My heart pounded in my chest. I sucked water from a straw, and though stale and lukewarm, it tasted like a rivulet of fresh snow-melt. From those numbers—

Barnet slapped my shoulder hard enough for me to spin and bump against the bulkhead. "I told you I had a good feeling about this mission!"

I took a calming breath. "Don't count your monopoles until they're hatched. Got the heading down?"

"Yup."

I thought at my neury. A 3d green arrow floated in my vision, pointing through a bulkhead in the right direction. A compass, and useful, but no help in navigating the maze of corridors inside this ship. "Me too. Let's—"

He hurried off, stretching for handholds and yanking himself along.

"Careful!" I said, and went after him.

Exertion mixed with glee in his voice. "Did you see those numbers, Mac!"

"Even if the signal's accurate, we can't sell monopoles if we're dead."

He hesitated, then extended his gloved hand to a stretch of pipe and pulled himself even faster.

I hurried after. The corridor curled, taking his head out of sight. The light of his helmet lamp cast dancing reflections over alien alloy.

Finally, he stopped at a T-junction. A cross-corridor curled away from the green arrow. The arrow wobbled like a confused bloodhound as it pointed at a slab of bulkhead to our right. What might have been melted screw heads or globs of adhesive ran around the slab's perimeter, all under a skin of billion-year-old dust.

I drifted closer and jutted my hand against a flat part of the wall to stop myself. I used the magnetometer again, moving it back and forth to verify. The signal came from a source right behind the bulkhead slab.

"It's in there, all right." Worry leaked into my voice.

"You could be a little happier."

"We have to be careful with laser cutters. If the derelict has any working defenses...."

"Big if." He angled his head at the blobs ringing the slab. Then, with a shrug, he reached for the slab and tried to pry if up.

My brow crinkled. "What are you doing?"

"Maybe it's loose."

"Stop. We'll use the cutter—"

He sucked in a breath. "What the?" His arm froze in place for a moment, then slowly he pulled it back to stare at his fingertips.

Dust drifted around us in straight lines. Except where motes passed his fingertips, and some force pushed them away.

Blood drained from behind my face. "Suit puncture."

"What?"

"Hold still. I'll get the puncture kit."

His breaths roared over the radio like a torn bellows. "Oh God oh Christ—"

"Easy," I ordered. My hands went to the puncture kit. "It's a small tear."

"I'm losing pressure, Mac, hurry!"

I worked quickly to open the mesh bag, pull out the kit, open it. Focusing on my hands put a lid on panic. Plenty of time to close the puncture.

And if the dust drifting around us held alien nano, activated by his body heat, it was already too late.

I worked finger by finger, covering the tip with a one-centimeter square of translucent seal material and shining the UV lamp to shrink the seal into place. Index, middle, ring. "Is that it?"

He didn't reply.

I shook him. "Hey, talk to me. Your suit telltales show steady pressure—"

"Yeah." His voice wavered. My neury popped up a message in vision, *data streaming request.* "What does the cam in my helmet show?"

I accepted the request. Impossible for the alien nano to have hacked his neuronal interface. I faced no risk. But Barnet....

My neury spliced his in-helmet cam's feed into my view of his visor.

Pale scalp clammy with sweat. His eyes showed whites. His mouth gaped in his brown beard, sucking in breaths that heaved his suited chest.

"You look fine."

"All my, what do you call them, vital signs are jumping all over the place—"

I put more authority in my voice. "Calm down. Most of the time, dust is just dust."

"Oh God oh Christ." His words almost trampled over one another. "I saw Erdmont."

On our previous mission together. "No. You were part of the crew that stayed on *Yolanthe*."

"Pics. Somebody shared pics. Oh God oh Christ you couldn't even tell it was a human being anymore!"

I rested one gloved hand on an arm of his suit. He relaxed a little. I then watched his gray eyes. Frightened eyes, but still human ones.

"Show me your face, Mac."

"Sure." I let my neury stream data from my in-helmet cam.

"Take care of me."

I patted one of the bags hanging off my suit. "I've got a suspan canister in my medkit—"

"You could put me in hibernation now and not do any damn good." His breaths rasped in the radio. He looked at my right hip, at the holstered pistol. "You know what to do."

I swallowed once. "It won't come to that."

"But if it does."

Erdmont's bloated humanoid shell, roiling with nano even after his body quit moving and he stopped screaming. I nodded once. "If it does."

It didn't. His helmet cam showed his normal color returning to his cheeks and bald scalp. His gray eyes didn't fill with blood and his beard stayed wiry. Within five minutes, his breath grew calm and his pulse and blood pressure dropped to normal. "Thanks, Mac."

I eased my grip on his arm. "Ready?"

"Yup." He glanced at the slab of bulkhead. "It's why we're here."

"This time, I'll use the laser cutter."

He kept his face turned away from me. Dealing with everything his fear of nano death had brought up, I guessed, and I gave him room to do that while I got to work.

I held the cutter in both hands. It grew warm against my gloves as I worked the beam along the alloy. The slab was thicker than usual. My earlier squeezebulb of coffee, combined with jitters from Barnet's close call, made the laser line waver. Still, though it took three passes in a couple of spots, I cut through it.

As I pulled the slab away and sprayed dollops of adhesive to stick it to the bulkhead out of our way, Barnet peered inside the opening. "That's it?" he said with disappointment.

I shifted closer. My motion jostled one of the mesh bags hanging from my suit.

The opening held a single floating cube with rounded edges, about eighty centimeters on a side. The cube nearly filled the opening, like a votive in a niche. Its skin was mostly intact, but a closer look showed the edges and corners were not simply rounded, but ground down and blunted from a billion years bumping against the walls of the niche.

"Looks pretty standard," Barnet said.

"Yeah," I said. My tone was flat until the very end of the word.

"What?"

The mesh bag jostled by my movements pointed like a hunting dog toward the middle of the cube. I reached into the bag and found a horseshoe shape just large enough to fit around a gloved finger. I hooked the horseshoe with the last joint of my index finger and pulled it out.

I had to pull my arm back to keep the horseshoe magnet from sliding around my finger and racing into the niche.

"I've never felt this strong a pull from a magnetic monopole before."

"Ha ha! I knew I had a good feeling about this mission!"

"We aren't there yet. Maybe it's a typical amount of monopoles but the cube's containment has degraded over time. Maybe it's a trap and the monopole signal is bait."

Barnet eased back. "You know how to piss on a man's cornflakes."

"We can't sell monopoles if we're dead. Time to run some more scans." I shoved the horseshoe magnet back into its bag, then we got back to work.

Neutrino scans showed the usual amount of condensed matter coiled around the cube's center. The electric field detector picked up an unusually strong current still racing around the superconductor loop after a billion years. Our eyeballs, and taps with a plastic rod, showed no signs of explosives or defensive nano.

"It's real," Barnet said. In his voice I could hear him already spending the profits.

"Looks like it—"

"Christ almighty, get excited for once! There's a mother lode of monopoles in there!"

"Looks that way. Let me run some numbers." From the magnetic and electric field data, I ran calculations with my neury. Then double-checked them because I didn't believe them the first time.

My beard stubble stood up on my face. My heart thudded. "At least two hundred milligrams."

"You know I'm not good with that micro, macro stuff."

I put it in terms he could grasp. "About seven thousand times the mass of the monopoles in *Winona*'s drive and conversion reactor."

His breaths huffed in and out, but from the sound I could tell he grinned from ear to ear. "Seven. Thousand."

"Give or take."

"At least."

I nodded. "I've never heard of a haul even a tenth as big as this."

His next breaths turned ragged. His voice then burst out, affable as ever. "Ha ha!" He slapped my back, hard enough to get me spinning, then used both his hands to stabilize me. I thought nothing of it as he said, "At the market rate, that's—hell, I don't know, but it doesn't matter, does it?"

The beam from my helmet lamp danced around the niche and flung deep shadows of the monopole cube into the corners. "We might even get above market," I said.

"Above? How? Wouldn't we get less for flooding the market with so many?"

I felt a little fatigue—no surprise after days of hard work—and sipped lukewarm water through the straw. "Some government might pay a premium to snap up all these monopoles. It could use them to build thousands of ships. Enough to change the balance of power over fifty, a hundred, star systems."

He whistled. Something about it sounded forced. I peered at him but he'd dropped the stream from his in-helmet cam.

I shrugged. "Time to get the cube back to *Winona*."

"Yup." Hastily he extended his hands toward it. Then he hesitated, with his gloves near the cube but not touching.

"If it had a pressure-sensitive booby trap," I said, "we would have set it off already."

"You sure?"

I chuckled, mildly confused. "Just now you were gung-ho to pull it out, and now you've grown cautious?"

He took a moment to find words. "Been thinking. What you said. Dead men can't sell monopoles."

Together, we worked it out of the niche. It seemed to have more inertia than any of the mostly empty ones I handled on my previous missions. Two hundred milligrams couldn't make that much difference.

So why were my arms aching?

I yawned. We started down the twisting corridor, Barnet in the lead. I yawned again. More tired than I thought. I tapped the cube to steer it down the corridor, then grabbed at a bulging pipe to propel myself along.

My hand slipped.

Spots of yellow and gray skated around the edges of my vision.

"Hey," I said. "Need to catch my breath."

Barnet halted. The bronze mirror of his visor reflected the monopole cube and a portion of my headlamp. "No problem."

The bronze color faded to sepia. Color leached from everything else. The spots rushed toward the center of my field of view.

"Something's..." My head swam. I took a breath but the feeling of fainting grew worse. "Wrong...."

Everything I saw turned a darker and darker gray. Barnet turned his visor away from me, tugged the monopole cube, and hurried toward the sled as my vision went black.

———

AIR IN MY FACE. Fans roaring. Beeping.

I opened my eyes. Words in augmented reality crossed my vision. *CO₂ emergency detected. CO₂ scrubber functional. CO₂ scrubber high-throughput mode activated. Emergency O₂ tank opened.*

Groggy, I drifted for a moment. What? Where?

My heel bumped something hard. Things came back. I'd passed out. A suit malfunction.

I groped for a handhold but couldn't find one. Where was Barnet?

My back bounced off a snaky conduit. Somewhere near the external panel of suit life support controls. It reminded me of his slap on the back after we discovered—

Everything rushed back.

That son of a bitch. After all I did for him.

Anger gave way a moment later to fear.

If he can get to Winona *without me—*

I reached to my left, found a handhold. propelled myself down the corridor. My right hand pulled my pistol from its holster. The low-power laser aiming dot skipped over the alien bulkhead like a red flea.

The next hole in his suit's coming from me.

How long was I unconscious? A thought to my neury gave me time-stamps. Four minutes.

A pit opened in my stomach. I pulled myself back from the brink. Maybe I could catch him.

I pulled myself faster down the corridor. I ducked my head to avoid braining myself on a bulging conduit. Soon, I came to the last bend in the corridor before the meteor puncture.

He wasn't here.

I went to the meteor puncture. Part of me wanted to grab the jagged edges to stop myself and get the best look out, damn the consequences. But I stopped myself with my fingertips against a bent flange. I looked out.

The backdrop of stars wheeled behind trim, blocky *Winona*. Except for one constellation of red and green pinpoints near her airlock.

I squinted at a widening rectangle of light. The interior lights of the airlock, opening.

Barnet squeezed inside with the monopole cube in his hand. He shoved the sled away from *Winona*'s hull.

I brought up the pistol. Drifting in free fall, I looked down the sights. Reflection from the aiming laser got lost somewhere across the three hundred meters between us. An impossible range in an atmosphere on a planet.

But not here.

I braced myself with foot and free hand against the bulkhead. Fired. Gas spurted out of the muzzle and the breech, ruining my aim for the next shot. But I fired anyway.

Too wild. Better one shot on target than spray-and-pray my last dozen.

I took a breath. The rectangle of light narrowed and a green pinpoint blinked.

I fired at the constricting rectangle.

Barnet kicked his leg. Did I hit him? Did he lose his grip on the monopole cube?

The rectangle of light turned to a sliver, then winked out. The blinking green light turned solid red.

He'd shut the airlock door.

Even if he'd lost his grip on the monopole cube, it stayed inside with him. Only the sled, tumbling against the stars, remained outside.

If I'd hit him, if he were wounded, if only I could get there....

I could jump. The airlock would recognize my voice and the RFID chip in my suit.

Jump, with no chance to change my vector. Any error would doom me to drift through the void until my suit's life-support systems failed.

Jets of gas puffed sideways out of *Winona*'s bow and stern. She spun, slowly catching up to the wheeling stars behind her. Preparing to burn.

My fists clenched. Rage boiled in my gut. *We could have shared it fifty-fifty and both been set for life.*

But prepping for burn meant I'd missed him. A wounded man would straight to the medkit. Unless so much guilt weighed down his conscious that he wanted to flee the scene of the crime.

Winona's spin matched the stars now. I fought to keep my bile in my stomach. Then came a brightness. No pinpoint, but a vague glow from *Winona*'s drive dish. And she nudged forward.

Barnet fired up the drive.

I ducked away from the meteor puncture, into the corridor of the alien derelict. The hull would shield me from any stray gamma rays coming from *Winona*'s drive.

Just in time. The glow brightened, overpowering my helmet lamp, casting sharp shadows of the puncture's edge against the interior bulkhead. The glow spiraled toward me. I scrambled away from it. A burst of sweat stank inside my suit.

The glow from the puncture faded. I worked my way toward the puncture, to show my monkey brain with its own two eyes what I already knew had happened.

Winona was a tiny pinpoint of light, receding more and more every second.

Maybe I'd shot him. Maybe badly enough that his delay in treating it would kill him.

But even if he bled to death inside *Winona*, the ship carried a king's ransom of monopoles and picked up speed away from me every second.

The slim chance I'd killed him gave a tiny trickle of comfort as I stared at the ship vanishing against the cycling stars.

———

I'M ABOUT to inject myself with the suspan canister. I know, even here in the shielded heart of the derelict, that radiation will slowly poison me. If no one finds me in about fifty years, I'll die in hibernation.

That's why I've laser-etched these words on the bulkhead. If you read them after I'm dead and Barnet lives, go after him. Blackmail him, prosecute him, guilt him into suicide if he has any conscience. Whatever you do to him, the son of a bitch had it coming.

If Barnet is dead? Or a billion years pass and the whole human race is dead? So be it. This is my best play, even if the odds are lousy.

But if you rouse me from hibernation, I'll make it worth your while to get back from him what's mine.

With interest.

—*Faraday McCandless 7 October 2572*

BODACIOUS URSULA AND THE PHONE CALL FROM HELL

BODACIOUS URSULA AND THE
PHONE CALL FROM HELL

THE CALLER ID on my desk phone read *Unavailable*, but the number was from a local area code and I needed a client so I picked up.

And heard the voice of a ghost.

"Ursula," he said in his voice too high for his straight-backed body, "are you still as bodacious as you used to be?"

I sagged back in my pivoting chair, suddenly thankful for the black mesh letting cool air touch my back. The view outside showed blue skies, gleaming office midrises, trees, the fountain in the roundabout, all in all a gorgeous summer day. But the cold sweat gluing my blouse to my spine was like the dead of winter.

"Who is this?"

"Who else ever called you *bodacious*?"

Ranger. Not his real name. As a kid, years before I met him in high school, he'd told everyone he was going to join the elite army unit when he grew up and the nickname stuck long after his army aspirations petered out in the juvenile court system.

A shiver ran down my back. But how?

"Hey, I thought you were dead," I said, trying to make a joke of it.

"I am."

"Get the hell out of town." My voice came quickly and lively while a black pit grew in my stomach.

"That's where I am, turns out."

"In town? When did you get back—"

"In hell."

Black spots swam in my vision. I leaned forward so that my brow was inches from the empty yellow pads stacked on the glass top. "I don't do immigration law and I didn't even know they have phones there."

"It's like the joint. You can get privileges."

"You're learning big words in the prison library?" I said.

What the hell is happening? Your first boyfriend who you know is dead calls you up and you banter with him?

"You get time to think, down here." His voice shifted into a thoughtful register. Maybe it wasn't him after all, *Ranger* and *thougthful* were two words that never went together. "Time to think about everything you did wrong. Time to think about how to make amends."

"What's that got to do with me?" Lightly, but a hollow feeling that always lurked near my awareness leaked through.

"You were a good girl and you deserved a lot better than me. I want you to have the loot from my last job."

My reeling mind found a lifeline. "I'm a member of the state bar. Makes me an officer of the court. I can't take stolen property."

"Twenty years, bodacious U. The statute of limitations expired. Says a lawyer I ran into down here. And I stole it from a meth dealer and he's down here too. No one else deserves it. You ought to have it."

I angled my head to pinch the handset between my shoulder and ear. A pivot to my desk. I pulled a pen out of the cup and clicked it, slid a yellow pad off the stack. First thing, I copied over his phone number from the caller ID. "And where is the loot?"

"You remember the place we called Heiny's farm, off state road QQ?"

The black pit in my stomach grew into a chasm. The lurking feeling oozed out. For once, I was at a loss for words. "Tough to forget." Tough to forget parking in the woods, miles past the last subdivision. Tough to forget fumbling in the back seat of his dad's extended cab pickup, him working his hips for ten seconds and me thinking *what's in this for me?*

A missed period, that's what. And a trip to the clinic to take care of it. Ranger drove me there and back, and he paid for the abortion, I'll give him that.

The hollow where the baby had been got worse when Ranger got arrested. Turned out he'd paid for the abortion with money from a convenience store robbery.

He kept talking. "....halfway between the tallest sycamore and the fence line. Got it?"

I scratched notes. "Sycamore. Fence."

"Weren't you listening? In the back field, away from the creek." Something clanked in the background. Really did sound like he called from jail. "Look, they're going to cut me off. I won't get another call for a century and the phone lines don't go through to where you'll be then. Go out there with a shovel. Let me think I did something good for once."

A click. A dial tone.

I dropped the handset back in its cradle. Then I stared at the yellow pad. *None of this can be real.*

I GOT HOME to my condo five minutes after six. The early summer sun was high and dappled by the branches of the oak in the courtyard. The curtains in the front window shaded my living room. My flats clacked on the engineered wood floor and my purse thumped on the engineered stone countertop in the kitchen. Mr. Meow kept himself hidden under some piece of furniture while I microwaved a keto bowl.

While the microwave hummed, I pulled out the yellow pad and my laptop. Laptop, because even with reading glasses my eyes aren't good enough to work off tablet screens anymore.

I started with the phone number he'd called from. One site—thick with ads and stilted written English from some third-world country— said the phone number belonged to a mechanic specializing in Japanese imports. Another site, one I'd had better luck with in the past, said it belonged to a brewpub in a minimall near the interstate.

I called the number. Three tones blatted in my ear. I jerked the phone away from the voice saying *This number is out of service. Please check the number and-*

Unease crawled down my back. That didn't prove the caller had called from Hell. Software could spoof the phone numbers showing up on caller ID.

But it couldn't spoof his voice. And his pet word for me.

One of his buddies from one of his jail stints. *Bodacious Ursula. Yeah, I hit that. She's a lawyer now.*

Though what would an inmate gain by sending me to dig up a farm fifteen miles out in the sticks? And why now? Ranger had been dead almost two decades.

Unless he wasn't dead. I heard about it second-hand from a high school friend, my first year out of law school, when I worked for big firm in a highrise downtown. Some drug deal gone bad. Hey, didn't you use to run around with him?

I searched up obituaries and news stories. Zach Cantrell, aged 27, found dead in the back parking lot of a donut shop in south city. Shot once in the head, gangland style. His wallet in his pocket and the keyfob in the console of his rusted Corolla fifty feet from his body. Robbery not a motive.

Mistaken identity? I shook my head. City cops would have lifted the dead man's prints and taken DNA samples. Ranger's records had been in state and federal databases for years by that point. The dead man had been Ranger.

The smell of steamed protein reminded me the microwave had finished cooking my dinner minutes ago. I ate cold glazed salmon and kale and frowned at the yellow pad and laptop screen.

I shivered. Ranger couldn't have called me from Hell. I couldn't think of who faked his voice and why they called me.

Look at it from the other side. Why Heiny's farm on QQ highway?

I went to the tax office's website for that county. No *Heiny* owned real estate there, but lots of folks named *Heine, Heinrichs,* and *Heintzelmann* did.

None of whom currently owned any farmland on QQ highway.

Did we call it Heiny's farm because someone with a name like that formerly owned it? I scrunched up my face. It would take a while to trawl through the county recorder's website, looking for real estate sales going back, good lord, how many decades?

It was that or watch yet another rom-com streaming on the living room TV, so I got back to work.

Hours later, I found a sale forty years back. About 120 acres sold by a Heintzelmann to someone named Abbott. I skimmed through the legalese description of the property to its postal address.

I opened up another browser window and typed the address into a maps site. Up popped a satellite image. A patchwork palette of greens crossed by a curving gray line. An orange location pin marked a mailbox and entry gate on the highway. A gravel lane meandered to a small house and a barn with a sheet metal roof. The satellite didn't show but I remembered boarded-up windows on the house and heaps of empty beer cans along the side of the barn.

Mr. Meow emerged from his hiding spot to nuzzle my ankles and *mrow* at me for his dinner. Aloof until he wanted his needs met, like one ex-boyfriend from my years in the big firm downtown. After I petted him and fed him, I jostled my head around. My neck crackled and my eyes were bleary.

Find there's no sycamore, let some guy in prison laugh at you for wasting your evening on his prank, and then go to bed.

It didn't help my bleary eyes when I had to read the legalese on the property sale to figure out which fields and clumps of trees belonged to the farm. But finally I laid out the boundaries with mouse clicks, then zoomed in.

There, the back field, pale green with darker splotches. There, the creek. And there, alone in a field about a hundred feet from the rear fence, were the spreading branches of what could be a tall sycamore.

I centered the satellite view on a spot about halfway between the sycamore and the rear fence, then zoomed in. The pallete of greens turned pixelated. No sign of hidden loot.

Ranger's old buddy in prison is having a big laugh at you right now, but I still wrote down the GPS coordinates before I closed the laptop lid.

. . .

MID-MORNING SATURDAY FOUND me at a big box sporting goods store. Faded denim shorts, a concert T-shirt some ex-boyfriend had left behind years ago, hair pulled back into a ponytail. I dawdled in the aisle for fifteen minutes, flipping through websites, dithering about which model of metal detector to get. Finally I decided and manhandled a long, bulky box into the cart.

Time was when a passing man would have volunteered to help, but not that morning.

I wheeled to the checkout. Long lines of old guys buying golf balls and moms buying soccer gear while their kids tried to sneak pouches of sunflower seeds and protein goo into their carts.

No line at the return counter. A middle-aged guy behind the counter said, "Ma'am, I can check you out."

Ma'am? Did I look like my mother? But the sooner I checked out the sooner I'd get to the bottom of the whole Ranger phone call business.

I rolled my cart over and tried to figure out how to lift the metal detector out. The clerk came around the counter with a handheld scanner. "You can leave it in the cart." He found the barcode and scanned. When the register beeped, he said, "Looking for some buried treasure?"

While waving my phone at the payment scanner, I frosted my voice a little. "Want to add to my beer can collection."

He grinned. "Playing it close to the vest? Buried treasure it is. After you find it, come on by, I'll help you spend it."

I raised my eyebrow at him. A face with some creases, and his hairline receded around a tuft of brown hair in front, and gray salted the sides of his beard... but hair and beard were trimmed, and his blue uniform polo draped nicely enough over his arms and torso, and when was the last time a man had bantered with me? A live man, not in Hell.

"I have to find it first," I said, and wheeled my new purchase into the warm sunshine of the parking lot. I wrestled it into the hatchback with the help of a ten-year-old boy in a Blues T-shirt who dragged his dad into helping. Maybe they noticed the new, made-in-China shovel next to it, but they didn't make any wisecracks.

Off I went, cold air roaring out of the vents. I took a roundabout route, checking my mirrors more than usual for cars behind me. Maybe it wasn't a prank played by a guy in prison. Maybe my caller had just gotten out of prison, and knew where Ranger had hidden the money but couldn't get to it himself. Bodacious Ursula digs it up, drives back to her condo, and gets carjacked in the parking lot.

The stream of cars thinned out as the subdivisions and minimalls thinned out. I abruptly shifted lanes to take the exit for QQ highway. No one came down the ramp behind me. I pulled into the parking lot of a convenience store—the one Ranger had robbed to pay for—the one he'd robbed, no less. Checked the mirrors while I pretended to read emails on my phone.

Satisfied no one followed me, I set off down the asphalt two-lane.

The area had changed since I'd last been this way. Instead of farm fields and a couple of small vineyards, housing developments clung to the rolling hills along the highway near the interstate. Yet I remembered the bones of the place underneath the face lift. I didn't use the GPS and didn't need to. When I drove up the last hill, my stomach knew I'd almost reached Heiny's farm.

At the crest of the hill, my stomach fell. Where there had been a rusted mailbox and a fallen metal-pipe gate, a low wall of pressure-washed brickwork faced the highway. Stainless steel letters float-mounted on the face of the wall said *Sloboda Estates*.

I turned onto a concrete street with curbs and wound through a cluster of houses. New houses near the highway. In the front yards, saplings in chicken-wire cylinders grew on lawns where you could see the lines between sod pieces. Farther in, half-built houses with brick skirts showed blue construction wrap up to the roof line. Next came the newest houses, where skeletal frames stood on new concrete slabs like naked models on runways.

If suburban sprawl had bulldozed the sycamore, or dug up the site where Ranger had hidden the money—

Then I returned the metal detector to the sporting goods store. Maybe I would get a date out of all this.

The concrete street ended at a field jabbed with dozens of tiny red flags marking the next wave of houses. Dirt and torn grass gave me a path. I drove carefully. How would I explain getting stuck out here to roadside assistance? And would a tow truck driver get greedy ideas if he saw the metal detector through the window of the rear hatch?

I neared the end of the flags. Brush and thistles dotted the field beyond. Where I could see grass, the ground looked uneven. If only I drove one of those tall pickups with knobby tires. The rough field climbed up a rise.

Over the far side of the rise rose the sparse yet leafy branches of the sycamore.

I turned between two flags and parked in what would be someone's garage this time next year. I turned the front of the hatchback toward the subdivision and put up reflective shades inside the windshield. When I climbed out, no one watched me open the hatch or pull the metal detector out of its box.

Up the rise I walked with the metal detector and the shovel. Sweat trickled down my back. In the branches of the sycamore red flittered among the green. A cardinal.

At the top of the rise, the entire tree came into view. The trunk looked like a skin disease, mottled gray and pale yellow. Plates of fallen bark heaped at the tree's base, too neatly to have fallen that way. I dug the toe of my sneaker through the bark plates and revealed empty plastic vodka bottles and broken cartridges for vape pens.

A wry grin touched my lips. I wasn't the last girl to lose her virginity on Heiny's farm, was I?

The grin faded.

Maybe not the last one to get an unwanted pregnancy out of it, either.

From the sycamore's shade, I got my bearings. The creek downhill to my right. The fence in front of me, maybe two hundred feet away. I eyeballed a bush about halfway to the fence. As good a place as any to start the final phase of this fool's errand.

Even knowing it was foolish, I daydreamed of a paid-off condo and cash in the bank. Hey, maybe I'd look good behind the wheel of an extended cab pickup with knobby tires?

I reached the spot, pulled up the metal detector's app on my phone, and started looking. My earbuds played songs from my teenaged years and the app cut in with suggestions in a smooth male voice. "Nothing here.... I'm getting something to your left.... False alarm.... Ahead...."

At the base of a thorny bush with leaves as sparse as the store clerk's hair, the app said, "I found something. It looks big."

My heart pounded and I shook my head. A bunch of beer cans, or just maybe a Civil War cannonball. Pure chance to find something. None of this was real.

I set down the detector and dug anyway, while in my ears, a girl pined for a boyfriend who by now probably had a beer gut and far more interest in hockey stats than her. The blade of the cheap shovel soon wobbled against the loose screw holding it to the handle. Sweat matted my hair and I wished I'd applied sunscreen.

The pile of dug-up grass and dirt grew. The hole was a foot deep, a foot wide. That convict was having a hell of a laugh, wasn't he—

The shovel clunked against something metallic.

I snapped my head up. Someone must have heard that. But I was alone with the cardinal in the sycamore's branches.

I kept digging. Soon I revealed the outlines of a metal box about a foot and a half wide and half that long and tall. Military surplus, the paint was still dark green though dabbed with dirt and rust. A hinge on one short side and a clasp on the other. I pried it out of the soil with the shovel.

Squatting next to it on the grass, my hands hesitated. This still had to be a coincidence. Even if Ranger had stolen money from a meth dealer before he died, he couldn't have called me with directions how to find it.

I unsnapped the clasp. The hinge groaned with rust as I lifted the lid.

Two thick plastic bags, the kind you use to freeze leftovers that you never end up eating, one inside the other. Through the double plastic showed a ragged brick of cash bound by a zip tie running down Jackson's face.

I hesitated. That bundle of money, hell, this whole dream might crumble up and scatter like ashes if I opened the bags.

I opened them anyway. The bundle remained intact. I riffled through the corners. All $20s, all looking legit, all the serial numbers random.

My breaths heaved. All of this was real. Ranger, the phone call, Hell, his regrets, and mine.

My pale knees slumped into the grass and dirt and my eyes shut for a while. *Thanks, Ranger, for at least one thing.*

After a time, I caught my breath and dabbed at my eyes. Time to think about what to do with Ranger's gift.

I counted part of the bundle and used the width of my pinky to estimate the total amount. About $22,000, give or take. Not enough to pay off my condo mortgage.

But enough to do some good.

I kneeled there and pulled out my phone, then looked up local charities that helped teenaged girls with unwanted pregnancies. While the summer wind rustled the brushy field and the cardinal chirped in the sycamore, I found one and entered the address into the nav app.

Before I lugged the money, the shovel, and the metal detector back to my car, I slipped $200 out of the stack and into my pocket. Enough for the sporting goods clerk to help me spend it on a nice dinner for two.

SEVEN OUT

A CONTEMPORARY WEIRD TALE

SEVEN OUT

The whole Vegas thing started when my boy Jaymz came over for our usual Madden game before I went off to work.

There I was, my dreads tucked under the Chickenator restaurant ball cap, in a polo shirt the color of hot oil splashed out of the fryer. My name tag *Gordon* in the right spot and straight. On the TV, the team select screen had the Cowboys ready for his controller and everything. He really liked that one blue star.

Jaymz hurried in like he always did. Being on time was never his thing. But after we fist-bumped hello he ignored the bright glow of the TV. He angled his head up a couple of inches and his small eyes locked on mine. "Yo, G, I figured something out and I got to tell you." For a shorter guy, and let's be real, kinda pudgy too, Jaymz had a voice that could fill the room. "It's my homey LeRoi. You know how shit get all weird when he be round, right?"

I had to nod at that. All the way back in elementary school, LeRoi sat alone with thick-ass glasses and no one talked to him. Until Big Tayshon called him a punk-ass for acting white and whomped on his head while the Teach for America becky kept pleading for him to stop.

Big T did stop, and later that day he stopped forever. Slipped off the top of the slide and broke his fat neck. His momma and her boyfriend sued the school district but didn't get a penny. The school had maintenance records out the ass and some phone video of kids fatter than Big T going up the same ladder a minute before.

No one really believed LeRoi had made Big T die, but no one called him out for acting white ever again.

Not that he ever acted white. He just acted weird.

"I didn't know LeRoi had any homeys," I said.

"Hey, I mean, he a tough dude to get to know, but he all right. Especially when he showed me what he can do."

"What's that?"

"Tele-something. Not reading minds and shit. Making stuff move."

"Telekinesis."

Jaymz' eyebrows lifted. Creases in his forehead seemed to reach halfway back his shaven scalp. "That's a big-ass word, G. What you been doing, reading books or something?"

"Something. To know telekinesis ain't real."

He shook his head like he was faking a seizure. "I seen LeRoi do it. I rolled dice ten times and he made them come up sevens every damn time. You know what this means?"

"It means he got lucky."

"Thousand-to-one? Million-to-one? That ain't luck, G. That's real." He stared at me for a long moment.

"I still don't believe you." Jaymz had a knack for hustles going sideways.

"You don't have to. Just set me up with Sestercius' street game, aight?"

I'd played football in high school with Sestercius, until my Achilles snapped trying to make a tackle. After school, while I earned money frying chicken and waffles, he ran a street craps game. Three nights a week, moving from garage to garage around the neighborhood to keep out of sight of the vice squad and the Mexican gangs looking for a big robbery. Tough to get invited.

"He might let me in," I said. "But he won't let in you and LeRoi."

"He will if you come with us."

I rolled my eyes. "Come on, jones, I got better things to do than lose my money." Like pay for an IT class at the community college.

"You won't lose money. Just bet with LeRoi and me all the time." He must have read something in my face. "G, if you walk out of there down—if you walk out of there less than a hundred dollars *up*—I'll cover you."

I snorted and said, "You didn't even cover me half of last weekend's pizza."

"This is different. This is going to work. Just get us in that game, aight?"

———

A WEEK later I parked the three of us on a street in the old neighborhood. Next to me, Jaymz pulled himself out by one hand on the top of the door frame. In the back seat, LeRoi didn't stir.

In school, I never was mean to him. Momma always said people touched in the head were looked after by God, and whatever you do the least of Mine and all that. But after what Jaymz had said about Big T's accident, I was especially polite. "LeRoi, you ready?"

He wore glasses so thick you could see bacteria through them. A reflected street light dazzled across them when he turned to me. "Yeah," he said, in the world's softest voice. "I could use some money."

He and I climbed out into the humid night. Where Jaymz was pudgy, LeRoi was scrawny. His hair looked like his momma ran clippers over it. No fade, no style at all. No style to his clothes, either. Store brand jeans from Walmart and sneakers from China where they changed the number and angle of stripes so Adidas couldn't sue. At least he left open the top button of his tucked-in polo shirt.

We walked the sidewalk between five cars and three houses. Jaymz whistled at a Cadillac with hubs sticking out like a war chariot in some old movie about ancient Rome. The Cadillac had a crack running two-thirds of the way across the lower part of the windshield. In a driveway, behind a fence and gate of steel poles, three Mexicans worked under the hood of a pickup truck while a radio played a man crooning in Spanish over the squeal of an accordions. One of the Mexicans squinted at us and hovered his hand near the tail of his shirt.

I nodded and said "Good evening" as we passed by.

We got to the address. The norm for the neighborhood, one story, dingy brick, burglar bars on the windows and a steel anti-kick plate on the front door. Garage door down. Bass thumped through the walls so loud the burglar bars rattled.

On the sidewalk, LeRoi sucked in a breath and froze. He squinted like he was getting a headache.

Jaymz looked alarmed. "You good?"

"Don't like too much noise."

Jaymz put on a smile while bobbing his head and glancing toward the front door. "Yeah, but, you good? To play?"

"I'm good," LeRoi said, like he was trying to convince himself.

We knocked at the door. A guy in Sestercius' crew opened it and gave us the once over. I showed him the text on my phone but we still had to slip him a $20 each to get in.

Inside, the music rattled the dishes in the kitchen. The air smelled like weed and malt liquor. We worked our way through a crowd to the garage. A woman's flirtatious laughter came from the living room.

The garage was all men. Ten of them crouched around a long green felt with one end tacked two feet up the wall. A portable LED display hanging above the felt showed the point number. Along the sides of the felt were alternating boxes labeled *Pass* and *Don't Pass*. The dominant smell was tobacco. A window AC unit labored but we still sweated in moments.

Dice clacked against the wall. "Seven out!" Sestercius called. Cheers and groans followed in equal measure.

After he split the pass bets proportionally among the don'ts, and slid a couple of $5s or $10s into his clip, he stood up and limped over to us. He had a cigarette tucked behind his ear and he'd grown a neatly trimmed mustache and beard since I'd seen him last. He gave me a bro-hug, then raised his eyebrow at LeRoi. "I didn't know y'all run together."

LeRoi ducked his head, like his shoes were the most interesting thing in the room.

I leaned my head toward Sestercius. "Favor to his Momma."

"A game of street craps?"

"Time with the boys."

Sestercius thought for a moment, then nodded. He gestured at the widest opening along the felt. "Come on in. It's still early, just $5 minimum."

We crowded in together, me, Jaymz, LeRoi. The concrete slab was gritty under my knee and I was close enough to smell a bag of spicy fake onion rings on Jaymz' breath. The next shooter was three to my left. Plenty of time to get a feel for the game.

And see what LeRoi could do.

He pushed his thick glasses up his nose and put the minimum in the *Pass* box. Jaymz said, "I got a good feeling," and put a $20 next to LeRoi's $5. Three hours' wages, if he had a job.

I bet $5 on pass too.

The shooter, bald head and lazy eye, nodded at the three of us. "Y'all know a hot hand when you see one."

Everyone else bet. Sestercius eyed the money stacks around the table to make sure there was about equal action on both pass, a.k.a. do, and don't, then squatted next to the shooter with five dice in a dented tin cup.

Jaymz barely moved his arm next to LeRoi, twice. I couldn't tell how many fingers he pressed him with each time, but that's the code they worked out.

The shooter picked two dice and threw at the part of the wall covered by the felt. LeRoi grimaced at the translucent red cubes like he was on the toilet and hadn't eaten enough fiber.

I watched the dice hit and tumble. If LeRoi used powers on them, I couldn't tell.

"Yo-leven yo!" called out Sestercius. "Do, winner." Cheers and curses sounded around the felt.

LeRoi turned his head toward us. "What does that mean?"

Jaymz clapped him on the shoulder. "It means we won."

The corners of LeRoi's mouth turned up. I realized I'd never seen him smile, not once.

We won, but just one game. Still could've been luck.

The shooter stayed the same. So did Jaymz and LeRoi's bets. Instead, I took the $5 I'd just won and put it on the don't box.

The shooter raised an eyebrow at me. "Dog, my hand's still hot."

"Yo then no, ain't that how it is?"

Jaymz elbowed my side. "What you doing?" he muttered. On his other side, LeRoi looked at me like I stole his lunch money.

"Lose a few, it looks real," I whispered to Jaymz' ear. And hedging our bets if it turned out LeRoi lacked the powers Jaymz thought he had.

Jaymz moved his arm once.

The dice came up four-six, an easy ten. If Jaymz had told LeRoi to make one of the dice come up four, the pass line couldn't have lost the come-out roll.

A ten meant no instant winner. Sess tapped his phone and the number glowed on the LED board. If the shooter rolled the same number before he rolled a seven, the passes would win.

Two movements of Jaymz' arm. Two dice tumbled off the far wall. Two fives showed.

"Hard ten, do winner!"

The shooter caught my eye and shook his head. "Yo then no? Not this bro."

I shrugged. A far cry from Jaymz, who high-fived LeRoi and announced, "I knew this be a good night."

LeRoi didn't say a word, but that look on his face. When a girl ever took him to bed, he'd get that look again.

A shiver went down my back. LeRoi had powers. I believed it now.

They sevened-out the shooter and play progressed around the felt. I still didn't bet with him and Jaymz on every roll. Despite believing in LeRoi, my hand shook a little when I thought about peeling one of my few $20s out of my clip and I laid down $5s instead. Even with that, I won more than I lost.

On the other hand, Jaymz acted like a pig who got an extra helping in his trough. He high-fived every man around him and constantly talked about his luck. At least he had the smarts to put most of his winnings in his clip, rather than flaunt them.

Still, when the dice came to a musclebound guy two down from LeRoi, he tensed his tattooed neck. In a deep voice, he said, "Sess, your game clean?"

The chatter around the felt dried up instantly. The smell of tobacco became more bitter. The dice tray fell from Sestercius' hand.

He lurched backward and rose to his full height. He rested his hands near the sides of his untucked shirt. Over the long wobbling note of the dice tray spinning down on the concrete, he said, "I run a clean game."

My gut filled with ice. Even Jaymz shut up, turning as quiet as LeRoi. Sess had to be packing.

The guy with the neck tats stood up and face Sess. I figured he had a gun too. "Clean?" he growled, then jerked his head at us. "Then how is it these mu'fu'ers won every single time?"

I showed my palms and spread my fingers wide. "I lost my share. Yo then no, remember?"

"Your homies ain't lost nothing. How can that be?"

Jaymz stood up with an argumentative look on his face. "Man, c'mon, we just got good luck tonight, beginner's luck." He slapped LeRoi on the shoulder, who jumped like he'd chugged a Mountain Dew and watched a horror movie.

The guy with neck tats gave LeRoi a once-over. Everyone's breath caught. LeRoi checked out the fraying edge of the felt.

The guy wasn't buying it. "Uh huh."

I whispered to Jaymz, "Bet against him and lose."

Jaymz twisted his neck to me. "What? No."

"$50 life insurance."

The guy with the neck tats glowered at us. His voice boomed over the hum of the AC. "I didn't hear what y'all said."

I spoke. "I said our luck going to cool off sometime and we should go."

"No. Y'all going to stay." He kept his eyes on us while he put $100 on *pass* and pawed two dice from the tray.

Jaymz scrunched up his face but bet $100 on don't. LeRoi did the same. I put $20 on do. The other men around the game loosened up, but the bets were all small and no one offered a side bet on the next roll.

The guy rolled the come-out. Sestercius called out the point was six. Both of them spent more focus watching us than the dice.

A couple of rolls and sweat beaded on LeRoi's forehead. On the next roll, the dice showed three-three.

The tension in the room melted.

Jaymz hammed up his disgust as Sess scooped up his losing bet. I let out a breath as he put fifteen dollars next to my $20.

Sess shared a glance with the guy with the neck tats, then nodded to himself. "Boys," he said to us, "y'all done here for tonight. Next time, try your luck in Lake Charles."

———

A TWO-HOUR DRIVE EAST, exiting near the natural gas flares from the refineries, brought us toward the Babylon. The newest of the Lake Charles casino hotel resorts, sprawling on the drained marshland between L'Auberge and the Golden Nugget. A ziggurat of neon lights towering into the night sky and casting a glittering reflection on the lake under the bridge.

Narrow lanes and a cross-wind made me keep my hands tight on the wheel. "Why'd you pick the Babylon?"

Jaymz' voice sounded like I was too blind to see. "Man, it's *Babylon*. Painted ladies and shit, y'know? Plus, their players club gives us more free buffets."

We checked in. Butterflies in my stomach. Just like waiting at the mouth of the tunnel to run onto the field. Nervous, but anxious to drop our suitcases in our suite and get to the casino.

Inside, the ding and bong of a hundred slot machines sounded. Flashing lights and video displays made me blink. You see places like this on TV but it can't prepare you for the real thing. The stink of tobacco in your nose. The barmaids with too much makeup walking on high heels with drink trays. Wrinkled old women tapped the buttons of the penny slots like rats getting government cheese.

I shuddered. There's a high price for easy money.

Degenerate gamblers surrounded the craps tables too. At least they were more lively. And diverse. A scrawny white guy carefully turned the dice to boxcars, then pinched them between his thumb and forefinger to shoot. A Mexican in gold chains over a black designer T-shirt scowled at the tumbling dice as if he wanted to knife them. Older brothers, still pimped out despite frizzled gray hair and fingers stiff inside gold rings, flirted with the Asian woman working the stick as they placed the six and eight.

That table. Blue like some small college's football field and marked up with dozens of boxes. Like you needed a degree in crapsology to figure it out.

We'd read up, watched videos, practiced with a game on our phones where there was an ad before every come-out roll. But my nerves at the check-in desk came back. There's a hell of a difference between a no-pads practice and game conditions.

That first night we eased in to get the hang of all the bets we could make. Hop, horn, hard way.

Almost getting shot in the garage had made Jaymz play smarter. We'd worked out a good plan. We bet pass line every time and backed up every point with odds. Not going to get rich off that, but it kept us in the game for the long-shot bets. Nine-to-one on the big six, thirty-to-one on the two or twelve prop bets. And LeRoi didn't make his constipation face at every roll, just enough to win two-thirds of the time at the pass line and about every other time on the long shots. He'd learned enough about the bets and how to win them that Jaymz no longer had to prime him with the numbers we wanted. He made them come up all on his own.

My jitters soon went away. The first night, I turned two hundred into two thousand.

The next night, two thousand into ten.

Other players took notice. They whispered to one another and copied our bets when we played the long shots.

The crews took notice too. The pit bosses took notice. Casino security, white guys who looked like retired linebackers in dark suits and sunglasses, took notice. But even if they assumed something was fishy, they couldn't stop us.

They tried. Made everyone re-roll if the throws didn't bounce off the foam pyramids studding the back wall of the table. Changed dealers a lot, in case we'd struck a deal with one to work rigged dice into the game. And still we hit, again and again.

The third night, I turned ten thousand into thirty.

By now, not just crews and players took notice. That third night, a

Saturday, after Jaymz decided to stop for the night with a hundred K in chips, we ended up in one of the Babylon's bars, buying drinks and playing jukebox songs for three sorority sisters down from Grambling to celebrate the youngest of them turning 21.

The night wore on. The prettier girls steered the ugliest one toward LeRoi. Not that he minded. Thirty minutes later, I was right about that look coming back to his face.

After we woke up around noon and told the girls to leave our suite, I turned to Jaymz with a tight look on my face. It was Sunday, and my next shift at the Chickenator started in four hours. With the bright light of day coming through the windows, the big check in my wallet seemed unreal. Like the Babylon would stop payment on it before I could cash it.

I could make it to work, if we left soon. But Jaymz had said, more and more the night before, that we should extend our trip.

Instead, he dropped his fork onto the room service plate on his lap, then tossed the plate onto the rumpled sheets of his bed. "You right, G. We done enough here. Time to go to Vegas."

———

COMPARING Lake Charles to Las Vegas was like comparing a small-town high school's football field to a billion-dollar dome seating eighty thousand. Miles of neon in the clear, cool desert night. Jumbotrons advertising loose slots, French circuses, and magicians catching bullets with their teeth. More Bentleys on the Strip than at a rappers' convention.

Jaymz picked the Babylon again. It made sense. We'd racked up players club points. The staff at the front desk treated us, not like kings, but like the sons of dukes.

Maybe staying at the Babylon was a mistake, but I tell myself everything would have ended up the same.

Pregame jitters, like always. I gawked at the size of the Babylon's casino. A long walk around a circular bar in the center of the floor. A crowd at the table that made the players in Lake Charles look like kindergarteners.

If Vegas was the big leagues, the pit boss was a hall of fame head coach for the other team. A white guy with yellowed eyes, his slicked-back hair was a pale gray, but he still had plenty of it. The deep creases in his face converged on a nose you could open cans with.

"Yo, G, check out the bald eagle," Jaymz said, then laughed.

LeRoi didn't. I didn't either. My fingers felt thick when I slipped twenty $100s from my clip and dropped them on that blue felt for the dealer to convert to chips. A year of community college tuition right there. Cause even if I could make a killing at the craps table with Jaymz and LeRoi, is that what I wanted to do with my life?

Then the shooter sevened-out all on his own, we placed our bets at the pass line, and got to work.

Just like Lake Charles. At first. We won most of our bets for the first hour. But after I won twelve grand on snake eyes, and five minutes later Jaymz won thirty K on boxcars, the pit boss gave LeRoi a cold stare and muttered into a microphone tucked into the sleeve of his suit.

At a break in the action, I tugged on Jaymz' elbow. "Jones, slow your roll."

He scrunched up his face at me. "I'm a follow the plan."

We played another hour. Won a few, lost a few. I bet cautiously, despite Jaymz and the people lucky enough to crowd our table all telling me the table was too hot to bet small. All three of us made a nice profit —I was up seventy K for the night—but every time I saw the pit boss staring at LeRoi like a hawk soaring over a rabbit that didn't know to look up, I felt a hole in my gut.

Next day, I urged Jaymz and LeRoi to head into the casino in the afternoon instead of the evening. The bald eagle wasn't working that shift. Our first bets hit according to our usual system... then he showed up. With guys in suits who looked defensive linemen.

And a white guy with noodle arms, hair parted down the middle, a polo shirt buttoned up to his neck, and glasses you could see bacteria with.

To Jaymz, I whispered, "Oh, shit."

"What? Bald eagle again? He ain't nothing."

"Not him. Next to him."

"Nerd boy? What about him?"

I still whispered, but harshly. "If you were going to paint a picture of a white LeRoi, what would he look like?"

Despite my whispers, LeRoi must have heard. He cocked his head. "You think he's like me?"

"No, dog. I *fear* he's like you."

A grin curled up the corners of LeRoi's mouth. Jaymz' swagger had rubbed off on him. "Oh ye of little faith."

We all put chips on the pass line. Jaymz and LeRoi bet the max, $5k. I only put a thousand down and Jaymz nudged me. "Your turn to bet something on top."

The white guy with the thick glasses stared over the box man's shoulder at our stacks of chips. "Nah, jones. I'm good."

"Your loss," he said, and shoved another five grand at the dealer to bet the hard six. LeRoi nodded.

The shooter was a white woman with dyed blond hair and thick makeup over her wrinkles at the far end of the table. She shook the red cubes in her hand and flung them with surprising force. They bounced on the felt and off the wall under our forearms leaning on the top rail. Under LeRoi's scrunched-up face.

The dice settled, one and two.

"Three craps!" called the stickman. The dealer on our end picked up our stacks of chips from the pass line.

I looked at LeRoi. His swagger from a moment earlier had drained from his face. He met my gaze, then looked at the scrawny white guy. Didn't meet his eyes, though. Before the white guy could make eye contact, LeRoi dropped his head and got really interested in the felt. His hands clinked together his chips in the groove between his forearms.

Jaymz didn't notice. "That's alright, that's alright," he said to no one in particular. He placed another max bet on the pass line.

Our dealer spoke. "Sir, your hard six, on or off?"

Jaymz had the option to leave the bet on the table but neither win nor lose on the blonde's come-out roll. Most craps players took their bets off in that situation, more out of superstition than mathematics.

"Working, man." He bobbed his head in emphasis. "Working."

The stickman slid the dice toward the blond for her to make the next come-out roll. LeRoi scrunched up his face even harder than usual, like your momma would say it'll stick that way.

Instead of the dice, I watched the scrawny white guy. His face stayed calm.

"Easy six!" the stickman said. "Hard six loser!"

The dealer shook his head as he grabbed Jaymz' chips off the hard six box. "I can't tell you how to play."

"It's alright," Jaymz said, but he didn't mean it. He turned to LeRoi and muttered, "Just let me know next time."

LeRoi's voice dropped like he was in elementary school again. "Wasn't me."

Jaymz grew still and didn't say a word.

The blonde rolled again. LeRoi did his face so hard his neck tendons looked like steel cables.

"Seven out!" called the stickman. "Pass line loser!"

Our dealer scooped up our chips from the pass box. Jaymz sagged against the rail as another five thousand dollars went away.

The bald eagle stirred. He came our way. The scrawny white guy was at his side. Two security guys came around them and us, took up positions to box us in.

"Gentlemen," said the bald eagle, "Please come with me."

My gut was like a sponge getting wrung out. I imagine guys going to prison the first time felt the same.

He led us off the floor, down a hallway of offices, to a room that looked surprisingly comfortable. No harsh light in our faces, no clamps on the chair arms. Padded seats surrounded a big table with a half dozen water bottles slick with condensation. The security guys waited outside.

The bald eagle offered us seats and water. Even if it was a trick, my mouth was dry as the desert outside. I cracked open a bottle and took a deep sip.

The bald eagle and the scrawny guy sat opposite us. The bald eagle stared at each of us in turn. "We know what you're doing."

Jaymz put on a bluff face. "Doing? What you mean, doing?"

The scrawny guy pointed at one of the unopened water bottles standing on the table. It rose in the air, rotated upside down and back up again. It returned to the table like a billionaire landing on a rooftop helipad.

LeRoi drew out his next word with breathy admiration. "Damn."

Jaymz stared at the water bottle like he could make it disappear from force of will. But only two people in the room had powers, and he wasn't one of them.

"Here's how it's going to be," the bald eagle said. He turned his yellowed eyes to LeRoi. "You are barred from the floor of every casino in America—"

Jaymz shouted, "You can't do that!"

The bald eagle ignored him. "Unless it's for your job."

LeRoi stared him in the eye. "Job?"

"There's a place in the industry for people with your abilities." The bald eagle flourished his hand toward the scrawny white guy. "We can start you at our Lake Charles property. Pay relocation expenses for you and your family. Six figures a year, full medical, stock options, opportunity for advancement—"

"A job."

The scrawny white guy spoke. "A good job. You won't get knifed or shot in a street game. And you'll be part of a team."

"Team?" Jaymz said. "Shit, we're a team."

"A job," LeRoi said. "And family? I can move my momma with me?"

"Absolutely. We can add her to your medical coverage too."

LeRoi took a couple of chest-heaving breaths. "I'm in."

Jaymz turned on him with fire in his eyes. "You in? Just like that? After all I did for you?"

LeRoi flinched, but then he lifted his shoulders and leaned toward Jaymz. "I made you six figures." He swung his thick glasses toward the bald eagle. "They get to keep it?"

"This is a case we will not prosecute. All three of you get to keep the money you won. Your friends are free to go back on the floor. In fact, they're welcome to play any game at any of our properties. With double platinum players club status. For life."

I waved my hand palm-down over the table. I had enough money to move on from the Chickenator and never look back. "I'm done with high rolling."

Jaymz didn't say a word.

We sat for a while, sipping water, while a young Asian woman in a skirt suit and wisps of hair coming out of a bun brought in a tablet with screen after screen for LeRoi to review and sign. After the third page, Jaymz rolled back his chair with a snort. "I'm out. Coming, G?"

I guzzled the last of my water. "Yeah." I rose and extended a fist to LeRoi. "Good luck in your new job. Look me up if you ever come back to town."

He fist-bumped me, cautiously, like he didn't do it very often. "I will. You been a friend, Gordon."

Jaymz gave another snort. He left without a word.

We didn't talk until we were back on the casino floor. Bright lights and flashing screens. The ding of the slots, the cheers and groans of players at the tables. Stink of tobacco and alcohol. The Babylon. The painted face of the scarlet whore.

Jaymz' feet slowed and he cast his head around, scoping the place out.

"I'm heading to our suite," I said. "Going to try to change my flight. Head home early tomorrow."

His gaze landed on the craps pits. "I don't need LeRoi. If I figured out what he could do, that means I'm the lucky one." A grin crossed his face. He sauntered toward the craps tables, like they were a woman he really wanted to get with.

I never saw him again.

IPHIGENIA OF KHUFU

A SCIENCE FICTION SHORT STORY

IPHIGENIA OF KHUFU

SHE WANTED with all her heart and mind and soul to be someone else right then. Someone pretty, with straight teeth and a smooth voice. But instead, she was plain Iphigenia.

Iffy, indeed. Her booty too flat, her hair too nappy, especially here in the free-fall airdock where it floated around her head like a black dandelion. Hiding behind a tank of molten uranium salts, her chewed fingernails gripped the radiation shielding and her dark eyes watched the man she both craved and feared to talk to.

A white man. Iphigenia's father and the other leaders of Khufu had debated loudly enough for their shouts to leak through the closed door of Papa's study and reach her room. But no other spacejock with a big enough ship answered their bid, and the time had come.

His ship, a cylinder with *Lady of the Lake* painted on the side nearest her, looked big enough. The cavernous airdock was the biggest space in the colony, big enough that she felt the air pressure drop and the environmental pumps chug harder when they filled it for him. Cradle arms locked the front of it in place near the wall to her right, but the nozzles of the maneuvering and main rockets at the back end nearly brushed the airtight gate between the dock and hard vacuum.

Big enough to carry human cargo.

Iphigenia eyed him again. She knew all the stories, of Kentucky colonels with whips in hand and imperious blue eyes. The spacejock looked nothing like a slave master of legend. In the harsh work lights inside the airdock, he had an oval face that didn't go well with his haircut, buzzed on the sides and long enough on top for his brown hair to float like seaweed. He had a wiry growth of mustache and beard over the lower half of his face. Cargo pants and multi-pocket vest over a threadbare T-shirt. Not handsome, not at all.

She didn't care about his looks. The way he would care about hers, if he saw her.

But how could she ask without showing herself?

He stroked his facial hair with one hand while his other, clad in a thick glove, pulled himself along the outer hull of his ship. He stopped, ran a scanner over the seamless-looking gray metal, and moved on. From time to time he muttered something too low to hear. From his body language, a curse. Each time, he scritched a paint pen off its hook-and-loop home on his cargo pants, painted a circle around something she couldn't see, and kept going.

The spacejock was about to round the curve of his hull out of her sight when her fingers lost their grip on the shielding. She shifted her grip to her other hand. Soundlessly. She thought.

Without turning his gaze away from his ship, the spacejock said across the echoing space, "Are you going to show yourself?"

Iphigenia caught her breath. If she froze and made no sound, he would decide he'd heard something that wasn't there.

"It's normal for an asteroid colonist to want to look at an inbound ship," he said.

Her back stiffened. From his voice, he wasn't much older than her, and he condescended her like a child? Or was this the arrogance of his type coming out?

She pulled her head and shoulders into his view and steadied herself with a hand raised to a coolant pipe. Brow scrunched, she called out, "What do you know about asteroid colonists?"

He blinked, took in her figure. His blue eyes met hers. "I was one."

His tone made her tense up. Not how this was supposed to go. She would say what she wanted, not pleading for a yes and not shouting at a no. Instead she couldn't speak.

The spacejock filled the silence. He craned his neck up and down and said in a raised voice, "Be it known that this young woman entered the dock without my knowledge and I'm asking her to leave right now."

Iphigenia drew in a breath. He was scared too. "Don't you worry about cameras and microphones. I took care of them before I came in. I'm worried about my—the elders—too."

He jerked his right hand to his chest above his heart. Where most people wore their patch computers. "I'm going to record everything." He blinked owlishly. She couldn't see tiny patch cameras stuck to the top of his eye sockets, but they had to be there, along with microphones stuck to his dangling earlobes.

Her heart jumped into her throat. "Don't tell the elders I was here."

He showed her the palm of his right hand, fingers spread, and she realized the thick glove on the other hand was magnetized to hold him to the hull. "Don't give me a reason to."

She wrinkled her nose. "What do you mean?"

His body language eased. "Most colonies get twitchy about male spacejocks chasing their young women. Some young women know that, entrap a spacejock, and then lie that he forced himself on them."

Iphigenia raised an eyebrow. *Most* colonies? There were thousands around the solar system and he looked too young to see more than ten of them. "You've run into a woman like that in your many years of piloting?"

He jutted up his chin. "There are a thousand spacejocks around the solar system. We share what we've seen. It's a brotherhood." He angled his head, narrowed his eyes at her. "You want a ride away from here."

She rolled her lips in on themselves. How did he know? "What makes you say that?"

"That's the second most common reason colonial women approach spacejocks on the sly." He scratched his scraggly beard. "You know why I'm here, don't you?"

She hesitated over the words, as if saying them aloud made them a good thing. "Your ship's the orange blossom special."

Her father and the other elders, men and women alike, said it was a tradition that couldn't be broken. Colonies were small, their founders went through a genetic bottleneck, and cosmic radiation damaged genes no matter how deep colonists burrowed into their asteroids and moonlets. Long term health required periodic influxes of genetic variation.

Some colonies used genetic engineering techniques for that genetic variation, but Khufu couldn't. Mad Scientist Yaqub had used genetic engineering to create white people on Earth ten thousand years ago, and look what came out of *that*. Khufu had to get genetic variation the old-fashioned way. But the elders were choosy about whom they let in, especially when most people off Earth were as white as this spacejock.

3362 Khufu and two other asteroid colonies founded by African-Americans, 500027 Nkrumah and 62201 Marcusgarvey, worked out a solution. About every twenty years, ten young women from one colony went to the next in the chain. Women from Khufu went to Nkrumah. There they became wives of men they'd never met or even seen. There they lived out their days.

It sounded tolerable, when talked about in a classroom or around the dinner table as a child. Especially when her own grandmother, Ruth, got a faraway look in her yellow eyes and talked about overcoming her fears as a young woman on her trip here from Marcusgarvey.

But as the day grew closer, and it sank in that girls she'd grown up with would be packed off, never to be seen again, the wrongness of it crawled down Iphigenia's back and made her want to escape this place more than ever.

"It could be your ticket out," said the spacejock. "Do you get to volunteer?"

Not all volunteers were accepted. Especially the daughter of Supreme Elder Robinson, who should know better than to make her father look bad by wanting to leave. "I could."

"Is Nkrumah a bad place?"

"Is it any better than here?"

He angled his head like he checked notes sent by his patch computer through eye socket projectors onto his eyeballs. "Beats me."

"Even if it is," Iphigenia said, "it doesn't matter. I want to leave on my terms, not the elders."

"I respect that. I shared the same sentiment when I left my home."

Iphigenia's heart swelled. A smile opened her mouth. "You'll take me?"

"Do you have permission from the elders to leave but not get off at Nkrumah?"

"Permission? To leave? Why would I—"

His blue eyes crinkled. "Sorry, but no."

A pit opened in Iphigenia's stomach. Dreams smashed a hundred different ways. *No?* "That's not right."

"If you're on the passenger list and you don't get off at Nkrumah, they'll force their way on board to look for you. When they find you, the best case is they drag you off and only damage my reputation, not me or my ship."

She could only blink.

He went on. "The hit to my reputation would be bad enough. Most colonies mistrust outsiders to begin with. If I flout one colony's leaders, a bunch of other colonies will refuse to let me dock or refuel. I can't risk that."

Iphigenia found some words. "What if I'm not on the passenger list?"

He extended his fingers, ticking off points. "I won't knowingly let you stowaway. You can't sneak on board. The airlocks are keyed to my biometrics and a password. And even if you did, we'll be weeks in transit to Nkrumah. You can't hide onboard from me and the listed passengers that long. You can't hide your disappearance from the elders here for that long, either. They'd radio ahead and I would have to turn you over at Nkrumah."

Her shoulders drooped. "That's that?"

"Sorry."

As if he meant it. "That's still not right."

"I have to take care of myself. Either find another ship to take you—"

"Ships don't come. We've got elemental separators and nanoassemblers, and all the metals and organic compounds we need. We don't trade objects and we don't accept unapproved immigrants."

"Self-sufficiency is a double-edged sword," he said. The tone of his next words sounded like he meant them kindly. "Maybe the best thing you can do is accept your life here."

"You didn't accept yours on your home colony."

"Hey now, that's different. They gave me permi—"

A noise to Iphigenia's right snapped the spacejock's head that way. She knew the sound. The near door of the main airlock to Khufu's living spaces opened.

She hunched down behind the tank of molten uranium salts. Her pounding heart roared in her ears.

The spacejock pulled himself toward the airlock with slaps of his glove against *Lady of the Lake*'s hull. He stopped and faced someone Iphigenia couldn't see. "How do you do?"

A male voice, young and deep. "Captain Bower-camper?"

Iphigenia shrank down further. She knew that voice.

"Close enough. Bauerkampfer. You're Vespasian Brown?"

"That's right. Khufu's Assistant Minister of African Diaspora Affairs."

She rolled her eyes. A puffed-up title, but it sounded more official than *son of one of the colony's elders.*

Vespasian went on. His voice carried through the cavernous space. "I came to inspect your ship's suitability for the mission."

"My apologies. I had that on my calendar for later today. I must have gotten the time wrong, are your clocks set to UMT?"

"We reserve the right to inspect any ship at any time it's docked here. Before we get to that, I overheard you talking to someone. Who?"

The spacejock hesitated a moment. "I didn't catch her name. Miss —?" He waved in her general direction.

She hunched down further. Wished she could burrow into the pumps and pipes around her. *Damn him.*

No getting around it now. Iphigenia slipped between the uranium tank and the coolant pipe. She showed herself to Vespasian but kept her distance from him.

Vespasian had broad shoulders and small, close ears. A fine-looking young man, her father always said. Pairing her off to him would strengthen the political alliance between their fathers.

But nothing seemed fine about him now. He gave her a look of a man ready to slip a fighting dog off its chain. "Iffy. Should have known." He swung the look to the spacejock, Bauerkampfer. "What she doing here?"

Iphigenia held her breath. If Bauerkampfer told the truth—her back tensed against the lash of her father's belt—

"She was curious and wanted to look at the ship. I was just about to show her the way out of the airdock."

Relief flooded her. Until Vespasian spoke. "Curious about your ship. Should have known that too." His dark eyes took measure of her. "She doesn't have to leave now. She can join me on the inspection."

Iphigenia froze. Only her eyes moved to the spacejock. "Unless Captain Bauerkampfer minds?"

"I don't mind at all," the spacejock said. His gaze met hers and held it for a moment.

What was he trying to tell her?

She found out after he unlocked the hatch by retina scan and keycode and led her and Vespasian into his ship. Big as *Lady of the Lake* looked from the outside, fuel tanks, radiation shielding, and folded-up radiators filled most of its interior. Human accommodations seemed to be afterthoughts.

Cramped cubical cabins four feet on a side. Each cabin had a sleeping bag bungie-strapped at each end to padded hooks jutting from the corners. The sleeping bags floated like empty cocoons stuck to cobweb.

Vespasian extended a ropy arm and tugged on a sleeping bag. The straps flexed but held. "Good enough."

Queasiness filled Iphigenia, and not just from free fall. Bigger and more comfortable than chained benches on the slave ships crossing the Atlantic, but not by much.

The tour went on. A single communal bathroom and kitchen. Pervasive odors, dust warmed by waste heat, the dead smell of white people.

Even if she could sneak on board, she'd have no place to hide. Or eat.

Unless she could persuade Bauerkampfer to hide in his cabin? Which would mean buying her passage with her body.

She shuddered. Yes, white men lusted after black women, even women as plain as her. But paying for escape with her dignity?

It wouldn't do any good anyway. The authorities at Nkrumah would search his whole ship and drag her off, no matter what.

Tour complete, Bauerkampfer led them back to the airdock. Iphigenia and Vespasian grabbed flip-up handles around the hatch to keep from floating away.

After locking up his ship, the spacejock turned to Vespasian. "How does it look?"

"It meets our needs. I expect you have numerous things to do to get ready. I'm going to leave. Iffy's coming with me." Vespasian clamped his hand on her elbow and pushed off for the hatch out of the airdock. Her fingers slipped off the handle and for a moment grasped only air.

A firm look on his face, Vespasian led her out and down, away from the airdock at the spinning colony's hub. Only when a whiff of hot plastic came to her from the colony's main 3d printer, and the spin gave enough centrifugal force for them to walk, did he shove her elbow away from him.

"Hey!" she said, anger in the muscles of her face.

Vespasian bounded ahead and blocked her path. His dark eyes locked on hers. "Iffy, I don't know where you get it. Maybe you've got some Louisiana voodoo in you from that grandmother of yours from Marcusgarvey. But you don't act like a daughter of Khufu is supposed to act." He shook his head. "Curious about a ship."

Her back bristled. "I'll be curious about what I choose to be curious about."

"You think because your father runs Khufu you get special rules? Maybe you do. From him. But you won't get them from the rest of us."

His tone brought her up short. "What do you mean?"

"My parents have been pushing me to jump the broom with you. I just saw that look cross your face, your parents are pushing you the same. Good for our families. Strengthen the alliance. I never wanted to go along—"

"Because I'm not pretty enough?"

"I could get over that. Because you don't act like a lady. The man who runs Khufu needs a wife who's charming and gracious."

"Who knows her place." She spoke it as a challenge.

"That too. But you go messing with the cameras so you can go into the airdock without anyone noticing? Because you're curious about a ship?" He crossed his arms. Here, the floor curved up so tightly, it seemed he was a stone statue and the corridor, a wave bearing him up to pummel her. "It's the last straw, Iffy. I'll never marry you."

"You're not man enough?"

"You aren't woman enough." He turned his back and strode away, leaving her with the stink of molten plastic and a hollow core in her belly.

———

SHE NEXT ENCOUNTERED Vespasian the following day, when he and his father, Trajanus, came to her family's quarters to visit her father. She sat in a plush armchair in the sitting room. The cushions conformed to her body. A cup of coffee cooled on the side table, under the lamp with the nanoassembled linen shade. Her computer and projector patches superimposed an old file on the far bulkhead of the room, next to a painting of Black Athena bringing wisdom to a Pharaoh.

The old file had nothing to do with that. Copied from the library of the ship that brought the founders to Khufu, no Minister of Information ever censored it, the way they did current news from the wider solar system. But censor the file they would, if they knew its contents. Mission description, passenger manifests, and photos of the first settlers of a science colony at 1855 Korolev. Baggy flightsuits, confident gazes, men and women standing shoulder to shoulder.

Black and white doing the same.

Warm hope lifted her chest. More proof the solar system outside Khufu, Nkrumah, and Marcusgarvey wasn't a wasteland of white supremacy.

More proof her father and the other elders lied.

Even more than that. Judging by the job descriptions in the old file, at Korolev, a woman could do more than be charming and gracious. A physician armed with nanomedicine to fight radiation damage. A scientist doing exoplanet imaging, turning a giant telescope to worlds around distant suns.

Which one was the exception? Korolev or Khufu?

A pneumatic hiss sounded in the next room, the foyer to her family's quarters. The main door to their quarters swung inward.

Iphigenia's hopeful mood remained until her mother bustled in to greet the visitors. "Trajanus, Vespasian. Please do come in."

Deep male voices answered.

Adrenaline snapped Iphigenia's eyes wide. Her gaze darted to the time. The meeting of elders to pick the young women to be exiled to Nkrumah wasn't scheduled for another hour. Why were Vespasian and his father here so early?

Quickly she swiped and tapped virtual icons. Hide that file. And don't forget to touch a bunch of other files, so the one she'd been interested in didn't stick out if someone looked at the library's files by access date.

"I'll ask Iphigenia to join us and sit a while," her mother said. Iphigenia knew the jump-the-broom tone in her voice.

From the way he answered, Vespasian knew it too. "Thank you, Mrs. Robinson," said Vespasian, "but we have business to conduct with the Supreme Elder before the main meeting."

Iphigenia's mother paused only a moment. "I'll lead you to his study. I'll have the kitchen make coffee? Sandwiches?"

"No, ma'am, but thank you...." Vespasian's voice trailed off, lost in the cluster of interconnected rooms.

Although the cushions underneath her now felt rigid, Iphigenia couldn't move. Vespasian would tell her father what he'd told her the day before. Papa's temper would grow foul. She could already hear his belt sliding out of the loops in his pants as soon as the meeting of the elders was over.

She jolted out of the armchair. Out of the room. Out of her family's quarters. Her feet knew where to go without her having to think about it. Down to the nearest spiral ramp, then up a level, to an apartment with the warm smells of fresh bread and clean linens.

The door opened for her. Granny Ruth called for her to come to the kitchen.

Iphigenia entered the cramped space. Comfort filled her. She walked through the sitting room, her steps light in the lower spin-gravity. A loaf of basil and oregano bread cooled on a wire rack and a cup of hot coffee steamed on the slate gray engineered stone counter-top. Perched on a narrow stool where her skinny legs barely reached the floor, Granny looked up from whatever she watched or read projected on the countertop. It only took a moment for her eyebrows to jump toward her puffy white hair and sympathy to fill her yellow eyes.

"Iphigenia, what's gone wrong?"

Iphigenia's pent up emotions came out with sobs and tears. She bent her head to Granny's shoulder. The old woman's spindly arms held her surprisingly tight.

The feelings soon subsided enough for Iphigenia to tell Granny what had happened. Not about wanting to leave Khufu on her terms—that was a secret she barely dared think, let alone say aloud—but about Vespasian refusing to marry her.

"Lord Jesus. How sad that is." Granny stroked Iphigenia's hair for a moment. "Just means we have to find you another young man."

Iphigenia pulled out of the old woman's grip. Fire burned behind her eyes, but she couldn't get angry at Granny. "There's no other young man for me. Vespasian's going to badmouth me to all the elders' sons of marrying age. I'm too curious. And I have Louisiana voodoo in my blood. What does that even mean?"

"That's what they called the old ways of knowing that survived and took root down there. They called them magic. There's no such thing as magic, of course." Granny's yellow eyes lit up. "But a woman doesn't need magic to be powerful."

From anyone else, the word would have mocked her. "Powerful."

Wistfully, Granny said, "I had the power once." She gestured up and down her wizened body. Old photos and videos, those yellow eyes paired with a slender figure with just enough curves, bubbled up from Iphigenia's memory. "When I arrived from Marcusgarvey, I found the best young man here I could and made him want to marry me."

"Made him?" Iphigenia peered at the old woman. Grandpapa was three years gone to the recycler for his phosphorous to feed the plants in the hydroponic farm. He never acted manipulated. He'd loved Granny. She'd loved him.

"He wasn't sure about this strange girl with a name out of the Bible. I had to help him come around." A glint in her eye made Iphigenia blush and turn her head.

Granny laughed and laid her hand on Iphigenia's arm. "And though the power changed, I still had it, years later, when I helped your mother catch the eye of a man who was going right to the top."

The old woman looked serene, certain that she had done the right things. Iphigenia looked to the lipstick marks on the bone-white rim of the coffee cup. Powerful? At playing the only game the elders let women play.

"The bread should be cool enough," Granny said, "and I have a fresh tub of margarine from the food synthesizer. Stay with me a time?"

Iphigenia wanted to get away. But the bread smelled good and a second, padded stool waited empty next to Granny. She forced a smile. "You stay in your seat. I'll get the bread knife."

They sat over bread, margarine, and coffee and talked for a time. Granny talked, mostly, while Iphigenia listened. The old woman, voice still clear despite her age, told stories of just how she'd caught Grandpapa's eye and kept him from straying.

It took ten minutes before Iphigenia realized Granny gave her advice on how to land a man of her own.

One time, as Iphigenia reached for her cup, the one lacking lipstick stains, more words came to her. Bauerkampfer, the day before.

Maybe the best thing you can do is accept your life here.

Would it be so bad to smile and nod at a man? To cook and clean for him and his children and grandchildren? To become his widow, at the end? That man might not be an elder's son, but the technicians who converted Khufu's atoms into food and finished goods cut a good-enough figure and carried themselves with justified pride. Papa would approve a marriage down the social ladder. What other choice did he have?

The scents of warm bread and herbs faded. The last crumbs cooled on their plates. Granny told more stories, about babies on her hip and the joy she and Grandpapa felt after they earned approval for a third child.

Ponderous musical tones suddenly sounded in Iphigenia's ear. The first notes of the Khufu anthem.

"Sounds like they're announcing which girls will be sent to Nkrumah," Granny said.

"Already?" Iphigenia noticed the time. She'd been here three hours. Time flies when you're in the only place you feel loved.

An image forced itself into the air in front of her. Papa, front and center. Dressed in his most serious attire, a chalkstriped gray three piece suit and a black necktie held beneath the Windsor knot to his shirt by a thick gold clasp. The other elders, also wearing suits like they went to a funeral, lined up to his sides a step behind him. Both Trajanus and Vespasian Brown stood among those backing him up. He looked confident, as always, and spoke with a voice heavy with authority.

"The time has come for us to continue the great chain that preserves our genetic legacy and strengthens our ties to our brothers and sisters elsewhere amid the desolation of space...."

He read names, voice ponderous. ID-card photos and captions appeared over his shoulder. Iphigenia knew the first nine names and faces. Most of them, young women she didn't care about. Vain ones, and ones who were far too brazen in the way they flirted with young men. Two brought out a pang. Young women from the working classes. Though not well, she knew them. She would never see again. Ripped away out of a custom the people of Khufu didn't need. A custom that mainly served to cement the elders' power.

After the ninth name, Vespasian's face turned stony. A cold glint formed in his eyes.

Iphigenia's blood ran cold. She knew that look. He'd won, and someone else had lost.

Papa's image grew even more stern as he spoke the final name on the list. "...and Iphigenia Robinson."

———

THREE DAYS LATER, Iphigenia curled up in a sleeping bag in one of the tiny cabins on *Lady of the Lake*. Through eyes blurred with tears, she watched the view from the ship's rear cameras. Despite the blurring fog of flash-freezing radioactive steam roaring out of the drive nozzle, details stood out clear. A diamondoid cylinder fused with a lumpy ball of ice and rock rotated briskly against the deep space backdrop. Rings of solar panels, near-perfect absorbers of light, blocked out the stars behind.

Khufu, her home. Never before had she seen it from outside. Already small, and receding more every second.

Tears dripped from her eyes and fell slowly in point-four gees of thrust. She moaned softly and hugged her crossed arms against her chest. Her home. Never again would she walk its halls. Never again would she see Granny Ruth.

You were hoping to never see her again starting today anyway. What's different now?

Her tears slowed. She sniffled back snot. She was going to live in the Nkrumah colony now. She could cry about her fate or make the best of it.

The acceleration burn away from home lasted nine hours. After the low thunder of the nuclear salt water drive cut off, and after Iphigenia kept her empty stomach from dry heaving and rehooked her sleeping bag, the spin gravity kicked in for the coasting phase. Three weeks to cross the asteroid belt. Even though Bauerkampfer stayed locked inside his cabin and the control room, he gave the passengers full access to the exabytes of files in *Lady of the Lake*'s media library.

While the other young women passed the time with movies and music, Iphigenia read everything she could.

With cautious hope, she read up on the colony at 500027 Nkrumah. The asteroid had been named for the first post-colonial leader of an independent country in West Africa two centuries before. In his honor, the founders took up numerous facets of African culture, from day names and kente cloth to boiled yams and oiled rice.

Her stomach fell. Could she marry a man named Kwame and learn to cook fish stew and bean cakes?

Iphigenia lifted her head to the gray alloy bulkheads. Granny Ruth had done comparable things. She could do them too.

She kept reading. The primary religion in the Nkrumah colony was a sect of Islam. *"Christianity was the religion of slaveholders and we reject it."*

A frown creased her brow. She looked up something she half-remembered.

Yes, Muslim Arabs had taken slaves from Africa a thousand years before ships of white people ever showed up.

Despair ran cold down her face and neck. Lies. Stupid official lies. As false as Black Athena and Mad Scientist Yaqub in the public mythology of Khufu.

Lies told for the same purpose. To cement the power of the colony's ruling class.

She sat in the corner of her tiny cabin, with the backpack holding all her possessions behind the small of her back, and shadows cast by the sleeping bag shifting back and forth across her eyes.

"Lights out," she said. The cabin answered.

Plunged into darkness, her head slumped forward. Her body curled around a new pit in her belly. Silently, so the other young women from Khufu couldn't hear from the corridor, she let herself cry.

Maybe Granny Ruth could make a life like that. But she wasn't Granny Ruth.

Iffy, indeed.

After her tears finally subsided, she turned with desperation back to the ship's media library. Maybe there was some fact, some key, that could unlock a future life on her own terms. Maybe a way to get spinster status and get out of spending her days pleasing a man. Or become a woman men feared. A witch, a medicine woman—

A voodoo priestess.

Days of reading made it clear voodoo was another set of lies, like all magic. Maybe there were kernels of truth in it, like the tomato seed from *Lady*'s hydroponic garden she sometimes found mixed in with a gallon of pasta sauce extruded by the ship's food synthesizer. Old ways of knowing. Natural medicine, like the drug cocktail that supposedly made zombies: pufferfish toxin to paralyze the victim and, after the toxin wore off, a neuroactive chemical to make him believe he was an undead slave.

Her head rose. Hope trickled down her chest.

"White people stole our ways of doing things and exploited them for their profit."

She stayed up late that night, tracking down facts she half-remembered or guessed at. Deep space exploration missions, far past Neptune's orbit, with no uranium refinery at the far end for refueling. Round trip times measured in years, not months. Saving mass on crew amenities and reducing the risk of cabin fever through suspended animation.

A drug cocktail. Slow the heart and breath rates to near zero. Drop body temperature toward hypothermia levels. For the deep space missions, hook up intravenous bags of nutrients, electrodes to stimulate the muscles, and catheters to carry away body wastes.

Her pulse quickened and she smiled for the first time since *Lady* left Khufu. She wouldn't need that extra medical equipment. She wasn't thinking months or years. Her plan would call for hours, maybe a day or two.

Her smile crumbled.

Her plan needed Bauerkampfer's help.

———

HEART THUDDING, Iphigenia stepped out of her cabin the next night. From the muffled sounds of movement and chatter and the trickle of light under cabin doors, most of the other young women from Khufu were awake. She had her excuse in place—*just going to the restroom*—but didn't need it. She walked alone down the up-curving corridor and no one saw her turn right for the nearest passageway toward the captain's quarters.

She twisted and stooped to get past thick pipes jutting out from the passageway. She emerged into a walkway a little wider than her shoulders. Hatches, utility panels, and storage lockers lined both sides. Red LEDs blinked next to biometric panels and security keypads.

Iphigenia followed the curving walkway until she saw two things that froze her. A locked hatch with the words *Command Deck and Crew*

Quarters - No Admittance in peeling maroon paint. And Artemis Merriwether, a woman with straightened hair and buxom curves squeezed into a tight green dress, clacking her long, crimson fingernails on the bulkhead next to the security panels.

Artemis pivoted. Her eyebrows arched, skewering Iphigenia with mockery. "You think you got a chance?"

Iphigenia's stomach clenched. Of all the people to guess at her hopes... "What?"

A sly shake of her head, then Artemis said, "He turned down all this." She writhed in place, showing off all the curves Iphigenia lacked. "He must be a sissy-boy."

Iphigenia sluffed out a breath. Her hopes remained her secret. She gave a smile she imagined Granny Ruth putting on decades ago. "White people like some strange things."

"Even as strange as you?" Artemis spoke with a teasing tone. "Good luck." She turned and sashayed to one of the other passageways back to the passenger cabins.

Iphigenia took five deep breaths. She patted her hair, smoothed her blouse over her belly and hips, glanced at the camera over the hatch.

More breaths. To make her hopes a reality, she had to do this.

Her finger pressed the intercom button near the security panel. Some grime in the switch resisted her finger.

Ten seconds. No answer.

Her heart knocked. Did the button not work? She pressed again.

Bauerkampfer's flat voice came out of the speaker grill. "Good evening, Iphigenia."

She spoke over the rattle and clank of the ship's systems around her. "Can we talk, Captain?"

"Looks like we're doing that right now."

"I mean, in person. Face to face. In your cabin."

"You're the last passenger I saw coming to proposition me. The answer is no."

His scruffy beard, his dead smell... she shuddered. "That's not what I want. I need to talk to you about something else."

He gave a long sigh. "I'm willing to talk. To you. But it has to be like this."

"Why?"

"Part of my contract requires me to deliver all of you to Nkrumah with—" His voice shifted higher. "—your virtue intact."

"Are you blushing, Captain?"

"I have to show the authorities at Nkrumah camera footage of every encounter I have with any passenger. But not audio. So we can talk."

Her mouth felt dry. She looked up and down the walkway. Hardware and the curve of the rotating ship blocked her view of the passageways back to the cabins. Would her voice echo? Or would *Lady*'s background noise cover her voice from eavesdroppers?

"Can you watch if anyone's coming this way?"

"No problem." A second later, he said, "I turned on motion sensors in both ways to the passenger deck. If they see someone coming, they'll let me know."

"Thank you." Iphigenia hunched over the tiny hole next to the intercom button, which she guessed to be the microphone. "Can you hear me?" she said softly.

He lowered his voice to match. "Yes. What's going on?"

Her words gushed out. She would use the ship's nanoassembler to synthesize a cocktail of suspended animation drugs. Take them during the deceleration burn to Nkrumah. Write a suicide note.

Her voice caught. One thing to think these things, but another to say them out loud.

"Then...?" he asked.

He'd declare her dead and she'd hide on *Lady* until they left Nkrumah for his next destination, wherever it might be. "That's it." She eased back her head and shook out her jittery arms. Cold sweat glued her blouse to the small of her back.

Silence for a moment, followed by a sigh and soft words. "You've overlooked a lot of problems. Suspended animation drugs are a controlled substance. I have to green light you to synth them."

She landed her fingertips on the mesh over the speaker. "But you can authorize them."

"The contract also requires me to look out for your health and safety. If you're declared dead, the Nkrumah authorities will put me under the microscope. If they impound my fab records—"

"They'll see that I ordered a couple of sleeping pills every night these last two weeks. I'll leave the empty packs next to the suicide note. You tell them cause of death was an overdose. Can you get your medkit to spit out a false blood chemistry report?"

A pause. If only she could see his pallid, stubbly face to guess at his thoughts.

"I can make that work," he finally said.

Her body wanted to melt, like butter in Granny's skillet. In the rush of relief she missed his next few words. "—unless I can find a place that will take you."

The word came out like the last air of a deflated balloon. "What?"

"I could get you away from Nkrumah. And one passenger wouldn't be a burden on mass or consumables. But it's not as simple as you leaving at my next destination."

"Why?" She forced her shoulders back and higher. She had something to offer any colony.

"Because nine colonies out of ten are full of fanatics for some cause. Like Khufu and Nkrumah, but for different causes."

"You mean they're white supremacists."

"A few are," he said, in an off-hand tone. "But even the ones that aren't are obsessive in different ways. You don't want to conform to the culture and religion of Nkrumah? Most places, you'll have to conform to whatever culture and religion the colony's founded on. Are you willing to do that?"

She leaned her forehead against the bulkhead above the speaker grill. "It depends..."

"That's assuming they'll even take you in the first place. Outsiders are a bad influence. They can lead people away from the faith or the proper way of doing things. Even if they don't mean to. Any colony would vet you before they'd let you in. Your odds of getting in are low unless you have something in common with the colony to begin with. Religion. Culture. Ethnicity."

Her head felt so heavy. A good thing, too, or else she'd lift it to slam it against the bulkhead. If she had to go someplace where people were like her, she might as well get off at Nkrumah. "Isn't there some colony that would take me?"

"A few might. Especially if you can show them your skills by pulling off this trick."

She lifted her head. "Take me to one of them."

"Do you have the millions in cryptocoin to pay for the fuel?"

"Take me to one of them. Any one. Please."

The sound of breaths came through the speaker. Bauerkampfer went on, voice mild. "If I can arrange a mission to one of those places, and if they show interest in taking you as an immigrant, then I'll take you there."

Waves of hope washed through Iphigenia. Tears misted in her eyes. "Thank you. Thank you so much."

"I said *if*. And if I can find a place to take you, you'll get off *Lady* there and make the best of it. No turning back."

"A chance. That's all I can ask for." A tear trickled over her smiling lips.

"Stockpile sleeping pill packs. Come by here this time every third night. I'll give you an update. If I find a colony that will take you, I'll synth the suspended animation drugs."

Hope felt so foreign to her. "And if you can't find a colony?"

"Then you get off the ship at Nkrumah."

Or she overdosed on the sleeping pills instead of throwing them into the recycler during the deceleration burn.

Iphigenia sucked in a breath for fear that even one exhalation would let the words out. The bulkhead between them gladdened her now for veiling her face from his eyes. She angled her ear to the speaker, listening to his breaths for any hint he suspected she might actually commit suicide.

"Three nights, Miss Robinson."

"I'll be here," she whispered. She turned and went back through the narrow walkways to the passenger deck. Before she went to her tiny cabin, she stopped at the passenger fab and dialed up a two-pack of sleeping pills.

———

CAPTAIN BAUERKAMPFER FLOATED in the airdock at Nkrumah. His magnetic glove held him in place on *Lady*'s hull next to the main hatch. Nine young women filed out of the ship, blinking a few times at the bright lights and cavernous space, holding queasy stomachs against free fall, before turning shrewd dark eyes to the press of waiting middle-aged men in kufi caps and robes in bright shades of green and yellow.

One of the men drifted closer to Bauerkampfer. Kofi Jeffries, master of Nkrumah's port facilities. He stopped himself with a puff of air from the front vent on his belt. Two younger men whose facial features suggested they were his sons or nephews took up positions behind him.

"It is good you brought these nine daughters of Africa to us," said Jeffries, "but it is very bad that one died."

Bauerkampfer tensed. "She was clever. She fabbed two packs of sleeping pills during coast phase. Any more and I would have seen the red flag. I didn't think she'd ask the others to fab them for her."

Jeffries' eyes narrowed. "You were not negligent in monitoring the young women's fab requests?"

"I'll share the passenger fab records with you."

"Yes. Also, you will give us her remains."

"Excuse me?"

"She was a daughter of Africa. Her potassium and phosphorous should enrich our biosphere."

"No," Bauerkampfer said. "She died on *my* ship, outside your port. Her trace elements belong to me."

"Your medical kit couldn't pinpoint her time of death that precisely. You were piloting. You didn't know she was dead until after you docked. At *my* port."

Bauerkampfer swallowed. "Do you want other ships to ever dock at your port? I'll tell every spacejock in the system if you try to take her remains off my ship."

Jeffries regarded him for a moment, then gave a cold smile. "Must be my grief talking. My son—" He flicked his thumb toward the young man behind him on the right. "—had hoped the daughter of Khufu's chief elder would be a good match for him. Even though we can't take her, he wants to see her, at least once."

A sympathetic wince, then Bauerkampfer said, "I'll show her to you."

The last of the nine passengers, escorted by men and women of Nkrumah, left the airdock. Bauerkampfer led Jeffries and his young kinsmen into *Lady*. Down twisting corridors to the passenger deck. To Iphigenia's cabin.

Bauerkampfer's nose wrinkled. Jeffries and the young men screwed up their faces. The stink of voided bowels and the first whiff of decay came from the woman slumped inside a dangling sleeping bag.

The spacejock pinched his nose with one hand and squirmed past the foot end of the sleeping bag to a duffel lying in the corner. He slid a piece of paper with smooth cursive writing from between the carry straps. "Here's her note," he said, voice more nasal than usual. He turned, pushed off the wall, and handed the note to Jeffries. His movements stirred eight torn-open foil packs of sleeping pills.

Jeffries glanced at the note, then at the woman's face at the sleeping bag's opening. Eyes closed, face slack, she almost seemed asleep. "We've seen enough," he said. A puff of air turned him to go.

"Pop, wait." The young man who'd hoped to marry Iphigenia spoke. A wheeze from his belt brought him into the tiny cabin, closer to her face. He raised a hand and touched her cheek with fingertips the color of yams.

He jerked his hand away. Eyes wide, he said, "Oh, damn, she's cold." A couple of breaths later, his eyes turned from scared to sad. He touched her cheek again. "Damn, girl, why did you do this? I'm a prince. I would have treated you like a princess."

"Are we ready?" Jeffries asked his son.

"Yes, Pop." The young man blinked rapidly, then shook his head and followed his father away from the cabin.

Back in the bright lights and broad space of the airdock, Bauerkampfer said, "I'd like to refuel as soon as possible. And get those seeds you were talking about on board."

"You should stay for the festivities," Jeffries said. "The group wedding will have a hell of a party afterward."

Bauerkampfer shook his head. "I'm not feeling festive, after...." He angled his head in the direction of Iphigenia's cabin.

"Your choice," Jeffries said. "Open up your fuel port and your cargo hatch and my teams will get you on your way."

The spacejock took his leave. Jeffries and his kinsmen jetted to the exit from the airdock. After it closed behind them, Bauerkampfer went back into *Lady* and carefully locked the passenger hatch.

He hustled to the medkit in his cabin, grabbed the preloaded syringe and a rubber strap, and sped through the passageways to Iphigenia's cabin. He pulled down her sleeping bag's zipper. Cinched the strap around her arm. Jabbed the syringe into a vein.

It took a minute for her eyelids to flutter open. She looked at him with groggy eyes. "We did it?"

"We did."

She inhaled, then winced and shook her head. "Lord, that stinks."

"Get out of the sleeping bag and take one of the other cabins. I'll throw this bag and the stink bomb straight into the recycler. Then I have to let the dock crew refuel and load up cargo before we can go."

She moved her legs, feebly inside the foot of the sleeping bag. "I'm so weak."

"I'll help you out." He grabbed her by the armpits, braced his feet against the bulkhead, and pushed off.

Iphigenia floated in the air and caught her breath. Arms and legs bare outside her blouse and shorts, a shudder racked her body. "I could use some hot soup."

"I'll bring you some in a couple of minutes. Look for another cabin. Got it?"

"Yeah. Wait, one thing. You found a colony that will take a chance on me. Which colony?"

"A science colony," Bauerkampfer said. "Korolev. Do you know anything about it?"

She shivered but managed a smile. "I've heard a thing or two."

RETURN BLESSING

A SCIENCE FICTION SHORT STORY

RETURN BLESSING

THE FLYING INSECTS the size of his fist, swarming around him every time he went outside his tourist flat? Annoying. More annoying? The natives of Valoduria shoving unwanted handicrafts in his face every time he stepped through the Development Assistance scanners lining the gate of the human zone, and into the alien city of thatched roofs and mud bricks.

Jeffrey couldn't even tell what the things were supposed to be. The handicrafts, not the natives. The aliens resembled the gigantic bugs except for lacking wings. Yellow-green skin, two compound eyes on the sides of their heads, a sinuous neck, and too many joints in their four arms.

All that articulation showed in the fine details they put in their handicrafts. But all the details in the world couldn't help him figure them out. Was this one a religious icon or a sex toy? That one, a brimless hat or a floppy drinking cup?

Actually, that last one probably was a hat, because when he drank from it, he spilled vodka and orange juice all down his shirt. At least it cooled him off in his flat, sweltering that one day when the repair company's robots took their sweet time coming to fix his air conditioning. And it made a fun conversation starter at a party in the human zone, starting off perched on his head, ending up at two in the morning as a fig leaf.

The morning after that, he woke up with a rash down there, and couldn't tell if he'd caught something from the hat or the woman with dyed green hair and belly tats snoring next to him. A lotion from the pharmacy kiosk took care of the rash. The hat ended up dangling from the wall rack near the door of his flat, along with a crinkly sack with a brittle drawstring, where he ignored it every time he grabbed a ball cap and left to shoot 3d video as part of his xenology "work" in the alien city.

All that meant Jeffrey had no idea what the native hissed in pidgin Standard. "Return blessing."

The orange rays of Epsilon Indi beat down on his exposed ears and arms. Not much UV, so he wouldn't sunburn, but still hot. It had rained the night before, which meant the sunlight turned the puddles along the curbs into sources of extra humidity.

"Sure. God—or whatever you worship—bless you." He took two steps away from the alien, on extra-padded sneakers and legs thick with muscles after months in Valoduria's gee-and-a-half.

The native hurried on its two spindly legs. Its splayed feet clacked on the human-taught waterproofing on the brick-paved street. The native loomed in front of him. Pungent scents, sweaty sheet mixed with burnt onion, clogged Jeffrey's nose. "Return blessing."

The things he did to keep his father adding cryptocurrency to his account were bad enough. But now, instead of pretend xenology, he had to talk to one of the natives? "Blessing?"

"We give blessing. Return blessing."

One of the handicrafts they'd shoved on him? Jeffrey forced a smile. "Hey, friend, have we met? No offense, but you all look alike." He reached up to give the creature's upper right shoulder a jocular shove, then thought better of it. "But humans look all the same to you, am I right?"

Poor alien. Confused about something. Good luck with that. Jeffrey stepped around—

"Return blessing, Cheff-ree Be-orn-son."

Jeffrey's raised foot stumbled to the brick street. Not because the alien mispronounced *Björnson*—most humans did too. How the hell did it know his name?

He put his fake smile back on. "I got to confess, when we met earlier, I didn't catch your name."

"This one Eyokviwex. Return blessing."

The street had seemed empty a moment ago. Now, Jeffrey glanced around and felt surrounded by a dozen aliens watching him with those gigantic insect eyes. Watching and edging closer.

Jeffrey turned back to Eyokviwex and spread his palms. "I'd be glad to. Two things. I don't have it on me. And I don't have a clue what it is."

"Is blessing." Eyokviwex leaned closer. "Return blessing."

The stink of the surrounding aliens made Jeffrey's eyes water. Words tumbled out of his mouth. "Yes, it sure is a blessing, and hell yeah, I'll return it. Next time I come to your city. And if you tell me what it is."

Eyokviwex worked its mouth parts from side to side. "Is blessing," it said, as if its identity were the most obvious thing in all the Consortia worlds.

GENTLEMAN JOHNNY'S was a bar in the human zone across the street of living asphalt from the planetary headquarters for Development Assistance. Most Devas were earnest young people, about Jeffrey's age, with degrees from the better sort of universities on the better sort of worlds. The men viewed him with distrust and the women tended to be frigid, so he usually avoided them. Jeffrey was a tourist, so the Devas usually avoided him.

A good arrangement.

A damn shame he had to break it.

Four days since Eyokviwex accosted him in the alien city. Six days since he'd last shot footage of aliens and uploaded it to the next ship bound for the jump point.

"A minimum of one upload every seven local days, or I freeze your account and buy a ticket on the next ship out." Spoken with eyes like iced sapphires. When Dad said something like that, he meant it.

The awning over Gentleman Johnny's shaded him from Epsilon Indi's late afternoon rays. The doors swung open. Conditioned air billowed out. After walking three blocks in the thick, hot air, the coolness overcame the last of Jeffrey's hesitations.

Polarized windows shaded the interior. Some tedious emo music played, overwhelming the chatter of the only group in the bar. Three Devas sat at the table nearest the door. They looked up at Jeffrey, looked disappointed, looked away.

He sauntered to the bar and smiled at the tender, a brunette with a pixie cut. Even if he couldn't get help, at least he'd get a drink out of this trip.

He raised his mug of bock and inhaled its malty scent. His last drink on Valoduria? His smile slipped and he forgot to ask the bartender for her number.

The clack of a stick against a cue ball caught his attention. In the back, a solitary Deva guy with bushy eyebrows and a neck beard stooped over a pool table.

Not Jeffrey's preferred company in a bar, but desperate times and all that. He wandered over. Balls thudded off rails. One clattered onto another ball in a corner pocket.

Jeffrey took a sip of his beer to fortify himself. "Looking for a game?"

The neckbearded Deva looked up with a squint. His voice sounded like a concrete mixer. "I don't play for money."

"Me neither. But I'll play for info."

The Deva raised an eyebrow, then gave a little shrug. "I'll rack."

Jeffrey talked as they played. He left out the part about how he pretended to be an amateur xenologist. Focused on getting accosted on the alien street, asked to return the blessing.

He slid the stick over the chalk on the webbing between his left index and middle fingers. The cue ball smacked a stripe that rattled around the mouth of the pocket but stayed on the green felt. "But he wouldn't tell me which thing it is."

"A hat, a... what were they all again?"

"Can I show you?"

A nod. Their wearable computers came to some data transfer agreement. The Deva, named Sedgwick, held his stick like a walking stick and got a faraway look on his face. Looking over the photos his wearable presumably showed him through the projectors like warts around his eye sockets, beaming visual data onto his retinas.

"Sedge, what's going on?" warbled a woman's voice.

Jeffrey looked up. Eyes set wide apart, two braids dangling to her shoulder blades, and a diamond studding the right side of her nose, all wrapped up in that Deva earnestness. Not his type, but he wasn't here to flirt. "Sedgwick's helping me better understand our alien hosts."

The woman softened a little toward Sedgwick.

"Wanya," he said, and Jeffrey needed a second to realize that was her name, "have you ever seen—may I share?"

"Yeah. Of course." Jeffrey reached for his bock while the Deva couple conversed.

They bent their heads together for a time. "Hmm," Wanya said. "That's a shroud for a fungus pot. Isn't it?"

"That's my guess too," Sedgwick said. "I've seen photos of similar ones in the messages I review—" He looked up and raised his shoulders. "I work in the Penpals Between the Stars program."

"That's great," Jeffrey said, with enough fake enthusiasm to fool a normal person. "You're talking about what I thought was a hat?" A fungus shroud? Maybe that explained his rash. "Is there a religious significance to their fungus or something?"

The Deva couple shared a look. "No." Sedgwick drew out the word.

"None we know of," Wanya added.

"So which one is the blessing?"

Wanya looked pained. "We wish we could tell you."

"Do you know someone else who might?" Jeffrey said. His voice sounded needy and he hated it.

"We can ask around," said Sedgwick. "Back to the game. My shot, isn't it?"

The need in his voice grew thicker. "I need to know. Now. If I go back out there—"

"Oh!" Sedgwick's eyes lit up. "You're worried the Valodurians will harm you if you don't return the whatever-it-is? No. They never have hurt a person who didn't attack them first."

Jeffrey jerked his head from side to side. "People get irrational sometimes about religion. Don't the Valodurians?"

Sedgwick cocked his head, then shrugged the question off. "I've never heard of them imposing any of their taboos on people. They figure their gods only care what they do. What are gods demand of us is not their concern."

"Unless...." Wanya said.

Jeffrey seized on her word. "Unless what?"

"Alien cultures sometimes undergo disruptive change despite our best efforts to manage interspecies interaction," she said. "Like the ghost dancers or the *maji maji* on Earth in the 1800s. New religions, or new ways of practicing old religions, can rise up."

"Honey," said Sedgwick, in a tone that showed she usually got her way, "I think we would have seen some sign of it before they asked Jeffrey to return the blessing. Right?"

"Sedge...." She drew out the word like it was a garrotting wire.

The Deva couple played out the roles in their recurring drama for a time. Jeffrey ignored them. His own troubles mattered far more than theirs. Would the Valodurians kill him? Better to go home and become an indifferent employee in Dad's business than risk dying here.

He raised the beer mug to his lips. Something in the repetitive action brought him back to himself.

If he didn't know which handicraft was the blessing, why not return them all?

THE NEXT MORNING, before Epsilon Indi rose too high in the cloud-flecked sky, Jeffrey hurried through his flat. Every alien handicraft he could find went into his backpack. He even lay on his belly on the concrete floor and groped under the bed in case something had fallen down with the dust bunnies and empty bottles.

Satisfied he'd found everything, he strolled through the gate, whistling a catchy tune played in a bar a few nights before. Everything would be fine. Go in, shoot some 3d, find Eyokviwex, hand over everything, then spend six days sleeping in and drinking before having to hit the alien city again.

It took thirty minutes, passing a gaggle of pupae throwing darts at the fist-sized flying bugs, a butcher stropping a knife of human-formula steel, a farmer walking beside a cart of baskets pulled by a pudgy white beast that looked half cow and half shmoo. No sign of Eyokviwex. Or that anyone spoke to Eyokviwex.

Word got out somehow. A crowd of natives formed a semicircle on three sides, hemming him against the windowless mud-brick wall of a school. Which was Eyokviwex? He couldn't tell.

Didn't matter. His heart beat a little faster, but in a good way, like when he challenged a guy to a game of beer pong while some women watched him. The chorus of skittering voices coming over the wall from the alien children sounded better than the music one ex-girlfriend liked. And the aliens didn't smell much worse than hours-old spilled beer.

One of the aliens stepped closer. "This one Eyokviwex. Return blessing."

"Glad to." Jeffrey shrugged off the backpack. It almost fell to the ground before he grabbed it like he meant to do it that way. Nothing inside was fragile, but why take the chance?

He set the backpack down, unzipped, spread the panels far apart. "Here's all the blessings. Take back which ever ones you want. I'm sure your gods are happy with you for loaning them to me."

Eyokviwex looked down. It reached into the opened backpack. Long fingers with too many joints sifted through the fungus shroud, the crinkly sack, the phallic symbol, and the other things.

The alien lifted its head. The compound eyes showed a dozen distorted reflections of Jeffrey's grin. "What these?"

The grin faded. "I'm returning the blessing. Like you asked."

"I no ask return things. I ask return blessing."

Jeffrey's mouth hung open far enough for one of the flying bugs to land inside. "I'm trying to."

"No. We give you, you give us. Byukh!" It darted forward. Hot dank alien breath filled Jeffrey's face. Mouthparts snipped skin on his forehead.

Jeffrey lurched back against the rough wall. "Hey!" He reached to his forehead. His fingertips picked up a trickle of blood. He stared at it for a moment, then looked up at the alien's unreadable face.

"We give you." Eyokviwex gestured with both its lower arms at the handicrafts jumbled in the backpack. "You give us."

Jeffrey's voice rose in pitch. "You want human tech? Christ and the robbers, why didn't you say that to begin with? I'll get you some."

"Good things. Not for pupae. For adults."

"Of course, of course." Dammit, what had he just done? Crypto out of his hardware wallet to buy something the aliens would want? Less money to live his life of leisure?

Money. "I can bless you by crediting your account with the humans who help you." Uncommon, but not unheard of, to give gifts of crypto to individual aliens to buy approved items from the Devas.

Eyokviwex paused. Maybe it didn't understand?

When it spoke, it showed it did. "Helper humans no sell what adults want."

Something illicit, then. Jeffrey's shoulders slumped. Which meant he'd have extra costs dealing with the gray market and smuggling it into the alien city.

A breath brought his problems back into focus. Even half a life of leisure beat the pants off of earning a living back home. And facing Dad's cold-eyed judgment.

"But then we're even," he said. "You blessed me, I'll bless you. After that, no more blessing one another. Deal?" He jutted out his fist to fist-bump on it, then opened his hand and let it hang in air like he meant to.

Eyokviwex angled its head at his hand, then mimicked his gesture as best it could with its right upper hand. "Yes." It clicked its mouthparts together like a craftsman sharpening a knife.

"Great. Six days. I'll be back," Jeffrey said. "With a blessing for you."

BACK IN THE cramped bathroom of his flat, Jeffrey covered the nick on his forehead with an antibiotic and liquid bandage, then figured out what to do.

He couldn't ask Sedgwick and Wanya, of course. The tech the Devas permitted people to give to the Valodurians had to get pre-approved by multiple levels of algorithms and human judgment. And clearly, the Devas would immediately reject whatever Eyokviwex wanted.

What did Eyokviwex want, anyway?

Tools seemed an obvious choice. But what sort? The Devas had given them some basic alloy and the knowledge how to work blades from it. But knives weren't the only tools aliens might want.

How was he supposed to know what the Valodurians might want?

The answer came to him. He actually had data. Dozens of hours of it. He microwaved a breakfast wrap and crammed hot tortilla, bacon, and eggs in his mouth while he reviewed the video he'd shot over the months.

The Valodurians used knives, yes, and buckets and stirrers to make mud bricks. In molds of sawn wood lashed together with twine. They would save time and get fewer leaks if they put together the molds with a drill and screwdriver.

Excited, he looked up the tools in the human zone's fabricator catalog. To rush the order in less than a week would cost much less than he feared.... until he factored in the price of the screws the aliens would need. No way could they make screws in their crude forges. He'd be on the hook to bring them screws every day, forever. Good luck keeping that out of sight from the Devas.

Jeffrey smacked his palm against his forehead. Who would want a screwdriver or a hand drill anyway? Eyokviwex said *for adults*, right? Some things were universal. *For adults* meant inebriating chemicals or porn.

In all his hours of video, he lacked footage of Valodurians drinking, smoking, or otherwise inebriating themselves. The fabricator probably wouldn't have any of their chemicals in its catalog. As for porn, he didn't even know how many sexes the Valodurians had.... let alone what body parts, smells, or sounds would arouse the one Eyokviwex belonged too.

Late in the night, with half a dozen empty beer bottles littering his living room, Jeffrey realized exactly what Eyokviwex wanted.

Weapons.

Not stuff with peaceful uses, like knives or hammers. Instead, tools designed solely to punch or pierce with great power. Maybe Eyokviwex wanted them for self-defense. The Devas might well be arming some native faction with advanced weapons in the name of peace and order.

Jeffrey's fingers drifted to the dried shell of liquid bandage on his forehead.

Eyokviwex didn't want weapons for self-defense. Street crime? Armed rebellion?

Did it matter? Hell, more violence might be good. Not for whichever natives were innocent, sure, but if it bled it led. Dad might keep him filming on Valoduria in hopes of getting footage to license to a media conglomerate. And Jeffrey could demand a bigger allowance every month.

Unlike screwdrivers and hand drills, though, he couldn't dial up a sling or a sword from the human zone fabricator. Eyes bleary, head drooping, he searched for articles and videos on weapons you could make from common items in any fabricator's catalog. Some pieces of metal, wire, and a hand crank, along with some effort, could yield a crossbow propelling a dart through a watermelon ten yards away.

He ordered the parts and fell asleep.

The next day, around midday, a clatter against his apartment door woke him. His wearable popped a delivery notification into his vision.

Jeffrey lurched out of bed and pulled in the packages. Spread parts on the coffee table, unpacked the other things, and left cardboard and airbags in the hallway for the building's robots to pick up for recycling. Toasting a bagel made it less stale, so he did that, then wolfed it down with gummy cream cheese.

He reached into the fridge for a beer but drew up short.

He had work to do.

The long afternoon and most of the evening passed before he completed the crossbow. His fingers lacked practice at making tools—at making anything, to be honest with himself. Frustration gripped him but he powered through it. He turned down two invitations to go drinking at bars other than Gentleman Johnny's. Eyes on the prize. Give the crossbow to Eyokviwex and he could go out drinking every night forever.

By the end of the night, Jeffrey had a piece that dry-shot just like the how-to video. He set up a case of gelatin snacks against one of the concrete walls. For the best these didn't have vodka in them. He cranked back the wire, laid a nail in the groove. Took aim, one hand on the grip underneath, the other at the release toggle on the crank.

The nail thunked against the concrete wall. The scent of lime gelatin filled the air. He tapped his finger on the empty groove. Friction warmth lingered on his fingertip.

He grinned and ate a couple of unpierced gelatin cups washed down with his first beer of the day. Eyokviwex would get its blessing, and he had a trick he could pull out at parties.

JEFFREY APPROACHED the gate scanners sweating. From the humid air, not his illicit cargo. Yes, he could be barred from exiting the human zone if the Devas caught him. But they wouldn't catch him.

The machines extended robotic arms around him. They didn't linger over his backpack containing metal bits any more than usual.

The bored-looking Deva inside the air-conditioned booth looked into space where Jeffrey guessed the data from the scanners was projected. The Deva smoothed down his bushy mustache with one hand.

Jeffrey's cheeks felt warm. Was the Deva taking longer than usual?

The light over the gate turned green. The clear plastic panels swung open. The Deva didn't give him a second glance.

Jeffrey entered the alien city. Eyokviwex seemed able to find him anywhere, and after months of fake xenology surveys, Jeffrey knew which quarters had little Deva presence. He sipped water from a bottle as he strode. Important to stay hydrated, especially today. He passed a construction site with the Development Assistance logo on a thin blue tarp stretched over a flimsy fence, then deeper into a zone of brick-makers and thatchers.

Aliens looked up from their work. He said *hello*, or what he thought was hello, in the local dialect. He sometimes wondered if he accidentally insulted their mothers. None of the aliens responded to his greeting, but none took offense.

He finished his water and gave the empty bottle to a legless beggar. Its four arms curled around itself, which he thought meant it was grateful.

Jeffrey walked on, smiling, please with himself. Returning blessings everywhere.

He found a pile of jumbled bricks where some Valodurian's house had collapsed and not been rebuilt. Rain had already softened the edges. Devas never made it this deep into the city. As good a place as any. He teetered his way about five yards across the pile. The heavy gravity and the weight in his backpack made his balance even more precarious.

From his pack, he pulled out a shrunken plastic bladder. He unscrewed the cap, turned his back to the street, and filled it with the only liquid he had.

He sat the thick-walled, bulging bag of golden liquid on a high brick backstopped by an even higher one, then picked his way back to the street. He sat on a brick and laid out the other contents of his backpack in front of him.

As he pulled out the last item, a crowd of aliens arrived. Half from his left and half from his right, hemming him in.

Jeffrey gestured at the pile of wire and metal pieces. "Here's your blessing."

Eyokviwex angled its head. The alien's stink clogged Jeffrey's nose. "Bring pieces. Not blessing." Its mouthparts worked with a faint scritch.

"Just watch. I'll turn the pieces into a blessing." He kneeled at the pile.

He'd practiced over the past few days. Assembling the crossbow by hand was easy. Harder was describing what he did in a pidgin the Valo-durians could understand. This many wraps of wire to lash together the pieces. So many cranks. Where to release the pressure on the wire.

"Watch," Jeffrey said. He cranked the handle again and pulled the wire taut behind the groove. He pulled a nail from the pile on the brick pavers and laid it in the groove. He stretched out prone. Sun-baked bricks warmed his belly and sweat stuck his shirt to the small of his back.

No problem. He aimed the crossbow at the bag of pee. Flipped the toggle.

The nail clacked against the brick backstop. His pee dribbled out of the punctured bag.

He grinned. Give a man a six-pack and he can get drunk today. Teach him how to brew and he can get drunk for the rest of his life. Something like that.

Jeffrey stood up. The aliens stayed in two clumps with a gap between them to the middle of the street. He faced Eyokviwex and extended the crossbow. "A blessing for you."

The alien's compound eyes reflected the crossbow in his hands like a funhouse hall of mirrors. Its four arms remained by its side. "Blessing?"

Jeffrey's mouth felt dry. "You can use it for all sorts of things. Target practice. Hunting small game. Self-defense. Uh...." Wasn't there something more? There had to be something more.

"Cursing," Eyokviwex said. "It curse to hurt other of us."

It paused a moment, then its four hands shot out. It yanked the crossbow from Jeffrey's hands. "Curse to hurt other." Its compound eyes met his gaze. "Of us."

Jeffrey sweated more, cold and clammy on his cheeks. Despite filling the bag with pee just minutes earlier, his bladder felt like it would burst. "Hey, hey, you don't want it, no problem, I'll get you something else."

"No more something else, Cheff-ree Be-orn-son." Eyokviwex spoke over its upper left shoulder to another Valodurian on its side of the crowd. It said something Jeffrey didn't understand.

He didn't need to, when Eyokviwex held its hand behind its thorax and the other alien handed over a dart like the kind the pupae had hunted flying bugs with.

Jeffrey's vision shrank to a tunnel focused on the gap between the two groups of Valodurians. He ran. The aliens hissed and shrieked in their language. He ran faster. From behind him came the ratcheting sound of the crossbow crank being turned.

Jeffrey turned a corner. A dart thunked the mud-brick wall behind him.

He ran, flat out, ignoring the ache in his shins and the burn in his lungs, until the gate of the human zone opened for him.

TWO WEEKS LATER, Jeffrey slumped through the concourse of the spaceport in low Valoduria orbit. The spaceport spun the concourse at 1 gee, and all his possessions fit into the backpack he'd bought to replace the one he'd abandoned to Eyokviwex. Despite that, he felt heavier than he ever had down on the planet.

Dad won again. Dammit.

The ship he rode outsystem also carried messages from Valoduria, including one automatically transcribed from words spoken six days prior by a native of the planet to a computer kiosk run by the Penpals Between the Stars program.

From Eyokviwex.

To Mister Björnson.

Your son come last time eight days ago. He give us weapon throw dart fast. We act like he do bad thing and scare him.

I no understand you story of prodigal son but I hope he return a blessing.

ABOUT THE AUTHOR

I'm **Raymund Eich.** I use my Middle American upbringing as a launchpad for journeys to the ends of the Universe.

Growing up in the Midwest prepared me for my academic career, culminating with a Ph.D. in biochemistry from Rice University. It helps me help inventors prosper from their progress in medicine, biotechnology, and life sciences.

Above all, it inspires me to write science fiction and fantasy about ordinary people facing extraordinary wonders and horrors, battling enemies both foreign and domestic, and building better lives for themselves, their families, and their societies.

My last name has one syllable and is pronounced "eye-sh." I live in Houston with my family.

Connect with me at **www.raymundeich.com** or follow the QR code below.

Online and brick-and-mortar bookstores around the world list millions of books, with thousands more published every day. I'm glad you discovered this one.

If you'd like to know when I release a new book, instead of leaving it to chance, join my Readers Club. I'll email you every two weeks with publishing news, book recommendations, or a short personal update.

Yes, please! I'll go to **www.raymundeich.com/mailing-list** or scan the QR code below.

No thanks. I'll take my chances next time I look for your books.

OTHER BOOKS BY THE AUTHOR

Available wherever books are sold.

Learn more about these titles at our website, **www.cv2books.com,** or follow the QR code below.

Orbital Maneuvers: The Complete Science Fiction Stories 2019-2020

Come and join–

- A mission to terraform a lifeless, rocky planet
- A private detective uncovering the ultimate crime
- A woman called by an ex-boyfriend... who's been dead twenty years
- A President breaking his country's highest law
- A star athlete discovering the true price of a championship

And five more tales, in the third installment of the Complete Science Fiction Stories of Raymund Eich.

––––––

Extravehicular Activities: The Complete Science Fiction Stories 2021-2022

Leave the safety of your space capsule for the dangers of billion-year old alien derelicts, intelligent insects with mysterious motives, espionage in an alternate 1920s Paris, and rogue reconstructed dinosaurs.

These wonders and more await in the fourth volume of the Complete Science Fiction Stories of Raymund Eich.

Novels

The Progress of Mankind

Stone Chalmers, Book 1
Complete four-book series available

Stone Chalmers. Spy. Assassin. Instrument maintaining Earth's dominion over all human worlds.

Opposing him? Hostile forces on colony worlds... and within the Earth government itself.

———

Take the Shilling

The Confederated Worlds • Book 1
Complete trilogy available

Tomas seeks an escape from his backwater planet and his widowed mother's rigid religious home.

'Taking the shilling' - enlisting as a space soldier - is only the start.

———

Exploration 2127

The False Flag War • Book 1

Two men from opposite sides of divided Earth make an interstellar discovery that could destroy Earth's fragile peace... unless they come in war for all mankind.

New California

After New California's founder committed suicide, two men clash to rule the colony.

One, Ashwin George, supported by the colony's elite and the Chinese company dominating half the settled galaxy.

Against him, Desmond Park, nanotechnology engineer, armed with the most formidable weapon of all.

A single idea.

————

The Reincarnation Run

Skeptical spacejock Landry Krieger knows exactly how to smuggle the "reborn" spiritual leader of an oppressed people past their conquerors... but the boy's priests—and governess—shake up his orderly plans.

www.ingramcontent.com/pod-product-compliance
Lightning Source LLC
Chambersburg PA
CBHW060702190726
48289CB00002B/501